GOING HOME

Volume One

FEVER THERAPY,

2nd Edition, January 2015.

Jim Burnside was born in Belfast, grew up in Glasgow, Peterborough and Leeds and studied at Middlesex Polytechnic and Cardiff University. He worked as a teacher of English in Wales, London and Bradford, before specialising in developing the communication skills of disabled and autistic students.

Visit his website at:
www.jimburnside.com

Proof reading by Karamjeet Nahal-Macdonald www.FinalDraft.co.uk

Editing by Jessica Macdonald www.FinalDraft.co.uk

Website and cover design: Chris Marshall
Website: www.marshallmade.co.uk
E-mail: chris@marshallmade.co.uk

Cover image original photograph: Antti Pietikainen
www.northframe.net / antti@northframe.net

1

Forthcoming titles in the series GOING HOME by Jim Burnside:

HANNAH DUFF, published September 2014

GOLDEN DAWN, due March 2015

TALLY LONG'S PIE, due June 2015

Other forthcoming titles in this six book series:

LOOKING BACK

BISMARCK ON THE MANTELPIECE

For Karamjeet.

With thanks to Jess, Joe, Maria, Libby, Hugh, Peter and Violet who variously offered positive criticism, moral support, large glasses of wine, or helpful recollections.

Contents

Chapter One - *Love's Dream*

West Port, Edinburgh 1893.

Early May sunshine warmed Edinburgh's Grass market, bringing a
flood of Saturday-morning late risers out from their wishful slumbers.
Queues were forming where traders called their special offers over the
chat. Gigantic Clydesdales nudged their way carefully through the
gathering crowd of shoppers, drawing commercial traffic of all sorts.

Two mounted Bobbies saluted John Harper as he walked back
against the flow towards the West Port. Tucking greaseproof paper
containing fresh Finan Haddies under his arm with a Granary loaf he
smiled amicably, returning their tongue-in-cheek gestures with a
parade ground salute of his own. Harper stopped to exchange
pleasantries with Lennox and Macdonald about what they had to do
to pull the early shift, but Elsie took Elizabeth by the hand and his
daughters began to run.

"Mammy, Mammy, that's our Mammy playing the piano!"
shouted Elsie, Elizabeth chorusing her cry.

"I'd better head them off boys 'afore they cause a stampede! See ya
now!" said Harper shrugging at the missed opportunity for casual
banter. The two policemen smiled down at him as they both turned
their heads back to pick up the somnolent, cascading melody. Their
friend Harper ran after his bairns. A dray horse waiting with his
delivery wagon outside the Black Bull turned his head, seeming to
smile as Harper ran past. The rising and tumbling emotion of 'Love's
Dream' slowed passers-by - leaving a smile of approval on the faces of
everyone who heard it. Harper knew every note because he'd heard it
played a hundred times.

Feeling, not contended or combined with thought.

Most had no idea that it was a piece by Ferencz Liszt, though they
could hear the intensity of expression. If they listened long, it filled

their souls. Harper relaxed his pace as he could see that the girls had run beyond the crowd and milling livestock into safe familiar territory. Their little elbows swept outwards as they ran out of puff on the gentle slope at the West end of the market.

He knew that Hannah would keep on playing though the delight on their girl's faces would demand her attention when they made the basement room. She was warming up prior to her first lesson of the day. The subliminal effect on the crowds passing by was more inspirational and more productive than a card in a shop window, or word of mouth. Out in the street Harper could hear celebratory laughter and welcoming surprise from the basement room as the last resounding cadences fell to the cobbles and continued to echo in his mind. Turning into the basement steps of the tall house he laughed to consider the simple joy that very young children bring into daily routines. He was proud that they were his and glad to be so alive. Harper waited until Hannah had seen him and stopped playing.

"Hi Woolly-Bird. I got everything you told me to. I'll take the girls upstairs and make breakfast."

"Fine, I have a lesson in five minutes and another at half past. Don't forget to feed Molly or she will go next door to steal from Mrs Stewart's cat."

Hannah Wilson Drummond Harper's ten o'clock tutee was a thirteen year old named Lavinia from a grandiose town house on Melville Street. Checking her pretty wrist watch, a gift from her grandmother, Hannah confirmed the imminence of her student's arrival. The girls were ordered upstairs as the basilisk manifested at utterance of her name, as usual scolding the maid accompanying her for walking too fast.

Lavinia had outrageously stubby fingers matching an extensive girth. Hannah had genuine fears that the young lady would never lose her puppy fat and that surliness projected this very same perception back at the world. But the girl wanted to play the piano. It did not matter that she found difficulty spanning chords or was striving for attainment she might never reach. Her desire to play was a virtuous ambition and Hannah made a point of telling her so.

Lavinia was one of the new, wealthy elite of young women who might choose to study and enter one of the professions. Hannah could imagine her rise within the management structure of some charitable organization or local government bureaucracy, perhaps as a tough matron at the infirmary or a job interviewer sticking carefully to the questionnaire at one of the glass factories. The girl's redoubtable energies simply needed channelling in the right direction. But Hannah feared for the underlings Lavinia would one day seek to crush with her turbulent frustrations and intentionally spoke to her all the more sweetly for that. A long suffering housemaid in uniform black coat and bonnet waited to accompany her back to Moray Place, her hands folded in quiet supplication beneath a serious face. The time passed quickly for all three: the maid because she had respite watching the world go by from where she sat by the basement window; the frustrated child because she met with approval through Hannah's tailored encouragement and for Hannah because she was doing what she loved.

At the end of the lesson Lavinia left as always with an exalted smile on her angelic face. The maid turned to Hannah to thank her quietly, with watery blue eyes conveying unspoken respect for her intercession.

"You're most welcome," Hannah replied with benign formality. The maid, not a handful of years older than her charge, smiled warmly in return.

Hannah's next eager pianist, twelve year old Joe Hammond, was standing at the doorstep with his portfolio under his arm.

Harper opened the tall cupboard purposefully as he organised his daughters in a quiet session of drawing and colouring, then turned to his breadcrumbs and frying pan. As he made breakfast his eyes were drawn constantly to the imposing fortress atop the basalt stump. As ever the conduit of timeless electricity stirred him to wonderment. He stood gazing for a while, feet splayed like a good copper, saving his back, contemplating earth and sky and the tides of fate.

Rental for rooms above the book shop in the West Port had been a little too much for a police constable with two children – three prospectively - to afford but Hannah loved them. He reminded her that they had some money set aside and her searching smile had spoken of thoughtful commitment. In truth she loved the flat a little less than he did, though Harper had never been the most sensitive soul. As long as she didn't complain he was not about to state the obvious – it was less than a hundred yards from where he worked. Even so, the generous space of the top floor with its four rooms and a well-received option on the basement fell short of the ideal for bringing up a family.

The 'Newbygging' had been constructed at a time when even Edinburgh notables accepted cramped living conditions. Such people had long since migrated to the self-conscious grandeur of the New Town of course - then successively to manicured suburbs or the coastal resorts. The main attraction of the old rooming house was its proximity to West Port Police Station, where PC Harper was based and to the nearby heart of the Old Town – the celebrated stomping ground of Burke and Hare and Greyfriar's Bobby.

They had taken the basement as well so Hannah would have room for her piano, though both agreed this was a temporary situation. Harper had persuaded her to look for a bargain locally, rather than risk consigning her recovered Bechstein to the railway at Rothiemay. There were plenty of second hand pianos to choose from and fees from the lessons she gave covered the outlay, helping to pay the additional rent. There was drainage in the basement for washing and a water closet. She could also store odd items of second hand furniture for the house they planned to buy some day and there was a work table for Elsie and Elizabeth's arts and crafts. Life was not easy but it was full of small, daily delights. They'd had a fine start to their life together. John and Hannah Harper held a brave plan in their hopeful hearts.

There were excellent markets within a stone's throw and the burgeoning city of Edinburgh with elegant hotels and shops, international entertainments and glorious railway stations was a short walk away. His location soon made Harper feel very much an important part of the scheme of things. There was harmony, movement and occasional sunshine smiling through the billowing clouds of this dynamic capital. There were fire-lit corners with intensely garrulous people – most of them affable or droll, some as piercing as the north-easterly wind. A few were harder than the castle rock itself - but none of them were ever dull. They drank and argued and occasionally they fought but they always looked forward in hope.

Harper knew well that at twenty four he projected a cool swagger in his pressed uniform, his quiet Northern drawl belying an iron will with an equally fierce temper. He was not tall for a policeman but had dormant muscles from years working at the Milltown forge.

Before that time as a teenager, he had worked the land for as long as he could remember. Harper had been raised on a farm at Auchterless in Morayshire, overlooking a sweep of the river Deveron. So much time had passed with so much imperceptible change that now at least with many good things to appreciate, it was no longer painful to think what had happened to that lonely boy.

Seven years on, John still showed brawny contours bequeathed by all the hard graft under his police uniform. That tight fit could in itself give pause to unruly revellers in the streets or noisy pubs around the Grassmarket. Locals recognised PC Harper, respecting him because he lived on his beat and itinerant traders and seamen tended to defer to the residents they'd fallen in with for the evening. Occasionally, seasonal drovers took over the place with the easy audacity of Bonnie Prince Charlie's Jacobite army and unspoken tensions would follow. Local farmers would inevitably be loaded in every sense of the word – having tearfully parted with their beloved livestock. Typically the atmosphere in pubs would be garrulous and friendly, until somebody accidentally spilled a pint. Then someone else would whip out a boning knife and the fun would start.

Edinburgh in 1893 could be a tough place to speak out of turn or show a disrespectful manner to 'the Polis.' This wiry little Bobby had a hint of danger in his pale blue eyes, suggesting he knew how to use his truncheon to help make an arrest or wade into a brawl with fists and boots judiciously flying.

John and Hannah's two girls – Elsie, who was almost five and Elizabeth, in her third year, loved the West Port house as much as their parents. They constantly ran up and down steep stairs from the street or the basement, shrieking and giggling in excitement. First time visitors - neighbours, friends and colleagues alike - commented with open approval on the house, its location and the heartening accommodation it offered. They supplemented what John and Hannah knew of the voluminous history of the area and its approaches. Laughing as they drank, some offered gruesome anecdotes of ghosts, murders and executions. Others pointed to the nearby locale of mass graves or the pounding of the devil's carriage, even the position of houses demolished in desperation to give a field of fire upon the besieging English. Resolving any doubt that they lived in the stage-set of Scotland's tortured past, the view from the upstairs back window was of Edinburgh Castle itself! What could give greater security – a legendary, almost biblical sense of time and place and a flourishing modernist dénouement to St Margaret's millennium as the turn of the twentieth century approached?

"Daddy, daddy, look!" Tugging at his shirt sleeve was his eldest child, smiling, dark-eyed Elsie.

"Oh, what's that darling? Is it the Loch Ness Monster?"

"No, don't be silly. It's you on your Police Horse, Blackie!"

Elizabeth came with a picture too - remarkably for a child her age not just a scribble of colour but an amorphous collection of loosely enclosed shapes.

"What can we draw next Daddy?" demanded four year old Elsie.

"Draw some trees, or the park. Maybe the beach, or the castle?" Harper's mind went out of time, back in a swirl of random impressions - many of which had been too painful to allow into his reckoning until now.

Milltown of Rothiemay was one of Scotland's myriad of scattered, uncut diamonds. The moody river Deveron coursed through a broad stream; sometimes gently, often with force, occasionally with fury. On the left bank bordering the Milltown, concrete culverts diverted the flow to power enormous wooden paddle wheels. Workers cottages lined both sides of the street back from the river to the warehouse at the crossroads. A bright hotel and grand estate made up the rest of this bucolic scene. The town lay among emerald farms and dense forests, echoing with the determined scream of industrial lumber milling. In an undulating wooded river valley, beneath low hills to the south and a broad fertile plain to the north, Harper broke ground to drill seeds, cut barley, howk tatties, wrestle sheep at the shearing - deliver new born calves in spring. He also knew well the cutting and handling of lumber and black arts of the family owned sawmill. Even as a schoolboy he'd grown used to labouring every holiday and weekend.

His young frame had matured early from the outcome of a curious sequence of events he least liked to remember, affecting Hannah Wilson's wider family.

Brodie Robertson, who had once been the Wilson's close friend and farm manager had leapt into the Deveron in full spate of the snow melt, drowning himself in the early winter of '85. This tragedy succeeded 'a long battle with depressive mania and cirrhosis' - alternatively with 'The Glen Moray Whisky Company, whose stock he was attempting to deplete,' depending on which account Hannah listened to – her father Frank's honorarium for his friend, after raising a glass with the coroner from Elgin or Jessie's Sunday morning sange froid after they had recovered Brodie's body and held a quiet funeral.

Frank Wilson had fallen out with Hannah's mother Jessie over virtually everything that it was possible to fall out over, including the implication that Brodie had more of a reason for drinking than bills he couldn't pay. When finally confronted after years of playing away from home, mutual anger turned to spite and Frank Wilson slammed the door on Jessie to walk over the fields to Mary Robertson's bed. He promptly fathered another child, Elsie, before suddenly dropping dead over the anvil after a bad coughing fit. Harper had been helping out on a Saturday morning and had witnessed the awful suddenness of Frank's face turning blue with cyanosis at the forge, at the age of forty eight. Hard work and hard drinking seemed to take men young but Harper had been proud to step into Frank's shoes. Consequently, when John voiced his intention of learning the family businesses of farming and lumber production, there had been more than a little resistance from the elders, especially his ma.

John couldn't quite grasp why they were apparently steering him away from succession towards a softer or less capital intensive profession. Perhaps they thought he was too small or weak for the punishing demands of farming. But John was a fine athlete who was as strong as any of them, although he had always been a little confused about this question of physique. All the other Harpers were rangy, long-boned people and as a child John had felt self-consciously tiny in the midst of his own family.

When the thrombosis had taken Hannah's father, the legendary Frank Wilson, in July 1886, John 'the help' turned up at the forge the day after his funeral. 'It was bad luck,' the pundits held, 'The work drove Brodie Robertson to drink and suicide for ruined health and now Frank, not two years on - still in his prime!' Young Harper was less than half a year past his sixteenth birthday but the critics were immediately silenced. Every visitor gave John friendly advice and even the horses seemed to approve of his touch. For some reason though, his brave efforts had not been good enough for his ma and pa. Their smiles of approval were too brief, their praise somehow stilted. John beat frustration out on his irons. When his younger brother, Alex arrived with orders to work alongside, 'to fetch and carry and stoke, or tend the horses,' at first John poured scorn upon him. He was still overwhelmed by the incoherent perception that he had actually begun

14

to hate his own mother. For some reason John did not feel himself to have equal status within the younger generation of his wider family - cousins Douglas and Ewan, or his elder sister Callan, who all worked as required on the Harper farms in Rapplaburn or the sawmill at Rothiemay. He felt intensely jealous of what he had come to see as favouritism shown by his father John towards his younger brother Alex.

It was nothing explicit or tangible at first – just an endless series of impressions and contrasts that had mounted up over the years, until young John's mouth curled in an angry sneer of sullenness and contempt at preference shown to Alex. Not naturally envious any more than inclined to be aloof, in truth the lad was naturally genial. John was also smart enough to quickly learn whatever he was shown and thus came to realise he was being discriminated against because he did not belong.

By fourteen, John had incrementally learned most of what was worth knowing about the fine art of tailoring. For as long as he could remember, his 'Uncle' Zach had indulged John's interests. Master Tailor Zachariah Williams of Elgin, formerly of South Shields, had voluntarily invested a great amount of time with young John Harper over the years. What had astounded Harper was the degree of adamantine resolution that the seniors - his Uncle Hugh who had joint ownership of the farm and sawmill with his nominal father John - and even his mentor, Zach, had shown over the years in never talking about this.

John's anger soon petered out and when he had whacked a few horse shoes into shape. Pondering the bluntness of the stone-hearted people who had raised him, he thanked God for his own sharpened sensibilities. Young, strong and proud of himself, John knew what they could not say. Imagining whispered confutations and how his parents might justify their secret using pompous language, he basked in their tacit support – welcoming pained efforts to step around imponderable moral ambiguities, 'for the sake of his feelings.' John learned to control those very same feelings and love every member of his family conditionally, as they had loved him.

First he resolved to treat twelve year old Alex as he deserved – as a dear brother confused by John's anger and contempt. They turned out to be picture-days at the forge: in all five years of hard graft with relative independence and decent wages, all of it annealed with frequent hilarity and bloodless battle. It was the commercial centre of the Milltown, visited at various times by virtually all of its hundreds of residents and John Harper's skills were highly acclaimed.

When Harper had time to walk alone through the woodlands of Glen Barry or down to Milltown, he found himself uneasily conjecturing about the past – his own as well as that of the community he had grown into. He would stand and wonder at the ruined church near the crossroads at Rothiemay. It had been burned by one group of fervent Christians who felt nearer to Truth and the Almighty than another equally fervent group of Christians. The heinous act of arson had happened less than thirty years prior to his birth but no-one he asked could give him a satisfactory reason why.

Ever more curious about his parentage and the intermediary role of the benevolent tailor, John had asked Zachariah about England. He had overheard a burning rumour repeated by his nominal cousins Jim Lorimer and Andy Murdoch that his true father had been visiting the area from Bristol or Bath. His pa was not John 'Senior' at all, he was heartbroken to discover - when Zach gently prompted him to demand answers from his mother, Isobel. Nor for that matter was his Uncle Hugh, as she asked him to believe in hushed tones when he pressed the matter. Evidently something shameful had been concealed in connection with his adoption, so John had let the matter drop – for the moment.

It hadn't been any English connection that might have shamed him however, since it was commonly noted that the Morayshire aristocracy directed much of their thoughts upon how to emulate them. The English were an ever-present element in the larger coastal and growing market towns, commanding grudging respect for their money, if not for their mores.

No - it was an entirely spiritual matter John concluded that his true parentage was not talked of openly. He was a bastard in a community that could not resist the fulfilment of its carnal urges but which resolutely patched up holes burned by tearful misfortune – diseases of the farm and the forge; accidents of the distillery, shipyard and sea - with open arms and alacrity.

If in lore Campbell might have stayed while his wounds healed and accepted the inconvenience of temporarily becoming 'Macdonald' in order to fit in with the very people who had inflicted them, then who would ever question the duality?

Harper's was a community that discreetly vaunted ancestry, in adding surnames to children with no parentage. Lately highland neighbours over the mountains on the horizon were advised to keep their true names secret, by changing them from McGregor to Brown or Smith. Double standards no longer surprised John. He learned to take hypocrisy for granted.

Harper reflected upon an increasingly confusing societal shift, in which Scotland these days actually had more people called Smith than the once ubiquitous Macdonalds. Flourishing contemporaneously were a generation of lovelorn bairns, some with as many honorific names as a Spanish infanta. He knew also that this modern confusion over forgotten ancestry facilitated an influx of southern sheep farmers. They had invested now where displaced Scottish crofters had loved and lost – moving on to Glasgow or Canada in their tens of thousands.

John resented the English but utterly despised the Scottish aristocracy - because he understood the land that had surrounded and spoken to him all his life and saw clearly how they neglected it. Denuded hills interspersed with random forests of conifers made his farmer's blood boil with hatred for the despoiling, landed elite. One more elevated side of a road would be cultivated, assuring private millions - while the less exposed acreage opposite was abandoned to the rain. Blackened stones poked through the moss. Here and there a bleached ewe's skull reminded him that this is a world of men, lacking thoughtful design - geared more to demand than supply.

One fine summer week in '86, when he pulled a ligament working in the forge and Alex stepped in for him, Harper rode with Zachariah north westward into the stunning glens above Dornoch. Near the roadside above the loch he saw a torn fraction of regally patterned wallpaper, clinging tenuously to the face of a blackened stone. A hint of grimed gold, sheltered from rain by hopeful rye grass, lay kissing the impoverished earth. The vain hope of it pierced the young man like a bayonet in his gut.

"Oh dear God, will ye look at this man?" he entreated his mentor, sliding from his horse. As Harper picked up the boulder bits of plaster fell from beneath the rotting paper. Zach dismounted to join his protégé, letting the horses graze.

"Uncle Zach . . . can you imagine the woman's white hands as she smoothed this wallpaper out? Can you feel her moment of satisfaction?"

"Indeed son, yes. This was once high quality wallpaper. A trifle seen in the town, maybe advertised in a magazine, or a shop catalogue."

"Hah! Good money wasted on a London fashion."

They both caught a sense of her living aspiration, the same bright hopes any loving heart might have for their family. Then it struck John that despite history lessons in school he'd never really let the tragedy in before.

They had not been poor as long as they had their cattle.

"How could they afford this?" he demanded turning to Zach. His mentor replied with gentle understatement, "Every fashionable commodity of the cities came directly to them from coasters, or across the ocean. It had been that way from time immemorial, for centuries before Calgacus berated the Romans. This forgotten family could easily afford the rent John. There was a market for imported brandy, as well as more costly items, such as tea from India and sugar from Jamaica."

John knew the evil before him had only been about the expectation of increased profit and the greed it aroused. The injustice of it all staggered his mind, as he imagined the scene invoked by the sad pile of stones. Seeing the plough lines across the top-land around the place the house had stood, he marvelled at the hardiness of the people who had been driven away. Favouring cattle over sheep, they had built traditionally on high pastures so they might observe the approach of diverse strangers as they toiled on the slopes. John could see and hear them in his mind's eye. He imagined sitting down to eat and drink with them, shaking their warm hands - but he dared not probe further at the demolished walls even in curiosity. Veneration gave him pause. This was a grave site to an entire nation.

Such sad piles were obituary to tens of thousands who never relinquished their right to the land. They had been given no time to remove timbers or furniture. When they resisted they were beaten down and thrown bloodied into the jailhouse. Some were burned alive in their sick beds. Many died from shock or exposure in the freezing rain.

"Some of the houses were only built in the forties and fifties you know," Zach told him, "Imagine that? Something constructed to a modern, high standard with a Welsh slate roof and raised wooden floors. It was all destroyed for political and economic reasons John - a design to get rid of recalcitrant Highlanders, off to the colonies where they were needed. By the same stroke investors secured a cheap supply of wool for Yorkshire mill owners."

Zach wiped his thumb across a piece of vitrified sandstone which he held out to the speechless Harper. Its charred crystals were silent imprecation to thuggery directed by an aristocratic owner; of jurisdictional wickedness carried out by his factors.

19

"In all the glorious centuries of the Highlanders, who might have foreseen lamentation riding up the lane, brandishing an injunction from The Laird?"

Harper stood silently as Zachariah stiffened in meditation, muttering a prayer in Hebrew. John's voice thickened as he growled a declaration, "This was not Colonialism at work here Uncle Zach, that's what you're telling me? This was done in the name o' what . . . 'Modernisation' was it no'? Increased profit for less effort?"

Zachariah nodded with his head and shoulders, as though praying for the souls of victims he imagined watching from another place. At length he glanced over at John, moisture rising sympathetically in his eyes for the boy's palpable sorrow. Zach smiled wistfully, moving to embrace the lad firmly. Then without a word he reached for the bridle of his garron, Sophie and swung back up into the saddle, turning the surefooted mare down the lane towards the road. It was natural for John to empathise with the victims of the clearances but Zach knew his distress went deeper than that. He knew precisely why. This forsaken land reminded the lad of his own abandonment.

John dried tears on his sleeve then carefully mounted his pony Merlin, though his eyes were still misted with rage. Kicking the horse gently, he drew level with his friend's. Zach patted Sophie's neck as she listened apprehensively to the tension in the men's voices. He spoke quietly of a fiendish concept, "This word Modernisation is a 19th Century euphemism for the fundamental ruthlessness of Capitalism, John." Zachariah slowed his horse to reach out for John's bridle. His two familiar carriage horses snorted, nuzzling each other. John was silent as Zachariah pondered something important he was about to add. He cleared his throat, then spat onto the metalled road they were about to join. There was fire in his steel grey eyes – a hard wisdom and what suddenly seemed to John an almost superhuman energy he'd never seen in another man. Zach suddenly seemed the equal of anyone he had ever met. John loved and revered the old man but now the elderly tailor showed a compassionate understanding no preacher or old father had ever expressed so clearly. Shivering in the cold morning air he listened as Zach spoke with vehemence.

"Remember what you saw here today, dear boy. Hold it fearlessly in your heart and bring it to mind whenever you encounter those with wealth and title – more especially those who wish to emulate them. Such people will bend every enterprise to their own interests. They abuse and corrupt the Law, dominate the political arena with deceitful slogans and dirty deals. Fortune and influence allows them to turn justice into lies; commit every crime - including rape and murder."

There was a moment of silence as John gazed at Zach in amazement, "Rape and murder, Uncle Zach?"

"Oh yes," he said firmly, "With impunity, son, because their victims are helpless. Nobility conspire to wage foreign wars, often taking what they will never need, to spoil it for others . . . like this beautiful land all around us here, John. Such discord is in the nature of empire. But never forget, all conflict is spawned by individual rivalry and greed."

He paused as he thought what more to say that might edify his charge. Harper listened in silence, certain of Zach's broad experience in the world of commerce. Zach nodded again to himself, musing over the truth of his revelation, "Make no mistake, the people who enacted this barbarism all over North Western Scotland own everything and control everything. They own towns and cities at home; control colonies abroad. Half of the banks and businesses in the USA were set up to extend their interests there by proxy. They dominate a global realm of dependencies. They own all the companies which procure government contracts for harbours, roads, bridges and railways. Public money is diverted to them through this conduit. There is an unseen 'Old-Boy network' awarding themselves contracts to erect every type of public building; office-block, hospital and school throughout the land."

John sighed heavily, shocked at the old man's fervent tone. Zach held tight to the bridle as Merlin chewed his bit then shook his head

21

as if in agreement with his master. John was smart enough to realize this revelation would never happen again, unless he showed a discreet level of interest unbecoming of his youth. He had never heard this thoughtful and passive gentleman talk so freely.

"Please go on, Zach. I want to know."

"The elite are small in number, but everyone in employment works for them. Your taxes are paid indirectly to them because their profiteering soaks up the expenditure of every annual governmental budget. Every penny you save in the bank makes more profit for them. They hide behind every line and layer of authority: robes of Ministers and Rabbis; the regalia of Town Councillors and Judges; the false smiles of self-seeking MPs and the disingenuous frowns of Cabinet Ministers, dealing their way through a term of office like commodity brokers, thinking only of personal advantage."

John knew there was something more. Zach's diatribe sounded more like a confession of guilt than evidence against a recognisable common enemy. Somehow Harper knew this was about the tailor's associates near to home, or near to him. The old man lowered his voice but ploughed on in his rancorous soliloquy, "Often individuals with controlling interests within our institutions use secret affiliation to subdue imagination and enterprise, steering innovation back towards the status quo. Private wealth blinds the majority to the truth, creating a wall thicker and taller than any castle, behind which they can conduct any act of selfishness and greed. From beginning to end it is all about money. Not merely the love of money but Money as an Absolute. Money as God."

Zach pushed down on his stirrups to stretch up in his saddle. For a moment Harper imagined him Moses returned and mounted, carrying some barely perceived New Commandment. John was abashed by the unaffected candour of his mentor. He told Zachariah that he suspected everything he had said to be true. All around them as they rode along the south side of the Dornoch Firth, they saw evidence of hundreds of burned out homes. John was speechless as he tried to imagine evil fires that must have lit up such a beautiful place and the thousands whom they made destitute at a stroke. Never in the long history of Caledonia, that Zach and his school teachers had taught him of, had law and entitlement served injustice so completely - plainly without any due consideration of humanity, in even the slightest degree. Zach talked about recent riots in Skye and the forthcoming Crofters Act, soon to be passed into law. He explained that the Act of Parliament was designed to give rights of tenure to marginalised Highlanders, although he sounded sceptical. Harper wondered if prospects might indeed be better in the Carolinas, or Cape Breton.

That night Zachariah and John booked into at a small hotel in Tain. They walked for miles along a magnificent deserted beach and Zach promised to hire clubs and equipment to take John for a round of golf the following day.

At supper, John pressed his Uncle to give an explanation of why he had spoken so censoriously about the wealthy elite he clearly knew so well.

"You don't need to know the details. It would give you a sleepless night."

"You're toying with me – you know them."

"I am a master tailor with a reputation. In time they all come to me," replied Zach sipping his claret, looking askance at John.

"You have connections – you helped them with their dirty deals?"

"You ask too many questions. You'll give me indigestion."

"It's true though, isn't it? That's how you know how they operate."

"Yes, you're right, now eat your steak."

"You settled here to get away from it. I know. There are things you say that are open. You can't hide the past from me like that."

"I'm not hiding anything but in my . . . in our profession John, if you choose it over farming, or being a blacksmith . . . the first thing you learn is never to repeat what you hear in private," Zachariah looked straight at John, "Understand?"

"Why is that such an imperative, if you actually know about the things they get up to? Rape and so on?"

"Because they'd cut your throat quicker than a Bashi-bazouk."

"What's a Bashi-bazouk Uncle Zach?" asked John with a disingenuous smile.

"A Turkish mercenary John, like a Legionnaire. It means free-headed, disorderly."

"He was one of them wasn't he?"

"Who was one of what?"

"My father . . . he was one of your cut-throat business associates."

Zach poured John some more wine. He was seventeen but he looked twenty one.

Chapter Two - *Children of the Barley*

One morning in the stormy winter of 1886, as she went to feed the geese at the pond between the two crofts Hannah had seen two year old Elsie Wilson still wandering around the farmyard in her pyjamas, at eleven o'clock in the morning. She immediately realised that something was wrong.

With the cold instinct of a brood parasite, Mary had conceded that she could never fulfil her commitments or make ends meet without a man in her life. The only touchstone for the survival of her young family was a croft she had neither strength nor commitment to work. Mired in scandal and tragedy after Frank had wronged Jessie and exited stage left, Mary Robertson felt she could never again find happiness in Milltown. Like Brodie and Frank she went to the pub too regularly and drank too much. Old friends found it hard to talk to her, yet new friends found it all too easy - when exposed to her one enduring asset – Mary's attractive persona.

Not long after Frank had worked himself into an early grave, Mary met a foreman road mender from Aberdeen named Danny Swale, in the Forbes Hotel. He was smitten by her genial, feminine allure but he left - and she pined for the fellow, recalling the infatuation of youth.

But Danny returned eighteen months later between jobs, to work on Mary's divided moral conscience. The next day the pretty cuckoo had flown for good. She left three bairns - two of Brodie's and one of Frank's but she never left a goodbye note. Elsie was half-sister to Frank Jnr, Jeannie and Betsy Wilson and step sister to Kate and Fiona Robertson – all three inherited by proxy, or some might formally say adopted. All told, it had made twelve mouths for Hannah Wilson to feed daily.

When Mary disappeared, John discreetly salted away the bulk of the profits from customers at the forge. Happy in modest transition he began to eagerly anticipate the next direction he was to be steered by his 'mother.'

Less than a week later Isobel Harper came walking down the lane with arms folded and a purposive momentum in her gait. Knowing from her expression and rarity of her social visits that this was business, John handed the tongs to Alex, turning to listen as his brother plunged the hissing shoe into a cooling tub. Isobel nodded curtly at Jim Lorimer, the apprentice carter who seemed to be a permanent fixture at the forge. Jim politely raised his cap as he stood holding the reins of a huge Clydesdale. Isobel was visibly shaking and her voice trembled with the importance of her request.

"Jessie Wilson asked if ye'd help out over at Ramsburn."

"Why, is Mary no coming back?"

"No, forget Mary son, she's on the road to ruin, what wi' drink an' men. Great Gran has told the Parish Council she tak' in the Robertson girls, Kate and Fiona, as well as Frank and Mary's daughter Elsie."

"So the Wilson's ha'e three more bairns tae feed and need help wi' both crofts?"

"Aye, son. The laird's factor has agreed to let them run the Robertson place too. They're mostly women, even wi' the efforts o' eight year old Frank Junior," she informed him, "and they need a keen labourer, though none of those three women would see you in their way. You'll be back at the forge by ten or eleven every day at the latest and Jim can help Alex if it's a broken wheel."

There was a softness and a tone of affectionate appraisal in Isobel's voice, betraying what she truly thought of him. John was overwhelmed by what his mother did not say - mesmerised by the beautiful logic of her simplistic insight. He knew the family in question as well as he knew anyone and the Wilsons of course knew John. He understood that they were desperate and the transaction had already been made - that a deal had been done between the two women and the landlord that would depend on John's willingness to work hard, without questioning the details. He did not know why but the shadows seemed to lift as Isobel spoke gently in the light thickening around them.

"I trust your judgement, Isobel and I love you very much," John averred, looking in her clear eyes, as one adult to another, "It's nae more than Brodie Robertson and Frank Wilson did between them. One was too busy boozin' and the other too busy chasin' skirt tae work a full day!"

"Good, so I'll tell her aye."

"That'll be fine, tell Jessie Wilson aye, ma." John was flattered to be so highly regarded at so young an age by a neighbour and close friend. Nonetheless, he would never again be able to bring himself to call Isobel Harper 'ma.' Both knew his affirmation was also an understated 'farewell.'

His plainspoken cousin, Jim raised an eyebrow as Isobel made off as quickly as she'd come.

"What? Go on, say it man, ye will onway, next time yer half-cut in the Forbes!" demanded John.

"Three women, six bairns, twa crofts an' a Blacksmith's shop tae run – ye'll need tae call upon Goibne the God of the Forge fer protection boy!" Harper looked askance at Jim as he pumped the bellows to bring his coals back up to a working temperature. Alex watched Jim from across the workshop, seeing a smile playing on the older boy's lips. Lorimer was tall, forthright and hardy but Alex knew that John was someone even he was wary of provoking.

"Spit it out, Jim. D'ye think I'm no up tae it pal?"

"No, nothin' o' the kind. You'll find oot soon enough man."

"He means the eldest daughter, Hannah," put in Alex, "even I can see that."

"Aye an' your balls hae no e'en dropped. But he's right John. There's a queue longer than the ale tent at the August ceilidh. They say she's saving hersel' fer Reverend Blair tae discover ees manhood."

"Get tae fuck, both o' yis! An' start pulling thon tyre affy the cart. This micht be a meetin' place fer aw the local gossip but I've nae time tae stan' aroun' talkin' scandal, especially concerning a man o' the cloth." Sardonic laughter closed the conversation.

When young John Harper came to stay it had been, in more ways than Hannah Wilson could count, a blessing sent by God. For most of her twenty five years till then, Hannah had been a slave to conscience and misfortune alike. She had been young and able bodied when the two other men in the extended family had passed away within five years of each other – now she was exhausted.

John Harper tethered his black garron, Dalryimple to a hitching bar on the far side of the barnyard and carefully avoided cattle droppings as he approached the door. It was little after five am but knowing how bairns need their sleep, he was reluctant to knock in case the family had not all risen. He gently pushed at the glass top of the half door and was surprised to see it swing open to reveal Jessie Wilson at her bread baking. She smiled gloriously and invited him in for a cuppa.

"No, no, I'll get on with the routines Mrs Wilson. Just tell me where tae start."

"Start by callin' me Jessie. If ye like ye can help my mother up on the hillside wi' the lambs. Hannah took the herd up onto the top pasture by the road, so I know she will need tae clean the barn ready fer the next storm."

"You make it sound like a certainty." Jessie looked at him askance, "Aye, so it is son. Add it tae the list, along wi' death and taxes!" Jessie's comely face glowed with welcome for Isobel's son and she crossed the kitchen, wiping her hands on a tea towel to greet him affectionately.

Twenty minutes later two eager collies rounded the barn entrance to scrutinise Harper from a distance without fuss, followed by Hannah Wilson, equally keen in the fullness of a pleasant summer morning. She wore blue denim dungarees, like an American rancher and her light brown hair was tied back.

"Oh, hello John!" she strode towards him with her hand outstretched and he pointed the hose away from her as he reached out to shake it.

"Thanks for this, I ruddy hate doing this job! Which is probably why you've done it in half the time it normally takes me."

Her eyes glowed with fond recognition of a lad whose reputation preceded him. John was instantly charmed by Hannah and she welcomed his presence warmly, speaking to him respectfully like another adult.

In all the accommodations of grace and circumstances Hannah believed in revelations of the Holy Spirit, commonplace as well as miraculous, even though she had nothing material to gain but the easing of her burdens. Harper had seen enough of living to know that a man might be struck by lightning out in the field, while contemplating nothing much of anything. His taking a share of the workload was blessed relief for Hannah however and in the most disarming style she made a point of telling him so.

"Never repeat this John but I was jiggered even before Mary left. She had me baby-sitting her bairns years ago. That's why we took them on. They were always part of our family."

There seemed to Hannah to be very little prospect of anything worthwhile ever happening in her life. Sure she'd had status in the family. Everyone loved her, especially her grandmother and the younger children. The bairns all flocked around her when she sat down to play the piano. They waited patiently for her offerings at mealtimes, when school and chores made them ravenous. Between daily routines they obediently helped around the farm. But the work never ceased and at times Hannah felt she was nothing more than their skivvy.

She gave piano lessons occasionally in the evenings or Saturday mornings. Local parents were happy to part with hard earned cash or pay in kind, as they knew Hannah was exceptionally talented. She was also honest in discouraging children with poor motivation, regardless of whether they had ability or not.

For some reason she'd acquired a reputation for deterring men who sought her hand in marriage. Grandmother Hannah and Jessie had not spoken of her looking for a partner for a few years – in fact since the age of seventeen when young Frank had been born. There had been quiet speculation amid the wider circle of friends, with more vocal and indiscreet gossip through the local community, as to why she was unmarried although perhaps in retrospect it should have been obvious. She felt morally bound to her mother's family.

Seventeen year old John didn't give a second thought to Hannah Wilson's reputation for playing hard to get. If anything it simply added to the allure. For a larger than average woman she was lissom, if a little care-worn before her time by too much hard graft. Her facial architecture was strongly harmonious and she possessed the most captivating green eyes it was conceivable for a lad who'd never been in love before, to imagine being anything other than matchless and unique.

He immediately began to watch Hannah from a distance, to empathise with her similar predicament, even though past twenty five that February she had been more than seven years older. It was clear to Harper that no matter how hard she worked, Hannah Wilson had a younger brother Frank who would one day inherit title to the two small farms. He would gain the wealth that would accrue to the family through the fruits of all their labour.

Moreover, John knew himself to be nothing more than a child of uncertain parentage although he'd come to terms with the benign manner in which the Harpers had brought him up. Apparently John and Isobel Harper had adopted him despite his being illegitimate. Also he could see that such unquestioning generosity was very much a commonplace in the tightly knit, enfranchised community of Morayshire. Most crofters did not own title to their own property and there were no secure prospects for those who grew up in the area, except to work as domestic servants or farm labourers. Young people were surrounded by nature. Trained to respond to her rigorous calendar of flowering and decay, parents, teachers and Ministers steered their minds in abstraction to spiritual messages from the pulpit. They were expected to control sexual urges until circumstances beckoned and opportunity arose. John Harper had incrementally come to despise the inverted snobbery of a society he felt to be economically and socially at war with itself, as piece by piece he had put together the bitter truth about his own status.

When Hannah received an official communication through the mail regarding a music teaching post at Elgin Academy, in the spring of '87, John noticed it was addressed to one Hannah Wilson Drummond although her mother Jessie's maiden name had been Barber. Great Gran was a Drummond but Hannah was too young to be her daughter. He knew not to ask about this but realised immediately they had a secret in common. He was only seventeen but he knew he had fallen instantly in love with her. John Harper swore a private vow in that very moment he would have her, or never look at another woman.

In his heart the young man could see a future of uncertainty in a community of endless intermarrying for one simple unavoidable material goal - the right to break the land and get a crop to grow. Life was hard even then - nobody outside of the farming community with its tightly knit order of accommodations and rank could ever understand the accession. There was a market value for everything: cattle, sheep, grain and people.

Hannah told him that she had been provided by Frank, ten years before he died, with a decent piano - a German upright, previously languishing in a barn near Huntly for years. Essentially it was as good as new although it had come at a bargain price. But this magnanimity now seemed no more than token encouragement.

Despite her consummate musical talent, her mother and Grandmother wanted Hannah to stay to help raise the extended brood of two closely interdependent families. She would never leave of her own volition. They all depended upon her too much, both old and young. Harper realised that she felt morally bound. Ultimately all their lives were in feu to a wealthy landlord. It was this invariable social pressure within all the farming families he knew of that he had come to resent most.

As he worked the months and years away for the Wilsons, John fantasised about the English father he had never known, supposing him to be some coastal trader or merchant. He also began to secretly envy the autonomy of the tailor and the road dresser, the grocer and fisherman. Such people might have to rent properties along the main streets, but they could take their labour wherever they wished. They no longer tipped their caps to a man looking right through them, just because he sat on a fine horse.

With its relatively diverse and thriving economy, John knew that Morayshire represented what little was left of the real Highland lifestyle. Clearances elsewhere had shattered towns, leaving them in ruin. Cattle had been replaced by sheep and the farmers driven away. Natural diversity, the symbiosis of people with land, was now utterly destroyed and forgotten. The Garden of Eden had finally become a wasteland. The Highlands were devoid of flowers and insects, birdsong, dogs barking at laughing children - of people working and living. Caledonia was bereft of the good people who had truly belonged here, borne of this land. What promise could it hold?

Despite the desolation of Inverness-shire and Sutherland, John knew that throughout Moray and Aberdeenshire there was work to be had. Wages were relatively good for those who laboured and never turned the word on their employer, whether ship owner, brewer or crofter. But in his situation as a farm servant working for three generations of widowers (Hannah's grandmother he noted was still active at seventy two and was as lissom as a teenage girl), John felt like some minor Royal waiting in the wings for death to take the Great Ones, that he might then take his place in the sun.

Harper threw the last bundle of straw and stood back from the potato grave on the west field. Stretching singing back muscles, he drank deeply from his water jar. Sitting on the ground in the summer heat, he looked around at the shimmering horizon.

How many tired minds and broken bodies have these hills engendered over recent millennia? How many family disputes have there been over marriages with inheritance? How long have sneering landlords sat back to rake in proceeds of so much hard graft, underlying so much private ambition?

He imagined the cries of war-painted Pictish forebears - Calgacus' reckless hordes running down a nearby mountain slope onto lines of redoubtable Roman invaders. Nothing had really changed in over two millennia – the Romans left empty-handed and even the English feudal system barely scratched the surface of a mediaeval clan hierarchy favouring a bellicose elite.

Now of course the Old Fathers were hiding behind banks of imported rhododendron in their baronial houses. Some had flitted to London to organise diverse businesses; more effectively overseeing the management of vested interests by attending the House of Lords. They no longer took responsibility for people residing outside of their private estates. Salaried land agents collected and banked their rents for them. Ensuring the profitable distribution of lumber, cargos of grain, casks of whisky and shoulders of lamb mattered more than the prospects of any struggling tenants. Inequality in the Highlands was a well-run industry.

Looking back in the direction of the two farm houses at Ramsburn, one with its traditional low stone walls and thatch, the other larger and restyled after the growing fashion of Nairn and many other Scottish towns - with Norman style peaked gables built around strong chimneys and surrounded by outbuildings and gardens - Harper realised that he was a pawn to Jessie's Queen. Despite the outward signs of status with all that might be taken for granted in the provisioning of a farmstead, the Wilsons, like the Harpers, sustained a fearful, almost religious parsimony in all their dealings. It struck Harper as dubious that people with money would never talk about it.

The farming community simply and unavoidably reflected the elitism and division of the greater society. Ownership was everything to Jessie Wilson. She would no more divulge her broad intentions to Harper than she would unhand the tenure of her houses and land. This was never a matter of why, so much as what. It was a fact of life, a matter of her personal survival. People here hung on tightly to what little they could call their own.

If he stayed, Jessie and her mother would smile and demur while they ran rings around him. Eventually they would drive him mad with chivvying and unsolicited advice, like they had Frank. It was no-one's fault particularly but John knew even at seventeen that whatever he worked for, whatever he achieved, would never be enough.

With an angry shock he noticed a hardened look of dismay in Hannah's expression as she looked out over the market garden when absentmindedly stirring through pans in the sink. That letter from Elgin College disturbed her, despite the promise carried by its official nature and relative bulk. She had been offered a job – but they had prevailed upon her to turn it down! It struck him like a bolt from the blue sky above his head and shoulders. She was too noble to act purely out of self–interest, to weep or complain, putting career before dedication to family. John knew in his very soul he would never find a better reason for loving any woman than such selfless altruism.

At that moment Harper decided that this glorious amphitheatre of pain – of warfare and work and ownership - would not contain him. It was fine country but it did not seem to inspire the soul to anything so much as hardness, envy and longing. John resolved that if Hannah agreed to marry him, he would fight Jessie for her eldest daughter, to take her away from this place.

He had to have her or leave with his anger and a broken heart. Loving Hannah had become a fact of life. John couldn't recall when it had happened. Like the mountains and the sky, his adoration of her seemed to have had no beginning and would have no end. John felt a

liberating purpose that eventually brought meaning to his life. This
best intention he was to pleadingly make clear to his beloved when
she later fell pregnant with their first daughter Elsie. Although taking
Hannah away hurt the whole family deeply, that is what he ultimately
managed to persuade her to agree to. Harper reflected upon the fact
that Hannah was twenty five the day he had whispered in her ear and
she walked with him hand in hand, deep into the forest at Moss Side.

She was stunned by his precociousness and sincerity both, but in
the curl of her lips was the answer. He had then been only seventeen
but spoke to Hannah like a man of the world. Hannah recognised
that in turn everyone she knew spoke to John Harper respectfully,
despite his relative youth.

Now there was an avid gleam in his eyes, a robust balance to his
frame and the lightly elegant pace at which he walked made her slow
to look at him anew. She laughed repeatedly at every joyful, engaging
comment her young suitor made. Hannah was as tall as he was. With
her almond hair tied for work she habitually never slowed her pace
except on the way to church, where she still arrived first to take her
place behind the pipe organ. Being persuaded to this diversion, to
walk with Harper on the return home from Sunday morning service,
was novelty itself.

John Harper had been offered the job by her mother over a year
before and Hannah had been watching him ever since. At first this
had been for professional reasons but then her interest had taken on
another purpose. She was subconsciously evaluating him, not just as a
labourer but as an individual. She had watched him playing shinty
and football and seen how he moved like a panther, shrugging off
challenges and tackles. Word was that he was an excellent boxer too
and that none of the rough farm boys would challenge him. He had
worked for two years as a tailor's apprentice before taking on the
forge. His Uncle Zachariah, who owned a shop in Elgin had taught
him much even as a small child. Now Harper had career options.
Hannah listened with interest as he talked about making his own suits

- which of wool lighter in weight and darker in colour than the grey favoured by many men locally, made him stand out from the church congregation. His attire also served to raise comment and laughter in a crowd. They named him 'the man in black' with all the superstitious connotations. Once, even the minister had mistaken him for a visiting cleric, perhaps because previously he had not been a regular churchgoer.

Hannah's obvious interest in John seemed to stop abruptly some three months prior to the walk in the forest, when she blushingly realised he was doing precisely the same in return – weighing her up. His had been a lingering look, not of false ardour or concupiscence but with a gentle smile of recognition. She knew this immediately for what it genuinely was – mutual interest – not the pecuniary variety she had seen at livestock markets, ceilidhs and church meetings, blatantly projected from groups of farm hands she vaguely recognised.

The locals had looked at her the way they looked at cattle at an auction. She could even tell how much they were prepared to bid by the way they pinched and stroked their throats above the Adam's Apple, alternatively how little interested by the way they leaned or slouched while waiting for the next bovine offering to be prodded through the kirk gate for cursory evaluation. Such presumptive men were abhorrent to her – red necks scrubbed up, bursting through collars that had fit them perfectly when they were less seasoned, less smug and less corpulent. Given the opportunity, they would have gripped her calves; peeled back her eye lids and squeezed open her mouth to look at her teeth.

Hannah and John talked, naturally . . . and in the workaday routines there was always opportunity for him to approach and appeal gently to her mood. Hannah was self-conscious and her mother Jessie was instantly, almost intuitively aware of their nascent courtship, as much evidenced by shyness as their politely controlled responses to one another.

Harper amazed Hannah by his certainty about her and his candour regarding their future together. He was not the gold prospector she had been warned about and had so often witnessed, without love in their eyes. He was genuinely taken with her - for whatever reason she could not quite fathom. Whatever else might be inferred they were comfortable in each other's presence. The harmony of their friendship was reflected in arduous daily routines that invariably went smoothly by.

On that wonderful, never to be forgotten day in the summer of '87, as they returned from morning service in Milltown of Rothiemay, it became clear in a glance with mutually dwelling smiles that she was available and he was in need. That was all that seemed to matter when he steered her up the lane past Hugh Harper's Sawmill and turned left along a forest track leading them to nowhere but each other.

They stepped over a ditch into woodlands, to stroll through broken sunshine and shade where leverets hopped into cover and a squirrel raced to hide behind a tree. John had waited for months to embrace Hannah's obvious and welcoming interest.

As a preamble to coupling he averred breathlessly that he would be hers for evermore. She blushed as she leant back against the tallest, most beautiful fir tree near the top of the hill and kissed him energetically. Yellow sunlight spilled down the length of its trunk. He kissed her in return, sweetly on the lips. As she pulled him towards her breast, Hannah smelled the Sunday morning soap flakes in his hair. They were innocently but painfully in love. Although each hesitated a moment at the thought of history repeating itself, they soon resumed their explorations with fervour and much laughter at the obligation to avoid tearing or soiling one another's best Sunday clothes.

A darker more ponderous section of Chopin, beyond the juvenile haste of Joe's forceful fingers, seemed to accompany Harper's conflicted recollection of a family quarrel.

"You o' aw people should ken better," Hugh Harper grumbled through his supper.

"Oh aye . . . an' how would that be?"

"Ah ken you know whit ah mean boy."

"Oh sure, hold on now . . . I ger it, 'cause o' aw the dutiful interest you've shown in my moral education, pa?'"

"Dinnae talk like that to your elders," put in Hugh's wife, John's sometime 'Auntie' Bonnie, whom he could not now accept the idea of - and outright refused to call his mother.

He knew they were all lying – merely transferring responsibility for his uncertain parentage away from John Harper senior to avoid scandal and disputes if at some point in the next few months a birth certificate had to be produced for the registrar.

"You'll marry the girl either way," declared Hugh with certainty as assured as his next mouthful of mutton stew, which he popped in just to confirm his decision.

"Oh! I'll marry her if I choose to do so an' if she'll accept ma proposal – no' if you declare it be done to ease your conscience," stated young John with a manful hardening of his voice.

The blow that came from behind to the base of John's skull was as fierce as it was sudden. Emerging through the doorway to the kitchen of the farmhouse at Auchterless was his sometime 'father' and namesake John, "You'll do as yer faither says and no back chat or ah'll tak the wind oot o' yer sails boy!"

"Oh, so . . . let me get this right - You're no ma faither. Uncle Hugh's my faither now . . . and what does that make you then?" demanded John rounding on the man who had raised him as a child. Harper's eyes filled with tears and his voice began to choke with the fury of enduring injustice.

The brothers were silenced by this – Hugh stirring his stew with a spoon, a piece of bread hovering in his other hand, looking down into some inner knowledge he had to now prudently step around. John Senior turned his shoulder as he paced into the kitchen. There was a long silence as Harper rubbed a grubby thumb and forefinger into his watery eyes.

Typically it was the women who took over in expressing an easy summation of an impenetrable design, with a simple reassertion of what is. Jessie Barber Wilson, slightly built, cheerily candid in her usual manner, looked at the confidently obese Bonnie Lorimer Harper, whose matronly, generous mouth was held for once open in hesitation, allowing the younger woman to speak first.

Hannah's mother turned her attention to the boy standing contrite in the doorway, "Ah didna come here te level accusations at ye son, or God forbid, cause ye t' fall oot wi' yer family John," she pleaded, holding her hand up to place on his shoulder, as if to confirm that she had been guilty of doing just that, "Ah came because Hannah telt me you are the faither of her unborn child."

She paused to consider her words diplomatically in order to steer all concerned past anger and conflict to the desired outcome, "An' she telt me that you want to marry her, is that no' true son? If it is that's a cause fay joy an' celebration son, no' fay raking up sorrows o' the past! Why don't we aw set doon an' talk it o'er?"

Bonnie Harper and young John sat with her at the table, with Hugh sullenly finishing his supper at the far end by the fire. John Senior mumbled something to himself and went away to wash before eating.

As no-one interjected, Hannah's mother continued but the folded arms and tight lips of the other three told Jessie she was still on stony ground, "There is no other man at Ramsburn apart frae eight year old Frank . . . an' twa crofts to pay wir dues on – ye've a'ready shown us ye can do the rounds. The bairns can help us when they're no' at school. Elsie is able to fetch and carry now . . ."

Harper hammered his fist onto the dining table so hard that Hugh's plate and the condiments jumped and rattled, "Shut up will ye woman fer Chrissake!" They stared at Harper aghast as the tide of anger rose in his eyes and voice, "I will say this one time, and we will ha' nae arguments or repetition." He looked from one to the other around all the faces in the darkening room before speaking again with heavy emotion in his voice.

39

"I will make my ain decisions . . . and if only to show ye. . . each of yis . . . the importance o' this to me, given my questionable status over the years in this family. I will love Hannah's child and . . ," he paused for maximum effect, looking now at his legally declared 'father' Hugh, then feeling his bruised neck he glowered defiantly across at John Senior who had come back into the room, "Let me make this crystal clear . . . . I will raise the bairn as ma ain, with Hannah always by my side. But I will no' marry her till I've income an' position away from this place. I will hold ma heed up an' be proud. I will teach my ain bairn tae do the same. All three of us will be Children o' the Barley together. At least no-one will lie tae us!"

Harper's anger petered out but his fists were still clenched, his chest heaving as he rose and turned to the door. He stood in silence looking out across the fields. Hugh Harper moved uneasily in his chair at the dining table, stretching his long legs. He sighed as though a great paradigm had been revealed to him and he had been forgiven by the Almighty. His younger brother stood in silence, staring now intently and disapprovingly at young Harper, his legs bent slightly and arms folded as he propped himself in a neutral corner over by the living room door, too angry to eat. He looked like a boxer catching his breath between rounds.

The two women were stunned into silence but Jessie reflected for an instant that things might have gone to plan if only she had insisted that Hannah had come with her to this meeting of the families.

Harper lowered his head slightly as his breathing settled. He regained the poised, understated clip of his Moray dialect, "I have decided no' to marry Hannah yet. So don't be talking aboot it again. I micht lie tae the preacher but ah'll nae lie to the registrar. One day ah may want to join the Polis. There's work to be done the noo' . . . so I'll gan on," he said, turning once more to Hannah's mother with laboured politeness but a smile of genuine affection in his eyes, "See you now, Jessie." He spun off the weathered porch stone, out into the flagged yard.

"God, there's pride for ye. Young bugger!" exclaimed Hugh.

40

"Pride yer arse! You didnae live wi' him for seventeen years. He's a stubborn wee bastard," John declared.

"Just like his faither," stated Hugh's wife Bonnie, with a hint of irony.

"Ye mean he has a fancy notion o' himself, like all the bloody English?" ventured Hannah's mother.

"No' so much the notions," cut in John senior, regaining his natural humour, "It's just that he canny keep his willie in his breechs."

They all laughed. Jessie laboriously jacked her weather-worn frame up from the table, pushing down on the flat of her hands, reminding them all of the gesture that gave sudden authority to Harper's ferocious outburst. No one spoke for a moment but with hospitality and further diplomatic planning in mind the conversation naturally drifted in the direction of Jessie Wilson staying for a drink.

Hugh's eldest son, Douglas was despatched to fetch Hannah for cross-examination. He was to invite Hannah's grandmother also, then alert his aunt Isobel. They might yet create an excuse for making a night o' it despite the 'wee bugger's' refusal to marry the girl.

Hugh briefly explained to Hannah's mother the awful secret that had lain dormant for so many years - the obligation he and his brother had felt back in 1870 to their cousin from Bath, a visiting merchant and father of young John.

"He regularly brought valuable cargoes to Banff frae England. Expensive cloth. Brandy. Thoroughbred horses for the toffs. He even persuaded Zach Williams, his tailor to come up frae Gateshead tae meet the local gentry. He and Sir William Forsyth helped Zach establish premises up in Elgin."

"Aye, so all the nobs could buy angora frock coats an' silk evening gowns, while the Hi'lan weavers could go penniless," put in his wife Bonnie.

"No woman, that's not the way of it at aw. The English gentry flaunt their tartans. They have a Scottish Society that pays good money for aw that stupid regalia. An' they filled up that vessel frae Bristol wi' whisky, lumber, horses and cattle for the return, so wheesht wi' yer nonsense!"

"Can't I have opinions? Can't a woman speak?"

"No opinions and no speaking . . . get that distillery malt and the glasses."

"Get it yersel' ye old bastard. Jessie an' I expect Champagne."

"Well yer goony ha' te send oot fer thon' – a poor crofter canny extend to storin' up they kind o' riches."

"Poor my arse; ye've more butter than a Jersey coo! Whit else dye ha'e tae spend it on?"

There was laughter around the table. Hugh Harper feinted a slap on his wife's voluminous backside as she rose to make for the carved mahogany bureau.

All eyes were on Hugh as he resumed the story of Harper's father, "There was great potential for the souring of relations here d'ye see – if ony word o' it got back to my cousin's family in Bath, d'ye understand?" He looked down at Jessie from under professorial eyebrows to emphasise his point.

"Family in Bath? Aw! You're saying he was marriet? John's father was already marriet? In Bath?" put in Jessie, her voice raised musically with the scandal of it.

"Of course yes, to a real beauty, with considerable wealth and ken . . . connections on both sides," acknowledged Hugh, rolling his head slowly from side to side, as though arbitrating a difficult case with the candour of a Jedburgh Justice. He paused before fixing his eyes on Jessie, audibly hissing with dismay through his long nose, "No' tae mention the good reputation of Sir William Forsyth," he said with reluctant finality.

"What do you mean?" asked Jessie, warming to Hugh's account as she waved away the offer of the precious malt, "How did auld Willie come intae it?"

"No' at aw, except that the goings – on, if I may call it that, took place under his roof and that . . . well, his business partnerships here

42

in Morayshire possibly stood tae suffer, whit's the word? . . . an hiatus . . . as a consequence."

"D'you mean he ended up with a hernia? I hope no' as the result of some sexual profligacy. Oh jee whiz, imagine that in the Daily Herald!"

"Hold yer tongue woman!" scolded Hugh, beginning to wish he'd never started the exposition. "The scandal involved a man invited by him to his fine house, to partake of his hospitality, sharing wi' him extensive, mutually rewarding business affiliations. Add to that the shame of a girl o' tender age in Sir William's employ getting intae trouble."

"So?"

"So, it could never be spoken of. Sir William was always a kind and honourable man. He'd tak' in a wandering piker an' gi' 'im his ain supper if the sleet was in the man's face an' chill in his bones. He'd gi' 'im his ain fine shoes if he saw the soles were walked oot o' the man's." As he spoke Hugh gestured with his long arms, something Jessie had never seen him do before. She was warming to the man, even if he was a tight lipped old hypocrite.

Hugh looked into the middle distance as if recollecting details he had actually witnessed himself. He sniffed his fine whisky and sipped it slowly. At last he continued, "So when the lassie died in childbirth, I registered it as mine. John and Isobel agreed to foster the bairn wi' certain assurances."

"And John's faither, where was he? Gone home to his loving wife nae doot, the fast jerker!"

"Oh aye, you're right Jessie . . . despite his love for Sir William and Moray Society, he's been a little reluctant to return since then," put in Bonnie Harper.

"Though at least he stumped the pew," added brother John, sitting down now at the end of the table.

"Oh God, aye, regular. Guilt is a powerful thing, as I'm here te tell ye," agreed Hugh solemnly, "An' there was private business over the years – log-rolling, quite literally in case you never noticed, has put food on the tables o' aw the boys roon here."

"So, wee John Harper's illegitimacy benefitted everybody but himself?" concluded Jessie Wilson for the record.

There was a tangible sense of relaxation in the room as they all agreed the history, "There are a hell of a lot o' sawmills nearer the coast they could hae gone tae," intimated Hugh.

"Aye an' there is also. . . , " said John hesitating as he realised he was taking a step too far. He deferred to his older brother.

Hugh looked as sternly as he could at his good friend and neighbour Jessie. If nothing else the mild sincerity of his handsome face assured her receptiveness.

"You're no' tae breathe a word o' this woman – d'ye understand? No' tae the old lady, an' especially no' tae him. Nor to that fine girl of yours," demanded Hugh Harper with gravity, "I ken Hannah's nae gold digger but money's always trouble if ye hae' it or no. Whit ahm gonae tell ye is no' tae be repeated, until legally permitted." Jessie sat hunched in silence, her azure eyes unflinching but Hugh waited.

"Women are incapable o' keepin' secrets Hugh, surely ye've learnt that by noo?" croaked John through his whisky.

"A'right ye hev ma word on it, whatever it is he'll no hear it frae me!" exclaimed the lovely Jessie at last, detestation of this overly cautious man welling in her chest. She reminded herself that she had been brought up a Catholic and was now a good Episcopalian, which amounted to the same thing amongst the people of the book in these parts. He'd forgotten that, the old cud, or no doubt he wouldn't even talk to her at all. She could always go to confession afterwards. With a smile teasing at her lips, Jessie resisted the temptation to bless herself before telling a conscious lie.

It struck Hugh in the instant how unlike her daughter Hannah Jessie Wilson was, with her straight black hair and slight frame. Hugh was suddenly abashed with the realisation – he guessed he was talking to the converted.

The guilt rose in him again and he mumbled as though the mere mention of money might bring the devil to the door, "There's a sizeable trust fund held in John's name by Christie's in Banff."

Hugh sipped his Glen Livet, allowing it to burn a pathway down into his belly, recoiling mentally from the prevailing irony of Hannah and Harper's circumstance. He would much rather have simply told them all the truth, especially as he knew Jessie would never believe him, "He's ony te hae it if he marries, or at age twenty wan, no afore then. You heard whit he said aboot makin' hees ain mind up."

Hugh paused to allow the point to sink in. At that moment John's wife Isobel came into the kitchen from the interior of the house. Evidently she had walked up the lane and entered through the front door. She sat down silently at the table next to Bonnie Harper.

"The young couple will hae five years o' hardship an' whitever we say or do, in the end we'll be in the wrong!" complained Hugh. Jessie ignored Hugh's pre-occupation with money and morality – she had other fish to fry.

"Why John and Isobel? And how did you two, Bonnie and Hugh, get involved so late on with his upbringing?" she asked, looking from Hugh to his wife, "I mean wi' the greatest o' respect, you were nae responsible for yer cousin takin' advantage o' that girl! Who was she ony way?" Jessie appealed to the other three adults sitting around the room.

"Le' it alone Jessie," advised John with a hint of menace in his voice.

"Oh sure, pardon me fer askin' – but d'ye think the boy will le' it alone?"

"She has nae living relatives, Jessie – that's aw ye need tae ken," Bonnie Harper reassured her.

Hugh prevaricated, returning to her first question, waving his hands wide in defence, while mumbling something about financial support for the orphan and an accommodation involving a big contract for lumber which had required him to visit Bristol; certain

45

people at the Scottish Society with local connections who'd asked too much about his personal circumstances, who knew him too well.

Hannah's mother nodded her head slowly. At length she inferred, "Oh, I see! It micht ha' been bad fer business, well that explains it all," she gushed with blatant sarcasm, placing both her hands palms down on the kitchen table, as though she was dumb and it had been obvious all along.

Brother John and Hugh's wife Bonnie tried to help Hugh along with his vague and painful explanation. Then almost as an afterthought Jessie interrupted the hesitant conversation again, to politely re-state the question, "Why, over all the intervening years, were your brother John and his wife responsible for bringing up the child and not you, Hugh?"

She looked at John who turned his head at an angle and glowered at her mutely like a prize fighter at a weigh-in, "Ah, well," Hugh intoned, choosing his words carefully while looking over at his brother who still looked dangerously compressed. John was sternly silent as he spun the fine whisky in a wide glass tumbler, "Eh, they didn't mind, I mean they were . . . marriet an' had a child - Callan and . . . I, what wi' the saw mill and the Grange Farm, had my hands full, ken? Travelling back and forth getting contracts for the lumber an' aw that . . ."

Hugh ran out of words and turned his hands up, raising his eyes to the ceiling but no-one interrupted. They wanted to feel his dilemma and share it but saw only his doubts and pecuniary self-interest, although for a moment Hugh had a look of intense sincerity, not unlike Da Vinci's Jesus at the Last Supper, thought Jessie.

"I love you guid people, the Lorimers too," Jessie Wilson affirmed, turning to look at Isobel, "An' aw yer family Hugh . . . yoos are nothing if nae decent hard working folk, an' respected sure by everyone . . . but why in the name o' the wee man would yis aw continue tae lie tae a teenage boy o' sich character and intelligence, for so many years?"

46

Childlike, Hugh Harper hung his handsome head in shame, forgiveness of his transparent guilt shining dimly like the halo of a fallen angel around his angled, sunken shoulders. He was an uncomplicated man, equally incapable of deceit, or of complete alacrity. He wanted to give young John Harper the birthright and fortune he'd always intended for him, the love he deserved too, but there had always been competing interests. Too much responsibility. Too many mouths to feed.

Hugh explained that the only option left to him, when the lad had started asking questions about the rumours, was to claim him as his own from his volcanic brother John and long suffering sister-in-law Isobel. Brother John, so it happened - although five years junior - had married Isobel two years before Hugh and Bonnie had exchanged vows. They'd already had a daughter. It had just seemed wrong to Hugh to start a family with an adopted son. His wife had agreed with this objection at the time.

This most recent twist of adopting Harper had been at least a plausible lie on paper, "For the registrar ken and the Kirk? And for young John Harper himself," explained Hugh with sombre rectitude. Hugh showed them all the birth certificate, nominating himself and Bonnie as John's legitimate parents. He had been thumbing the folded document throughout his tortuous explanation.

Inevitably their adopted son, with the wisdom and perspicacity of youth, had come to see through it all; as had Callan and Alex, who'd conferred with him as bosom pals. The one thing Harper in turn failed to see was the simple humanity of the two hard men who had owned to him without ever deigning to offer an explanation. Then again, he had never imagined any explanation which could have been so labyrinthine or unfeeling.

Unwillingly he had grown to be just like them, especially John who had reared him and shaped him in his own image and to whose home Harper still gravitated for all social events, when not working for the Wilsons. Like him he was leathered and taciturn but with the heart of a lion for all that was moral and plain to see. Yet Harper still failed to see compassion in himself – how would he ever learn to allow it in?

There was the sound of hurried footsteps dodging puddles of ordure on the flagged courtyard opposite the cow shed. The latch flicked upwards as the split door, snibbed for the cool evening burst open. The breathless and quite stunningly beautiful Hannah, clearly having been well briefed about the unseemly argument by Douglas, stood wide eyed and red cheeked panting before them. The conversation stopped immediately. Hugh had exonerated himself at last. Besides, with the arrival of her beloved daughter, Jessie had suddenly run out of thorny questions concerning legitimacy and inheritance.

Naturally enough Jessie Barber Wilson made her daughter Hannah aware of what so deeply affected Harper – of the secrets that burned and the pain that would not go away. In short, of the impasse she herself had witnessed between Harper and the elders of his family. She also made Hannah aware that John's status in their home was merely as her labourer; and that John and Isobel's son Alex, or maybe one day Hugh and Bonnie's younger boys Douglas and Ewan, would be inheritors of Grange Farm and the sawmill, not John.

She explained the legalities of inheritance and custom of taking on existing tenancy agreements - that this was the 'English Way,' now accepted reluctantly as the 'Scottish Way.' The newly imposed tradition was that the eldest son was the assumed inheritor – unlike the Highlands of olden days or its once powerful ally, polyglot yet romantically Celtic France.

She dared not breathe a word of Hugh's revelation regarding Harper's wealthy father. That was a locked chest buried in sand on a stormy coast – that all the world knew of yet none had seen. She was off the hook either way, although she did not want Hannah and Harper to leave. When that day came she knew her old heart would break. Harper's financial surety would be delayed by his own determination to act independently.

Implicit in her mother's vague explanation Hannah understood, was the notion that perhaps her half-brother Frank would be shown the same unwarranted privilege as John's adoptive brother Alex, even though it was she who did all the hard work of managing the two farms at Ramsburn and Frank was still an unstructured schoolboy.

She tightened her lips, pouching her cheeks in resignation but the reddening of her face under wavy almond hair and the moment of fire in her green eyes told their own story. From that moment onwards Hannah said goodbye to all that was borne of sentiment, all that was childhood and all that had been taken for granted at home. She loved her ma and her grandma and of course Jessie's bairns, all of them: Frank; Jeannie; Betsy, whom she had gone out her way to spoil when Frank had left; Kate; Fiona; and Elsie - but from now on the truest bond and Hannah's greatest trust lay with Harper, as she began to habitually call him.

Chapter Three - *Fault Lines*

After Sunday dinner they sat in the living room at 'the new house' as she had declared it to be, even though it had been constructed in the sixteenth century, "From now on I'll just call you Harper . . . How does that strike you? Eh, Harper?"

"As guid a name as any I suppose, an' I'm proud o' it!" He lied barefaced without a hint of irony. She laughed the more so because of his casual duplicity with a brightly resonant, quite voluminous laugh. She put her hand up to her mouth to constrain delight at his irreverence. Her magical green eyes shone with beauty he could only gaze at incredulously, so uncommon were they.

Harper wagged his crossed leg, unselfconsciously comfortable in her presence, then reached across to the hearth to tap ash out from his pipe. When he glanced back at her sidelong, Hannah read the look of whimsical acceptance in his expression.

"You're lucky to have two names at all laddie. In the good old days only those with a grand title had such. So from now on you'll just have one name, Harper . . . "Harper!" She affected the Edinburgh English tone of a portly laird, "Here my man! Harper, play a lament for us!"

"Ah but that's no' a forename Hannah – a Christian name was aw they ever had or needed, no' a surname. Surnames were fae the gentry."

"Oh, what the hell is in a name anyway but the burden of humanity? When I was an innocent soul, first ushered into this world, I knew no name and found it alien when I learned it!" He was enthralled by her vivacity, even when she laughed at her own conceit.

She had great strength and solid natural beauty which overwhelmed him, though he affected restraint. Hannah would go with him, he knew now and they would find their life together somewhere on the road that headed south. Harper was bursting with excitement to possess her, to live the wonderful life that intuition told him lay ahead. She played for him on the recovered German upright with its broken candleholders and cracked inlay. Harper was swept away in love and harmony, completely out of time and mind.

The Bechstein upright had been purchased for five pounds – less than a tenth of its original cost. It was transported and tuned for a guinea - outlay which seemed monumental at the time even for the overly magnanimous Frank. To Hannah it seemed then as indeed it did ten years before at the age of fifteen, unbelievably good fortune and the greatest kindness ever shown her by her considerate father. She knew it was Frank's way of saying, 'I'm sorry for my pathetic sake that you are not my daughter and I'm sorry that you are not a boy. I could not possibly have cherished you more as an individual if you had been both!'

The gentleman farmer who owned the sumptuous German piano had inherited his father's estate at the age of thirty one. Gary Walker was a huge, boyish fellow who sounded more English than Scottish. Walker gave the impression that whatever he did best it was not work. Active in the theatrical society around Elgin, he seemed a predictable if dignified bachelor, who at some time in his youth had dabbled at the keys.

When Frank began to negotiate determinedly but playfully at somewhere just below the piano's estimated value, it quickly transpired that Mr Walker was deeply embarrassed by the condition of the yellowing Rosewood Bechstein. He would not hear of Frank's raised offer commensurate with anything approaching its original cost.

"Put your money away man!" Walker cried out disarmingly, to the now discomfited Frank, "Don't you realise it will cost a small fortune to restore and polish. It needs retuning twice for the damp," he wisely cautioned the now overawed and trembling Hannah. When she had thoroughly explored beneath the cobwebs under the dust cover and a permanent smile registered across her ecstatic face, they went into his parlour for tea.

Gary pointed out regretfully that, "The candleholders are long gone. No doubt pinched by bar room rogues who had no concept of the insult they were delivering to highly skilled craftsmen who'd worked over this classic instrument for months in their factory." Walker was ashamed almost to the point of tears, as though purviewing the desecrated tomb of a beloved mentor. He had explained to Frank that he still played but now favoured his Spencer – a more strongly voiced, steel-framed English piano, for use amongst chattering audiences. Frank nodded his distracted approval, absently regretting the fact that he'd not taken Jessie to the occasional show over in Keith.

"The Bechstein is easier for a girl to play though," Walker assured them, "In many ways it's a much nicer instrument, with a softer tone."

Standing in the dusty storehouse with the sunlight slanting through weathered timbers, Hannah's heart leapt into her mouth. Tears of joy began to well into her eyes as she realised this was her dream about to be fulfilled. She quivered with the kind of delight only a young girl can experience as optimism is fulfilled. Hannah looked at Frank in awe but he spun away without comment, inured to life's expectations, to shout for Brodie Robertson to climb down off the wagon. Sensing a bargain, he was eager to get his rig loaded and pay the man before Walker changed his mind.

Frank and Jessie's prodigious daughter was already the talk of the town for her musical ability, long before she had left school. There had been much ado about sending her to Elgin Academy for her last year in full time education. The establishment was generously equipped and had a great tradition in all aspects of music. The distance had been too great however – she was already making a twelve mile round trip each day to her school over at Keith.

As a consequence of her disappointment, Frank wished to complete the gesture to the satisfaction of all: the Minister whom he thoughtfully avoided but who seemed to have a say in everything locally; Hannah's music teacher, who happened to be the wife of the

52

doctor to whom Frank owed a small fee for treatment for a persistent cough neither man had forgotten; and above all his fiery better half Jessie, who might never forgive Frank's drinking and carousing but would be choked at such generosity towards their daughter.

Years went by and Hannah excelled beyond even the most optimistic expectation. The doctor's wife had been a wonderful teacher – without question superior in every way to the tuition available in any regional school. She recommended graded studies offered by the Associated Board of the London Academy but only as a touchstone for the most profound, magical adventure.

The doctor's wife, Judith Payton taught Hannah technique and movement through performance, not practice, "I will play for you and then I will listen as you play for me – but you practice in your own time. Practice every day, just as you feel Hannah - as much as you wish or as little as you have time for. Push when you want, idle when you want. But always practice every day. Look for inspiration and new challenges. That will guarantee progress. One day you will be a master. You will know what you need to do and precisely how to do it - whether technique, composition, structure or intonation. But always listen. Listen to yourself. Listen with your heart. In the last five minutes or so I may comment on your technique and how to improve it." This was her first and only pedagogy.

Hannah marvelled at how this delicate and lovely woman would lean shoulders and arms, head and fingers into the piano keys - merging and flowing with the poise of a prima ballerina around synchronisations of Schubert or Beethoven. Above all Judith Payton inspired Hannah to absorb what she heard into her body – to listen with her eyes closed, 'then play with energy and heart – with love - experiencing love.'

In the interim, Frank found Mary Robertson and faded from the days, then from memory but never from Hannah's beating heart. Each time when she sat back, mentally exhausted from her exploration of what she knew to be the language of the heavens,

Hannah saw Frank standing before her with a warm grin of recognition, arms outstretched ready for an embrace. Tears of gratitude and forgiveness were never far away when she remembered Franks' gift. Somehow, she reflected, her music had also helped to heal Jessie's bitterness.

Hannah had often seen it in her eyes – a kind of pensive acceptance. Jessie Wilson voiced it only once, many years before Harper had his feet under the table, when listening to Hannah's playing, "The old cud is gone – but at least he left something good behind!"

On a glorious Sunday afternoon in April '88 with spring sunlight slanting through the windows of the sitting room, Harper marvelled at the most prolific demonstration of musical virtuosity he had witnessed in his eighteen years.

"My God woman, that's astounding. Tell me what it is and who taught you?" The bright, mellow tones of the German upright piano were quite exceptional for its specification. The time in the barn, as since then in the fairly evenly humidity of the Morayshire farmhouse, had done it no harm at all. Harper was no expert but he knew he'd never heard a piano tone so mellow or sweet, or for that matter such energetic playing of romantic and inspirational music. Equally he would not have been surprised by the fact that the instrument was worth at least twenty times what Frank had paid for it. To Harper it all seemed very exotic and other-worldly.

"Oh sure, thanks for the accolade!" answered Hannah genially.

"Oh . . . well, I didnae mean it to sound like I would actually know the difference . . . maybe though . . . Hey, I'll shut up before I trip on my tongue."

Hannah laughed again. Harper felt overwhelmed with joy just watching the voluptuous contours of her neck and chin. She seemed to laugh all the time. Whenever she played for him, Harper would catch sight of her Grandmother waltzing with the children in the Kitchen, keeping out of the way of the courting couple but listening in. The children hummed snippets of the tunes Hannah played. They laughed more than usual too, infected by the mood of the lovers. Harper knew that she loved him, that it was he who made her want to laugh so easily.

"It's a higher level test piece I had to learn for my matriculation – to be allowed to teach, or charge people for lessons."

"Let me guess – It's by Johann Strauss."

She smiled but was careful not to sound condescending, "Good guess, but not quite – it's a Chopin waltz and I know the section you are thinking of that sounds a bit like Strauss." She played both pieces brightly, one after the other. The door burst open and the younger children, Betsy, Fiona and young Elsie flooded in, clapping and trilling, followed by Jessie their mother, who promptly rounded them up and chased them away to allow the young couple space and time for their romance.

"Dr Payton's wife, Judith studied music in Glasgow," Hannah informed him, "It's where they met when he was at the University. My Daddy used to give him coal that he bought for the forge, for the stove in his surgery. He would get a cart load delivered wholesale and take a bag to everyone he had offended when he was pished, or cuckolded when he was feeling randy."

"Ye mean he was shagging the Doctor's wife?" Hannah shrieked with mock offence at the scandalous idea.

"Well she's a fine looking woman . . . maybe she likes a firm hand when the sun goes down." Hannah laughed again at the pastoral imagery, for some reason remembering her father Frank sitting grim faced alongside her on an upturned milking pail, on a late afternoon many years before.

"Stop now Harper, speak well of the dead!" she demanded, whacking him on the shoulder with a rolled up Strauss folio, suddenly serious now at the memory of Frank's passing, "But she does seem quite a handful for poor old Doctor Payton," intoned Hannah after a moment's reflection.

"Hmm, there you are! What did I say? Women can never resist a man with a look of childlike innocence. Who else round here was man enough tae even try? Maybe they bags o' coal were fer more than cough medicine and your piano lessons."

Hannah laughed again at the preposterously salacious image of a tumescent but over-committed Frank servicing the delightful Mrs Payton. Again Harper got a hard whack across the head with the rolled Strauss pianoforte score for his filthy mind, not to mention a sense of humour that knew no limits.

Hannah and Harper were powerfully, deeply in love - somehow comfortable with the pressures and illusions which surrounded them, delineating their simple lives in this pacific, ordered place.

Hannah realised she had not felt sensitive to Harper's awareness of Frank's weakness for the tender sex. No-one had mentioned it before, other than her mother in a rage many years ago when Frank had left. In truth it had always been more the other way round - girls had a weakness for him, although Frank did have a tendency to become embroiled.

It was not simply that her late step father had been handsome – Hugh Harper was handsome but most women despised him. Harper was handsome but most women found him smouldering and dangerous. Frank, by way of contrast, had had the natural look of perturbed innocence of a toddler who's lost his teddy. It appeared that any female with maternal instincts could not ignore him, even though they might not know him. Add to that quality of form the fact that he was a six-foot, faired haired gigolo with an insatiable appetite and inevitably trouble would follow. At one time before Jessie had tamed him, Frank Wilson reputedly had five women in tow, all of them eager for his attentions. Frank had been a Tom Cat.

Hannah and Harper finally married on the 2nd August 1890, a month after Harper's twentieth birthday but almost two years following the birth of their daughter Elsie. On the eve' of the nuptials Jessie took Harper to one side to tell him about his inheritance. She also told him in detail, including her own deepest convictions, about the matter of the conversational exchange the night they all got fuelled up in Hugh Harper's house.

"Why didn't you . . . why are you telling me this now?" asked Harper, incredulous at the idea he was soon to be a wealthy man.

"Because the information will not affect the outcome either way. You will marry my daughter and you will no longer hate your adoptive parents. I would have told you the truth years ago. I just wanted to be the first to tell you John, as a matter of principle."

"Let me think about this."

"There's nothing to think about."

"Did Hannah know?"

"Absolutely not."

"Grandma?"

"Well yes . . . but despite John Harper's opinion to the contrary and the rogue's insulting attitude towards women in general . . . I'll have you know Hannah Senior is a woman who would hold back scandalous information at the Final Judgement." Harper laughed heartily, hugging Jessie.

"Welcome to the family by the way . . . in advance," she whispered through tears of joy.

"Welcome to mine," replied Harper, rapturous anticipation welling in his heart.

As he sat back with a glass of sherry, Harper smiled wryly at recollection of Hannah always attending regular church services. After they'd posted the banns Reverend Blair announced a reservation for their date. Suddenly from being on nodding terms with the majority of the Kirk community, they found themselves held in warm esteem with dozens of people in the wider locality. Citizenry approached in random numbers over the intervening weeks to congratulate John and Hannah, to smilingly declare their approval.

Their frowned-upon and much gossiped about age differential; the fact that to some with a trained eye Hannah was obviously pregnant again; Blair pointedly delivering his homily about restraint in the run up to the Harvest season when teenagers would spend time unsupervised in the fields, the annoyance of two-year old Elsie clambering over worshippers' legs to retrieve copies of the Official Prayer Book to stack into a neat pile during Holy Communion - all of this litany of transgression and judgement was now of no consequence and best forgotten.

The response of local people who hailed them or approached across the street in the tiny mill town, or accosted them when they had a chance meeting in the market at Keith, caused naturally discreet Harper to mumble self-consciously over his words. Hannah took it for what it was though, responding in kind. These were well-wishers, so it was only proper to extend every courtesy to them.

Hannah's mother and grandmother were nothing short of legendary for matronly integrity and good manners. They knew and indulged everyone who resided or worked in the area, rich or poor. They had won their own battles in their own time. Now it was Hannah's turn.

They arranged hire of the Forbes Arms hotel for the afternoon of their wedding. All and sundry were invited to open-house in the evening at the Ramsburn crofts. Come the day Reverend Blair could not resist dipping into the obvious supporting characters from the Old Testament: who had sinned and been saved, who had wandered from the fold yet returned to the flock, with a pointed stare and cough at Elsie. He was blatantly canvassing for more business, on the presumption of a series of 'yeses' from Hannah. An arrangement was made for Elsie to be baptised within the month.

Warm, effulgent summer light slanted through untainted glass into a whitewashed interior, making the smiling faces and dark wood stand out clear. In the centre of the starry-eyed picture stood a woman in the fullness of her bloom but not yet showing the child forming inside. A posy of red roses contrasted embroidered Spanish lace of her mother's restyled wedding gown, more cream with age than self-conscious white.

Looking in her eyes, tight-skinned from the summer sun and dapper but without a hint of age, stood a man for once wearing conformist grey of the finest cut. Harper had many unresolved issues with the world, as with himself but this was his one instant of complete certainty. They gazed into each other's eyes and for an eternal moment the world diminished and everything seemed right – fixed, not broken.

In an instant the truth faded and illusion returned. They re-joined the carnival with all its distractions. Outside the church a generous congregation watched with baited breath as Hannah carefully detached a neat little wreath of wax blueberries from her hair. It had allowed her to look, for a while, a sylph from Christina Rossetti's painting. Hannah tossed it with a broad smile towards a knot of girls standing together on her left. She looked away quickly, avoiding embarrassment to whoever was most eager to catch it.

Many people had approached them that day to offer congratulations and assure them this was the best wedding they had ever been to. There were endless conversations rolling against the kaleidoscope of incidental backgrounds and movement – the churchyard and the main street, the Forbes Arms Hotel with its bedecked interior, horses milling in the town, the shaded lane with a dozen carriages and later the warm interior of two houses with parties - one for elders and the other requisitioned by the youth.

There were children running everywhere, restrained only by wariness of spoiling a best frock or breeches but wild nonetheless. There were bevies of sumptuously prepared women of all ages, smiling and laughing; men telling tales and smoking in groups. There was music behind the chink of cutlery and glasses, easy laughter amid storms of loud conversation and repartee.

As the afternoon wore on, amateur talent had successively stood to play or sing. Before too much drink created an atmosphere of uninhibited ribaldry, as she knew it soon would, Hannah left the near family group to slide unnoticed between chatting guests onto the piano stool in the alcove. She tapped middle and high C to avoid embarrassment with tuning then began to play quietly.

Hannah looked like a feature extracted from a pre-Raphaelite painting in all her sylvan finery - Joan Beaufort perhaps, ready to weave her feminine magic and capture the heart of a poet king. There was amusement in this image. As she worked the keys, the walls echoed with her version of the most noble and subtle harmonies ever to make a travelling girl rise to dance around a fire.

No-one present ventured to suggest the entire scene was extremely bizarre, or that Hannah energetically hammering out bass chords against delicately poised trills in the style of Chopin, while still wearing her matching hat, veil and wedding dress, fringed upon the lunatic. An anthropologist from the immediately previous generation would have marvelled that so much of tradition had evidently changed.

Elsewhere the highlands had been depopulated and anglicised as an adjunct of the woollen industry but this was the garden county of Banff. Ever since Cumberland's army had been rested and enthusiastically pointed Westward they had been allowed a Passover. The most talked about changes recently had been mechanical threshers; harrows and ploughs, yet this community was nothing if not open minded and appreciative.

Hannah began sweetly with the practice pieces she had learned years ago and once she felt safe in her skill, the nervousness in her chest died down and she ventured on. She played three of the more well-known Chopin mazurkas. Although nobody knew a highland dance reel in those precise time signatures, some of the younger children invented their own adaptation on the spot.

They pranced in and out of men chatting or making their way to the bar with dramatic sweeps of their arms, the elders standing back to watch with approval. When she finished there was rapturous applause - especially from the bairns. Shouts came from around the room of, "Play on lassie!" and "More! More!"

"Thank you for indulging me on my wedding day," Hannah responded with laughter in her voice, "You are too kind. . . . Maybe I'll play some more this evening, if you're lucky and I'm not too pished!" She stood and bowed, her face flushed with ardour and quiet joy at this, the most humble zenith of her private occupation.

"There's many here would indulge you on your wedding day lassie!" shouted one drunken sage from the open bar.

"Aye, but I think John Harper would have a say in that," came a response. No offence was taken. The innuendo was lost in a gale of laughter and ribald affirmation as fifty conversations resumed at once.

There were many familiar faces of the wider family – Duffs, Cowies and Wilsons, Robertsons, Drummonds and Barbers and of course all the Harpers. A fight was started by Jim Lorimer, the pugilistic carter's apprentice, with his marginally elder cousin Andrew Murdoch, over who knew what precisely. Predictably each accused the other of the wrong choice of words. Some said it was over the touchy politics of Andrew mentioning an unpaid bill, which both vehemently denied – but the fracas was certainly fuelled by too much drink. At least they had the decency to take it outside.

Many guests were still arriving as others left, grappling the bride or groom; paying respects directly but without disgrace. They had come in rotation with other members and generations of the same household – farmers inevitably tied to routine. Many left with a promise of, 'See ya later' and for sure many did just that.

Beer and whisky flowed as gentle urgings and challenges were issued around the throng but especially from over at the bar, for noteworthy characters to tell funny stories, recite poetry or eulogise about love and marriage. There was generous applause, flowing banter and many speeches as the evening wore on, all with toasting and salutations.

Ewan Harper opened the score as best-man, speaking politely and tentatively about his cousin and his exploits – his sporting prowess and his charming bride. As Hannah had no-one other than her Grandma to give her away, every notable mother's son under the age of ninety five stepped up in turn to speak to the credit of the loveliest girl ever, bemoaning the fact that it was not he standing in Harper's shoes.

Some plaudits tailed off into drunken incoherence, accompanied by derisive jeering or gentle mockery. Who cared if feelings were hurt? It would all be blamed on the drink and forgotten in the morning. There was a surfeit of increasingly disinhibited pedantry, as a succession of important speakers: Harpers; Barbers; Wilsons; Drummonds, tapped the table with a spoon as they rose to introspect through whisky induced idealisation for la mot juste.

In his absence all and sundry felt free to wax lyrical about the legendary, belated Frank, although one or two had been cuckolded by him back in the day. They praised Hannah's wider family and her remarkable husband. A succession of speakers delivered dryly hilarious anecdotes; recited poetry; made scandalous putative assertions.

Stirring Highland music served to punctuate the general, helping to bring it back to the particular, giving contemporary substance to legend. As the evening progressed a tightly played accordion silenced more than one drunken fool talking nonsense. Equally there was nothing quite like the challenge of hopping around to the Eightsome Reel to confirm whether or not a man was on the verge of stupor.

John Barber, aged patron of an extended family of minstrels - himself an exceedingly deft fiddler- hammered out a succession of Highland and Strathspey reels. Even the most elderly and infirm abandoned their walking sticks.

The volume of conversation and laughter rose with the tempo. Floorboards bounced to the tight rhythm of fifty pairs of dancing feet. Barber, the true professional ever keen to involve his audience, made a cursory crack at playing one of the familiar Chopin waltzes which Hannah had just performed so consummately. Hannah was seized by her younger fans and dragged to her feet to respond to the fiddler's intuitive mastery. Barber had *Valse Brilliante* in his head and what he missed he bluffed with dramatically poised changes in tempo. Raucous applause hid Hannah's embarrassment when he'd finished.

With a smile the supreme fiddler flourished into a medley of familiar waltzes and classical melodies, lifted irreverently from a range of popular composers of grand symphonies.

Secretly, the bride and groom planned to consummate their nuptial flight propped against the same King of Fir Trees in the woods where they had both lost their virginity. As their hired carriage was due to be returned before nightfall and none of the bridesmaids could be torn away from the party to accompany them back to Ramsburn, they had the perfect excuse.

Best man, Ewan Harper was too far gone to notice their absence, so Harper told Rona Hendry, daughter of the Maitre de Hotel, whom they encountered in the kitchen as they sneaked out the back, "If anyone asks, we've gone back to our respective homes to change into our evening wear." Rona looking slightly confused. Appealing to Hannah, she muttered something about them, "Surely not crossing the threshold without Mr Barber."

"What darling? Spit it out," voiced Harper a little impatiently.

"Well, I hoped to be there for the dance. You know the reel, as you cross the threshold - when I finish up here that is. I've kind o' missed it all. Da said I could have the evening off."

"Oh, oh . . . yes Rona, naturally. That's a time – honoured tradition. We will be back! Anyhow tell Mr Barber that I would like him to play *The Marquis of Huntly's Farewell* for the Cheymnes Reel up at Ramsburn," agreed Hannah, extemporising to spare Rona's embarrassment. Without another word, bursting with restrained laughter at her innocence, they left Rona to her sandwiches.

The act was more insouciant and memorable for the complexity of buttons and bows and the irrepressible laughter that welled up in both. Mid-summer light bathed the silent forest in promissory evening fondness, as sparse cloud and hills beyond shimmered and blazed in glory.

"Reverend Blair has given us his blessing," Harper reminded her laughingly as he nuzzled his face into her hair, "so we can do whatever we feel."

"Yep but hurry it up, we've only got five minutes," she chided, deftly releasing her petticoat.

"Oh, I think I might need seven or eight. Wouldn't ye rather I took my time and did the job manfully?" he teased without even a hint of his wry smile.

"We'll be missed," she cautioned with an ostentatious flick of her gloves upon his shoulder. He responded by stripping all his clothes off in front of her, boots and all, as quickly as he could, strewing them carelessly around the forest floor.

"Ah, be careful man, that's your new wedding suit!"

"Oh, I won't need it again will I?" he said finally, pretending to 'humph' while hanging socks and underpants on the stub of a broken branch.

Hannah's hearty abandon rang through the forest with peals of wanton hilarity. She rested her forearms across his shoulders as Harper bent his knees, looking up into her face with a saucy smile. As he penetrated her the old grey carriage horse Charlie, who had been passively cropping long grass at the edge of the track, snorted loudly, causing Hannah to squeal, thinking perhaps they had been discovered in the unrestrained consummation of impatient desire.

The business was done, despite the laughter of both, in considerably less than seven minutes. Their confidence in one another - that same energetic joy of giving and of loving, the salubrious oil of mutual engagement always resulting in pulsating laughter when they looked into each other's eyes - continued with Harper and Hannah wherever they went together for the rest of her life. Their love was as expansive as an iridescent Moray sky on a spring morning, when every fir tree and flower, every blade of new grass and every creature under the sun celebrates life.

Of all the events of that day, one specific image surfaced in Harper's mind the instant he finally lay back and closed his eyes, just as birds in the bluff behind the new house were beginning to stir at around four am. Harper knew there was something important he had missed which would haunt him for the rest of his days. Three gentlemen and a lady who had arrived late stood together observing the celebration from the periphery but did not stay to join the party at the Forbes.

The tallest of the three had been sitting astride a thoroughbred stallion which looked every hand a potential Derby winner. White curly hair and saturnine gaze as he surveyed the crowd outside the church seemed to suggest the optimacy of the patrician. Hugh and John Senior had both gone over immediately to shake hands and speak with this fine gentleman. Although no-one said it directly, Harper knew this man to have been Sir William Forsyth. His name certainly hadn't been on Jessie's guest list, although in retrospect, had relations with Hugh been anything approaching the ideal, perhaps it should have been.

Another he knew well was Zachariah Williams, the tailor who had mentored him as a boy and whom he regarded as uncle and his dearest friend in the world after Hannah. It irked Harper that he had been so much in demand that he'd not had a chance to speak to Zach or his wife.

It had been a time–honoured tradition that John would spend part of every summer with Zach and Annie up until his mid-teens. Zach had started to show Harper the fine art of his trade from the age of six, when the old man's eyesight was still perfect and his fingers deft. Young John proved an assiduous student and soon became a consummate tailor.

Harper had been more disappointed by not having the chance to celebrate properly with Zach than the wider implications of his mentor's aloofness, an annoyance he planned to remedy at the first opportunity. The other two gentlemen were clearly Zachariah's close associates and the Williamses had evidently withdrawn early for their sakes. Although the clique stood at the back of the church during the wedding ceremony, they had not ventured to push through the congregation to introduce themselves. To Harper's chagrin the group had left before the festivities began, although his curiosity had been aroused more by their departure than their appearance. With so much to pre-occupy him, Harper forgot about them until after the last of their guests left in the small hours of the morning. Now among all the people who smilingly embraced him through the laughing parade of his wedding day, Harper's tired mind could not let go the image of these emissaries from another world.

Harper now realised that there had been something oddly familiar about the smallest of the three men he had observed between Forsyth and Zach. This third individual had been dressed in a top-hat and beautiful blended angora-silk town coat. Though he looked like a type of local man, dark and tightly packaged with round neat features, Harper had never actually seen him before.

Something Hannah said to him when opening cards and letters as he attacked the mountain of crockery and uneaten food in the kitchen at two a.m. struck a dissonant chord. She explained with incredulity that Zachariah had handed her an envelope, containing a letter wishing them well in their new life together. Folded inside was a bank draft of five hundred guineas, a fortune even by Zachariah William's comfortable standards. Now Harper realised who the man was and why he had seemed familiar.

He slid soundlessly out of bed into chill morning air to sit naked in front of a three piece hinged mirror, crowning a finely crafted locally made mahogany dressing table. He noticed with displeasure observable signs of strain on the face peering back through the watery morning light but that didn't worry him much - that was down to too much drink and lack of sleep. Harper was more interested in examining the roundness of his own skull; broad lines of brow and chin, the compactness of ears and mouth.

"My God, only the eyes are uncertain," he whispered to himself as Hannah groaned softly in her dream, ". . . because he was too far away for me to see them properly." Harper put his hand up to his head to hold back the long black curly hair that he'd neglected to have trimmed before the wedding, "If this mop was removed, or began to fall out with old age and worry? Well hell, I'd be his spit and image."

Harper's days had been full of love – with an expectant wife and vibrant two year old child; wider family - many sage, larger-than-life people who all now respected him, appreciating his views. There was hard work to occupy his mind, a warm hearth, good food almost taken for granted – yet even now he felt emptiness in his heart and a deep need for connections that had never before been made.

The finely dressed man with Sir William was my father! Zachariah, throughout all the years has acted as nothing more than a discreet conduit for his beneficence! The cheque was obviously from the Trust Fund Jessie tried to tell me about.

"Oh God, don't turn your back on me!" whispered Harper. His own breath seemed to energise an unwanted but inevitable feeling, making sorrow tangible. He stared into the mirror for a long time, trying to imagine the face he had never known; the voice and manner of the man who looked so like him, while fighting back anger and condemnation.

"His failings gave rise to my inadequacies," he opined to himself pessimistically over and again, until finally he formed all the fragmented impressions into a resolution to just let it be.

Unable to sleep Harper checked on the listless Hannah, then grabbing trousers, pipe and tobacco pouch padded softly from the room. In order to avoid rustling or a heavy footfall, he went without shirt or socks into the breaking midsummer dawn some distance from the house, intentionally out of sight of any windows he might be observed from.

Leaning against a windbreak chestnut, sucking at his pipe like a baby at the tit, he held back silent rage and unwelcome tears. In the pit of his stomach Harper carried a hollow sense of forfeiture for everything in childhood he had never known and he wept a little in silence for the pain of yearning itself. How could he not want to imagine the relationship that had been denied or simply stop his mind in unquestioning dumbness?

His sadness was for the disappointment of conditional love that at times had seemed no love at all. He would gladly have handed back the five hundred guineas just to have spent one day standing in the shared love of the mother and father he had never known. Thwarted by what he could not visualise and had no desire to concoct, Harper came instead to endorse the fate that had brought him to Hannah.

Sorrow quickly turned to gladness at his coming of age in such fruition. Finally, unwelcome but irresistible tears turned to joy, for the fulsome love of a woman he adored and the consecration of that tie in such fine Highland tradition.

The sound of Jessie's mother pumping water from the well snapped him back to reality – she had work to do every day at this time. There would be no exceptions, apart from sudden death.

"Shite!" intoned Harper to himself, stretching his vest to dab at watery eyes, "Fucking spawny old goat!" he spat out vehemently, thinking of his shadowy father. Tapping out the hot ash on a fence post before spinning away from his secret sorrow, he shuffled back along the lane towards the farmhouse with short, rapid steps over protruding stones.

"Maybe Hannah will be in the mood when she wakes, if I make her a cup of tea," he mused optimistically.

Harper's shambling gait and seeming consternation gave Great Gran Hannah, who had a witch's power to read people's minds, the impression of a deranged Chinaman attempting a break-out from a life of incarceration at Sunnyside psychiatric hospital. But if she had overheard Harper's cursing of his father from a distance, she would have echoed the sentiment precisely.

I know. We all know. All except that poor lovely boy . . . English bastard!

The weeks that followed their marriage at Rothiemay were full of inexplicable tension and unfulfilled transactions for Hannah and Harper. The subtle dynamics of seemingly fixed relationships began shifting like bending rock along a fault line. Hannah wore a mantle of visible but impenetrable surliness, disconcerting to all but her own mother, who for her part adopted an equally uncharacteristic and chiding pettiness.

Jessie manifested her longsuffering attitude as gently as the rain. But she was determined with an ant like single-mindedness to anticipate and proscribe Hannah's every thought and action. Jessie reasoned backwards from every outcome, successful or otherwise, to arrive at and question neglected alternatives. She offered unwelcome advice for every workaday option, however trivial or obvious. She was nagging, sparring before a fight, without knowing or necessarily wanting the prize. But she couldn't leave it alone.

In a way Jessie wanted Hannah to leave Rothiemay for her own good. What frustrated and began to anger her was the fact that Hannah would not bite back at her imperious pettiness, much less throw her own heartfelt desires into their exchanges for discussion.

In her quiet moments, Jessie prayed for the good grace not to resent the husband who had failed her or the son-in-law who one day soon would break her heart. She indulged little Elsie Harper's every whim, treating the child like her own, even to the neglect of her normally essential routines, while fussing vocally over arrangements for Hannah's confinement.

Jessie prevailed upon Dr Payton that Hannah be given a bed at the new Stephen Cottage Hospital in Dufftown, because she had complained of abdominal pains and bleeding after the birth of her first child. On that occasion Jessie had been impressed by the gynaecologist, Mr Mitton. He had unequivocally voiced concerns about her daughter possibly having a pre-cursive condition that could develop into ovarian cancer.

At last, as the first frost whitened the new slates and smoke from chimneys rose in narrow vertical columns straight into the blue crystal sky, the postman delivered Harper's acceptance letter from Edinburgh City Constabulary. There was a cry of jubilation from within, like when one of Harper's team mates had scored at football, "Yes! Yes . . . I've got it! I've to report for training in the New Year," he shouted. Jessie had only ever heard the boy raise his voice once before. Clearly he was very enthusiastic about leaving and joining the Police. Although saddened by the prospect, she was quietly impressed by his zeal.

There was a tangible if understated relief for all, if only because family tension was now resolved. Love, as well as loss, poured out from Jessie's arrestingly beautiful blue eyes as she smiled through her tears. There was nothing she could say or do to prevent their leaving, although her heart was breaking and Hannah's baby was due quite soon. Hogmanay loomed large too and the lambing that would soon follow, "But what aboot the lambing?" she croaked weakly.

"Oh, wheesht woman," commanded Hannah senior, "We'll manage fine. We always do. Ewan is looking for a full time job and Alex will come over if I ask his ma. We're two families now remember, no' one!" added the old witch with a broad smile.

Harper hugged Jessie, holding the letter in his hand as he whispered in her ear, "We love you Jessie. It'll be alright."

Elsie Harper hugged both their legs as she offered the only empathetic expression to Jessie's deepest concerns, "I'll stay here wi' you granny and help wi' the lambs. I'll no' leave you!"

The move followed quickly in late January 1891, with lunch for all twelve members of the family at the Railway Hotel in Keith. There was a tearful farewell on the platform, overlooked by seagulls fleeing ahead of an approaching storm. A huge granary glowered down upon the trivial sentiments of the little group. Harper remembered that he had felt so awkward that he had been pleased to note a fair number of fellow travellers to lend distraction and a sense of urgency that might gliss over the hollowness, the monumental sorrow of separation. He had been dreading this departure for months. In the event he felt much less embarrassed than he had expected.

As the train shuddered and rolled southward he even had a brief moment of self-doubt, tinged with regret. The true cause of much of Hannah's introspective moodiness, their second child Elizabeth nestled like a tiny kitten, warm inside the open lapel of Harper's frock coat. He ignored the faint smell of milky vomit, welcoming an opportunity to explore Hannah's lovely face as she sat opposite with Elsie lying under her arm, watching magnificent scenery roll past the window. The amused curl of her mouth told him it was all okay, though her complexion appeared bloodless and drawn.

Chapter Four - *Wheels of Fate*

The music from the basement stopped and the tall cupboard door banged as Elsie pushed too hard against it. Harper snapped back from his reverie, calling over his shoulder for them to wash their hands and help him set the table. He looked across at the castle as he waited for heat to die down in the frying pan.

He'd travelled through a vortex of painful years; such that the glowering stones and eternal sunlight on emerald grass returning his gaze might be watching him, reading his recollections with dispassionate understanding. This old building they occupied opposite the castle felt strange. The room was benignly alive somehow, venerably old and wise.

Harper put a warm plate on top of Hannah's breakfast. He slid them into the warmed oven before dishing up shallow-fried fish with salad: radishes, tomatoes and lettuce with Lee and Perrin's sauce 'for those who can't resist a splash.'

Molly the cat immediately appeared on cue, rubbing her tail by way of greeting against Harper's leg. She wanted to make her presence felt without getting in his way but planned to get in his way later if he neglected to feed her in short-order.

Elizabeth had forgotten to put away the tin of coloured pencils, so the last part of the clearing away routine was repeated with another vigorous bang of the tall cupboard door. Harper pretended to scold, bearing upon them, brandishing the frying pan with shirt sleeves rolled and a dish cloth folded purposively over his left arm.

"More coloured pencils!" he said pointing across the table with the pan.

"Oh!" answered Elizabeth.

"Oh!" repeated Elsie.

"Where's the satchel I gave you from work?"

Elsie scooted back to the tall cupboard to fetch the large leather evidence satchel that had seen its day in a thousand Police investigations.

Hannah entered the room silently with a smile, to witness squeals and laughter, "In the name of the wee man!" exclaimed Harper, "More of them on the floor!" Elsie went under the table to collect three stray crayons which had rolled off when they'd been busy drawing. She grabbed them and stood up, bumping her head on the underside. Elsie immediately dropped the crayons, holding her hand up to her head. Elizabeth giggled at her misfortune, "Silly! You're too big . . . let me do it!"

On the neatly pressed table cloth were buttered oatcakes, warmed plates and sweet Indian tea steaming in burgundy red, patterned china cups. For the girls there would follow a trying time of bones and crumbs and where to wipe fishy fingers.

"Oh boy!" enthused Elsie, "This looks great . . . I could eat a man off a horse!"

"I could eat the horse too!" declared Elizabeth, ever keen to emulate her older sister. Elsie laughed raucously as she fetched two cushions for Elizabeth and herself, so they could sit up at table height on the mass produced bamboo chairs.

In the three years that had passed since the Harpers had left the farm at Rothiemay Elsie and Elizabeth had grown, each of them into a different but very distinct phase of their lives. Elsie played teacher to her sister's constantly exploring mind. For her part she was proud to be Elizabeth's guardian and shepherd - the one who responded to her essentially tactile needs: the pointing finger with a perplexed or questioning look, which if neglected might result in a little too much experimentation.

Elizabeth would open kitchen and sideboard cupboards, remove everything and climb in to see what was at the back. She might fall asleep against the forgotten film of invisible dust and gossamer. In purposeful exploration she climbed narrow mountainous stairs, with treacherously shortened 'go' as assuredly as a squirrel on a washing line, taking rind intended for the blue tits. Her backward glance from the landing had met with a gasp from her mother, echoed of course by Elsie.

Elsie could form thoughts into questions, give explanations and lead by example. Routine was everything and all their lives were busy and full. Elsie had a professed role to play – 'helping mammy and daddy.'

The demands of starting her own family had come for Hannah on top of the endless toil of having been one of only three adults – herself; mother Jessie and Grandma Hannah – between them working two decent sized crofts. Until the age of twenty-eight, back in '91, she had been used to managing her mother Jessie's accumulated brood of six: three of her own: eleven year old twins Frank and Jeannie – Betsy aged eight, but also the adopted Robertson girls, Kate aged six and Fiona aged five as well as Frank senior's child by Mary, Elsie, then aged five. She could never quite recall when obligation had bound her in loyalty and breathless fatigue had become a way of life.

Sitting down to breakfast, Hannah felt a twinge of pain in her abdomen, reminding her of a problem intentionally sublimated. She consoled herself by thinking of the palliative phenomenon discovered by each successive generation of physicians. The spreading cancer they'd warned her of had seemingly disappeared after she had fallen pregnant . . . but she was almost due. Maybe she had been sitting too long on the uncomfortable piano stool. Smiling at Harper, she lovingly pressed her open hand on his shoulder.

Nothing would spoil this moment for her. Nothing. More alive than ever before in her life she loved every vibrating, rightful day. Hannah felt that everything she did, every plan or deed however small had purpose. This fine handsome man, poised and thoughtful, always roguishly funny and these luminous, gentle bairns were Hannah's channel for living. Joy they reciprocated affirmed the vessel of her being. The goodness of her inmost thoughts had become actualised in many small ways through a relentless life of both ease and pain. It really didn't matter to her which she felt. In full awareness of her inescapable mortality, Hannah's heart was filled at that moment with a reconciled, wistful love she knew to be the only worthwhile thing the human soul can aspire to. She wiped a tear from the corner of her eye before tucking into her breakfast.

'Great Gran Han' as Elsie had entitled her mother's mentor, came from Rothiemay. She stayed for a month but it seemed more like two. When Harper returned from his late shift on the Friday night of her arrival, he was disgruntled to find the two bairns sleeping in the back bedroom. Leaving the gas light off he made a meal over removing uniform and boots in the dark, rocking backwards on top of the exhausted, half-aware Hannah as he did so.

She was almost full-term, spread out in the centre of the hollowed out mattress. Harper's elbow fell heavily against her abdomen as he rolled onto the bed. Even before Hannah protested there was a kick in response to his clumsiness causing him to immediately sit up in bed, startled by what he had felt.

The girls were burned out by the excitement of meeting their mum's gran at Waverley, followed by an afternoon spent shopping for the holiday weekend. They breathed softly in deep slumber across the room, as Hannah listened indulgently to Harper's incredulous account of what she had come to take for granted.

"It kicked me! It must be a boy. He will be a grand footballer wi' reflexes that fast. Gan' on . . . he kicked me again! He kicked me in a different place, when I put my hand on you!"

"Shush now, you'll wake the girls an' we'll never get them off to sleep again."

"Naw, woman listen . . . you felt me lie agin' you? Well, he kicked me!"

"I've told you before Harper, it's another girl."

"How the hell dye ken woman?" he hissed in the dark.

"Wheesht man, will you!"

"How do you know?" he whispered lower, "Here," he continued, lifting the heavy eiderdown quilt, "put your head under, so they won't hear us." She laughed silently as he probed his left arm under her pillow, resuming the conversation with his mouth close to her ear, "How the hell can you know such a thing? It's the old lady isn't it? She's organised a witch's coven while I've been out on the beat!"

"Oh yes? And meanwhile who do you think was out shopping for your Easter Sunday dinner?"

"What did you do, dangle a needle on a cotton thread? Or that amber pendant I got for ye?"

"Don't be silly. I just know."

"Well onyway hen, she kicked me!"

"I'm not surprised you clumsy clot, you woke her up! You should take more care getting in and out of bed in the dark."

Harper slid down under the sheets until he was at a level with Hannah's ample inclosure. He gently placed his hand to the left side of her belly button. Kissing the warm smooth swelling, he whispered an affected apology to the unborn child in a comical voice. A third kick came, as suddenly and fiercely as the first two. Harper recoiled, unable to resist exclaiming aloud with an incredulous laugh, "Ah! She's done it again!" The blanket domed up over his arched back.

"Shut up will you!" hissed Hannah, "Now they're wide awake for sure." She tapped him firmly on the top of his head with her knuckle. Elsie stirred in her wood framed camp bed, moaning softly.

"I'm sorry for waking ye at this time o' night," Harper crooned to the unborn infant inches away from his face – sincerely this time – though the recipient of his apology lived nameless in a disregarded dimension of darkness and indeterminacy.

The following morning as Harper worked with Great Gran Han preparing breakfast, Hannah was obliged to lie still for a full ten minutes, as Elsie and Elizabeth examined her bulging abdomen, listening for fluid movements while chatting sweetly with the now rested, less cantankerous child inside. Not entirely satisfied that they had fully experienced Harper's degree of interaction, they booked another appointment with their mother, "For the same time tomorrow."

"Let's buy her a football next time we go shopping. Harper will teach her," suggested Elsie, as she took Elizabeth by the hand and led her to the bedroom door, "Girls play football too you know!"

There was a minor medical complication, soon forgotten and much confused as to its precise implication, amid social activity around the time of Hannah Wilson Drummond Harper's arrival into the family. Throughout Hannah's pregnancy there had been bloody discharges. To confirm obvious concern, the GP, Foxworthy - an endearing, mousey little man with rimless spectacles balanced half way down his stubby nose – had made diagnostic rumblings in a tone of mild surprise. Foxworthy followed his diagnosis with the assertion that, "Hannah will lose the baby if she does not take complete and extended bed rest."

Essentially Hannah bled a lot and kept on bleeding, even when matron sternly ordered her to, "Spend more time breast feeding." She was finally discharged from hospital on Tuesday 11th of July 1893, towards the middle of the driest summer on record and the most glorious holiday week Harper had seen in over ten years of working life.

'The first-named' as Harper wryly referred to her, stayed to help her Granddaughter who had often complained over the years of back pain with great and irreducible fatigue. The old lady attributed Hannah's current stress to the drought, which had stunted barley and slowed growth of the lambs at home. But nobody listened to her elliptical reasoning, however well intentioned.

So this was how it came to pass that Granny was still there managing home and family two months later for which Harper was notionally if not eternally grateful, although for the most part his mind was elsewhere.

Counterfeit bills had appeared in the city. All hands and ears were employed in talking to shopkeepers and market traders about their origin. There were many leads, followed by great urgency in finding a bona-fide source of information, whilst maintaining proprietary confidence. The accuracy of copies of Scottish £1; £5 and £10 notes, plus the flood tide of their distribution, implied seeding from a highly organized foreign source – quite thorough – even grudgingly admitted to be professional in their planning.

The criminal mastermind behind it had been here and gone within a week – making contacts within Edinburgh's ubiquitous and adaptive underworld, who by all accounts had been delighted to seize the golden opportunity to clean-up. The painful admission was that no-one could speculate as to precisely when that week of activity had been.

There were people who knew people – several dubious informants and one or two forced confessions from men who essentially were known intermediaries for any type of contraband. Such men were like seagulls around a purse seiner – nothing more than cackling opportunists. Their information would never lead to a criminal mastermind, or even the gang itself – rumoured to have been tough merchant sailors said to have plied the Danube as well as the Seven Seas. But they had talked little of themselves, or their origins.

All sorts of inferences had been made about three or four close associates: a Greek or Turkish Captain; his Romanian Bosun; a couple of Russian or maybe Serbian sailors, who had given no real confirmation of who they were – and in any event all of these men had acted merely as delivery boys for the fake money. It could have come from anywhere.

Even if a ship and crew might have been identified retrospectively, its complement was now on the high seas, or maybe even scattered across a different continent. Despite this hopeless scenario for detection, the only policing effort possible was done through legwork, countless discreet interviews and much sampling of paper currency tendered.

As the weeks dragged by, Harper grew increasingly detached and morose the more he became involved in the pointless activity surrounding the relatively high value bills. The people who passed them as exchange, or flicked through them in piles after closing time, were surprisingly not only too numerous and diverse as a group – everything from travelling merchants, to grocers, to hoteliers - but as a section of the public were notoriously difficult to interview.

Relatively well-off suspects were sophisticated, defensive, invariably pressed for time and likely to bleat to higher authority if rattled. Harper's compass was spinning. Worryingly the supply of counterfeit money had not dried up as anticipated. His frustration at work seemed to reflect his feelings about home life.

When he arrived back at the house in West Port each evening, the old lady fussed over him too much, making him feel he was dependent upon her. The girls seemed to him to be constantly making urgent little demands, conducting territorial disputes, or were fast asleep in bed so that he felt guilty about not showing more interest or affection when he did see them.

In the past he had compensated by picking up odd trinkets for the girls – hair slides; mirrors; badges or even odd things seen lying on the street or in the park. Once he returned from patrolling Holyrood with the corm of an enormous Blue Spruce in his greatcoat pocket. They had been delighted with his thoughtfulness. They dried it in the oven so it would open. Then Great Gran helped them find plant pots for the seeds. She told them they could take the saplings to Ramsburn in the holidays to plant along the lane on the north side of the 'new' house. They came to look forward to Harper's return from late shifts and would run to greet him. Elsie took to searching his pockets in her endearing style, even as he walked through the long hallway.

When Harper let out some of this dilemma of tiredness and disinterest to his beat partner Aleister Macdonald, dry worldly introspection came back at him, instantly serving to frame the ironical mind set of his colleague, "Ah, hell I can see it John . . . Ye didnae tell me ye were hag–ridden! That's enough to sour any man's beer."

Harper laughed gently, with an inner light that had not shone for weeks. He glanced up at the taller man as the more experienced Bobby nonchalantly strolled through a melee playing out in the narrow reception area of the imposing Police Constabulary building at number 50, West Port.

It was a market day and the pubs were overflowing. There was a great deal of angry cursing from an arrested man requiring the impatient and unexpected involvement of the duty desk Sergeant, which it was best for all concerned wearing a uniform not to witness.

Ali Macdonald complemented Harper in many ways: he knew nothing about horses, so Harper taught him everything that basic training had left out. Macdonald knew Auld Reekie - its patrons and popular haunts, as well as how to handle himself in a tight corner.

Again, the training was not on any schedule and most of it had to remain off the record. Tall, open-faced Ali was strong-minded yet soft spoken and amenable. Harper had liked him from the outset. Over the past two years they had become true friends. Now was the time to seek honest advice. Once the business of harnessing and mounting-up was out of the way he intended to broach the subject of Hannah's confinement, as well as her grandmother's concern over the underlying illness. Harper was not at all sure how to deal with the old lady's emotional concerns.

As they emerged through the gate of the stable opposite the Police Station both remarked how quickly the furore had died down and were glad to see the street scene had returned to complete normality.

"No blood on the pavement either, eh?" ventured Harper.

"Naw, the poor bastard micht ha'e tae lea' aff sex for a month though."

"Aye, best no tae lea' a mark the magistrate micht see."

"Right enough, Harper, but naebody should drink at lunchtime."

Mounted and paced in a tight pair, the horses controlled both themselves and to all intents the crowd in the busy market for the two policemen. They were alert and fearless, bringing an essential presence to policing. Elevation afforded from atop their broad backs lent a certain neutrality and comfort in space and time.

Harper felt he could relax and talk to Aleister, which he now attempted. The conversation was terse and mannerly, in the convention of tough men everywhere but this time went deeper than love into a timeless seeing, stripped of sentiment.

"Cancer you say?" echoed Macdonald, looking straight across at Harper from under the peak of his uniform riding helmet. He dragged the nose of his mount to the right, away from a barrow the horse was browsing on. Harper just looked back at Macdonald tight lipped, aware that his words were intended as neither repetition nor rhetoric. Both men were silent as the implication sank in fully and each thought ahead to how the conversation might go.

After several minutes Macdonald spoke again as the horses turned into the approach to the North Bridge, "How is she taking this?"

"Oh Lord, we haven't even talked about it . . . what with her just having had the baby and Great Gran still here. The old lady is heading back home next week but her mother intends to come instead as soon as they sort out business at the farm." There was more Harper wanted to say but he held back, unsure of propriety with this relatively new friend.

"I imagine you feel you've already begun to lose her?"

Macdonald said what Harper had wanted to say. He had expressed the torment in one simple question. The profundity and honesty of Ali's insight struck Harper like a bolt of lightning. He felt mortifying panic rise in his throat. Tears began to well into his eyes. He looked away towards Waverley Station below the ornate parapet of the bridge, then as the moisture occluded his sight, over towards the castle on the skyline. When he glanced back Harper realised Ali was looking out of politeness in the opposite direction, at pedestrians and traffic moving in and out of the parkland to their left. Macdonald was avoiding comment upon Harper's obvious embarrassment. Ali knew that despite the tough little man's stoicism he must have been in turmoil.

Drained of energy, Harper felt his spine collapse into the saddle of the mighty horse. He stopped in the middle of the bridge where there was fluid movement among passers-by, therefore less interaction for them to get involved with. He gulped air - fighting his emotions, "Imagine what it's like for her?" he asked Ali, with obvious distress, "Her GP has given her Tincture of Opium for the pain. He's referred her to a cancer specialist."

"Ye have to talk to her man. Go with her to the hospital and . . . and yeah . . . . get rid o' the harpies . . . that's what I would do . . . they can help later if you actually need them."

"Yeah but understand - they come all the way frae Aberdeenshire. Up there they live close tae nature's cycle. Everything is a matter o' routine to them – even life an' death is business as usual." Harper relaxed on his mount, staring into the middle distance. Ali gave him time to think. Traffic flowed past them down towards the banking area of town. At length Harper composed himself to continue his explanation, "They are worthy people Mac: Great Gran Hannah an' Jessie, but they are deadly in the attack. They dinnae scream and shout but they will freeze me out if I'll no' defer tae their advice."

"Well, if they are so business-like, they'll understand your need to stick with your normal routines as long as possible. Play it aw doon. Dinnae discuss what's too personal wi' them. When they've outstayed their welcome just put their suitcases in the street."

Harper forced a laugh then breathed out audibly through his teeth. There was perplexity and sadness in his tone.

"Yes . . . thank you," he said. Harper pondered deeply as the horses clattered onto the cobbles of Waterloo Place, "You are right . . . ken, all I need is to get proper access to my own wife again - tell her that I love her."

"Boy, I know all about that one," agreed Ali with conviction. Harper knew Macdonald could probably tell some tales of his own about in-laws and visitors turning up unannounced to see 'the new-arrival.' That could wait for another, more relaxed occasion when Harper felt he might be able to see the funny side of it better.

"Sing out, John and my Marion will come over and help out with daily chores, shopping an' such, or just drop the bairns off with her. I know that she will be delighted to help. I will speak to her tonight."

Harper looked at Macdonald thoughtfully, knowing this was a man he could trust. His heart rose slightly, despite pressing circumstances because he knew he had made a good friend.

He had heard that Ali was from a large and notable colony of second or third generation Western Highlanders, based around Dunbar; Haddington; Musselburgh and Portobello. Families had migrated incrementally into the mushrooming market towns via East Lothian and its unrivalled farmland, where they had first sought work on leaving their island homes.

Formerly, Ali explained, his broader family and cousins were from Trotternish in Skye. They were closely linked with the ubiquitous McSweens, from the area around Portree. Harper remembered talks with Zach about Highland Clearances. He recalled the unwarranted economic pressure put on most families to leave. Harper decided that he had a lot in common with Ali.

Ali had many brothers and sisters, aunts and uncles he talked of and more cousins hailing from the north of Skye than Harper could shake a stick at. He was garrulous and proud but no fool. He obviously liked people in general, celebrating their actions with compendious, wry humour. But the flow of anecdotes would quickly cease if no interest was shown. Harper chose to encourage the flow.

Harper and Macdonald reviewed the crowds of people and carts wheeling around the top of Leith Street in silence for ten minutes. They were watching for the sharp faces and casual inactivity that belied theft and racketeering. Turning their mounts in an instant like rehearsed Lipizzaners, they headed lazily along Princess Street directly into the blazing August light.

Harper felt the wheels of fate crushing him more with each daily cycle, slowly grinding away youthfulness and optimism, dragging even attenuated strength out of his wiry limbs. His mind constantly raced for a plan, even when he was pre-occupied by the routines of work: crouching with Ali behind the corner of the Vennel, truncheons in hand waiting for a purse snatcher to strike; writing up a statement from a remorseless Norwegian sailor who had beaten a whore to death in an alley; all the wasted while he spent chasing money with no validity, with no ultimate meaning beyond the discrimination it served to undermine. He thought of Hannah all the time. When she wasn't with him, she was slipping away.

Chapter Five - *The Auld Firm*

It was early October when Harper decided to ask for the holiday entitlement which had accumulated but his request was momentarily declined by Inspector Brodie - who gave a brusque explanation that it was, "too late for that." He was still pre-occupied with tracing counterfeit money. Harper stood in front of the grand mahogany escritoire, feeling sweat trickle down the inside of his uniform shirt into the bulge of his waist. He felt the constraint of his collar, reflecting that the women were perhaps feeding him too much. He struggled for what to say next.

"It really concerns the health of . . ."

Brodie was not even looking at him. He was warming his hands at the fire. As Harper waited at attention, his senior officer poked at the glowing coal in his ostentatious, white marble fire-place. The Inspector occupied the second floor office on the right hand side of the double fronted West Port Constabulary. Brodie had chosen this location for his own self-interest, as a man of importance in the establishment. He was out of the way but also able to observe all comings and goings by a glance into the stairwell, or from the front window overlooking the stables opposite.

He could hear every conversation from the reception lobby below, especially those he was not meant to hear. Loud exchanges tended to echo too much for effective eavesdropping, but they were probably not worth listening to. In contrast more noteworthy, whispered confutations tended to drift languidly up the broad stairwell. Except for when he was sleeping, Brodie always kept the door slightly ajar and the fire well stoked to counter the constant draft circulating up from the street.

This morning was cold and crisp, with a slight, almost autumnal mist after a weekend of rain. An early chill presaged clear blue sky above and continuation of an Indian summer.

"You get yersel' sorted out lad," replied Brodie, as he replaced the poker in its niche alongside shovel and brush on the brass implement stand. The man was clearly proud of the privileges of rank. He required the cleaners to wash and polish the fireplace regularly. Brushing off traces of coal dust with both hands down his uniform trouser legs and inspecting them with clear, sharp eyes that missed nothing for any deposits of soot, he glanced at Harper before sitting back in his chair. Harper thought Brodie looked ridiculous. He guessed he could feel Brodie's personal deadly sin – 'Vanity' rising and looking out through the tough little man's eyes.

"You just take as long as ye want man . . . an' no questions asked. We'll call it compassionate leave," stated Brodie with aplomb, "Pop in and see me if you're passing but don't worry either way."

Harper coloured up with embarrassment, confounded by the ambiguity of Brodie's words.

"What's wrang man, is that no' good enough for ye?"

Harper stumbled over words he had not expected to have to say, "No, no!" he almost shouted, "That's very kind of you Inspector Brodie, sir! Forgive me, it's the change of temperature from the cold outside. I don't feel one hundred per cent."

"Okay Harper, go home now. Take the rest of the week off and the following week too. Spend time with your family and get whatever help you require for Hannah. Take Macdonald up on his offer too."

Harper looked at Brodie in amazement. He felt uneasy that his superior officer always seemed to be able to throw him off balance.

"You know about that sir?"

"I know everything that happens here lad. I make it my business. The City Constabulary look after our own Harper. We're the 'Auld Firm.' Think of us mair like yer greetin' granny son, on'y wi' hobnailed boots. I regard it as a fundamental part of the role of an Inspector to look after my boys, John."

"I didn't . . . I mean . . . I thought . . . I mean thank you sir."

"You stated on your application that you were Church of Scotland, right?"

"That would be so," acknowledged Harper, shuffling his feet and looking down in embarrassment, "What of it, sir?

"You don't hold with any of this 'High Church' Catholic nonsense?"

"Can't say I know what you mean, sir," answered Harper, who'd come to see himself more as a heathen than a practicing Christian. Brodie kicked back in his chair, clearly about to give Harper a lecture of some sort, "The established traditions go down well for a man seeking a management career of some sort . . . up to a point, if you catch my drift. The Lodge will accept anyone who is not a 'Teague.' You're not an under-cover Jacobite Harper, are you?"

Harper was startled again and could read no humour in the fierce blue eyes, levelling at him from under clipped, uniformly white tonsure.

"God no, sir! And thank you sir. I'll make it up to you . . . I mean I'll work it all off . . . when this thing is . . . I mean as soon as I return, I'll volunteer for every graveyard shift," vowed Harper, before he finally ran out of words.

"Just go Harper, before you trip over your tongue!" Harper saluted fiercely like a military man, then spun on his heel towards the open door. Making a mental note to question Ali about Brodie's stance regarding Catholics and Jacobites. He suspected that it would not be entirely favourable.

As he skipped down the stairs, pretending to give full attention to the business of arranging uniform, helmet and greatcoat which he slung over his arm, Harper felt overwhelmed with the stupid, dysynchronous nature of existence. He felt unable to connect with anything objectively in the material world.

Through their dependency, his children had become his oppressors. His in-laws represented the unsmiling face of a traditional authority, which served to intimidate. His employers wanted all of him – body and soul and his colleagues suddenly seemed like wooden puppets. The woman he adored was in limbo – an aberrant kind of physiological confinement, serving to generate inversely the social duties and obligations in her mother and Grandmother which smacked of a continuation of their former lifestyle at the farm.

He should have had time for all of this worldly nonsense, with interludes to laugh or dream, forget and just get on with living – but he had none. Harper had time only for quick recollection of growing despair; the soulful searching of a man who has just accepted the extreme improbability of rescue and the imminent likelihood of drowning. There was no palliative. He had no plan. No universal schematic to inform direction.

As he slowed to a dolorous pace and his baleful eyes reviewed the Grassmarket for people he knew and did not want to speak to, Harper kicked an idea into shape with every heavy footfall on the worn cobbles.

Tomorrow he would round them all up early and head for the beach at Portobello. The cry of the gulls and the squeals of children were in his ears now, already speaking to his soul. There would be no argument or discord, no curtailment of choice or measuring of necessity. He would lead them in one last, smiling dance into the light before violin and accordion played a hauntingly measured, poignant lament. Let time and nature heal what it might.

Even Hannah's mild objections to the day out at the beach were a change of tone. In his sullenness and internalised conflict, Harper could hear an elevated harmony in her voice which immediately gladdened his heavy heart. The human mind can tolerate only a certain amount of reality. In the bright morning he observed the busy interaction between Hannah and her mother as they wheeled about the kitchen area.

He noted the graceful manner with which the old lady had demurred. Harper realised that Great Gran Hannah really was a gracious individual. She sat and watched Hannah and Jessie prepare a splendid picnic. Savouring her favourite Earl Grey tea, she resisted the desire to comment on Hannah's expenditure of energy, which darkened eyes betrayed.

Elsie wore an emerald green frock with white lace trimming and Elizabeth pink satin with a white bow. The old lady knew that their beautiful clothes had been made by their mother, no doubt with direction from Harper. Everything they wore, from hard wearing sailor suits to party frocks, were shaped and cut by their father then machine sewn by Hannah. Great Gran thought of her granddaughter working late at night on the Singer machine they had been given by Zachariah Williams. She commented on how delightful their clothes were but held back from saying how much hard work it must have involved.

As he pondered how to help, Harper was left with the baby. He found himself grateful for the warm contact that kept his nervous hands full. Harper felt self–conscious and uncomfortable – guilty of having pre-judged the situation from a working man's point of view. He felt embarrassed by his own stupidity. Bitter-sweet delight rose in his heart as the energy of love began to dance soothingly around him. His own needs and conflicts were being subjugated at last. In this moment of acceptance he felt a paradigm shift, to new questions and new lessons.

Harper attended well, watching and listening with his entire mind. These women took empathy for granted. They knew how to let love rise and flow when and where it would, without anger or defiance. The crooning baby in his arms seemed to question him in the same sympathetic tone used by the adults. Her tiny hands were opening and closing in what appeared to him gestures of fondness. Her bright eyes searched his face for a response. In her peering innocence, baby Hannah reminded him of Manet's Folies Bergere girl, unwittingly reflecting a universal communion. She was innocent and unstructured – yet somehow as old and otherworldly as the Castle Rock he could view through the window. Her eyes were mesmerising in their comfortable absorption of all that was offered.

Harper did not know how to react, he was so far down in the crypt. The normal patterns of interaction demanded play but he had lost the ball. His heart was burdened with incoherent sorrow, as he tried to make conversation in turn with the adults and then his children, each pre-occupied, hurrying in the growing excitement.

"She's talking to you," Great Gran Hannah informed him, from across the table. He looked at her in surprise. Her watery eyes reflected yellow sunlight pouring through the window, as it searched the Old Town for signs of life. Her thinning silver hair was curved into the loose permanent waves that only a professional stylist can achieve, set off with a becoming hint of make-up. She was legendary in her assuredness and now the old lady was setting the seal on him.

Harper knew her statement was also a question and a lead for him to follow. It may have carried a hint of understanding and reassurance. He nodded in acknowledgment of the advice, realising with embarrassment that he had been nervously rocking back and forth himself. He stopped now, gently lifting the baby up into the crook of his left arm, gazing into her eyes, not knowing how to act.

She cooed at him and her wet lips stretched into a flashing smile. The baby's eyes lit up with recognition and pleasure as she studied Harper's face. She gently touched his cheek, probing the thin line of his moustache. He was transfixed. Had he missed something with the two elder children, or was this experience unusual - somehow unique or different?

Elsie had been premature and there had been a deficit in her early responses. Hannah loved her the more so for concerns and a bond that grew during a long stay in hospital. Since then, dark eyed smiling Elsie with her long platted hair had become everyone's mascot – the symbol of a loving family. With guidance, Elsie made lists of the things she could do to help others. At the top of the list was attendance to the needs of Molly the cat but there were no omissions. Every member of the family was on her charitable itinerary.

Elizabeth had been born into this world with all the penetrating shrewdness of a Sibyl. She had been entertaining as a baby but had moved on fast. He couldn't recall the details because he had been working too hard while planning their house move, with several visits to Edinburgh. Harper had missed his chance.

Women had a natural ability to bond with babies that escaped him. He had seen it many times with cattle and sheep. Though he numbered every one, looking to their care, ever cautious in his handling, their offspring never required such bonding from him. If they appeared etiolated they were wiped clean and a bottle shoved in their mouth. Within an hour they were up and running around the pen. Though he had tried, he could not recall his childhood experience of this kind of dependent relationship.

What little Hannah offered was pure magic: 'Feeling not contended or combined with thought.' This was Harper's impression, yet he had no words to express it. How could there be a distinct quality of wisdom in his child's eyes? It felt like he was the one who had taken some narcotic tincture which was now slowly releasing through his brain. He was engrossed in dependency upon this new-born in a way he had never before imagined possible. It was more than the passionate love which his involvement with Hannah had offered him through the years. This selfless granting was the conferring of mutual trust without condition. In a curious way it occurred to him that this blossoming love was led by his child. All he had to do was reciprocate.

He looked away, chatting across the room to the girls and women but he came back again ever more frequently, to see the eyes that studied him. In an instant he laughed, despite all his surliness. He spoke to baby Hannah with the tone reserved for a favourite sheep dog. Great Gran Han shook her head at his clipped muted calls and whistles.

 She was a renowned trainer of Border Collies and knew well why they merited high esteem. She knew one or two of them who'd figured more highly in Harper's affections than some of the people he knew. They were more innocent; more genuine and a bloody sight smarter.

"Ridiculous. A baby makes a man ridiculous in his range of behaviours!" she observed, laughing across the table at him. Her bright eyes were suddenly animated with cautious relief. Harper smiled back at her, for the first time in several months.

The gestural dialogue with glimpses of expression from little Hannah became ever more subtle and warming. Harper lifted her close to his face as he dandled her. He whispered in her ear and sang to her. She gently displaced the hairs on his left eyebrow with a pointing finger, probing the skin beneath. Conjecture was confirmed with fingers, eyes and mouth. Listening and tracking conversation across the room, she raised her tiny hand to make gestures. The bairn delighted in being lifted above his head, or spun gently in a circle.

When her name was called, or spoken softly by Hannah or Jessie, she would call in return. If a momentary visitor, Elsie or Elizabeth was near the door, they called to her and waved. She opened her hands and raised her arm to try to wave back. She would crank her head, bouncing on long powerful legs, glad to be lifted if her mum or Gran approached. Baby Hannah never cried. Hunger was conveyed with a single articulated groan, with welcoming eye contact directed to the provider. There was a backdrop of constant verbal assurance from her mother or grandmother. The concern they projected upon little Hannah was well received. She already knew how to play the game.

Finally, Harper made a brave fist of feeding and changing the baby, gallantly playing down quiet hilarity that circulated among the five other females surrounding him as he did so. He turned their cautions into slapstick as they bombarded him with advice.

"Women's work is simple," he declared with his Morayshire dryness, "That's why it's ca'ed 'women's work.'"

"Oh, how so?" asked great Gran Han, glad to engage with Harper.

"Cos it's easy," he returned with casual reassurance.

"You'd better watch boy," warned Hannah, turning from the sink with a smile on her face.

"That's why a woman's brain is on'y three fifths the size o' a man's," he added, dropping the wet nappy onto the dining table instead of the bucket provided on the floor.

From their loudly voiced repugnance, he gathered that the girls were giving their full attention. Elsie and Elizabeth stationed

92

themselves at the end of the kitchen table, to watch close up as he fumbled with the gigantic safety pins.

"Next time I'm gonny charge admission," he cautioned them over his shoulder. It struck him that he had only a meagre understanding of young creatures. Harper's natural detachment - his 'pulling the wheel out of the rut' approach to everything in life, had left him ill-equipped to deal with the crisis looming immediately in front of him. Suddenly he felt overwhelmed.

He stood silent for a moment over the child. When he looked across to his wife standing at the sink, she had caught his mood and his eye. He was in a gyre. Water trickled over her hands as Hannah rinsed the mud from radishes, her white lace cuffs pushed back tightly on well-proportioned arms. A long twine of light brown hair hung free from a shaped tortoiseshell clip at the nape of her neck. Harper wanted to say that he belonged to her completely. He desired her so much in that instant that it made his mind reel and his entire body flush with excitement. If only she could throw him a line and tow him back into the current. Hannah reflected only a telepathic look of concern, though he read in her gaze the need and promise of later engagement.

To avoid comment upon the desperation that surrounded this moment he diverted his pique inward once again. In a stupor, Harper gave his attention again to 'Heaven's Child.' Little Hannah pedalled her legs and tried to clap her hands, as she latched again onto his clouded eyes. He could only repeat over and again, "Aren't you a little marvel? You are amazing! Yes, you are – amazing! Me? . . . I'm just an old duck in thunder . . . but you . . . you're Heaven's Child. Yeah, no question . . . you've lived before, an' no question."

Then in an instant – his mind racing ahead to the next imperative, so that the day would all go to plan, he lifted the baby and proffered her at Jessie who had her hands full packing the wicker hamper they had hired from the Co-op. Jessie never hesitated; she just smiled wisely, throwing the greaseproof paper onto the pile. Quickly wiping her hands she embraced the child with a smile, switching on her own baby chat.

Harper turned on his heel, speaking urgently of hiring a cab up at the station. He sped away before they could raise objections, or closely examine his incoherent, plough-boy frustration.

The women carried on preparations for the day at the beach without further comment, gestures to one another or lingering eye contact – nor in fact any outward acknowledgement of Harper's strange behaviour.

"What's wrong with Harper?" asked Elizabeth twice, tugging at her mother's voluminous bustle. Hannah looked down from the sink, smiling wistfully but did not deign to reply. Elizabeth would find out all too soon what was wrong with Harper.

The town and beach at Portobello was awash with people by the time they got there. The Indian summer had brought Edinburgh locals out in droves. They agreed to leave the hamper with Mrs Laing at the imposing guest house on King's Road, where Harper had persuaded Hannah to stay for the weekend. They would return to Mrs Laing at around one in the afternoon and decide, weather permitting, to lug it across to the beach or make use of her fine dining room, as offered.

The girls would all head back before dark under the auspices of Gran and Great Gran Han, as they had begun to refer to Jessie's ma, to their home at West Port. This was their chance to be alone together at last, to attempt to broach decisions that cruel fate had forced upon them. Hannah looked long at Harper as they stepped down onto the pavement, her tender eyes reassuring him that despite doubts he anticipated, they could find agreement.

The old lady strode ahead, watching the girls as they squealed and ran headlong for the promenade at the end of the street. Elsie stopped near the round tower house to rub the flat of her hand upon wind-blown sand that had accumulated against a dwarf wall fronting the fine Redstone terrace. Elizabeth tumbled over her in her haste to be 'first to see the sea and win a farthing.'

She laughed, manically shouting, "I thought ye were playing leapfrog!" She bent over to rub her hands in the sand also, even though Great Gran Han cited the fact that, "There are a million tons o' the stuff right there at the end of the street! We'll have to get ye a bucket and spade." Great Gran gently drew their attention to the wide expanse of beach beyond the prom. Again they squealed with excitement as they left this transient, microcosmic novelty for another all-embracing one - presaged by the distant cries of wheeling gulls, already glutted with processed flour and chips.

Cheerful organ music reached their ears underlain with the distant cacophony of a thousand children at play, their bright voices mingling with the gentle plash of breaking surf. Jessie had caught the mood, following swiftly with baby Hannah cradled high in her arms, looking back over her shoulder at her mum and dad. She watched them turn to one another in an avid embrace. The bairn put her hand to her mouth to blow them a kiss, as they had all been teaching her but only Jessie saw it. She told them later she had been around children for all of her fifty one years but swore she had, 'never seen such a prodigy.'

Harper knew not to speak of their sorrows with Hannah. He had read signal pain even as his adored companion alighted from the cab and walked up the steps to the guest house. He noticed that she had taken to swivelling sideways on her broad hips, waiting for others to go in front. It made her look like a popular heroine of the western frontier, stepping out from the shadows to shoot down a baddie, except for the silken weave she favoured in place of the denims worn by cowgirls. Hannah sipped tincture from a tiny brown medicine bottle. Pulling a face, she briskly returned the vial back into her handbag.

Nonetheless, for all that restriction of movement, she cut a dash. With a confident smile on her face, Hannah looked as alluring with her voluptuous contours as any woman he had ever seen. But Harper knew from the pause she made between each movement, in which she carefully steadied her weight over the knee before bearing down, that she was stiff with pain. Her eyes were bright, too bright perhaps, as she approached her physical difficulties with a self-conscious flourish.

He was aware that she was never going to admit defeat, much less burden another with her sorrows. This was not the decrepitude of old age - so Hannah would fight until exhaustion finally overcame her. But to Harper it was all the more alarming for that. He headed for a bench, adjacent a guest house on the promenade for her to sit on. If need be, he was ready to politely displace other promenaders. There were cafés nearby that would serve this purpose also. He could mask his real intention, avoiding embarrassment to Hannah by citing the needs of her elderly grandmother or the children, to rest awhile.

He had money in his wallet and a cheque book too, which the Royal Bank had been pleased to issue. Pierpoint, the branch manager in town, had treated him like a big-wheel, speaking of 'investment opportunities and assurances.' The enthusiastic suggestions struck a chord – people with money can afford to be interested in how it accumulates, but right now Harper was more interested in the journey than the destination, "Let that come when it may," he told himself. This was Hannah's time, Hannah's family, Hannah's moment of glory.

Harper actually prayed for the first time in years, silently but from the heart. His invocation was as assiduous and humble as any supplicant's in a state of grace. Or for that matter a condemned man begging forgiveness.

Lord, let there be laughter and sunshine for her; Harmony; an end to searching. Let there be love between these gentle people young and old I am responsible for. Today let us find the golden thread of delight surrounding all things temporal, broken and blindly human. Let us forget for now the road ahead, to see instead the eternal smile of God.

He stared out across the broad vista of Portobello beach, as if he might yet see it there.

"Stop worrying now!" scolded Hannah, offering what seemed to him the maternal comfort of the contemplative, "All our prayers will be answered," she added, as though catching his thought, perhaps reading red–eyed fever in his eyes.

"In weakness I have strength," he replied sardonically, at a loss for anything more appropriate to say so preoccupied was he with her illness. He stood up to avoid the discussion he had not yet mustered the grit to endure.

"What?"

"Oh, nothing," he replied, resisting distress he felt rising again in his gut. Harper folded Hannah's arm inside his and they marched bravely along King's Promenade.

Little Hannah did not so much imagine herself at the centre of all things, as being an honoured observer within a magical theatre. Her face was all astonishment, so great was the contrast with the tenebrous interior of the apartment she was used to. Even noises and smells of the bustling Grassmarket were predictable compared to this.

This was different in so many ways. Warm, gentle sea-breeze caressed her cheeks, playing with germinal senses, tuning them to the sweetness of a concert violin. Little Hannah thrilled and laughed as her innocent, watchful eyes were charmed by every movement.

The beach at Portobello was an open-air symphony of sensual elements, populated by freely moving souls. Everywhere she looked children ran shouting with glee, as if this day might not last forever.

Elsie and Elizabeth ran to paddle in the cool sea, returning momentarily with stones and shells to burden Grandma Jessie - the newest best friend in their lives. Her presence had been bracketed by recent renewal of their memories of Ramsburn and through the tenure of Great Gran Han at West Port. They had been excited by expectation of her arrival and had grown to love Hannah's mother within the week. She was gracious in indulging them. Like her mother, she was expert at turning a crisis into a drama.

Glorious autumnal beams of light fell bravely from a crystal clear sky. Leaves in the gardens were still, for the most part, strongly green. Fruit trees were laden with an unpicked bounteous surfeit, which galled Jessie the farmer.

Every smile tightened to a glower in the glare, then back to a grimace that might still pass for a smile. Harper remarked that the toffs wore sunglasses. No shadow fell. No heart was darkened by malice or hostility under the mid-day sun.

Promenaders laughed as they dodged a man dressed in riding gear and deerstalker, cycling past precariously on an old penny farthing. A stilt-walking clown came towards the dense crowd, emerging from Beach Lane. He made no progress at all through a gathering mob of children, keen to engage with him. They bombarded him with questions.

"D'ye bump yer heid goin up the stairs mister?"

"Never, we live in a bungalow."

"Whur dye sleep? I bet ye need two beds!"

"Nae bother, son. I sleep standing up."

"Is yer wifey as tall as you?

"Naw matey, she's a midget."

Cheeky banter and the stilt man's practiced drollery filled them all with raucous, infectious laughter. He convinced them he was, "A descendant of the Biblical Nephilim, just arrived from the land of Noah," as he handed out flyers and free sweets.

"They have a twenty-five letter alphabet!" shouted one smart fellow from the verge of the group.

"Absolutely," confirmed the giant, "No "Ah," he chimed with the lad.

There were squeals of laughter from the recent elementary school initiates. One girl turned to explain the in joke to her little brother, "No letter "ah" – get it? Noah!"

"Oh aye," he told her doubtfully, holding her hand tight in case the giant stooped to make off with him under his arm.

Parents waited indulgently nearby while other children older and less patient turned away, only to fall into the ambit of ticket vendors who followed the stilt man in teams. The training mantra was, "Let him work on the young ones. You persuade their parents while the bairns are still watching. And never target a man without his wife." Some beat a rapid retreat, hiring deck chairs to spread out onto the sand as far away from the crowd as possible. Others dug deeper into their pockets, committing to an evening at the circus on Abercorn Park.

The Wilson - Harpers all reluctantly paddled in the sea with whoops of excitement from everyone including Great Gran Han. At first she demurred about the new fashion but following encouragement from Harper concerning a precedent of kicking off shoes and wading in attributed to, 'The Glasgow People,' Great Gran Han declared thoughtfully, "Weell, if it's good enough for Glasgow People, it must be a'right for me too!"

For Great Gran Han the pejorative Edinburgh term 'Glasgow People' still connoted with forced economic migration from her beloved Highlands. Although no conceit was intended by Harper, still they all laughed. Jessie dandled baby Hannah in the water, the bairn kicking and splashing with her dimpled legs. She 'Ooh oohed' softly, peeing unselfconsciously into the foaming ripples.

As the adults looked around they were noiselessly confronted by a tanned, scantily clad fellow in his early twenties carrying four folding deck chairs. He warned them of the high water mark, toting his burden to the best place as the ladies followed. Taking his advice they made camp, peeling off layers of warm outer garments as the girls ran madly about. Harper was pleased to note that they had picked a spot close enough to the guest house on King's Road for him to collect the hamper. Without a word of discussion he set off.

There were slices of steak pie with chopped potatoes, onions and salad. There were sandwiches of various kinds made from Jessie's marvellous seeded, home-baked bread. There were delicious pieces of roasted chicken wrapped in greaseproof paper. The ladies had used some of the original hamper contents – pate and smoked salmon-but had removed the tinned ham and bottles of wine. Harper planned to consume those nearer to the winter festival, on arrival home in the dead of the night. Nothing made him so hungry for the rich jelly of tinned gammon as persuading a belligerent youth of the error of his ways at three o'clock in the morning.

Jessie fetched tea and cream soda for the girls from a kiosk on the promenade. There was an apple for each of them which, due to their size and sweet sugary snap, both girls managed to drop from their mouth into the timeless, laughing sand. Harper mockingly stated that he felt obliged to eat what the others wouldn't eat, as he would have to carry the heavy hamper back later. When they offered to help out, he said they could, "help by eating the ruddy food!"

The women laughed easily, eating more than they would have liked. Jessie railed with levity against the impossibility of having a picnic on any beach, "without getting sand in your mouth!" A warm thermal suddenly whipped off the Forth, as though to reinforce her point. For two bizarre minutes the fine dust pinked into open eyes and settled on lips. They turned their deck chairs to back into this unexpected mistral, protecting their food with their hands like starving urchins.

Jessie and then the other two women hooted with indecorous laughter as they overfilled their mouths. Harper told them he thought their childish behaviour was, "Scandalous," and that, "Anybody looking would think ye'd never seen food . . . An' yis never even said Grace!" he reminded them, like a true Episcopalian.

"Oh, I know," agreed Great Gran, taking Harper's new found piety seriously. The two younger women looked at him with broad smiles, signifying quiet scepticism.

Checking the sky above the beach resolved any doubtful prospects voiced by Great Gran Han concerning the weather. Only a scattering of light cloud in a warming sky chased by a light breeze, spoke of any long term prospect of change. Seagulls circled, encouraging Elsie and Elizabeth to hurl fragments of unwanted food - apples and pieces of crust they were determined not to consume, despite advice about healthy eating and futile cajoling from their mother.

Jessie the provider chose not to be offended, as the gulls snatched morsels of her preparations in mid-air. The girls were advised by Harper to take their activities elsewhere, so Jessie volunteered to accompany them nearer to the water's edge.

Keening as much as Harper, Jessie watched the mood of her eldest daughter from a safe distance but with anguish in her heart which she dared not show at close quarters. She walked the girls to the ice cream kiosk, then pretended to show interest in a photographic lecture on the pier. Harper caught her eye and came up with her, to evaluate what was on offer.

He spoke to his mother-in-law of acquiring one of the much vaunted hand held cameras which the lecturer proposed to discuss. She knew that Harper's interest was leaning in the same direction as her own, in her watching of Hannah from afar. He could not help turning to stare, with concern visible in his grey eyes. Jessie knew that in his mind the lad was already trying to hang on to something that had begun to slip from his hand.

For her part, Jessie Wilson gave space emotionally to all matters pertaining to the daughter she felt in her water would soon return to her care. Jessie never once voiced this expectation, as she knew Harper would fight it all the way. She loved Harper but knew that this desperate dilemma could make or break him as a man. Jessie knew that in time Hannah would come home to her.

Great Gran rested in the strong sunlight, as baby Hannah settled like a cat in her lap. The old lady thrilled to the movement and aroma of the mite in her charge. For her this was the time of silent grace - of reflection upon plodding physical compromise and the inevitable extinction they would soon lead to.

Hannah Drummond was beginning to feel old and careworn, knowing that events of recent months had taken their toll. She felt that all the disasters of a long life had re-emerged to shape into a new, deeply personal trial.

"Parents should not outlive their children, much less their grandchildren," she declared with vehemence to Dr Payton shortly after Elizabeth had been born. Hannah's symptoms had promptly returned. The local GP was a Man of Science; a skilled medical practitioner and prominent Hebrew. If anyone might have an answer to her crisis of faith, perhaps it should have been him. All he could offer Hannah's grandmother was a silent hug before he picked up his bag and walked to his carriage.

There was a relentless natural evil - an imbalance in this world, familiar throughout her time yet never quite reconciled. When she looked at her ailing granddaughter now, outwardly so full of graceful tenacity with elegant form and gorgeous complexion, a somniferous voice charming to hear and always full of modest wit and laughter – Great Gran Han felt completely robbed of sense and purpose.

But here in her lap was a moving being whose very presence seemed to give both pointed resonance and alacrity to all the old lady's conflicted thoughts. There was nothing to do but carry on with a smile on her face that might hide wretchedness.

Great Gran had been around many babies and children in her life. She knew that each one had uniqueness and charm but also knew from this tiny child's demeanour and alertness that she was, in some indefinable sense, very special. She felt a sudden sense of loss when Harper unlocked the tiny hand from around her thumb, offering an excuse about 'taking the baby on her first shopping adventure.'

Jessie spilled the beans about Harper planning to buy a hand camera. There was an immediate spat of mocking controversy aimed his way, including a predictable one about Lothian Constabulary evidently paying their police officers too much from Great Gran, the model exponent of financial organization and prudence.

"Aye, Great Gran Han, you always keep yer money close," acknowledged Harper with disarming candour, adopting the tone of a small boy while winking at Jessie.

"Oh true an' aw," replied Great Gran Han, sitting forward in the deckchair, rubbing her hands on her distended knees, "but I always pay the rental in advance."

"Oh, you're only jealous o' me takin' the bairn aff o' ye!" mocked Harper, feigning annoyance.

"What's worth photographing around here anyhow?" the old lady demanded, clearly scandalised at his plan from the high tone of her voice.

"Oh, I never said I was going to buy a camera. We're just nipping up to the High Street to take a look! Besides, here's you, your serene highness, with your natural, golden curls and azure eyes."

She seemed embarrassed by his familiarity and put a hand to her mouth as she paused to think before replying, not sure whether to be charmed or offended by the audacious flatterer.

"Why not save your money for a rainy day? Get a family portrait done by the man at the pier," put in Jessie, looking up from the hamper she was busy re-packing, "What's his name, the man preparing for the talk?"

"Patrick, wasn't it? John Patrick I believe. The other gentleman from the shop in Portobello was Mr Lees."

"Yes, why not go and see him?"

"It's me he wants to get pictures of, before I die and leave him a widower at twenty five," Hannah stated with conviction.

They all stopped speaking and the smiles on their faces froze. Great Gran put her hand to her mouth again. This time she was genuinely shocked.

"I just think that is so romantic, don't you two? And I love him the more for it, so Harper . . . come on, help me up. Let's you and I go an' find a bargain!" Hannah held her arm up from the deck chair in an authoritative manner that silenced all objections, to logic as to fancy. When the mite reached across to her mother as she brushed crumbs out of her wrinkled dress, she stopped to take the child in her arms, brooking no caution or hindrance.

The girls were deployed peremptorily by Harper to, "help Grandma with the hamper." He gave them each a small amount of money with instruction to fetch tea and scones for Great Gran Han, "As soon as she likes. Get yourselves an ice cream - also for Great Gran Han and Jessie if they would like one." When these arrangements had been effected with due accommodation to the feelings of all concerned, the couple set off at last hand in hand, with Little Hannah waving from over her mother's shoulder.

They walked in silence, surrounded on all sides by the gentle tide of humanity resonating with the sea. A large lady, her skirts tucked around her waist, flopped out of the water with ungainly effort wearing a huge, self-conscious grin on her face. Her four small boys played in the surf, vaunting marine prizes - crabs and cowries. They competed to show their skills – throwing, running, wrestling and splashing, loud and raucous in their seigniorial challenges. Lilting tones betrayed their origin and recent arrival for a late season holiday in Scotland's favourite resort. Every gaze was averted from them for some distance around, save that of their proud mother, who watched now from her base on the dry margin of the beach, her man stretched out and snoring at her side.

"Glasgow weans!" whispered Harper, as they rounded the end of the pier. Hannah suppressed the urge to laugh out loud. She nudged him in the ribs to be silent, momentarily forgetting that Harper had become the great observer of humanity.

"You're off duty now, so please try to relax."

"Oh, you'll get no argument on that score from me woman!"

As they strolled hand-in-hand up the beach and across the promenade towards High Street, each of them glowed inside, confident in the warmth of the other. Hannah thought of the first time he had held her hand, as they had walked through the forest. Pictures tumbled through her mind of the precocious, graceful assurance of that young man and all it had led to in eight intervening years. She mused upon the profound trust their passion had engendered, for this present time of worry. Their vision had endured.

Yet she knew, beneath the romance lay deep concerns that seemed too great to voice in case they leapt out from the very walls to overwhelm them both with fear. She adored Harper and thrilled with pride in their daughters. Yet Hannah knew in her heart this delight was a golden summer day in its last brave hour before the long vigil of night.

Everything she looked at seemed phenomenal to Hannah. Colours seemed richer; sounds and actions more significant than their usual appearance. Every passing individual was imbued with a deeper purpose than superficial sense or mere perception would admit.

Heavenly light glowed it seemed, behind every scene in the bustling town. Men urgently laying granite and tar Macadam surfaces, excavating cobbles in preparation for a new urban transportation system which would link the coastal towns with the great city, disturbed all peaceful communication. Though not praised by the generality for the overtime they'd committed to on someone else's day off, to Hannah they were as enthusiastic and three dimensional as Angus Og's Islanders, turning up at Bannockburn in their Kingdom's hour of greatest need.

Hannah was fascinated by their sweaty brows and bright eyes which seemed to glow with bonhomie. She found herself suddenly engrossed by their coarse laughter, welling irrepressibly underneath the dust and dirt as they raked and shovelled. Even the blaring sound of massive compression engines they used to drill quickly through the top surface, seemed to her the clamour of momentous battle.

This impression of combat was confirmed as she stood watching the thoughtful rotation of exhausted men, operating monstrous leaping and plunging pneumatic drills. Hannah noticed with amazement that while spare men rested, activity never abated. The crew inched their way up the main road as determinedly as Roman legionaries – noisy pneumatic hammer drills at the front, followed by a small army of men swinging picks, or hurling cobbles into motorised dumper trucks at the rear.

Portobello seemed to Hannah the perfect microcosm of an industrial world. It had rail and sea links, extending markets for traditional work with fish and beef, pottery and glass. The little resort town provided world renowned beer and regionally famous dairy produce. It outclassed other model towns - New Lanark and Saltaire in England, for popular recreational facilities which drew visitors from across the country. This allowed all of Porty's citizenry to walk tall. The fact that it was proximal to the most beautiful city of Great Britain was an added attraction, frequently mentioned by the residents of Edinburgh who wanted to claim it as their own.

Hannah had heard fastidious talk of Brighton, Scarborough and Blackpool. She had visited Duff and Banff many times. Perhaps Nairn was her favourite seaside resort, so she had told Harper, with its starkly beautiful hills and endless sand dunes. People's talk, like railway posters, made her want to travel but somehow the knowledge that she never would had begun to turn her mind towards the qualities of her erstwhile home.

This place with its wheeling activity and earnest, quick paced people, made Hannah laugh out loud with incredulity, even as Harper stood at her side, patiently waiting for her attention. The infant in her arms amazed him again, with the rapt manner in which the child's gaze was now following her mother's.

Harper could not bring himself to interrupt with questions, or observations. He knew that his wife was living more deeply in the moment than an honest chorister singing a Handel mass. He could feel, see and hear the cymatic resonance of bliss swelling in Hannah's breast as she gazed at the tumultuous activity from the street corner.

Portobello had worked its magic for Harper also. The crowded beach under a splendid sky, the gay fairground atmosphere of the little town had been a wonderful respite. Great transport and gas engineering projects, employing an army of labourers, were also truly inspiring. These activities clearly subjected people in the same way as the seasons. The good folk of Porty were already well used to constant battle with the elements, in their working lives on the land or the sea.

It seemed to Harper that Edinburgh, the great hub of Scottish urban life, was spinning each individual experience. Auld Reekie was like a constellation moving its orbiting satellites into a woven tapestry of colours and sound. His little observer Hannah was gently introspecting impressions of crowds on the beach, seagulls wheeling in the sky and changing rhythms of industrial life in the town, just as surely as her mother.

There was an extraordinary connectedness between them as they gazed together at the cacophony of construction through a drifting pall of black pitch fumes. Evidently there was a spiritual bond, which Harper could neither gauge nor fully understand but which was charming and humbling for him to observe. He leant back to sit on a shop window sill, watching his glorious wife with amusement as she guided the attention of their infant. His mind suddenly reeled with grief - for time in uncertain decades ahead he knew she would never spend with her children. The burden of duty he carried for each of them could not be contained or supported. It made him physically shake with dread for the future. In that moment Harper wished with all his heart that it could be he who was dying and her to be left with the broken heart.

Yet in starkest contrast Hannah's heart sang with happiness as she silently admitted the impermanence of everything she could imagine, including the sweet, harmonious poise of her own tenuous existence. Her thoughts and vision, fears and resolutions dropped gently away. Her mind rose like a halo, another tube-torus joining the smoky billows wafting from factory chimneys stretching along the burnsides of the cohesive little town. Internally Hannah was preparing herself for the worst, rehearsing how she would handle the dénouement to her own tragedy.

It seemed to her that life's trials had merged into the ringing note at the end of a stunningly beautiful, unwritten symphony – the final cadence that touches every heart before it fades into silence – the long rest of eternal listening. Fear could no longer touch her. Reconciled to the future, she turned to Harper with a beam of accepting happiness on her face and they walked along the High Street away from the road works.

"Why so much activity Harper, what are they digging up the road for?" Hannah asked, handing the baby to him.

"Ah, who can say, there's so much not yet decided."

"You mean the cable-tram system?"

"Possibly . . . but they're probably extending the telephone network, or modernising the gas-main first. Maybe it's down to those new rare-earth filaments for the gas lamps. I've seen them in the hotels in town - and they are actually much brighter. Also there was an American company called Bush at the exhibition, showing off what can be done with electric lighting."

"Oh yes, I saw the electric lights on Prince's Street. The supply comes from a building on Dewar Place."

"Yep, described as, 'more beautiful than any stars in the sky' but just an advertising experiment I suppose, though everyone will want it. Ali Macdonald told me about the proposals to construct a cable system. It will pull trams along the coast road, between Joppa and Newhaven."

"Oh, I hope that won't happen - what would become of the poor old horses?"

"Having been raised on a farm you will already know the answer to that question, dearest. Perhaps I'd best say nothing!"

Hannah smiled and edged against him, blowing a raspberry into the palm of their baby's open hand.

The man in the camera shop showed them Voigtlander; Fallowfield; Kodak and Blair portable cameras. They were mostly second hand but all were offered with a guarantee plus reassurance of, "Expert processing as well as commendations from notable professional photographers." Hannah was unimpressed.

Harper looked into her eyes without speaking however and each read the other's thought. She would indulge his every whim, but never even attempt to use what she couldn't carry. Blair's *Petite Kamarette* was the only horse in the race – the others made obsolete in comparison to its fifty frame roll film and compact size. The salesman mentioned a photographic engineer based in Lambeth who offered rolls of 100. Harper told him to order a couple. He paid in advance and asked that the film be sent to his home address.

Unlike most of the others they were shown by the shopkeeper, Mr Lees the *Kamarette* was new and relatively expensive. Most ordinary working people would never dream of buying such a thing but Harper had the same look of determination in his eye she had seen when he got the job in Edinburgh. There was no point in arguing with him. Hannah's lips parted but she thought better of what she was going to say, smiling instead with her open face while imagining the offence this purchase would give Grandma – the eternal advocate of financial prudence and thrift.

In a way Hannah knew this was Harper's final gesture of defiance to the old girl. It drew a line under the shared but unspoken knowledge that, whatever urgent contingencies might arise with management of the family business before young Frank Wilson attained the age of majority, the two crofts in Rotheimay would never come John Harper's way. Neither would any other property belonging to the Harpers.

As he reached into his inside jacket pocket for the cheque book, Harper put his finger gently to Hannah's lips. She spun away in embarrassment to examine framed images of photographic backdrops. Covering an entire wall of the studio was a romantic couple picnicking in a bucolic summer scene outside a country pub. A wooden table for posing around would give the impression that the backdrop was genuine, with realistic vanishing perspective.

Stung by the perception that such an image might be all she would leave behind for them to remember her by, Hannah perused a finely attired lady with tooled leather travelling case, on another wall. The model's beautiful face smiled as brilliantly as the glorious sunshine streaming down over her shoulders. Heavenly light poured from the stained glass windows of a neo-gothic cathedral devoted to rail transport. Hannah caught the ingratiating tone of the shop owner, noting with dark pleasure the sudden reversal of authority that money invariably provides.

In that moment though, Hannah's bravura had stalled. She saw and was overwhelmed by the convincing beauty of these pre-eminent samples of photographic art - even where one image was obviously superimposed upon another. She realised that it was studio lighting that had created what seemed a breath-taking masterpiece of exposure.

Regardless, here was a quintessentially forward-looking poignancy of hope and expectation, which all who laboured and wished for escape would recognize. She so badly needed to be that lady of circumstance heading for her train. Yet in the back of her mind, Hannah already knew that the next train she was going to catch would take her back home to where her mother could look after her. And that excursion would probably be her last journey.

Trying to speak to her child, Hannah pointed to the fine lady, then to her case and then to the light from the windows. But her voice croaked with sadness as she spoke. When it finally tailed off the bairn looked at her, not at the photo she was pointing at. For once tears of distress welled in her eyes – prompted as much by Harper's sweet understanding, as finally being forced to acknowledge the heavy stone of truncated ambition beginning to tear through her abdomen.

They went to see Marion Macdonald, who made a great fuss over baby Hannah. She immediately struck the Harper's as being mild and sensible. Marion stood quite tall for a woman but was not physically imposing. Raven black hair and otiose brown eyes held a questioning softness, which spoke of confident upbringing and a considerate mind. She was well proportioned, if a little tired and wan though full of youthful kindness and enthusiasm, despite her twenty three years.

Although Marion's appearance gave a tantalising impression of the kind of individual who might well change beyond recognition in later years, perhaps into someone stunningly beautiful, to Hannah she seemed more of a girl than a mature woman. Marion clearly knew the situation and the dual purpose of their visit – it was more than just a routine social call, yet her reaction to Hannah Harper's need was to assume a role in assuaging doubts, rather than in talking about her concerns in any way.

Marion spoke effusively about what mattered to her - her own two small children Ailsa and Ross, and how they thrived in this safe, interesting place. Ali's family lived within a stone's throw of the High Street, with its proud new town hall and fire station, its numerous shops and nearby railway. Horse drawn trams into the city took an age to drag their passengers up the hill in the morning but there were also regular trains.

The Macdonalds clearly liked it here in Portobello, although they were drawn by aspiration – like everyone else around. In particular Marion told them, she dreamt of owning one of the spectacular new red sandstone town houses being constructed above The Meadows.

"They are so much closer to the West Port but it's hard to save and he works long enough hours as it is. I feel that we can bide our time."

Marion thought to mention cousins who lived on Brighton Place, who would look after a child too but held back until another occasion because that might give Hannah the impression that her predicament seemed desperate. Instead Marion said emphatically, "Look whenever you have a need Hannah, at short notice even, it really will not be a problem to drop them off . . . especially this one!" she added with exaggerated delight, reaching for little Hannah.

As Marion Macdonald gestured towards the child, she let out a loud chuckle of laughter that surprised even her mother. The bairn lifted her hand to point a finger of approval at Marion. Marion lifted little Hannah onto her knee, turning her towards her mother. The child's smile said it all.

"Well that's settled then. I may as well leave her here with you!" Hannah resolved and they all relaxed. As the three adults drank tea, they laughed about the camera Harper had bought, agreeing that it did not look much for the money. He made them all pose as he tried it out, then prevailed upon Marion to swap his handful for hers. The baby got in on the act, gently examining and probing the large box in Marion's hands with her fingers but not quite successfully with her mouth, although she did try. Then both Hannah and Harper each took a photo with Marion in the frame, holding the child who had taken to her so quickly.

Ali came home from his shift, greeting them comfortably without fuss. The men went to sit in the back room, where they might smoke with the window open to the small garden. They shared a large bottle of Dryborough Ale, Harper in his best Sunday suit, Ali with shirt sleeves rolled up and braces hanging. They chatted about politics and work.

In the sitting room at the front of the house the women talked about the practical business of managing three girls - should their mother be absent for any length of time. Various ideas came to both.

When the time approached for Marion's bairns to be rounded up and scrubbed down, Hannah hugged her, knowing that the trials of life had created a bond in an instant where under different circumstances a dozen meetings might not have done. Harper invited Marion and Ali to come over on Sunday with their children.

"It seems so long since we entertained," intoned Hannah wistfully, "We used to invite people all the time."

The Harpers departed with dignity and the perceived quality of energy renewed – at least outwardly. They took away a little of the hope that sustains the beginning of all new ventures for the bold – even when planning for hospital visits, deaths and entrances.

Hannah left Harper to deal with the baby and the camera, stepping ahead rapidly through the gate and burying her arm inside her day bag. In a swift moment she had pulled the stopper, bringing the dark brown amphora she craved to her lips to sip as Foxworthy had directed, 'When the pain is unbearable.'

Her hand shook as stiffness from sitting so long seemed to grind her bones, stabbing upwards into her belly. Taking special care, she made sure that not a single spot of the Tincture of Opium to fell onto her dress. Hannah had no idea why she was feeling guilty about taking it but felt the need to be discreet nonetheless. What at first had been a palliative for distress had in intervening months become a life line for survival.

The perfect harmony of the engineering project and the wheeling mandala of all that lived and moved, which she had previously envisaged standing on the corner before Harper bought the camera, returned to Hannah like the turning of a key in a locked door. Foxworthy's pain-killer had done more than simply subdue discomfort. It had returned everything she perceived to its pre-conditional, phenomenal essence, lending her complete perspective of things in themselves. Hannah guessed that this was how her baby daughter saw the universe.

Now under the influence of the Laudanum, her localised experience of the world was breathtakingly, mesmerizingly colourful - resplendent in harmony. She was completely detached as she drifted painlessly along, able to observe silently, feeling that she understood all wider attachments. As Hannah sensed her own individuality begin to dissolve, the drug allowed her to view mundane reality from a higher dimension without feeling or pain. Suddenly everything made sense.

We are immersed in the witnessing of astounding, eternal beauty.

She was reminded of opera glasses which she'd once hired at the Empire Palace and how Harper teased her for looking through the wrong end. She had burned with embarrassment at her own lack of sophistication, watching the show in miniature like a giant. But that was how the busy world appeared to her now. Her face was blank, while inside she roared with incongruous laughter.

As she walked easily along the street two paces ahead of Harper, every person and object was suddenly imbued with its own discreet physical existence and polite rationale. It was the purest entertainment, exclusively for her. She felt herself at one remove from the magic theatre around her. The being named Hannah Harper was endowed momentarily with the sublime objectivity of a Grecian deity. She was Demeter, presiding over the cycles of life. Warm, effulgent light engulfed her, body and soul. She was floating. Nothing intruded into her individual cosmos. Nothing could perplex her in any way.

Hannah was a child again, walking within a life sized doll's house. The world was sublime in that perfect moment, as she strolled effortlessly through it. She wished only to be able to reach out to touch those she loved with that same perception. But in that very instant of returning human desire, Hannah found she could not function precisely as she wished.

Her hands and feet had lost all sensation. She could not speak. She wished only to convey a summation of all that might fail to be understood otherwise, but in the very moment of revelation she became dumb. Hannah's fine mind was somehow detached entirely from her numbed body and floundering emotions.

Like Isaiah descending from the Heavens, her vision of the world was sealed in awe behind muted lips. Harper noticed her wallowing, aimless movement. Balancing the camera and the bairn he took her elbow in his hand as they walked back to the family.

As they approached the deck chair encampment, Hannah was heard to mutter something plaintively about wanting to sleep. Meeting an alerted Jessie half way along the promenade, an enormous cold hand rested heavily upon her head. Putting her last effort into trying to speak, she began to panic but found that her lips would not move. Hannah's eyes rolled to the heavens above as she raised her hand feebly, before crumpling to her knees.

Chapter Six - *Morpheus*

Harper watched Hannah devotedly as she slept, his heart ringing with the most human diatonic of giving and losing. At that moment he would have offered anything to save her – the world and all it contained, himself included - were it not for the fact that he really had nothing to give at all. He knew also that Hannah had given him the most precious gift of all. She had taught him how to live in the moment.

Hannah woke in the rented room to find the light from what had been a magnificent early autumn evening gone from behind the heavy drapes. She stared for a while at dim embers glowing in the grate. Then realising Harper was next to her in the bed slowly turned her numbed and marbled body into his.

It occurred to Harper in that returning moment of sensual relief for the woman who meant everything to him, that even the skin on the top of his scalp was flushed with blood. She wriggled into him for warmth, caressing his arms to indicate her willingness to be loved. His heart pounded in his chest with deepened breathing, even though his mind was still asking the question, 'does she really want this?'

Having not attempted to couple with her for months – since little Hannah had been born in fact, he was actually terrified of what it implied, imagining she might break like a porcelain figurine. He had been neutered by disillusionment, imagining Hannah's agony. Sexual fantasy had been replaced by visions of the tumorous mortification gathering inside his wife – of its dubious origins, location and spread. It was an evil mystery, the taint of which had served to cancel out the merging of all their mutual desires towards fervent union of bone and flesh.

Yet both had grown used over the years to an ecstatic, indwelling appeal for the other. Yearning, with ever more synchronous releases, had followed their harmonious experience of living together. That nurturing tenderness had been manifest, undiminished over many years, in thrilling sexual play.

Now Hannah encouraged him to make love to her, although he had been perplexed by her passion. The soporific tincture which had stilled her tortured body, uncovered the deepest sensory urges as it receded. Afraid to hurt her, Harper responded temperately, realising that above all she desperately needed reassurance.

Then suddenly Hannah was far away again, her mind torn by nebulous images at once cosmic and starkly mundane. As Harper studied her in the half light, she was pulsing through imponderable celestial spaces. Yet her mind and heart were compressed into the momentum of a deeply personal, subjective will.

In her tortured imaginings she was the Goddess of fertility, then the seed fallen on stony ground. In all her breathless, circumscribed dreams she lamented the injustice of her own dying with a mother's dangerous anger. Hannah started to consciously dread the Tincture of Opium wearing off.

When it finally did, she was relieved to discover terrible aches of the previous day had actually subsided with deep rest. Harper had risen, dressed and eaten breakfast although it seemed to Hannah they had been making love only minutes before. He had been for a walk along the promenade, bought a Sunday paper, but found he could not give it his full attention. He returned mid-morning to find his wife asleep again.

Hannah came back into full alertness with a cry into a grey, unforgiving reality. She began to weep like a lost child, for the dispassionate brutality of impermanence. Harper flapped like an old man as he lit the gas lamp, rummaging quickly for the narcotic amphora. But to his amazement, she told him she didn't need it.

"Then tell me what can I do for you?" he asked helplessly, seeing a tear roll from the outside corner of her eye across her right temple and onto the pillow.

"Oh, nothing Harper, it was just a dream."

"Do you want to talk about it?" He moved closer to her to stroke her cheek, wiping away the moisture with his thumb.

"No, I don't think I could find the words. It was more of a hellish vision. Don't let me take that horrible stuff again!"

"Try if you want to, it might help you to share it."

Lying silently for half a minute she squeezed his hand to reassure him. Hannah realised that something very odd had indeed happened with the overdose of Laudanum. Although she had been worried about the future and had for some time been sipping the tincture to alleviate aches and pains, there was a new element here.

Dr Foxworthy, she now remembered, had tried to warn her off excessive use of the narcotic tincture. With growing distress and the urgent need to hide it for the sake of appearances, she had increased the dosage. Hannah had suddenly felt a leaden torpidity. Then her mind as well as her body had fallen into the lap of Morpheus.

"Your hands are freezing even though the weather has been sunny."

"I know. I swear it is this stuff!"

"Hmm, whatever it is you are ill. Foxworthy came you know. He looked in the bottle and took your pulse. He said you would sleep it off. That you would be fine. It's my damned fault. I made you do too much."

"Nonsense man, I had a marvellous day. We all did. Are the bairns alright? They will be worried about me. Send a telegram to Great Gran and Jessie, tell them I'm alright, please!"

"Of course. First I will pour some tea and order you food in a sec." Harper banked the fire with a layer of sticks and four mighty lumps of coal, then slid open the vent below the grate to accelerate flames that licked upwards from the pink embers. Soon the blaze comforted them both. He narrowed the chimney flue to direct heat into the chilly room.

Harper warmed the remainder of a pot of tea he had consumed alone the previous evening after the girls had left with Jessie and Hannah's Gran for West Port. He rinsed his cup in the bathroom at the far side of the landing then returned with water to dilute the brew, before sitting again fretfully with Hannah. She sat up in bed, trying to smile but her face seemed ashen and strained. Dark orbs like bruised apples lay below her once beautiful green eyes, making her appear all the more alluring in her vulnerability.

Harper looked at her questioningly and in a moment she began to explain her trauma.

"It started before we bought the camera. It was like I was suddenly transported into a different world. At first everything was incredibly pictorial, like looking down from a high hill onto a little town. Like the Provencal Santons, or an elaborate Doll's House on sale at Jenner's. It's hard to explain, Harper – everything seemed so neat, so perfectly simple. Even the noise of the pneumatic drills seemed to have their own incredible, blasting harmony. As we walked up to Marion's house, even The Moon up in the afternoon sky seemed to make its own noise. Everywhere I looked there was movement, giving off swirling sound and colour. I had to keep stopping . . . do you understand? I wished that I could somehow become absorbed in the perfect beauty surrounding me. I had this overwhelming wish to just stop and simply watch the world going by."

"Why didn't you say so? I would have cleared some old hens affy a bench at Abercorn Park for you, Hannah."

"You don't get it, Harper. If I'd sat down, I would never have got back up again. I honestly thought I was about to sign out permanently last night when I collapsed at the beach. I wanted to talk to you but I couldn't even speak. Then in my dream last night," she stopped suddenly and held Harper's wrist, "Tell me it is Sunday . . . we have only been here one night?"

"Yes, yes. It's one o'clock in the afternoon."

"Oh, thank God. I feel as though I have been gone for days. I suppose that in a way I have. It has been building up for so long."

"Go on with the dream."

"In the dream I was just walking and walking and getting nowhere . . . You know something like strolling along the Royal Mile with bags of shopping. There were enormously tall lamp standards, shining down like a blazing hot sun."

"Hmm, it's the opium, sure enough. I have seen quite a bit of it coming in with Chinese sailors and the problems it causes. A lot of the Merchantmen bring it in as contraband. They sell it to others in the know - Asians and Orientals mainly but Lascars and increasingly Europeans have the habit. It's deadly. Anyone taking it who is not used to it, gets in a bind right away."

"I just wanted to get home and rest but the more I walked the smaller I became, until I was a bug crawling through the desert."

Harper ventured a laugh, as much at Hannah's little girl tone as his own relief that she was recovering her natural voice.

"Ho, sounds like moonshine to me. You're sure you haven't been at the Cream Sherry?" She hit him with her open hand across the arm and he grabbed her forearm to pull her forward, protesting. He kissed her as passionately as the first time he had ever made love to her.

She seemed to him as she might have looked in her mid-teens – a time when he had not known her well. Tiny orange freckles he always delighted to examine stood out either side of her stoical nose. He was overtaken with sympathetic desire for her. However gently it might have to be, he was inclined to make love to her again as languorously and sweetly as he possibly could and as soon as he possibly could. She laughed and hit him again as they broke off from kissing.

"I know what you're after Harper. I haven't even cleaned my teeth! Now listen to me! I'm trying to tell you something. This may seem inconsequential to you but this is precisely the point I'm trying to get across!"

Harper looked down from her eyes, to allow her to express what he had known instinctively for weeks she needed to say – partly because it would be difficult for her but also he knew well, because it was going to break his heart.

He wasn't quite ready for the discussion they had to have. They both needed this swan song of passion and exuberance. So he would listen with his heart but he would play the fool, to lead her out of sorrow. Hannah hugged her knees under the embroidered quilt as she struggled for words to continue describing her drug induced vision.

"I haven't the words to explain this . . . I felt . . . I felt cut adrift from reality itself. I was overcome with a sleep, like the sleep of death. But my will propelled me out into space, even as my burdens dragged me back down again. I was a rubber band - stretched to the point of snapping - but I flew higher and higher - spinning like a weaver's shuttle, up into the starry night."

"Good Christ! Where is that stuff woman?" demanded Harper, turning round and pretending to search in her bag.

"No, John, what are you going to do? I need it. I need something for the pain! Don't pour it away."

"Don't fret woman – I'm only going to try some of it mysel'," he said with mock enthusiasm, "I'll lea' a wee taste fer you."

Mumbling the apothecary's instructions from the label with an artlessly senescent Morayshire farmer's voice, he carefully poured a single droplet into his tea, trembling and sighing like Methuselah. Harper's face was deadpan, grey eyes expressionless, voice gently understated as ever when he acted the rogue.

Hannah roared with delight at his cadaverous bedside manner. Her joy at his teasing was the more pleasurable for him, knowing he could still make her laugh so easily. He had set the seal on her episode of distress. Now he tore off his shirt with a flourish, hopped out of his trousers then vaulted across her onto the bed. She beamed with anticipation. They lay together in gentle warmth coupling again each time they woke, sanctifying a precious bond that time and decay could place no limit upon.

In the afternoon they walked on the beach. Hannah took several photographs with the new camera, "To get the best out of such a romantic luxury," thinking she would probably never use it again. Her involvement served to deflect Harper's interest – allowing her to feel less self-conscious. She told him that she couldn't wait to see the results. The weekend crowds had thinned, giving them time to listen to one another at last - and to make their compromised plans.

Harper knew he had to accommodate Hannah's needs before his own career in the force. He talked speculatively about training as a

Life Assurance Actuary. They spoke freely, without irony, about money and the ways in which it can offer protection. He told her that the training would take years however. He would find it difficult to study in the months ahead, so he needed to think of something else in the meantime while the baby was small. He had trained as a tailor but again that required time and commitment to set up a business.

Hannah agreed that she would press Foxworthy to arrange the operation she dreaded. By implication, she could not manage to look after three children. They had plenty of money to fall back on but finding a nanny and arranging a move to a smaller, or at least less expensive house, seemed urgently pressing requirements.

They kept away from the difficult prospect of Hannah not recovering from the operation and the question of where she might end her days. But he knew what was coming as she stopped before the water's edge, with the crimson sunset hanging over her shoulder. He stood in the surf, gazing into her eyes like he had never seen her before. She knew what he was doing. It was why he had bought the camera.

Harper was studying her so he would remember every contour and wrinkle, every laughter line of her mouth and dark fleck in her green eyes. She rested her forearms on his shoulders as she searched his eyes in turn, full of compassionate humour. He remembered their wedding day when they made love in the woods, still feeling the same smoking passion for her that he'd had then. The bubbling tide flowed around their shoes but they ignored it.

"I need you to agree a couple of things with me, Harper. I have nothing much to pass on to the girls - jewellery and such. Jessie will deal with how they divide that up – what's mine is yours anyway. But I want to be buried in the churchyard where we were married – in Milltown of Rotheimay . . . do you understand? Promise me!" Harper was dumbstruck but she took his silence as assent.

"The other thing is, the girls will need a mother . . ."

"No! Don't do this . . ." Harper's voice thinned to a whisper as his masculine poise folded before Hannah's vision and foresight.

"I'm sorry, dear man! Harper, I know you love me with all your heart . . . but time will move on and you must move with it. Promise me you will allow yourself to be happy when I am not here!"

Harper's cracked vessel burst with sorrow. He trembled as he wept, aphonous and heartbroken, before the angelic compassion of Hannah's simple logic. He tried to speak but was humbled before her judgement. Only a childlike, halting treble came through the gasping anguish.

"Don't leave me, Hannah . . . you're not . . . going to leave," he sobbed. She hushed him, clasping his face in her hands. He shook with the unjust grief never fully admitted until this moment in his life. She stepped towards him and they embraced intensely without movement. Some passers-by watched them - an elderly couple, silently amused at lovers bound so tightly as the incoming tide gently lapped around their neatly polished shoes.

Foxworthy was reluctant to arrange any operation. He even seemed to have stepped back from making a firm diagnosis. While not doubting Hannah's painful symptoms, he fulminated about the pointlessness of surgery stating that, "nature has its own cures for this sort of thing."

Incredible though it seemed, he was apparently suggesting that the couple should have another baby and that it should be delivered by Caesarean operation. At that convenient moment in time Hannah could be kept in hospital for, "investigative routines and microscopic analysis, which would take only a few additional days." Harper's mind was reeling.

The old fuddy-duddy has gone quite mad.

Harper knew of doctors who had worked themselves to an early grave, eased in their passing by a rarefied professional weakness for malt whisky which might only be regularly consumed by the wealthy, or those on the road to ruin. Some had other peccadilloes, it was also clear to him, perhaps borne out of years of dedication to curing the sick, as a result of which they became obsessive or over-compensated for their natural depression.

The Edinburgh Police were the oldest establishment of its type in the United Kingdom. They had records that told the story. Harper and his colleagues were well used to keeping a close eye upon, not to mention laughing a great deal about the high minded medical elite that the city was famous for.

He resisted the urge to interrupt with a sardonic remark about Edinburgh's anatomical traditions, of Dr Knox's association with Burke and Hare. Harper tuned in again to the eccentric little man.

"Of course she would need to understand and agree that the gynaecological surgeon would have to act on instruction from the oncologist – that is to say, the cancer specialist, if any tumours were found."

"If any tumours are found?" repeated Harper with incredulity, immediately wishing he had spoken more softly.

"Look, Doctor Foxworthy, I can't have another baby in my state," cut in Hannah with earnestness that shocked Harper into silence, "Whatever is wrong with me, it is already too far advanced. I don't need an expert to cut me open to confirm that." Hannah had a desperate look in her eyes as she leaned forward in her chair, which seemed to mirror the look that the GP was giving back to her.

Dr Foxworthy's lips parted and closed no less than three times before he actually Hmmed aloud, but clearly to himself alone, as he was evidently musing over some clinician's perspective unsuitable for their ears. When he did finally get to the point though, Foxworthy was a force of nature.

"Look woman, it's not my place to tell you what to do – but this has been a life-line for others in the past." He placed his fine fingers curled against the right side of his mouth, crooking the thumb underneath his chin. Staring into the middle distance between the couple, the GP appeared to be looking for a solution they both knew wasn't there.

It struck Harper that here was a pause more dramatic than an ironic plot turn in a drama at the Royal Lyceum. Foxworthy was a nice man but he conveyed nothing so much as a sense of utter futility. Harper's heart skipped a beat. He knew they were getting nearer to some awful truth.

"Mrs Harper, I know what's wrong with you from the symptoms you've described," Foxworthy stated quietly, now looking directly at her, "I do not need a much travelled academician from the Royal College of Surgeons to tell me that." He thought for a moment before resuming, with his more usual blustering pace, "And yes, you may well be right," he stirred the air with his hand, as though mixing a witches brew for Burn's Night, "It probably is too far advanced to operate. If your last child had been born by section . . . had we known beforehand . . . the surgeon could have performed a biopsy. We never know with Ovarian Cancer until it's too late anyway . . . because the symptoms are non-specific. The point is . . ." he tailed off without actually making any point.

The hand came up to his mouth again. It struck Harper that this was the signal gesture of a man who is about to prevaricate.

"Yes, doctor?" Hannah prompted indulgently.

"Well, in short, it might have been worth our while operating under that particular set of circumstances but . . ."

"That set of circumstances did not apply - and now it's just too dammed inconvenient because of cut-backs due to the financial panic!" put in Harper, finally at the end of his tether.

"No, no! It's nothing of the sort. I don't want your gold fillings."

"Well what are you saying then? Get to the point man! We can pay for the operation."

Foxworthy took a deep breath before replying.

"Look, Mr and Mrs Harper, I understand your desperation," Foxworthy folded the fingers of both hands and rested his chin like a learned justiciar about to make a pronouncement, "But there has never been a good prognosis for putting a cancer patient under the knife. I've seen this a hundred times before. People just place too much faith in our medical elite – and please understand they are the very best in Europe, possibly in the entire world – but," he tilted his head to one side as he paused again in his sincere apologia, "we just don't know enough." Foxworthy looked perplexed. He knew the medical debate but felt unsure it was edifying for the public, much less the patients.

Harper was infected by the man's uncertainty. Now it was he whose mouth was half open, still angry but for now at a loss for words.

"And just why do you believe that is so?" enquired Hannah with alacrity.

"Well, if you will allow - it has to do with the way the ailment spreads," explained the good doctor, removing his spectacles to look at his patient with greater sincerity, "If it's left alone in one person, they may live for years; while another weakens rapidly, seemingly because of the operation. In other words the operation seems to advance the spread, unless there is a clear boundary and often the surgeon cannot see that. Microscopy is an old science and has advanced tremendously in recent years but we are talking about activity at a cellular level here. We are just beginning to understand the molecular chemistry. But research definitely shows that pregnancy reduces the spread of even tertiary level cancer."

"So what are you saying? Don't have an operation but do have another baby?" Harper demanded incredulously, looking hard at the man. Foxworthy's silence was confirmation enough, although his reply, after a measured hiatus was nothing more than an official disclaimer.

"Thank you Doctor," said Hannah, consciously omitting his surname, standing suddenly, shooting her hand out in a gesture of farewell, "You have shown great consideration and honesty. If you will be so good, you might facilitate my transfer back to Aberdeenshire by sending my notes with a covering letter to Mr Mitton at Elgin. I already have a GP there who will re-register me locally. I'll give their addresses to your receptionist. You never know, *I* may live for years," she added with a broad smile. Foxworthy's jaw gaped fully this time as he too stood up. He could think of nothing to say except, "But I, but I . . . don't see that . . ."

"She's still trying to think of ways of acquitting herself of the responsibilities she has to the three bairns that she has already got," explained Harper to the open mouth.

"Aw . . . yes, yes of course. If that's your decision," the doctor added as an afterthought.

Harper stuck out his hand in much the same peremptory manner as Hannah, who by now was through the door. Foxworthy shook it firmly then beetled across to the coat stand, to hand Harper his overcoat and trilby, smiling warmly as he ushered him out. Back in his practice room Foxworthy reached for his medicine cabinet and the fine Arran malt that nestled there, ever ready for such unresolvable medical traumas.

"What a nice man he is," Hannah remarked, walking back to the house at West Port.

"Absolutely, a real gentleman," agreed Harper, "So few of them are prepared to tell the truth."

"Yeah, if they did, they'd all be out of a job."

Hannah laboured on, 'like a fish wife or a machine minder,' so she thought of herself through the arduous, aching days – but though she mocked her circumstances, she never once complained. Daily walks with the girls past the Tollcross onto the Meadows to recline among her children on a bench where she watched truant schoolboys playing soccer or cricket, helped her fight the oppression of declining health.

She envied serious looking medical students from the University of Edinburgh Medical School sitting remotely under the trees, poring over their text books. They were totally absorbed in a future they took for granted. Some sauntered past in garrulous bevies down to, or back from the town. They tended to evaporate quickly like ghosts before the dawn, as the clock approached each hour and lecture halls began to fill. The noises of saw and hammer, the coarse shouts and laughter of builders and roofers echoed across from the new residential constructions stretching out in a broad arc above the parkland.

Hannah did not care about the pain in her legs or her back, as long as she had her Tincture of Opium to control and suppress it. She was determined to spend every moment that she could with Elsie, Elizabeth and Hannah, not to waste her time worrying about the end. Now that she understood its action, the soporific drug could not oppress her motivation to interact with her family. She knew that the parting would come soon enough but prior to that time she would give up only if exhaustion sank her completely without trace.

Harper had included Jessie in their planned strategy for survival. On her last night in Edinburgh, he explained to her the need for Hannah to return home to Rothiemay. With Jessie's agreement, as soon as Hannah deemed it necessary, she would leave along with their youngest child who needed her mother most. In the meantime, he suggested, it was best to avoid discussing these matters in front of the girls and for them all to carry on as normal. In short, for Jessie to go back home herself for now.

"Of course she can come, Harper! You don't even have to ask. Your cousin Ewan can move into the other croft, with my mum and the bairns." His mother-in-law looked hurt, as if about to cry, but Harper worked his charm as always. He explained quickly, before she could raise any objection, that they had agreed upon the purchase of a new house and had put down a deposit. They had also interviewed a seventeen year old trainee children's nurse who was looking for casual employment. Jessie was quietly impressed with the speed with which Harper had moved.

He added quietly, with a tinge of regret, that he had been offered work with Charles Jenner and Co. He was to start work in the New Year as a Draper's Traveller, for Kennington's - one of their major subsidiary wholesalers. The company supplied many of the local tailors, as well as competing department stores up and down the country.

He explained that Jenners were beginning a major recruitment drive, following their gradual recovery from the fire of '92. Kennington's had their assured business. Jenners new store was only a year away from completion. Harper explained to Jessie and Hannah that William Hamilton Beattie's creation was mooted as, 'The emblem of modern Edinburgh.'

Bemused caryatids had been hauled into the clinging pall of sulphurous air, only to be compared sardonically to naked fishwives picking their way through the crowded market with empty crates balanced above their heads. Harper knew when he said this, that it was really Ali Macdonald's Portobello slant on a modern kind of corporate empire.

Hannah laughed raucously but his irony failed to raise a smile with her mother Jessie. She had the third eye trained upon him as ever. She could read his disappointment at having to leave the City Police. Jessie saw again the fiery eyes of the tough little man who had replaced her former husband at the forge, still ready to do anything to prove himself. She looked again and the child was gone. Here instead was a suave man of means – confident and self-aware. Jessie always admired Harper and was truly glad to have taken him away from his parsimonious family and that he'd fallen for her adopted daughter.

Harper said he would have a decent salary, given his knowledge of the more lucrative refined end of the market - for his understanding of, 'best quality manufacturing, which always underlies fashion trends.' A reference from Zachariah Williams had no doubt swung him the job but everything he had said at interview had been true.

Simply put, Jessie knew that Harper was sacrificing his career in the force for a travelling-expense account. Neither of the women had anything to say on that score but they were pleased by his thoughtful planning. Both hugged him affectionately, if a little wistfully. Then they hugged one another, weeping sentimentally for the imminent goodbyes. Reconciled to the outcome, he cleared the supper dishes while the women discussed Jessie's train times back to Morayshire.

Harper felt guilty, for all sorts of reasons he could not explain but mostly because he found himself depressed and had begun wishing his life away. There were always plates and bottles in the sink. Always unwashed clothes and unmade beds. Worst of all was the plaintive look in Hannah's tired eyes, begging for mercy. What inspired him most also broke his heart – the sound of Elsie's boots clipping and running up the stairs for her next errand, her little sister shuffling behind. Elsie was equally glad to feed the cat, take out the rubbish, or fetch his truncheon and whistle before a shift.

Elizabeth stole his whistle every day to conduct timetabled affairs around the house with martial orders, peeps and drones. She was innocent enough in her mischief to be able to reduce all interaction, whether bad or good, and all attempts to sanction her behaviour to absolute hilarity. All the adults were under clear injunction to indulge the girls' behaviour – which for the most part was extremely good in any case.

Nonetheless Harper could find no real solace in either family life or police work. Now that he had decided to leave, the chasing down of petty criminals seemed more pointless and difficult than ever. Somehow he had come to see everything with an artificial sense of detachment - like an old pantomime he had seen a dozen times before. He wanted to drink himself into oblivion but he had seen the damage drink could do so many times that his policeman's perspective on that tragic weakness of humanity actually terrified him.

Harper felt that he had to persuade Hannah to go back to Foxworthy. He had to find out more about new treatments for ovarian cancer, even prevail upon her to allow the operation offered – anything but let her slip away without trying. He had to do these things without making her unhappy or acting unnaturally himself. It would all be very deterministic but he was good at that. All he lacked was a plan.

He thought momentarily of tickets that he had ordered for a performance by the stateless Polish virtuoso pianist, Jan Ignacy Paderewski for a mid-November Monday evening in Glasgow. He had arranged to work double shifts that weekend, overlapping into the Monday morning. This was never popular for it was certain to be busy but offering to do it meant he could grab a few hours sleep before they caught the train on the afternoon of the performance.

Georg Henschel was to conduct the newly formed Scottish Orchestra at Queens Hall. Perhaps they would play Chopin or Beethoven, which he knew would transport Hannah to another world - but let it be Brahms, or Handel, or Servian Romances it would delight her just the same.

If it made her smile, that was the narcotic he needed. He wished it could be Strauss, so that he could sweep her away in a whirling waltz that might transport them to heaven together and never end. Here on Earth, Hannah was complaining of constipation and backache. Although she appeared bloated at times, she was definitely beginning to lose weight. The cancer was eating her away.

Harper observed that often she would rise in the night, ostensibly to relieve herself; gallantly spending time trying to remove all traces of her vaginal bleeding. But she could not hide the scared look upon her face when she returned. All things being equal the simplest explanation was usually the correct one – the cancer was spreading, not healing.

He sat in the kitchen after arriving home from his night shift, waiting for Hannah to finish sluicing away the traces before the girls rose in the morning, allowing her the dignity afforded by time and space. He reached up into the kitchen cupboard to look inside the envelope at the Henschel tickets, to confirm the doors opening time for the grand event. Smiling to himself, Harper moved his hand in the assurance of Occam's razor to the bottle of Glen Moray waiting patiently behind the envelope in the corner.

The only forgetfulness I'm gonny find is in a bottle.

130

Although Inspector Brodie tended to dictate the shift pattern as he saw fit, Harper regularly volunteered for the night shift so he could help with chores around the house. He could talk to Hannah during the afternoons or early evening when he got out of bed. It also served to take his mind off another matter that arose frequently during nights they spent together. She could not be involved with 'goings on under the sheets' as Harper put it. But when she did feel like it, the Heroin pills which had been prescribed at the last meeting with Foxworthy seemed much more powerful as an anaesthetic and were agreeably less soporific than the Tincture of Opium.

Inspector Brodie was kind enough to leave his Scotsman behind at the end of each working day. As a matter of course it would find its way down onto the Sergeant's desk, after Jeanette the cleaning lady had had her cup of tea with the caretaker and between them they'd filled in the crossword.

When the nightly round of drunken brawls and the secondary wave of domestic murder attempts had been sorted and clarified in their minute legalistic details, or when Harper was still waiting for a witness to return from the infirmary or perhaps just sober up enough to be able to make a statement, he would continue his purposive search for vital information to help Hannah. Within a very short time he was overwhelmed by the sheer amount of medical research information regarding the treatment of cancer.

Whenever a piece came to light in the relevant medical science context he would tear out the page, fold it carefully and place it safely inside his jacket for perusal as soon as he could find time. When he rose from his bed in the afternoon it was the first thing that came to mind. He adopted the habit of strolling into the city to a newsagent's close to the more exclusive hotels, which would carry international as well as national press. On occasion he ordered American papers following discovery of a research theme.

Desperate to gain insight into conventional methods of finding information quickly, Harper started asking the detectives he knew,

Ian Harker and Bill Yeates about, "how to conduct background enquiries into a known killer in the medical world."

"There are some tricky bastards out there . . . I'd tread carefully Harper, old son," came the response. "Let us professionals know if ye come up wi' anything concrete eh?"

DC Rogers pointed out University Library buildings for Harper to visit, across the Meadows. He even gave him professional tips about, 'the softly, softly approach.'

Harper's life was no longer his own. In between night shifts and his medical research and trying to assist around the home as much as possible, he also had to attend interviews for more suitable jobs than the one at Kennington's. He was obliged to pursue the conveyance of a smaller, more affordable home. But as soon as he had paid the deposit on the terraced house at Lillyhill, the estate agent had ceased taking his calls and ignored all his letters.

Harper had not exactly lied to Jessie but felt so desperate to get rid of the encumbrance of having Hannah's mother and grandmother staying with them in relays that he had embellished the truth slightly about those necessary arrangements. At the time of Jessie's leaving he had not actually made a commitment to purchasing the house on the hill above Parson's Green that they had seen, simply because he needed to be sure of his income. He wanted a mortgage. All of Harper's instincts told him to hang on to his savings.

The job offer he knew was also tenuous, given the knock-on effects of the financial and economic Panic and the fact that Jenner's new store had not even been built yet. Prices for basic commodities of clothing and food seemed to have remained stable all the same, despite the disaster in railroad and banking industries on the other side of the Atlantic. He had been waiting for six weeks for a letter of appointment detailing his new salary but was still determined to give a month's notice to Brodie, less any holiday entitlement, only if and when such confirmation arrived.

Now there was another question on his mind and it occupied all Harper's thoughts. An exploratory operation might create a dilemma for the oncologist as to what more could be done; but if all they did was take a look, surely that in itself would do Hannah no harm? It occurred to him that there was a fine balance for the surgeon between giving best advice as against actually worsening prospects. The chance element of a patient perhaps falling pregnant would allow Mother Nature to weigh in on the side of the experts. He imagined the Catholics would approve of Foxworthy's cautious approach. In fact the doctor made no secret of that spiritual affiliation.

Harper could see it all now: this was not a moral dilemma for individual doctors giving advice on such tricky prospects, as much as an actuarial overview. Clearly 'policy' was to make concerned noises but do nothing.

A wad of cash might be useful in swinging the balance away from the business-minded seniors behind the planning of surgical procedures.

Sitting alone on a bench in Holyrood Park at three am, Harper looked up at the moon to gauge whether it cast enough light in addition to the sputtering gas lamp over his shoulder to read by. His trusted beat partner, Charlie Robertson had strolled on. He would keep out of sight of Sergeant Chambers for half an hour when he took his break entitlement back at the West Port. Harper decided that there probably was sufficient light for him to conduct his studies without interruption.

He was not reading the paper as such, so much as searching for cross references to two or three interesting articles he'd seen over recent months. There had been one headline in the New York Times which had immediately made his hands tremble but which there had been no chance to actually read. He reached inside his greatcoat for the articles he had collected from various heavyweight national newspapers, deciding to peruse them systematically as DC Harker had advised, in the date order he had discovered them.

The first was a full page spread about the use of radioactive elements for the treatment of skin cancer. He had heard of Marie Curie but had never made an association between her dangerous work and cancer – save for in the most negative sense. This particular article discussed the pioneering work of Neils Ryberg Finsen, and a new treatment described in the article as, 'Ultraviolet Blood Irradiation.'

Harper quickly scribbled the man's name with those key words onto his Policeman's incident pad. This was detective work he would not be forced to shirk under pressure of routine at 'The Port.' He would seek opportunity in short order to approach the matter through the best libraries within walking distance – there would be medical journals featuring this research for sure.

He decided to go back onto the day shift and take a beat, so he could use his uniform presence as an incidental support to his requests for information. He was prepared for resistance. Some of the chemical aspects of counterfeiting might give enough spin for a necessary detour. If there was no such reason, he planned to invent one. Maybe Ali Macdonald would help him identify some dissolute medical students to harass, ostensibly for their notoriously loud drinking parties.

He looked at his fob watch and decided he had time to continue reading before returning from his break. Dennis Chambers, the duty officer in charge would notice and make it known that he had, with a hard look or a raised eyebrow. But Harper doubted he would mention it to Brodie. Something had to give under all this strain and if it were not to be Harper's mental health itself – then it had to be the career that had once inspired him.

He pulled the next folded newspaper out of his coat and checking the index on the front page went straight to the section that interested him. This was a weekend omnibus edition of the New York Times. He had heard from Foxworthy that the newspaper sometimes presented pioneering enquiry into science, technology and medicine with an alacrity that failed to impress in London, or indeed Edinburgh. So strike one for the Americans. In Europe generally it seemed to Harper, the halcyon days were always in the past – primarily because no-one had money to invest in new patents.

Harper noted with dismay how Daimler's high revving motor engine had been held back and the poor man sacked, despite his pioneering genius and his health subsequently ruined by stress. Now a French company were making cars and no doubt vast profits with his invention, under licence from the board that had got rid of him.

Marie Curie it struck him, had been briefly congratulated then promptly forgotten by the patronising, male-dominated elite of French academia. No doubt the same would happen with Finsen's Photoluminescence Therapy. That is if nobody bothered to insist it be used on them as a patient. In the end Harper reflected, progress in medicine, as in society as a whole, was all about competing market forces. He remembered Zach's diatribe about elites with vested interests. No doubt such people would always have the final word. Harper had no idea who they were - but for Hannah's sake he intended to find out.

"Luminescence, humph," mumbled Harper to himself.

They even took down the fucking electric lights after the Bush demonstration, when everyone was on the hook. Now they say it might be twenty five years before we have it in our homes.

He stood up, stretching and yawning against mounting tiredness and gnawing cold in his bones. Harper's own health was beginning to suffer. He tried to imagine a futuristic Edinburgh with electric lights and privately owned petroleum fuelled cars, where every ailment – even cancer itself, was treated freely and effectively. He shook his head in doubt, turning his thoughts to his wife and daughters at home in their beds, feeling trapped in time and space. He wondered if every soul alive felt at some point this same wistful impression of being trapped – a prisoner to their own doubts.

A fox loped past along the base of the cliffs, its breath condensing in the air before it, forming glistening droplets around its angular whiskers and below its purposeful chin. It ignored Harper, listening instead for movement along the margin of the slope where the grass was longest. The hunter paused to flick an ear for any duck forgetful enough to have stayed off the water, before downheartedly accepting the onset of autumn's stark wisdom. He rolled the point of his cultured nose in a tight spiral, sniffing for what was beyond his reach, narrowing dreamy eyes as he did so.

"Ha! A fellow optimist!" Harper called aloud as he reached for his pipe, sitting down again to resume his research.

The article of greatest interest was coincidentally about bacterial injections having an effect on immunity to diseases. In particular, they reduced certain types of cancer. As he read Harper felt his pulse lifting. The hairs above his collar tightened into goose bumps. His eyes focussed attentively. He adjusted his frame for comfort, so he would not miss a single word. This was truly significant.

A clinician in the USA was successfully reducing the progression of second and third stage cancers by injecting his patients with toxins. Again Harper reached for his notepad to scribble key information with name of the doctor who had developed the treatment: William B Coley.

"Jesus, Hannah! They've found a cure for cancer!" Harper cried out. As he read on, noting that it was not a new discovery but was first observed in the 17th Century, then recently popularised independently in Russia, he whispered, "O Lord . . . it's a world full of secrets and lies."

Glancing at his watch, Harper realised he was already five minutes late. He paused for a moment as an unearthly squeal came from the long grass at the base of the cliff – the fox had found a meal. Harper stood up and carefully folded away his newspaper cuttings, before running all the way back to West Port Police Station.

"You'd better look to that, lad," advised Chambers as Harper lifted the hinged counter top, reaching for the key cupboard to put away the copy set for the park gates. He turned immediately out of respect for his sergeant, looking straight at him as Chambers reclined imposingly in the duty officer's chair. He slipped the keys into his pocket until later.

"Yes sir, I'm sorry sir. It will not happen again."

"Any use to you?"

"Come again sir?" asked Harper, immediately grounded, but consciously wishing he was more engaged with his colleagues.

Especially this good fellow in front of me.

"What you were reading about," prompted Chambers with a slight hint of exasperation.

Harper realised he had probably talked little, but yet had talked of nothing else. His colleagues and friends were no doubt all deeply concerned about him, and his delightful Hannah. Over the past three or four years she had welcomed them all into their home at one time or another. Intense exchanges of training days, followed by social integration with ranking officers and old hands based at the large and extremely busy station, a stone's throw from their apartment near the markets, had been exciting and reassuring.

Now Harper felt he had come up short. He could no longer show that easy bravura they all respected in him. His confidence as a Bobby had gone, along with his optimism. The camaraderie which inspired him was still there though, stronger than ever. He loved the guys he worked with, even though he couldn't stay with them.

"No, well yes," he said quickly, "there are actually a couple of radical new treatments, sir."

Dennis Chambers spread himself comfortably before the fire in the officer's rest room, an enormous uniformed thigh elevated at a wide angle, his expression demanding information as a matter of course. With policemen it was always this way. There was a parallel requirement for both prudence and alacrity, which carried a complex set of rules and conventions. It was important to learn them and not mix them up. There was a time to speak and a time to remain silent. This was the time to speak. "No wonder so many of them are in the Masons," Harper mused to himself, as he warmed to the man before him.

Chambers was sitting like a grandfather inviting a child to rest on his knee. It occurred to Harper that Chambers was barely ten years his senior yet a warm flood of embarrassment welled up as he realised that the Sergeant and many other colleagues genuinely cared about them.

Caring was sometimes a luxury it seemed, yet it was also clear that his researches were now a major topic of consideration amongst his comrades. This was after all, the age of the locomotive, the ocean liner and the diesel car. Every decent Congregationalist who affected an intention to educate himself, could be found at some point during the course of an ordinary day with his nose stuck in a newspaper.

Some folk, determined to read serialised novels by aspiring authors, even visited the bookstalls around Waverley Station, just to purchase popular murder and horror titles, which were increasingly churned out in syncopation with the rolling bogies of the overnight express to London. It wasn't just regular long distance travellers who were hooked on pulp fiction - it was the increasingly literate multitude of the general public.

Policemen were no exception to the norm. There was a need for realism tempered with scepticism in the force, which helped develop their superior worldly perspective on all heinous matters brought before them as agents of the law. It was no coincidence that the West Port was beginning to gain a reputation for an enthusiastic trade in second hand books, as well as every other kind of used, and nearly new commodity.

It surprised Harper that his personal challenge to the received wisdom of the high-minded medical elite, which everyone knew characterised Edinburgh at its very best, had become daily news for all his work colleagues. The fixed gaze of Chambers' massive head said all of this and more to John Harper. His activity was hot gossip.

If the dawn patrol dragged men in off the street to give account of their misdemeanours in the next few minutes, there could be hell to pay. Chambers was not a man to be deflected or taken lightly, whenever he took on a serious mood. Harper put the park keys away and pulled up a chair. Chambers poured them both enormous mugs of tea, shovelling several large spoons full of white sugar into his own.

The discussion was brief and to the point. Chambers invited Harper to outline his broad intentions, in respect to the journalistic medical research he had been conducting into cancer treatment and he obliged. The Duty Sergeant listened intently, sipping his tea, respectfully proffering a tin of broken biscuits when there was a natural pause in Harper's revelations. Chambers looked straight at Harper when he had finished his explanation of Photoluminescence and Bacterial Injection Therapy, avid questioning still clear behind his large eyes. But he said nothing.

Harper met Dennis's searching look and continued without a pause, although now there was a lump of embarrassment in his throat. He felt as if his entire life was rolled up into a ball of the waste paper he been generating recently in such prolific quantities. Why was he feeling so guilty, and at the same time so vulnerable to criticism himself? The one certainty in all of this was that as time moved on, hope for Hannah would probably fade. That made him angry. Somehow it was the isolation of his youth revisited, which he tended to shrug off with characteristic sullenness. The Sergeant's benign scrutiny demanded a fresh approach.

He explained all of this personal ambiguity first, to Chambers. This was a more honest reply than pretending that somehow he had a coherent plan and could take Hannah abroad for treatment – whether to the USA, or to Europe. He couldn't even remember where Finsen's clinic was – "Helsinki maybe, or was it Copenhagen?" Chambers nodded slowly, almost imperceptibly with his granite outcrop of a head. Harper felt a tangible sense of relief, which he then struggled to hide from his colleague.

"I don't know what to do, man. If I could get her to talk to the doctor again, maybe we could even ask him what he knows about these new treatments. That would be a start!" Harper's trembling voice gave away his true feelings of self-doubt. Dennis Chambers, the master of a thousand confessions, looked into Harper's soul with a sidelong glance, registering all he saw without judgement. He stood up to pour himself another half a pint of milky tea, ladling in three more sugars. At length he spoke with the sure voice of the responsible Sergeant – his back still turned to Harper.

"I hear that Brodie invited you to join the Lodge and you declined."

Harper was astounded and although his mouth opened, no sound came out. He was clear that if this was a question and not a statement, it was nonetheless rhetorical and required no reply. Chambers turned to stand before him, milling the crystal grains in the bottom of his enormous mug of tea. He was suddenly revealed in his buttons and blues for what he probably was - a trainee necromancer, refining rocky paradigms of obscure historiography into a palliative for eternal damnation.

"Well?" he said at last, raising his mug to his mouth, examining the recalcitrant Harper through the steam.

"Look, Sarge, clearly you're thinking of ways to help me but I don't think Inspector Brodie would want me to presume . . . I mean I'm not sure if I should discuss . . ."

Chambers sat down, placing the mug on the floor near a filing cabinet in the corner before turning over embers in the white marble fireplace. He threw on enough fuel to meet the dawn chill that would accompany the arrival of the early shift. Then he carefully looked around to business being conducted in the two interview rooms across the lobby; to ensure that no-one was within earshot, there or on the stairs, before he resumed.

"Don't be a fool Harper," he insisted without emotion, pausing for effect before speaking again, "This is Edinburgh, the home of Democracy. We wear our inequalities with pride."

"I've found it hard to think rationally just of late," remarked Harper, rubbing his cold hands together, "And I mean no disrespect to you at all, but I need you to explain what the hell you are talking about."

Chambers took a shallow breath and expelled it petulantly before he answered,

"Golf!"

"Golf? In the name o' the wee man . . . what the fuck has golf got to do with my predicament?"

"Men of circumstance used to commit calumnies and slaughter one another over traditional claims and blood ties; outrageous interpretations of the Word of God; notions of Sovereign Law and line of accession to the throne."

"So?" Harper was becoming increasingly irritated.

"So now they play golf."

"Yes . . . and your point is . . .?"

"This is about friendship and brotherhood lad; something that transcends political and religious affiliations." He paused to let wind out of his voluminous belly, politely covering his mouth, "Provided of course you're no' a Roman Catholic," he added as an important caveat.

"Aye sure; if you're rich enough in the first place for such things not to matter."

Chambers ignored Harper's minor objection, continuing fervently, "It's a kind of sporting commonwealth, where every member rubs shoulders with the elite . . . that and well, you know," he said leaning forward in his chair, "It's an informal meeting place for the Lodge."

"I don't understand sir."

"Brodie plays golf with John Inglis. Lord Glencourse to you and me, the Chancellor of the University of Edinburgh Medical School."

"Oh, aptly titled. Did they make that one up recently in the Cabinet Office, or is it an Ancient and Royal inheritance?" murmured Harper sardonically, grinning over his mug of tea, "So, what you are proposing . . . let me get this right, is that I should curry favour with Brodie and ask him to find out what the man might know about Finsen or Coley? That's a bit o' a long shot, don't you think, even for a handicapped golfer?"

"No laddie, that's just the very beginning." Chambers looked around again and lowered his voice as he explained, "These people have access to unlimited financial resources. They are part of a world-wide brotherhood. These ideas you talked about are perfectly plausible. Who knows what they might decide to do? They could pay for Hannah's treatment at a clinic in America and write it off against hospital running costs."

Harper stared at Chambers as his animosity faded. His nervousness had subsided and he was impatient to know precisely what the man might propose.

"Do you seriously think that the decisions affecting the growth of a big city like this happen in a council chamber, where they can't even reach the second or third item on a fifty point agenda?"

"No, Sarge. I take your meaning. They are made in the locker room at the club, or on the ninth hole where nothing can be overheard and attributed later. But what has that got to do with my situation?"

"Meet me at the Masonic Hall on Tuesday evening and I'll introduce you Harper. We'll take it from there."

"Look you know my situation. I cannot ask for charity. Maybe the Lodge is a big thing for the Police and I would have considered it if I was staying – but. . ."

"But you're a Catholic?"

"Fuck no! Not that I have anything against Catholics mind."

"What then?"

Harper looked at Chambers for a long time before he answered, realising the man had thought deeply about his hopeless situation and the stated intention was, outwardly at least, synonymous with his own quest – deliverance for Hannah.

He thought of saying,"I am just naturally suspicious of the ulterior motives of rich bastards, with all their devious strategies for extending control over ordinary people," but he held back for the sake of honour and philanthropy. Sucking his teeth before replying he said rather more ponderously, "I'm like you Dennis old son. I'm just a natural sceptic. But thank you, I will be there on Tuesday." Harper put his hand out to shake Chamber's, before voicing the intention of joining his colleagues in interview room number one.

Crossing the hallway he raised his arm and crooked the fingers of his right hand at a right angle, as Chambers had unexpectedly done when shaking his hand. Harper pretended to inspect the alignment of his fingers, as though by not reciprocating in the Masonic handshake he had committed a faux pas. Chambers, who was watching, smiled to himself brightly before returning to his paperwork.

Lennox and Hamilton had been interviewing a man recently suspected of an association with the counterfeiters whose product had recently hit Lothian like a tidal bore. Simultaneous arrests of known forgers, black marketeers and other intermediaries had followed. The interrogations were aimed at cross referencing information gleaned, to provide even a single useful name, or an address. Advice from Treasury officials was that the number and accuracy of counterfeit bills suggested the gang, always assumed to be an international syndicate, had now set up a printing press locally.

Lennox, born and raised in Musselburgh, now lived in Portobello. As a boy he had seen the entire world go by his window with the seasons. He was imbued with understanding of resident and itinerant populations alike with an ear for the grafters' slang of the fairground. As a teenager he'd worked with them for pocket money, quietly absorbing all the gestures and looks that spoke volumes of the robust world of the mumpers. He had watched young men of the itinerant community work and steal and occasionally fight like bantam cocks. Lennox saw how they blended in with the fixed community of the resort and its surrounding town, using it to operate an independent cash economy at every level. He had also seen the varieties of contraband and special entertainment available to a receptive adult male clientele over in Leith and Newhaven.

Lennox was white haired and blanched in complexion – tall, thin and wiry. A slender face belied adroit toughness, serving to immortalise him with the epithet 'Ferret.' He would have balked at this, had he not earned the reputation which went with the handle, for his ability to 'ferret out' ill-gotten gains of all kinds of criminal activity.

It had been Lennox's idea to look for a pornographer because, he said, "That's what I'd do if I was a counterfeiter, looking for a local printer on the wrong side of the law." Everyone in on the job of finding the pornographer and that meant by now almost everyone who worked out of the West Port station, had enjoyed a glib half hour of derision at Lennox's expense.

Harper recalled a couple of the choicest insults aimed at the man.

"Lennox is looking for porn!" Andy Magee announced to Jimmy Soutar.

"Oh aye, tell him to look in the bottom filing cabinet."

"No, Sergeant Laing has got the key and he's on his break."

"Aw, I hope to God he's nae smokin' in there at the same time! I hate the smell o' keech mixed wi' tobacco!"

"Ye could always nip across the street an' tak' a pee wi' the horses, Andy."

"Oh, no! No chance o' that boy. Ye'll no catch me takin' out ma member in front o' a horse, Soutar. Harper micht hae been used to the rustic delights up in Aberdeenshire, but I'd just frighten the poor animal an' cause it tae bolt. Besides, you bastards would talk about me so much, I'd probably end up ha'in' tae partner up with Lennox hissel', the filthy wee pervert!"

Another slight began more innocently, between McCauley and Booth, but with tongue in cheek, "I hear Lennox is going to be coming down hard on the printing trade Tam?"

"Yeah Walter, he will be coming down hard if he finds the right material."

"I just hope he'll let me have a gander."

"I usually go up hard and come down all soft and sticky."

"All right now boy, keep it clean! There could be officers, or women present tha' micht overhear ye!"

"Sorry, Walter you're right. That did lack subtlety."

"He should try some of the photo booths down in Portobello!"

"No need tae gan that far, there's a guid knockin' shop jus' the other side o' the Grassmarket!"

But everyone who laughed at Lennox, came up with a name for Lennox. It soon appeared there were dozens of candidates who might be his dodgy printer. Davy Lennox trailed the beat with his partner Hughie Hamilton for a week making general enquiries, until he found one man who appeared immediately defensive. To the experienced Bobbies he seemed a nervous individual, with the word guilt written all over his face.

Lennox, Nordically handsome in a boyishly disarming but therefore utterly deceptive way, observed closely, while Hamilton asked the questions they had rehearsed, in the bluntest possible manner.

Hamilton was an oblong, closed-faced Neanderthal, without any natural politesse. He had an effective treatment for shocking any potential suspect. It was legally worded insinuation, falling just short of direct accusation.

The litmus test for perpetrators would be tenuously couched in a carefully worded assertion, aimed at everyone and no-one – like a sawn off shotgun. 'Do you sell pornography here? If so we need to talk.' If a printer was not guilty, he might be offended but would not be defensive. The defensive one was the suspect. After all Hamilton was just asking a reasonable question backed by a broad statement.

"Are you the owner of this establishment?" he asked the man behind the counter of the shop on Dalkeith Road.

"Yes, I am. Why do you need to know this?"

The tall, thin man with slicked-back hair had just added himself to the short-list by answering a question with a question – also by having an unnaturally high and busy tone of voice.

'If his voice goes up he's lying,' Lennox had told Hamilton.

"We have reason to believe there is an illegal trade in reprographic images . . . of a sick, pornographic nature. We want to ask you what you know about this," snarled Hamilton, with the bluff animus of a mountain gorilla.

The man hesitated too long before answering Hamilton's insinuation. He looked at his hands and then looked at the till. Then glanced over his shoulder, before giving a considered reply.

"Look, I don't mind answering your questions but I have a business to run." He looked at the Bobbies pleadingly but they both just stared at him, Border Collies with a stray sheep, all three of them thinking about the wolf.

The printer's right hand slicked through his lank hair. He simpered quickly like a Latino dancer with a shift of his weight from right to left, then back to the right.

"Are you arresting me?"

"That depends on you."

The man squawked like a duck before struggling to get his voice under control, as a telephone rang somewhere in the back room.

"I . . . I am happy to co . . . to answer your questions, officers if you do not mind me dealing with my customers and my . . . my telephone enquiries . . . I have a large clientele, some of whom are connected you know . . . to the Post Office exchange." The caller rang off.

"Look Mr? What is your name?" demanded Lennox, eager to confirm identification of the new target and get out quickly before they blew it completely.

"Davidson, Fraser"

"Which, Davidson or Fraser?" asked Hamilton, playing the simple ogre which seemed to befit him more with each passing day.

"Fraser is my Christian name," the man replied with just a touch of petulance, having regained some of his poise.

"Is that yer full name?" asked Lennox, catching a whiff of the Jesuit.

"No, if you must know, my full name is Fraser Kentigern Ignatius Davidson. Ignatius being my confirmation name." Now the touch of petulance had become a hint of defiance.

Lennox intentionally took a great deal of time writing the name down in his notebook, while Hamilton stared straight at the man, like a giant Silverback impassively staring out a rival half-concealed in the undergrowth. Lennox licked his lips, concentrating a burst of pulsing excitement, before flipping over the page with his pencil and slowly looking up at his quarry. He paused for several seconds before speaking again.

"Sir, please just answer oor questions. We're no' interested which foot ye kick with."

At that precise moment the telephone rang again and also the shop door opened. Lennox restrained the urge to curse aloud. Davidson disappeared into the store room at the rear of the shop without another word. Hamilton turned his head towards Lennox like a navel gun traversing slowly towards a target. Lennox's inscrutable look gave his silent reply.

No, I don't think he is about to leg it!

The customer greeted Lennox with a cursory grunt then stared at the wall behind the counter. Clearly he had caught a glimpse of Hamilton and felt it wise to sublimate the dubious and threatening reality of his existence by ignoring him. Lennox turned again to his partner, slowly bringing his fore finger up to his lips.

The phone was just behind the door. Lennox could hear from its cursory nature that the telephone conversation was about repeat business. Davidson took a minute to confirm the order and state 'usual terms' before replacing the receiver. He returned through the door.

The walk-in customer was an office boy from one of the breweries out at Craigmillar, come to collect urgently needed office stationery.

Davidson scuttled around the back counter area until he found the bound and addressed packages that tallied with the boy's list. He demanded a signature with stage camp hauteur, then briskly tore back-copies of the invoice and consignment notes from his system pad. He brandished them sharply with his left hand - like Don Quixote delivering a *coup de grace*, with a slight rightward elevation of the chin.

Lennox's eyes clouded over with the workaday sanguine of the executioner, as he observed the relish in Davidson's eyes for the boy in the cheap suit. The lad strolled casually to the door, his parcels in a Hessian mail-sack slung over his shoulder.

Lennox wanted to shout, 'What kind of pornography do you print Davidson?' but his refined instinct for making a collar told him to do the opposite. In fact he said, "Look sir, we can see you are too busy to talk, so perhaps you would like us to return when the shop is closed. Then you can give us your undivided attention, so to speak."

"No, no, no . . . it's alright, really! I would never have any dealings with anything illegal like that. I do a fair amount of photo lithographic work, since I actually began my career as a photographer," he paused to lower his head, as though about to make the sign of the cross, for an instant looking deceptively pious, "and occasionally customers would make certain special requests, which, well without implying anything illicit . . . I have always felt it necessary to decline."

Hamilton was out of his depth, like a bear cub in a lake full of salmon, he had no idea how to focus on the kill. Lennox wanted to build Davidson back up before leaving, so he picked out a couple of misleading questions from the dozens that were suddenly queuing up in his mind. He began with a little invective, to offer as flannel to cover their retreat.

"Well, I suppose that's human nature sir. Who are we to question what goes on between a man and his wife behind closed doors? But, you know, there is a more sordid side to this illegal trade. It can have a corrupting effect on ordinary working men, not to mention the youth of today. We are approaching all the photographic businesses in the City with a view to warning them off well in advance of next summer's holiday season. There is a gang from Glasgow buying and selling the stuff wholesale. But let me tell you, they are living on borrowed time sir. Anyone foolish enough to trade with them will be put out of business."

Davidson grew visibly, like the rabbit that has just seen a ferret struggling away through the grass with a fresh kill. He knew that he would survive till another day, but had no idea how soon that would come.

Lennox asked him if he knew the exact location of another printer further out along Minto Road, whom they had actually spoken to that same morning. They thanked the man for his help then bade him good-day.

Mounting their horses slowly, Lennox and Hamilton headed out of the City past Davidson's shop front, to complete the charade. They were so pleased with themselves that they rode for some distance, enjoying the afternoon air, before comparing impressions.

"He's queer," stated Hamilton as a point of information.

"Aye, so maybe they have a hold over him."

"Yup, so they can blackmail him if need be."

"They already are."

"Aye, we can assume that much."

"And he's used to keeping a secret."

149

"Good point Lennox, yes, and he's well situated here in the quiet middle class suburbs. But he is also on a busy main route, where no-one asks too many questions about who comes and goes."

"Yep. His business is profitable and well organised. He uses a telephone and parcel mail, rather than employ travellers." They rode in silence for a distance before turning right, then right again, to head back into the city on a parallel route.

"But what makes him so different from every other poe faced bastard we've interviewed, Davy?" enquired Hamilton.

They rode in silence for several seconds, then both men spoke simultaneously with the conviction of Walsingham's inquisitors.

"He's our man."

"He's our man," repeated Lennox.

"Yup, he's our man," echoed Hamilton.

Harper did knock gently although he thought the room might have been vacated. He realised that the discussion with the printer had been relocated to another part of the building for convenience sake all round – even though no formal charges had been written up yet. He knew it was never good for the public image of Edinburgh City Constabulary if coercive methods were witnessed as they were being delivered. Nor for that matter were the broken teeth and blood spills which were the inevitable concomitant of such coercion.

Harper went down to the back basement cell block to offer assistance, or make them tea if they needed some. He was met near the bottom of the concrete steps by Lennox. Lennox was leaning back against the wall, smoking. Although visibly exhausted he looked elated.

"Harper!"

"How're ye doin?"

"Fuckin' great!"

"Are you ready for a brew?"

"Aye, yes we are, very much so. Three mugs please. Bring a pail with some warm water an' a mop."

"Fuck me, what have ye done to the poor bastard?"

"Aw, he'll get aff lightly. He's made a 'full and frank.' I wish they were aw' that easy boy."

"Tell me, dy'e think it will it lead to what we were aw' lookin' for?"

"Yes, it will!" declared Lennox, rubbing his hands, "Yes it will!" he repeated enthusiastically, in a hoarse whisper. His eyes were red. They glistened tiredly in the flickering gas light.

"Now, no more questions bonny lad, just gan' an fetch us yon pail o' water, an' the tea. Oh an' the prisoner could do wi' a wee spot o' medicinal . . .Tell Chambers to put the 'closed for Yuletide' sign on the front door an' bring doon a charge sheet an' his Parker pen."

"Anything else?"

"Aye tell aw' they cunts, nae mair Lennox pornography jokes! Frae now on yis can all line up an' kiss ma arse."

Harper smiled benignly at his dear colleague, who had spent much of the night terrorising and brutalising the hapless Davidson, or 'Saint Ignatius' as Hamilton liked to refer to him.

"Shall I tell 'aw they cunts' to polish their door kicking boots while I'm about it?"

"Aye, an' for their women to buy mince instead o' chicken, cos there'll be nay mair fuckin' overtime after this one boy."

Harper turned to set off up the stairs.

"Harper!"

He stopped and turned to face Lennox.

"Just kiddin' pal . . . No' a fuckin' whisper tae ony cunt but Chambers. Brodie will want the first word on this one."

"Aye, and the last. Well done though, Lennox eh? Even I thocht ye were a fuckin' pervert."

"Ah never said I wisna!" breathed Lennox through his cigarette smoke.

Harper waited for the kettle to boil as he made toast, which he smothered with orange peel jelly. He got out the China tea service Jessie had given them as a wedding present, tip-toeing around the scullery for fear of waking the baby. The other two children were more likely to resist waking these days, as crushing routines had already begun to take the shine off their Stirling enthusiasm for life and living.

Hannah no longer rose with the lark – her redoubtable energy for scooping up every chore had centred defensively, then shrunk into a pattern dictated by late evenings and late mornings. Her evenings were characterised by the logistical bombardment of pain, which was always trying to creep down the muscles of her buttocks, hips and thighs. It retreated under the cool hand of the heroin, only to prepare for the counter-attack which came the moment she lay down to rest.

Mornings were a swan song of stolen dreams and deep sleep - her mind's last rallying cry for earthly ambition and the vestiges of dried up self-realisation. Each day she talked of nothing more enthusiastically than the activities of her bairns, Elsie's artwork or Elizabeth's buns; who Harper had arrested, or had seen sent down.

Actually she found it difficult to find anything to say about gentle, smiling Elsie that was not mundane, and even more difficult not to praise Elizabeth's precocious talents in every context. But she engaged with them both wholeheartedly, taking everything each offered with approval.

Harper often speculated, as he did now with the comforting aroma of tea enhancing his sense of homecoming, how things ought to be different, and if he was failing his family in some way. Regardless of whether *things* 'could be different', whether *his role* 'should have been different', he just needed to know how to be a better father in the given circumstances.

Without deluding himself, he knew that good women had a superior feel for family than men ever could. They understood the emotional needs of others, placing it before moral equivocation and the exercising of discipline to reinforce power. They achieved recognition through compassion and compromise, regardless of authority.

He felt intuitively that, whatever terms his little family might have been offered by fate, it was his burden to be least amongst equals. He nodded to himself, deciding to muse longer upon this notion at some other time as he spaced the various items around the tray.

Grabbing the folded newspapers, he pinned them under his left arm. Pausing for a moment above the sink, he looked out at the Castle Rock, which had overseen a millennium of desperate individual traumas and resolutions, every one as earnestly involved as his. He stared at it, feeling these awesome tidal energies, imagining St Margaret kneeling at her prayers. Harper's internal dialogue spiralled into muted supplication, "Give us time Lord . . . Please give us some little cause to hope," he whispered.

Thinking to himself that the tea would be stewed, Harper glanced down to check that the hot water jug was full when he was startled to hear Hannah's voice at the door.

"I could stand there all day just looking at it too, especially on a fine morning like this. I never tire of looking at its turrets and windows . . . it makes me wonder about who lived inside it throughout all the centuries – you know, what they were really like."

Harper turned to greet her with a smile intended to hide his growing distress. He was annoyed to feel a drop of moisture escape to roll down past his cheek bone, "Oh, I think I'm coming down with the cold," he explained thoughtfully, which happened to be true.

"Well," she said, taking the tray from him, "I think we'll just put this down here and have breakfast without the wee ladies hearing our voices. You can get to tell me about this wonderful new cancer treatment that you think is gonny save this sad old wreck."

"What? When did you join a witches' coven? Unless . . . have ye been spying on me, in case I tak' on another woman who has mair time for her man?"

The smile from Hannah came as always, followed by a sensationally deep hug. She smelled strongly of perfumed emollient cream – a cheap mixture of emulsified petroleum fractions, musk and vanilla, which spoke more of hard work than luxury or leisure. But it was Hannah's characteristic smell, which overwhelmed Harper more decidedly than the most seductive rosewater perfume. Their hearts were in tune again. Though it disappointed him to spoil this delightful moment, he was resolved to show Hannah the newspaper cuttings and tell her of his last bid for her deliverance.

They ate breakfast purposively, knowing the door could open at any moment and the adult conversation would be over. They managed to talk earnestly for an hour. Twice Harper checked his pocket watch to confirm that they might have time to continue. He showed her the various articles which he'd found, and had spoken of briefly to Brodie and Chambers last Tuesday evening. Hannah was immediately sceptical about the Lodge, so he didn't push it. But he did remind her of his mysterious benefactor and his munificence at the time of their wedding. They both knew full well this had in fact been Harper's father. Both also knew that Harper had too much pride to ever seek him out to ask for anything.

"No! In fact, you would do that for me, I know. But although you would not be too proud to ask him for my sake, you are in actual fact too proud to take the trouble to find out about him, or contact him in the first place."

"No, you're right in that assertion Hannah, because he has a family and a life, which I was never a part of. I accept that. It's just the way it is. But at least I've been invited by people I trust and like to join the Masons."

Hannah laughed freely at his clipped sense of irony. They chatted loosely about this affiliation with the Brotherhood - bantering about age restrictions; whether they accepted queans - which Harper told her he thought was a decided advantage if you were an aspirational politician or a general, like Arthur Balfour or Hector Macdonald and whether haemorrhoids and halitosis were compulsory pre-requisites.

She told him she had lately become more accepting of his, "ludicrous, rough Copper talk." He realised this assertion was something different too, that under normal circumstances would not even have arisen. She would have had him under the thumb, so he told her.

"But there is no normal," he declared, "How can Freemasonry be classed as normal?"

"Well, you'll be alright then," she said in conclusion.

"Aw yeah," he said lunging at her, "Give me a marmalade kiss! I know you love the taste of butter on my moustache!"

They chortled as their teeth knocked together. He ran his fingers through her hair, to restrain her head from pulling away. Her belly and breasts moved invitingly with sumptuous laughter playing below her ribs. She stood up dramatically, moving with a girlish grace. Tying her cream woollen dressing gown, she padded over to the gas range, to refill the kettle.

"I'll look out one of my cooking aprons, and ye can borrow Elsie's Sunday school sash for a blindfold. Next time we're out we'll nip into Campbell's hardware and buy you a roofer's square and a window maker's compass. Remind me to rip the leg affy wan o' yer old breechs."

Harper stood up to intercept her as she lit the gas and blew out the match.

"And you have to agree to see Foxworthy again, and this time lay down the law to him. I'm not making any more plans for the future unless you are the priority."

They kissed again passionately then made love gently, standing almost motionless on the kitchen floor. They were inept, like two first time lovers; fragile marionettes waltzing to the interminable music of unseen stars pulling at them from overhead. Hannah laughed irrepressibly as Harper made great play of offering his seed without moving.

"Have you taken your pain killers this morning?" he asked innocently.

"Yes, I've taken my pain killers!" she replied through a kiss. Hannah felt nervous like a girl, lest they be discovered. She heard the music of a Strauss waltz in her head as they both came to a gentle

155

climax. As she gasped in abandonment, a white china teacup fell off the table and smashed on the kitchen floor.

The Monday afternoon of Hannah's surprise concert trip to Glasgow came around quickly. There was an unusual urgency about Harper's footsteps as he raced up the uncarpeted stone steps from the front door. He had worked the double weekend shift, never popular with his comrades, in order to get Monday night and the following day off.

He was glad to hear the voice of a young woman from the back room in conversation with Hannah but went into the bedroom to change out of his uniform, rather than waste time chatting with her. She was Margaret Kemp, the trainee nurse – the lassie recommended by Marion Macdonald. The important thing was to catch the Glasgow train in plenty of time.

Hannah was unaware of the surprise he had planned for her that evening. Marion had arranged everything discreetly with the help of young Margaret. Marion Macdonald had also explained Harper's plan, of taking their mother to Glasgow for the concert, to the girls.

Elsie and Elizabeth had agreed to keep it all within a secret tryst, "Cross your heart and hope to die!" They had also surreptitiously prepared cards for Harper to give their ma on the train.

There had been much earnest and heavy whispering in his ears about just what she might like in form of a design.

"Lots of pretty flowers, I think, because they make people well," suggested Elsie. Elizabeth went straight to the point, drawing a piano, with rows of people in seats listening. Harper knew Elizabeth was helping to define the moment. As ever she anticipated her own important place at the centre of things.

Hannah had risen to the occasion with alacrity, showing her uninvited house guest Margaret to the room where she could sleep. They had met before and the girl was already part of their medium term plan. Hannah shook her head, resisting the temptation to comment when Harper blithely announced he had already changed the bed sheets for their guest, on arrival back from work. Hannah pointed out to Margaret items for the evening meal, explaining the usual bedtime arrangement for the girls.

Seventeen year old Margaret Kemp sat at the kitchen table nursing a cup of tea, silently captivated by the busy scene. For the two girls she was a minor celebrity but for her the unfolding drama with its discreet purpose, was the quintessence of adult romance.

Hannah turned her attention to probing Harper about the nature of the evening's entertainment. Where were they were going to stay? Which travel and evening clothes would she need? Harper was amusingly disingenuous telling her only what she needed to know. Hannah began to feel like a child on her birthday, full of anticipation. There were ten minutes of happy chaos; then Harper ceremoniously handed the young lady his house key, confirming that his wife would bring along hers.

Margaret Kemp, sitting at the kitchen table flanked by Elsie and Elizabeth had evidently made an instant, smiling attachment to little Hannah, as well as the girls whom she had met previously. Soon it was time for the couple to set off. Four pairs of hands waved as they chorused, "Bye-bye!" Little Hannah waving with both hers. She knew that mum was going to listen to some piano music with dad in Glasgow and they would be back in the morning.

Harper expected the late afternoon train to be crowded with commuters, so he had bought First Class tickets.

Opening of the children's envelopes by Hannah was met with scrutiny and benign amusement from their fellow travellers. Opposite sat a quartet of old dears dressed to their nines, scented and pomaded with their twin sets and stoles, observing the couple's private exchanges as Hannah demanded to know where Harper was taking her. Their male counterparts were also turned-out for a special event in Glasgow that evening. They were sitting across the carriage, speaking volubly of business and travel. Their mutually appraising exchanges were overheard by Hannah and Harper but the couple were oblivious to them. Harper tried to ignore unsolicited remarks about his private conversation, giving instead singular attention to his beloved Hannah.

He knew that although Edinburgh had always been the dynamo of political change, Glasgow had occasionally decided the critical outcomes of Scottish History, without proper involvement. It had flaunted relative wealth in recent centuries, whereas Edinburgh had to plan with parsimony. Now the world's pre-eminent musicians were drawn to the largest city, with the wealthiest audience.

Judging by the proliferation of evening wear and jewellery, more than a few of the travellers on this train were Edinburgh socialites making their way to Glasgow to see Paderewski perform. With a sudden sense of alarm Harper expected to turn around to see Inspector Brodie with some of his golfing chums.

"So what else can they teach me, the poor farm boy?" thought Harper. He had no desire to share hackneyed views on the darkening political economy, much less a sense of his poignant love for Hannah with strangers, however personable they seemed.

Hannah expressed her joy sweetly at Harper's delightful reporting of the whispered discussions with the girls. She approved of the time and detail invested by Elsie and Elizabeth in the colourful cards, with an unusual amount of sentimentality. Noticing Elizabeth's grand piano and the rows of people in seats, she levelled the obvious question at Harper.

The nosey audience sharing their carriage were fully alert to his plan now, so Harper responded with the clipped official voice of the Bobby appearing in court as he handed over the next exhibit for her appraisal. The female passengers mused hawkishly upon his inscrutably stern demeanour.

The jury confirmed that the artefact was indeed a silver lame bag containing opera glasses and a royal blue envelope. Members of the refined commuter audience nodded imperceptibly, murmuring their conspiratorial approval to one another.

Hannah's delight was consummated in the moment she withdrew the concert tickets from the envelope, her exclamation confirming the nature of his gift for all who saw it. She gasped in amazement, then cried out in surprise. Standing up, she lurched across the rolling floor of the speeding train the better to hug him tight, congratulating him for his insight.

"Oh Harper!" she cried, "This will be the most magnificent adventure of my entire life!" Harper was speechless with pride. Fellow travellers smiled with gratification, looking ahead into the middle distance perhaps thinking upon the finer, less subtle connotations of how the smartly dressed couple might round off their evening after the concert.

One professionally attired gentleman lifted his broadsheet to hide a knowing smile. He folded it discreetly on the entertainments page to see if he could ascertain precisely where they going and what he had missed. Another whispered to his wife, who responded with a request for confirmation, "Paderewski? Yes?" He opened his mouth to ask, but Hannah interrupted him.

"Yes," she confirmed, turning to look at her audience, holding up the two tickets for all to see, with a laughing smile on her face, "Paderewski, Yes."

She sat down, smiling across at Harper, who finally dropped the High Court demeanour, to smile unreservedly back at her. Everyone else in the carriage reflected the same irresistible smiles. Harper was waiting for them to burst into spontaneous applause. Overwhelmed by Hannah's approval he suspended his natural reserve.

By the time the train reached Glasgow the new acquaintances in the carriage had pretty well exchanged the essential elements of their life stories, as required.

The Maestro worked his magic and for a thousand rapt souls in the Queen's Hall, time and troubles stopped. After his introductory smiles, the pianist's face became riveted with attention. Deep lines scored his genial face as Paderewski's hands thundered across the keys. Heroic phrases of musical discipline transcending anything martial, suggested to Hannah willing, honourable sacrifice. Tripping progressions conjured images of graceful feminine movement, at once both noble and balletic.

Yet more were perhaps rustically sexual in their appeal. Delicately spaced trills and pivots swirled into the huge auditorium to stagger minds, to bring soft gasps, even tears of joy to aficionados.

The vast concert hall echoed to the swelling pride of sublime personal brilliance, in the most persuasive of all intellectual forms. The composer's soul-cry translated into multi-dimensional geometry of bright sound. Paderewski's grand, shining Steinway threw a thousand aural paradigms of artistry and conflicted emotional reality into the ether - stunning listeners with resonant musical expression. Paderewski was Chopin reborn!

The early nineteenth century was alive again, to be generously embraced with the comfort of hindsight. Everything seemed right with the direction the world was heading. Here in this city of shipbuilders and tobacco traders, divided citizenry with entrenched opposition derived from failed monarchy and the compromise of Union, small enclaves from the empire and illiberal Europe; all could forget their assumptions to agree in listening that there was a quality of appreciation all mankind held in abstract, but in common.

That evening they all witnessed something inspirational, transcendent. For Hannah, the Hand of God could be felt in this most tangible form. Chopin was awesome; Paderewski sublime.

Hannah was overwhelmed with delight. She beamed with smiles and stood to applaud at the finale. Harper too was moved; converted forever by the ambiance of the concert, to both Chopin and to the virtuoso Paderewski.

The Maestro looked in their direction, smiling and bowing. Hannah waved effusively, as did many of her neighbours in the rows of seats to the side and in front. The whole atmosphere was magical. At last Scotland had come of age. This fine man was one of the honoured guests at the majority celebration.

Harper disappeared in a swift movement, which reminded Hannah of how he used to play soccer as a youth. Two or three members of the audience had approached the Maestro under the eagle eye of Henschel, but his benign smile under wild hair prompted an opportunity not to be missed and they pressed forward without hesitation.

Harper returned, bounding up the steps two at a time, holding the autographed programme aloft for Hannah to see – the name 'Ignacy Jan Paderewski' scrawled across her performance schedule.

"What better way to round off the perfect evening?" Hannah declared.

"Oh, I'm sure we'll think of something to surpass even that."

"Oh you mean you're going to take me for something special to eat?"

"Oh aye, we can get a fish supper an' eat it walking doon the street."

"Okay then, if that's all you want."

"You know, despite all the places I've visited on my travels, I have never once had room service, eaten a meal in my hotel room." Harper imparted with a smile.

"Aw, I quite fancied fish 'n chips. We could drop in at the hotel and say we changed our minds; catch the last train back to Auld Reekie. We could save the money and sleep in our ain bed."

"No, not tonight hen, ye can catch up with the laundry tomorrow!"

Hannah walloped him firmly, with her open hand on his upper arm for his impertinence. Two elderly ladies smiled at him from the row behind, as the standing ovation continued until Henschel and Paderewski disappeared. Harper led the elated Hannah out of the auditorium through the floating crowd. All the compressed melee of people moving through the foyer had been stunned into silence. One droll little man looked up to his gigantic friend to say, "I only came to hear him play Polonaise Number Six." It was preciously funny, typical Glasgow understatement but to laugh aloud would have broken the spell. The giant smiled all over his face but said nothing.

Harper shook his head in amazement. He had never seen so many of the most naturally garrulous people in the world with nothing whatsoever to say. There was nothing that could be said. Many were in groups - everywhere around were folks who knew one another well, or intimately. Family generations were there, couples, friends - all with music in their hearts and heads. They were the 'born again' coming from a revivalist preacher. These good people had heard the Word Made Music. They had been singled out, to be saved from Babel around them. Their souls were at peace.

Incredibly, it seemed to Harper, on the tram to the hotel there was the same silence. Harper's internal hearing rang with fragments of Chopin's elusive Ballades over and again, evincing bittersweet sorrow, dignity and joyous love – for him an entirely different way of looking at the world. In Chopin's musical statement, every individual failure and compromise was somehow forgiven - understood, resolved in tonal harmony.

Harper felt there was a kind of certitude to this graceful, passionate music that could only be revealed when time had rolled back and All was One. Paderewski's stunning rendition seemed to have spoken to his mood, transcending the very bones of his dilemma. Harper had no words that could ever express what he'd perceived, yet he knew Hannah saw it even more so. She knew these pieces and could play some of them superbly. He knew that all the people around them on the tram from Queen's Hall had also glimpsed something sublime.

Chopin's music is the sacred mathematics of life - of feeling, sentiment, and passion. Of supernatural love, rather than scientific rationalism. Divine harmony shining through into a world of oppression!

There was a culinary clarion call on the friendly autumn streets that night, but Harper managed to resist the moist aroma of frying potatoes, the piquant overlay of vinegar on battered fish. They were

163

hungry and had to be quick to catch the hotel restaurant before it closed. Giggling like schoolchildren, they hurried along Gordon Street to the Grand Central Hotel. Harper went straight to reception to confirm his booking and order room service requirements from the menu but they were to be held up.

Gazing at one another in mirth, they waited as the night manager dithered over finding a suitable room for an elderly couple from Alberta. It seemed they took precedence purely because of their novelty status and exotic accents. Their advanced years would not have impressed the manager otherwise, Harper imagined.

There was a new international elite in evidence, more Scottish than the Scots, who came to visit the Old Country from the colonies and the USA, and indeed as Harper knew well, from diverse parts of England.

Often they appeared soft with success but there was a quiet fierceness in their manner and eyes that commanded sympathetic understanding and recognition. They tended to be boat builders and engineers, administrators, soldiers, chemists or surgeons. All sought a homecoming, yearning with full hearts for a welcome in the hills.

These good people explained to the indulgent night manager that they had, 'made our fortune in lumber but we can't take it with us, so we're here for a long vacation.'

"What's that, vacation?" whispered Harper, "In't that a posh word for when ye empty yer bowels?"

Hannah poked him contemptuously in the ribs even though they stood several paces away out of politeness.

"Do you have family over here?" asked the night manager. The Canadians both laughed heartily.

"Oh yah, originally up around Aberfeldy, but they're scattered to the four corners."

"Well good luck tracking them down. I hope you enjoy your stay. Have a good night Sir; Madam."

They thanked him warmly and ambled after the swift moving porter. A glance from the man behind the reception desk intimated

164

an understanding that they must share the tip he had worked so hard for.

Finally the night manager turned his attention to Harper and Hannah. The last entry, with ink still wet was for Mr and Mrs J Campbell, "At least they had something to come back to," thought Harper.

The night manager searched assiduously for the misplaced room service menu then seemed confused as to the name and room number, which Harper gave him three times in all.

"It was one three two I gave you, not one two three?" he asked, all understated politeness, checking the diary listing for the second time, despite Harper's assurances. Harper indulgently asked him if he wanted the key back, to check the number stamped on it for himself. Hannah suppressed a guffaw.

Seven or eight young revellers surged through the lobby, laughing and talking loudly, heading to a reception room they had made their home for the day, their smart dress and ostentatious Highland attire hinting at the loosest of formalities – clearly a wedding.

It struck Harper that they had all evidently drunk far too much and there would certainly be trouble. Bagpipes and accordion rose and fell from an inner room each time the door was opened, gaily rallying scattered subjects to conjoin in the spectacle. Two or three women's voices could be held screeching with laughter above the pleasant rumble of anecdotal conversation and the chink of glasses within.

Nothing could detract from Hannah's mood. Harper thought his gorgeous companion to be feminine excellence personified. He wished to dwell in the moment, to understand fully what his mind had sublimated so often before when she was near him. He had seen Hannah ten thousand times, yet he still wanted to see her objectively, as through the eyes of a daring artist.

The architecture of her athletic hips fascinated him. They were sharply outlined through a plainly cut, ruby coloured evening gown. They were broad, rounded and strong, yet without any excess. Her breasts were generous – also rounded and full. Yet from a distance her shoulders seemed light and fast. Her hands were slender and elongated, her fingers like part of a child's bendy toy. It struck him that they were probably the perfect musician's fingers.

Hannah was not inclined to sports or leisure – unlike Marion Macdonald's circle of women friends at Portobello. Many of them competed at golf or bowls, went rambling in the wood, or swam in the sea to sustain fitness. Yet Hannah's physique surpassed any of them.

Her face shone with spontaneous delight for those who offered something of themselves. Indulgent good humour lay beneath, as a given. Her alignment to life projected a joyous, self-contained wonderment for all things. She would always be that enthusiastic, capable farm girl.

Despite the attrition of her illness there was usually a natural glow from under her skin, which was visible far across a room or from a distance in the open air. For Harper she always stood out in any group of women as the most strikingly fetching even at first glance, regardless of relative age and prettiness of their features.

 Harper had seen how other men noticed Hannah as they approached. He remembered an occasion they had climbed Arthur's Seat, not long after moving to the Capital. There had been a scattering of walkers around the top of the hill. One middle aged gentleman looked up from his efforts, as he emerged over the brow. The fellow stood in his tracks to stare at Hannah. It was a momentary observance which in no way Harper took as a challenge. But the man gazed at his wife – not at the view he had struggled up for. Neither did he show any interest in the rest of the scattered group of less appealing hill walkers. Her everyday beauty had arrested the fellow's attention more surely than any rare, highly prized picture hanging in an art gallery.

Hannah was aware of this – used to it, no question. She could pick and choose to whom she returned her attention and always could have. Yet from a sense of duty to her family she had been available, 'on the shelf,' until Harper arrived in her home to work for Jessie.

Now her darkly ringed eyes lit up again, animating her whole being. She spoke but Harper allowed her words to wash over him, as he often did – taking significance not from the import of what she was saying so much as warm personality her voice conveyed. He was transfixed by the flow of her warm energy. Absorption lay not in the fact that she was sexually alluring for Harper – but that he loved her totally as an individual. She was captivating, resonant and self-assured - right in every way. Her recent desperate decline made Hannah's company all the more sweet for Harper. Despite the pain Hannah endured there was spontaneity, joy and care in everything she did.

Why are there deep brown cups of pain beneath such gloriously soft eyes?

He wanted to gaze forever into those eyes. They were love and life, in all its bounds and imaginings.

Why is she losing her life to cancer, at so young an age?

At last the assiduous porter came briskly back into the lobby. After a purposive detour to the cash box in the office, to split the money given by the Canadians and pocket his own share, he came eagerly to interrupt Harper's romantic reverie. With a measured reduction in pace he collected their bags from the store room, ushering them with a sweep of his uniformed arm towards the lift.

Hannah smiled with her lips, linking her arm tightly against Harper's. Once again he felt the heady flood of desire for her as his pulse raced. So proud of her was he in every way that wanted to tell the world. It was obvious she loved him too. He smiled at Hannah, laughing aloud as they moved after the porter who coloured with embarrassment, wondering how long this avid couple had known one another.

Harper would come to reflect many times throughout his eighty six years, that he felt more alive at that moment in the Grand Central Hotel in Glasgow, standing proudly next to the beautiful and ever patient Hannah, than in his entire fortunate time on earth.

The porter came to knock on the door of room 132, with a trolley of freshly prepared food. Harper had his peppered steak, Hannah her fish n' chips – Halibut with tartar sauce. When they finished eating, Harper pushed the trolley out into the broad corridor and they settled to talk into the night.

"What would you have done if you had been free to do whatever you liked? Anything at all, even assuming we had never met?" Harper asked.

"I would like to have studied and taught music, like Madame Henschel."

"I would have been a Lightweight Boxing Champion, or played football as a professional.'

She laughed long, with her fruity laugh, slapping him on the shoulder for his deadpan, mocking insincerity.

"If I had been born five years later," he insisted, "I might have explored this leaning in a perfectly natural way. Soccer will civilize the world in future, even though James the First banned it back in the fifteenth century."

"It sounds to me like you still bear a grudge!"

"Aye, no wonder he got knifed in the tunnel. Tennis will never be as popular as fitba'! If he hadnae blocked off the sewer tae stop the balls he micht hae evaded Bobbie Graham."

"Oh, was he a defender, or did he play on the left wing like you?"

"Ye know me hen – I'm equally happy on either flank."

They stared at one another for a long time, each thinking of the most hurtful question of all, neither of them sure how to broach the subject they had always avoided. Then Hannah spoke, as she knew Harper never could.

"I was adopted at a very young age. I can barely remember my ma." Harper continued to look at her, stillness and silence conveying the utmost respect. She looked out of the window onto Gordon Street just below, thinking for a full minute before continuing. Harper waited but did not lower his gaze.

"Hannah made me her own child," she said with a sidelong smile.

"Your Grandmother Hannah? Not Frank and Jessie Wilson?"

"Oh yes, it was Grannie who took me in, and she who gave me her name."

"How so? Tell me what you remember."

"Through the Kirk, Harper. She was always involved. They practice what they preach up in Morayshire. Good works, charity and visiting the sick. And don't joke."

"And the Drummonds, where did they come in to it?"

"Drummond was just Gran's family name, which she passed on to me. My family name was Duff. I had forgotten most of the story, until I was old enough for Gran to explain to me. She kept it all from me, or allowed me to forget because it was too painful, until I was fourteen, or fifteen. Then she told it all. After a while, the memories actually came flooding back. It's incredible how the human mind works to recover what is buried, with a little prompting!

Duff was a deck hand on the trawlers; sometimes the big cargo ships. He was tall and handsome and strong. He had brown hair that would turn blond as it grew out. He had a beard whenever he came home, which he would carefully shave off."

Hannah spoke slowly and pensively, as though trying to separate accretions of memory from a living reality, reaching her hand out to a time beyond the grave.

"He wanted to be kind but he couldn't express it. Not in the usual way. I think the sea made him cruel," Hannah looked long at Harper, as though reinforcing some unexpected personal authority, "The sea does that to some men, they can't admit their weakness."

"Did he beat you?"

"No, never. I was his little darling, I suppose. For a week or two. Then he'd get drunk and shout at my ma. The money had run out. Then he'd be gone again. I remember missing him; crying at night."

"How did that feel, not knowing the truth all those years?"

Hannah turned to him again, drawing in her breath as she prepared to offer an explanation. Harper could see that there were tears running down her smiling face - tears of joy, not of sorrow.

"Amazed. I was amazed. I always knew, I suppose, in my heart. It was like I had been another person, in another world. It was all so long ago. I was staggered at how Hannah and Jessie loved me, without once mentioning what she was telling me then. Jessie never said anything, at that time you know, just Gran. I'm not sure Gran even mentioned telling me all this to Jessie. I respected that too. It was like no-one needed to know, or question it. Jessie's bairns don't know. The twins, Frank and Jeannie always accepted me as an older sister. Then Betsy came. They have no idea. Jessie brought me up as her own daughter. They love me and I love them. We are such a close family now. There is always harmony at Ramsburn."

Hannah paused to wipe her eyes on a little handkerchief. Harper watched her blow her pretty nose, with a smile. She smiled back at him. Again a flood of delight swept over him. He sat still, enchanted by her story as he listened.

"I am blessed to have had this experience. Blood ties are irrelevant, Harper. How we treat one another is of much greater importance."

This struck a chord with Harper and he spoke up, "I always wanted to know about my parents. That's what irks me, Hannah! John and Isobel never told me the complete truth, even though it was obvious to me. I hate that, when people can't express their feelings, even to acknowledge those of a growing child. I was a mild embarrassment to them. They were doing me a favour that I could never repay. You were privileged Hannah, you had two mothers. I felt like I had none."

"Oh Harper, let me give you a hug," she cooed. Although he wanted to talk he also laughed, accepting her affection. Harper needed the warmth she offered almost as much as the perspective of her understanding. They complemented one another perfectly.

"Some people go through their whole life searching for what we have now, you know." Cradling her in his arms, they sat together in a large padded armchair near the window. She was ready to sleep, but Harper was on the brink of something revelatory in nature.

Hannah buried her tired face in his neck and he thrilled to the caress of her soft breathing. Watching the darkness dance with the flickering gaslight for a few moments he felt ready to probe again, "Tell me more. Tell me everything."

"There is nothing much to tell, only heartbreak. Duff never returned. Black Agnes, the schooner he was on, keeled over trying to make the harbour at Peterhead in a storm. Some of those sailors went into the sea within sight of their own homes. Only three men were saved from the wreck."

"Good Christ, how terrible!"

"After that I remember my mother was always working, always worn out. Gran told me that she died of pneumonia. She was only twenty three but she couldn't cope without him. I think she really died of a broken heart."

Hannah lifted her head up to kiss Harper on the cheek. She continued speaking proudly, "I live for her, for both of them really. Spurn sorrow in your life Harper, no matter what happens. Never let it enter your heart. It will spoil your life and take you before your time." Harper remained silent, not daring to challenge Hannah's obvious consternation.

"Now I think I understand," he said to himself at last, imagining she had fallen asleep, but she heard him and she smiled.

"What would our lives be like now if we had never met?" she asked. Harper laughed at this new variation on wishful thinking. In this manner their conversation moved freely into the small hours. Hannah opened the window for him to smoke a pipe. They whispered as they watched dedicated Tuesday morning drunks, singing and carousing under the street lights.

Occasionally the sound of broken glass and raised voices could be heard intermittently through the early hours from the broad street below their hotel, mostly in bonhomie – once perhaps in anger.

Harper turned out the gas lamp. They lay in a gentle bond that was love, without the need of love making. One spirit, they had no need, no desire other than the constant affirmation of each other's company. Their minds ranged over all the images of a lifetime, finally resting in rediscovered innocence.

Harper hated being ill at any time, but now he was losing patience with the inert condition which resulted from the vigorous onset of influenza. He was subject not only to the good humoured attentions of the imperturbable Hannah, which served to make him feel guilty, and of course the girls who were deployed frequently in his direction with drinks and medicaments to ease his suffering but also those of Molly, the cat.

Molly was a feral cat who had moved into their basement three years back, not long after they had arrived in the area. Tired of thinking through interminable problems, Harper's mind drifted to the neutral and delightful subject of his devoted friend. Molly it seemed was a contradiction in terms, like so many of her gender.

What logic prevailed in her feline consciousness, to inspire her to select this family?

Sure, the girls had encouraged her as a kitten when there was wet weather. Hannah had tolerated her wilful determination not to be pushed over the threshold one particular evening. The following morning there had been no less than three dead mice scattered around the cellar. They were an offering accepted without great celebration but from that moment Molly, as they lamely agreed to Christen her at Elsie's suggestion, was henceforth a member of the family.

Molly had a wide territory and would follow the family, appearing suddenly when they went out walking. She had most of the markings and much of the behaviour of a moorland wild cat: black spots on her orange belly; black ankles, wrists and paws. She had striped flanks and hooped tail, joined by a black line from her head along her spine and wore symmetrical bands of black, white and orange fur on her legs. Molly was a true Scottish Tiger.

Constantly coiled to spring, with tension in her arched back even as she walked, she examined the world with yellow eyes and a salmon pink nose - outlined it seemed, with the stroke of an artist's fine brush and set in a Maori warrior's mask of a face. Her initial - the capital letter M, set upon her forehead - completed the biological phenomenon. From the front when she lifted her chin, a fox's white throat beneath long whiskers gave her a certain maternal grace, as she meditated now with eyes half closed.

When she stood, yawned and extended an arm with scimitar claws into the door mat, the soft illusion was gone. She had a small head with a bobcat's enormous ears. Her hind legs seemed out of proportion to her forelegs, much longer than those of an ordinary domestic Tabby cat. She moved with a slight sideward gait, gambolling, Spring-lamb like - seemingly ridiculous to the untrained eye. Yet her approach could be deadly to prey or combatants not anticipating how this shambling motion accommodated sudden changes of speed and direction.

Neighbourhood cats saw all of this in Molly instantly and tended to stay well clear. Her body had been engineered by nature for ranging over long distances and jumping vertically at unsuspecting birds. She could reach the top of any tree growing within a half mile radius of the West Port house, from ground level, in two or three seconds. In fact Molly didn't climb trees – she ran up them.

At first the undomesticated creature had the annoying habit of not burying her droppings. Harper went to some trouble to demonstrate to Molly that this was unacceptable. She could be destructful and fierce but was always more affectionate than any normal cat. Evidently she had moved in to stay.

Now at three am on Sunday morning, as Harper slept fitfully on the floor before the banked fire in the small lounge, Molly decided to demonstrate her love for him. Woken from a shallow slumber by her purring, he cursed softly to himself, resisting the urge to stroke her.

Her rear end, with tail erect, wafted gently past his forehead. He groaned as he tried to summon the energy to push her away.

174

Whenever he sat by the fire in the evening, his feet up toasting, Molly would arrive on the scene. With much thoughtful examination of any visible unevenness in his trouser material, or whether the elevation of his knees was acceptable, she would circle two or three times on his lap before finally settling down.

She would stretch full length if the fire was hot, anchoring her claws in his woollen socks, occasionally pricking the skin beneath. It would be difficult for him to fold a newspaper in order to read a chosen section. He was obliged never to move, despite his bottom growing numb. Harper was philosophic and staid in subjection to Molly.

Women loved him for his amenability and it was nice to be part of an extended social set but this cat did not understand him as well as he understood her. Did her feline instincts not tell her about contagion? Had she never stepped back from a rat too sickly to defend itself?

If he took her downstairs to put her outside he would have foundered by the time he got back up to his fire. If he just put her out through the lounge door she would scratch with her flat little truncated growling sound, to get back in. This endearing croak was part of her hunting repertoire. She made the alerting sound whenever she saw birds through the window, accompanied by broad sweeps of her tail to elicit assistance.

At mealtimes she might cry momentarily, like any ordinary cat however. Each day Hannah gave her pieces of fresh herring, mackerel or cod. But her strangulated mewing conjured up an image of a family of wild cats, ranging over a Highland fell. Molly reminded him of the ever watchful but unapproachable population of felines which even now inhabited the granary at Ramsburn.

Harper tried to see the funny side of the situation as Molly circled him for the fifth time, still purring and leaning against his angled shoulder. He laughed ironically through his puffy face as he rolled onto his back. The wracking cough came again, bursting through swollen lungs, forcing blood into his already aching temples. Life's lessons were indeed unpredictable – constantly shifting and layered – overlapping in sequential time, ever elusive in their quintessence. He was eager to attack Hannah's problem, while resolving his own transitional career arrangements. Harper also needed to complete the imminent house move.

He *had* to be available for Brodie and indulge Chambers one final time - and now this! He was too ill to sleep in the same bed as Hannah. Coughing and general restlessness would affect her, possibly even delay much needed exploratory surgery if she became infected with the same virus.

A combination of factors – Hannah's reluctance and discouraging noises from the doctors were delaying what seemed to him unavoidable. Now she seemed to be moving towards the same objection, aware that if she caught this flu and it sat on her lungs she might be too weak for them to allow the operation.

Harper felt all of this was intolerable. Now even the gentle demands of the good-looking, exceptionally confident cat made him want to throw up the sliding sash window and yell frustration into the night. The oppression of illness mounted as the hours wore on and the puttering gases of the fire's embers reduced gradually, like a failed vision of heaven. At one point Harper felt so ill he wished he could climb right into the fire.

Rolling the pillow to fold it along its length, he lifted his head into the radiant glow as the cat finally settled herself into a circle on his lap – her face buried in her own flank with ears pinned back, subliminally attuned to Harper's movements. Finally he also found a position where he might still his aching frame and actually breathe mercifully dry air through his inflamed nostrils. At this fulcrum point he could at last repress his own spinning, aimless thoughts to find serenity in the considerate embrace of sleep.

"Hey Sqwidge!"
"She's mine, I'm gonny dress her up . . ."

176

"Mammy says, 'No, yer not to do that, cats don't wear claes.' You'll make her too hot."

"She can play wi' a ball o' wool."

"Aahowww," groaned Harper softly to himself.

"Shush! Ye'll wake daddy!" Elsie cautioned Elizabeth.

'Ali, Ali, no more!' Harper thought he said. For an instant it was Friday night and they were drinking in Bobby's Bar, at Greyfriars. In fact no sound came from his lips apart from a moan of distress. His mouth was a non-functioning part of a mass of facial tissue and muscle that had apparently begun to resolve sense into a lower order, like a live lobster boiling in a pan.

Physically, this consisted of an internal hollowed out space containing ash and fire that was his mouth, throat and salivary glands. Externally, a limp hanging that had sometime been a face hung over two painfully swollen protuberances which had formerly been cheekbones.

As sentience returned to Harper it became evident that the roots of his teeth had also begun to protest with a dull swelling.

The girls are taking the cat, so it must be morning.

The constantly leaking eyes of last night had become salt encrusted lick-holes in a desert at sunrise. He was afraid to rub them, lest the weeping begin again.

Eleven minutes past ten was confirmed - as he opened his right eye to stare malevolently at the clock on the mantelpiece. If he could concentrate and summon the motivation, he might make the bed recently vacated by Hannah, whom he could hear moving about the house – ideally while it was still warm. He could not allow himself to be ill – Lennox would never speak to him again. He stopped at the scullery to issue a pleading demand, "Powders please woman! And the toddy – just bring a kettle of boiled water and the Macallen."

"The Macallen?"

"Aye, if you would. There's nothing else for it. It feels like bronchitis but I've been told by all and sundry that it's just the flu."

"Oh, I think we're above the pea-soup fog here. But we'll have to keep an eye on that."

"No, I have to be at work tomorrow before six at the very latest. Wake me at four thirty so I can have a bath. I want in early, for the briefing, and I don't want to end up sleeping through it."

"I'll wake you at five. I'll draw a mustard bath for you. What about food? Do you want me to bring something up for you, or just let you sleep?"

"Yes please," he muttered, leaving Hannah to wonder if that meant he was keeping his options open.

Hannah slept through her promise. When she rose at five thirty and went to check on Harper, he had gone. The glass with the toddy was untouched and the kettle was cold. He was ill – but not so ill he could not function on nervous energy.

Although he was starting the job with Kennington's in the New Year, something very big was about to happen at the West Port. Harper was determined to be there when it did.

They admired him, she realised, in many small ways. He still found time to play rugby and football for the City Constabulary in spite of his dedication to family routines. The infamous lock-in sessions were now severely restricted from his standpoint though. Too many excellent young policemen had been caught and sacked. Although temptation was always there to get involved in the drinking bouts, Harper avoided it with discretion. She could understand how much they meant to him. It was the Monday of his last week at the West Port Station and a time when everyone would work together for the prize.

Hannah looked out of her window at Edinburgh Castle and the valley to the east. She could see beautiful but life-threatening invection clouds, white against the slowly breaking dawn.

Today the hospitals will be full of the harshest sorrows. Loved ones taken just days before the Yuletide and Hogmanay holidays. Episcopalians and Presbyterians bonded alike to serve the new industrial demi-urge, despite potentially fatal risk in stepping over the threshold into that pall.

There was much talk of a man heading off to work in the morning, struck dead within seconds of waiting at the tram stop. Another fellow rushed into the street after a day in a warm bright office, his mind full of plans for the evening. A minute later he was choking and foundering in the scouring reek. An eye-witness report in the Courier told of a look of surprise and dismay on his moist, bleached face as he breathed his last.

Here at least they had elevation above the creeping miasma of deadly smoke from factories scattered around the south and east of the city. She had a feeling Harper would be okay. Today she was fiercely proud of him. Hannah had always joked that she was mother to him, as well as wife. Now she considered him like a father to her, as well as a son. Lastly and above all, he was her man. She had been glad to give herself to him. Whatever it was he was doing today that required duty and self-sacrifice – it mattered to her because it mattered to him.

Harper arrived early for the six o'clock briefing. He banked the fire in the upstairs conference room until he knew it would blaze for an hour at least, before positioning himself comfortably as near as possible to the big sash window at the front of the room. He might open it a crack for ventilation if he needed to, once the temperature in his runny nose and circulation at his chilled extremities had settled to the flow of ambient air.

He had with him a pocket stuffed full of spare handkerchiefs and a small bottle of pungent vapour jelly, some of which he had smeared onto his fine moustache. Chambers told him he smelled like, 'an exotic section of the herbarium at the Botanic Gardens.'

The Treasury officials from London were there already, with Brodie flapping around them like a mother hen, ensuring they had every requirement for support arranged immediately it was requested. They were business like and direct – above all wishing to be left alone to get on with preparations for the raids across Lothian. Noticing that Harper was infectious, the management were pleased to avoid close proximity with him. Nodding their greetings from a distance they were happy to let him be.

For Harper, the operational briefing dragged on interminably. He frequently interrupted with uncontrollable bouts of productive coughing. His lungs were wracked with pain and his breathing shallow, but he politely demurred when Brodie asked him if he was alright. He raised a Bobby's hand in both fealty and arrest.

You can see I'm fucked . . . just shut up and leave me alone!

The third floor conference room stretched the full depth of the West Port building. There were almost fifty officers and men scattered around. Many stood against the walls; others sat on desks, or at workstations. At the large conference table near the front presided the Brass, including several notables from other stations.

"It's clearly going to be a logistical nightmare," announced Somers, the Home Office liaison man, "To correlate information we will glean from international sources and target known offenders, who have a tendency not to stay in one place for too long."

Somers' counterpart and mirror image, Chatwin was invited to explain. Both men were small and rotund with neatly trimmed greying beards. Each spoke quietly and gazed interrogatively with watery blue eyes, at whoever spoke back to them.

Chatwin was slightly larger and younger than Somers, so Harper labelled him thoughtfully as, "Chat, Fat-Man One," and his colleague Somers as, "Fat-Man Two." Harper had a feeling they would be inaccessible to the direct approach, yet were somehow key to the job.

The mnemonic would work for his counterparts in the weeks ahead, especially Lennox, who liked simple, deterministic notions.

"We are back-tracking the illegal activities of an enormous, highly successful gang of international counterfeiters. Our task is analogous to salmon swimming upstream – but be clear - it is not only one stream we are interested in." He made eye contact with two or three individuals around the room, staring at the policemen for several seconds, making them all feel uncomfortable.

Somers came in on cue once this damning point had been made, "You are part of a very important, deadly serious initiative, to detect some of this criminal activity and put these men behind bars. Let's be absolutely clear – this is more heinous, more cancerous than any other crimes you will ever have prosecuted before gentlemen . . ."

Harper groaned audibly. The doppelganger paused for effect, staring at the same three or four individuals at the sides and far corners of the room before proceeding.

"Fuck me," whispered Chambers into Harper's ear, "I swear I'm gonny lose it if these two break intae a song and dance routine." Chamber's huge earnest eyes, floating behind large varifocals, undercut the stern atmosphere in an instant. Harper guffawed at the dry, comical image. He tried to disguise his laugh in a spluttering bout of coughing. Brodie scowled at them from behind the top table.

"Just because our operation forms a small part of a much larger scenario, does not mean it cannot be understood for what it is. These villains will take lives without compassion or mercy. They *will* be armed - if you get anywhere near the big boys. Even so, any one of the go-fors will cut your throat to protect their end. So watch out lads."

Another pause for effect . . . just get on with it man, so I can get out in the fresh air!

"They also crush the lives of the people they use to extend their network, like the man Lennox and Hamilton pointed out to us as a

181

suspect." Hamilton silently mouthed something to Lennox, which Harper thought might have been the word 'Wanker.'

Somers continued unabated. He was well used to stealing the credit for other men's hard work. He would be lucky to even get a gong when he retired, let alone any public recognition for years of dedicated undercover work – so what did he care?

"They look for patsies with high cash turnover. They use dark criminal organizations that stop at nothing, even indulge the vilest human weaknesses to turn a profit. They use the people of the night – petty criminals of course; the money launderers who service every illegal activity, black marketeers and bordellos. But they also look to compromise or blackmail pederasts and catamites, typically using them as printers and couriers. They actively seek out legitimate traders who might have fallen into debt. Any business proprietor with questionable morality can fit in with their plans – including bank officials and accountants. They like tourist resorts where there are well equipped local photographers, responding to the growing demand for holiday snaps – it makes our job all the more tiresome and protracted . . ."

"God, you said it pal!" whispered Harper to Lennox.

"Ah wish he'd shut the fuck up, an' let us go get some doors kicked in," retorted Lennox.

Harper smiled as he brought his kerchief up to his mouth again, to cover another bout of coughing.

"We suspect they are based somewhere in central Europe: Russian occupied Poland, Germany or Austria maybe, but have no way of pinning them down. Lately there has been a two-way traffic of counterfeit bills. In other words their operation is both mobile and international. They are manufacturing counterfeit bills of different denominations and possibly for other countries, locally. This might tend to dull the enthusiasm of local police looking for the currency of another country in a printer's warehouse. But we believe that you set the gold standard here in Lothian and in the United Kingdom generally. Not to presume we are more outward looking and more

182

conscientious than some of our counterparts in Europe, or the USA," Somers paused for effect again before adding, "But I happen to think we are."

Everyone laughed except Harper, who wanted to slip under the table. The patent aspirin powders and cough medicine he had been taking for the past two days were having an effect at last. He felt the desire for sleep creeping across the top of his head, down through his forehead. He was glad Hannah had not woken him at four thirty. He felt as though a bath would surely have killed him. The little man from the Treasury Special Unit continued to drone on, about everything they already knew.

"You can help with your thoroughness and efficient organisation. Inspector Brodie has reminded me several times over the past few weeks that Lothian has the longest history of successful policing and criminal detection in the country. Right here in this room are constables who have already given us the breakthrough that we needed to take back the initiative."

There was a murmur of approval from everyone. Hamilton slapped Lennox firmly on his shoulder. Ferret took a half step forward under the unexpected impact. All eyes were on him as he lurched like a guilty Dr Frankenstein, scowling back at his alter ego.

"Well done Ferret!" Hamilton announced, giving his pal the credit.

"Oh, did I fall asleep and miss something," cried out Harper, feigning being woken with a start. His comic timing was perfect. The outburst around the room was open and raucous. Lennox, Chambers and Hamilton all began to rock with laughter.

"Something funny gentlemen?" demanded Brodie with his Colour Sergeant steely voice, standing up to look at them, as if he was ready for a fight.

"Nothing at all sir!" answered Chambers, still smiling to himself.

"Right," intoned Chatwin through his permanently fixed indulgent smile, which seemed to encourage more banter, "So . . . ," he gathered his words thoughtfully around him, like friends who would not assume he was patronising,

"I'll just finally assure you gentlemen that we intend to chase these bastards across Europe and North America. We *will* eventually get them and put them where they belong. Can I say it again loud and clear? What happens *here* is pivotal to what happens *there*. I would suggest you read the papers from abroad. Ask your superior officers for confirmation of how your intelligence was used. Don't stop being vigilant of the suspect crews involved on your stamping ground.

I want to say thanks gentlemen, to one and all. Thanks for your thoroughness so far, as for the commitment I expect you will all demonstrate today. Incidentally that thanks comes from the very top, the Cabinet Office as well as the Treasury."

Chatwin, clearly the link man with the big-wigs in Whitehall looked over at Somers who smiled with tired eyes. He was flanked by two plain clothes detectives who looked like simians escaped from Edinburgh zoo. The little man sighed as he stood up to continue his directive.

"I call this a dragnet operation. I don't need to tell men born and raised in a seaport town what a purse seine is. We want everyone and everything connected with this pernicious business. We are looking for presses, with plates for paper bills. We are looking for wrapped or boxed consignments and the means by which they are hidden or disguised in other labelled containers. These will not be at the same premises, so we have to find and arrest the people who collect the bills and package them for distribution." Somers nodded at Brodie, who had been itching to take over, to impress the Brass from London. As he rose and stretched the fabric of his neatly pressed uniform, Harper half expected Brodie to scream 'Tenshun!' like a Guards Regiment drill sergeant.

"Lennox and Hamilton will advise you on the basic information they got from their informant before referring him to plain clothes. Offer your suspects the possibility of a reduced sentence if they co-operate at first interrogation – otherwise you will throw the book at them. You need that information immediately, in order that second –

"B wave" squads can be informed of our progress and make further arrests.

Above all we want information sifted quickly for hot leads: addresses, telephone numbers, bank accounts; all business contacts known to the people on the A list. Some names given will be false but record them anyway. We'll charge them later for hindering our enquiries. Your suspects might be the butcher, the baker and the candlestick maker, but I want them all arrested and booked for receiving. We'll sweat them slowly and if need be, take them off your hands so you can get back out on the streets to make more arrests."

Brodie had run out of invective so he sat down rubbing his hands affectionately on his own thighs above the knee. He nodded at Somers, who rose again to have the final word.

"We'll get the little fish that lead to the big fish. Search them individually before searching their premises. Look for their account books – the one in the back pocket first, then the official one in the desk drawer. Oh and take their wallets but also find where they hide their own little swag bag – don't leave the premises without it. It will be under a floor board, or in an attic, but get it.

The crime is the evidence . . . Exaggerated profits; counterfeit money and the money trail – record it all properly when you find it. Good luck," concluded Somers.

He stepped back as though fearing a rugby scrum. Brodie stood up like a cocky prize fighter, a hard glint in his eye, ready to challenge the growing animus from the impatient Bobbies in the room. He listened for inappropriate murmuring.

"Right, well that just about covers it then. If you have any questions address them to your team leaders. Just a reminder that we have Post Office authorisation, with private company technicians ready to cut off telephone lines into all the targeted premises, so ensure that you cover all exits. Any alert like a dead phone line and they will leg it, so timing is vital. Keep the lid on these arrests until all suspects are interrogated. Under no circumstances does anyone below senior command speak to the press. The conduit for public information will be through me, to The Scotsman crime desk and no-one else. Is that clear?"

"Yes sir," they all echoed with one voice, sceptical of Brodie's blatant reinforcement of the social hierarchy. There was a scraping of chairs followed by an instantaneous hubbub, as the body of police professionals rose like a pack of bloodhounds with their tails up.

Harper was a passenger all that memorable day, wishing he could go back to bed. He had been burning the candle at both ends for months. Now he was suffering from extreme fatigue, on top of a genuine illness. Apart from the one man he had found left in the basement of the illegal 'print shop' off Ferry Road, he participated very little in Operation Purse Seine. The prisoner had to go to hospital, as Harper had used his last ounce of energy to spread the unfortunate fellow's nose all over his face.

There had been five or six merchant seamen of various nationalities bunking down in the house. All were clearly aware of the sinister nature of the printing works in the basement. That much could be concluded from the speed with which they exited the building, through every feasible exit. Aware of the time forfeiture if caught, they ran like wild eyed horses from a burning stable. They employed feet, foreheads and fists to facilitate their leave-taking.

Two of the men vaulted through upper floor windows. Judging from personal effects left on the floor of the basement where they were kipping, two others went over the wall at the back of the spacious suburban villa, into mature neighbouring gardens and parkland. They had sprung to life as any trained unit of brawny sailors would when responding to a crisis at sea. They left the squad of half-blooded, corpulent peelers scattered in their wake.

PC Bradley, at post by the gated railings, suffered a deep gash across the left side of his chest from a rogue swinging a bill hook. In less than a minute the yelling, scuffling engagement had receded into the surrounding avenues and side streets backing onto Ferry Road.

Harper heard the sharp cry of agony from behind as he entered the house and knew Bradley was hurt badly, without having to look back.

Left standing at the top of steps at the end of the hallway Harper saw facing him from inside the doorway below, a balding middle-aged man with glasses. He was tall, with a pleasantly lived-in face, and was wearing a full length apron over his shirt. Rolled-up sleeves and long powerful arms covered in ink, showed that he had been hard at work, no doubt printing forged paper bills. His slightly quizzical, almost professorial expression belied a waning Herculean athleticism.

As Harper ran down the steps he said something in what sounded to be a central European accent, "This be what you looking for mister?" but the meaning of the words did not quite register through the rush of frenzied behaviour or Harper's desperately weakened physical and mental state. All Harper saw was something metallic in the man's raised hand, being pointed towards him.

As he moved briskly into the basement printing room, Harper put all his remaining energy into one well timed thrust of his clenched fist into the man's face. Given his bodily stiffness and general feeling of impotence, the blow was neither telegraphed nor tempered. But it was delivered with a righteous intensity, driven by more than a touch of fear.

The printer didn't groan or raise a hand – he just sank to the floor in a twisted, inert heap with blood gushing profusely from both nostrils. Harper handcuffed one wrist to the supporting frame of the gigantic press, before checking for a pulse. As he did so he saw an oil cloth containing three forged metal plates resting in the unconscious man's left hand. The forger was totally insensible, not even groaning. Harper felt a twinge of panic that he might have broken the man's skull, possibly snuffing out his life. He shoved the metal templates wrapped in the oil cloth into his greatcoat pocket without looking at them closely.

Running back up to the front of the house, he saw Bradley sitting in a bloody heap, his colleague's face creased with genuine distress. Harper saw in a glance there was nothing much he could do for him except call an ambulance, or just stay close while he bled to death. Remembering the purpose of their tribulations, Harper decided to throw his whistle to a concerned looking bystander then nip back quickly to check for evidence before securing the cellar door. There might even be another armed man hiding in the house.

"Run to the corner hen and blow the whistle hard. There will be a Bobby on point who will call an ambulance for me. If you cannae see him, head up the hill towards Drylaw Police Station!" Harper instructed the lady, "Give them this address; number three Chancelot Grove. Say there is Police officer at the scene and another one badly injured. Tell them there is an injured prisoner also. Go quickly and look after my whistle. Give the Bobby your name. What is your name hen?"

"Chalmers, Mary Chalmers," she smiled, seemingly flattered by her position of trust in the alarm. She was fulsome and strikingly pretty, for a woman apparently in her fifties. In a flash it occurred to Harper that this fine lady looked how Hannah might at such an age, should she endure her illness.

The tethered Police horse champed, flexing the muscles along his back, as he stood nervously at the heavy wagon. Mary rushed towards the mounted policemen on point a hundred yards up the hill on the main road.

"Fuck, where are they all?" cursed Harper as he left Bradley, spinning on his heel back into the house. Remembering his duty, he was alone for what seemed an interminable time as he checked again to see if the man handcuffed to the printing machine had expired, then moved swiftly around the large residential house. It was silent and appeared to be empty now.

He realised with annoyance that the counterfeiters had chosen their location well, to maximise opportunities for escape into the quiet suburbs of Leith. Concerned for the agonised groans of Bradley out on the street below, Harper briskly visited all the rooms, bolted the back door from the inside, then returned quickly to check on his colleague.

Expressions of pain were usually a good indicator of the potential for recovery, but Harper needed to see the extent of Bradley's wound. Carefully stripping off the man's uniform coat and jacket, he tore his shirt apart with a cursory apology. Blood was everywhere. It poured from the downed PC's chest, covering Harper's hands to form a pool beside them on the brown flagstones of the pathway. Harper cursed insensitively as his greatcoat dipped in the gore.

The sun was rising now, penetrating fog hanging beneath the mature trees of Inverleith. Golden rays reflected off the brown sandstone villas. The air felt slightly warm for the time of year, where flickers of light reached over the rooftops. Harper threw his blood soaked greatcoat into the back of the paddy wagon.

Alongside it he threw the spoiled uniform greatcoat and jacket of his colleague. Harper concentrated upon gently removing Bradley's necktie, before ripping off his shirt with another habitual expression of regret. He tried to talk reassuringly to his colleague throughout, though by now he was almost in a state of collapse himself.

"Don't worry Brad old son . . . ye've at least another eight pints where that lot came from. Sorry aboot the shirt."

"No, fuck, it's okay John boy. At least Jeannie won't ha' tae wash it."

A six inch gash was now visible, clean through to Bradley's rib cage and splintered bones beneath. White, chicken-soft muscle flowered in trembling, stinging pain, as new blood rushed past torn nerves, down onto Bradley's bulging waistband.

"You'll live to be an old man Brad. You've been lucky today," Harper informed the casualty, conveying bluntly with a sense of tangible relief what a more tactful man might not have voiced, "No major arteries severed and no organs punctured, although that was more down tae luck than judgement."

Harper rolled up the blood soaked shirt in a long strip, tying it tightly across Bradley's deep chest wound as they talked.

"Yeah, that cunt had a boat hook, Harper. Six inches to the right and I'd be contemplating a pile of my own guts."

"Six inches to the right pal and you'd be toting up the score wi' Saint Peter. If the boys find him, they'll shove the boat hook up his sphincter and pull out his intestines for you." Harper broke a strong new-growth branch from an apple tree in the front garden of the house. He twisted it into the shirt–bandage, for Bradley to tension as a tourniquet over his prolific chest wound.

"Well at least we got the printer and the plates. Now . . . I'm going back to check the house a little more thoroughly Brad . . . to see if there's anything else for the Treasury men, okay? You stay sitting to keep the blood flow down. I'm sorry if it's uncomfortable but I had to tie it tight. Wait for the ambulance and do not move. They were on alert for us, so they will be here soon." Harper found an evidence satchel in the wagon. He went back into the house to begin a more thorough search of the premises.

As Harper stood in the hallway his whole body began to tremble with exhaustion. He sneezed again, wishing not for the first time that he could simply fall asleep. He heard a gasping sound from the Printer and could see that the man was in a bad way. His mouth and nostrils were full of blood. Harper groaned aloud at the thought that the poor chap was his arrest. He would be obliged to attend the hospital with him to ensure that he did not abscond, if and when the man did come round fully. Then he would be obliged to conduct the initial arrest interview, before passing him on to the Treasury investigators.

Harper didn't mind intense activity – but right now he could not face a long wait at the Royal Infirmary. He tried in vain to resuscitate the villain, even by shocking him with an amount of cold water poured from a jug he found in the basement scullery.

Stretching out the Printer's crumpled frame, he unclamped the handcuffed wrist in order to straighten the man's folded legs. In that instant he felt a hand gently removing the strap of the evidence satchel from his shoulder. Harper looked up to see the smiling face of Sergeant Chambers.

"Your ambulance is here John. You go with him and Andy Bradley. Don't let this sack of shit out of your sight - even if he is in a coma. We've had four men down today – another with a knife wound; one with a gunshot and we've had to destroy a mount."

"And the other?"

"What? Oh, Hamilton broke his ankle jumping off a wall."

"Arrests?"

"Sixteen and counting across the city. That's in the first hour."

"What about these rats? Did we catch any of them?"

"Just one but that's enough . . . we're impounding their vessel and we'll arrest the entire crew. The Harbourmasters at Leith and Newhaven are in on the job. None of these shit-bags will leave the country the way they came in. The second wave of arrests is just getting under way. I believe that by the end of today we will have half the itinerant population of Leith in custody - as well as a fair cross section of the most loathsome of Edinburgh's criminal elite at our disposal, offering their undivided attention."

"Does that mean I can go home and die in peace Sergeant Chambers?"

"Harper, if you were a woman, I'd fuck you right here on the floor, I love you that much."

"But does that mean you will send some rookie to relieve me at the Royal, as soon as you see one not doing anything?"

"You have my word on it son. Now go . . . The stretcher bearers are waiting for you to give the nod up in the hallway."

Harper instructed the paramedic crew to recover the unconscious suspect, while he fetched his coat from the back of the Paddy Wagon. Then he went to join Bradley, in the back of the ambulance.

It was eight thirty in the evening when Harper saw PC McClenaghan striding purposively into the reception area of the Head Traumas Department at the Royal Infirmary. Although he had slept most of the day outside the operating theatre where surgeons battled for the life of the comatose printer, endurance had taken him well past vexation into a mute, self-consuming and caustic rage. The only thing that prevented harsh words to accompany a mood as black as thunder was the knowledge that he had almost killed a man with one blow earlier that morning.

The thought did not make Harper feel any better, so he gave no word of advice to McClenaghan. He just stood up and walked past him with a grunt, his coat tightly wrapped against the penetrating grips in his tortured chest. For a moment it occurred to him that he would have been better off saving his legs walking home, had he just stayed at the hospital.

Harper staggered towards his home in the West Port along Lawton Street, glad to be in motion but nauseous with fatigue and longing for rest. His feet and hands were numb and he could barely keep his eyes open. Harper knew that he must forego the delightful recounting of all the events of that momentous day, to allow the illness to take its course. He was due to leave his job at the end of the week but had three days of leave accumulated due to him and had to rest.

Regretfully, tomorrow was out of his hands. He was not dejected but a good thing had ended, and Harper felt a profound sense of love and loss. He was everyone's favourite, yet he would never bask in the reflected glory of Ferret's prize. It was enough to walk free with the respect of agreeable and decent men however. Now at least Harper could devote all his attentions to organising the house move, and to instigating Hannah's operation.

Dizzy and trembling, he leant against the door with his forehead, in the pale gaslight. He was trying to remember where he had put his keys when Hannah appeared in the hallway. She was aghast at his deathly appearance. Immediately removing his blood-stained coat, she muttered that it was, "Impossible to wash clean and fit only for burning, or the rag and bone man."

Harper was more interested in the need to collapse in front of the roaring fire. Dog–tired, he sighed gratefully as she returned from the basement, to pour him a brim-full tumbler of fragrant Macallen Malt.

Its glorious ether spiralled downward through his fragmented senses, quelling gold-hammered harassment with rapturous unction. Ghastly images of the day flooded back into Harper's mind's eye, as he groaned and fell into his armchair. He found it difficult to keep his countenance – uncertain if he needed most to laugh or cry. Hannah chatted with him as he rambled like a lunatic in his raging fever. He planned to knock over the bottle, but twenty minutes later, after three large glasses of the sensational malt, his head began to swim. Within another ten minutes Harper folded into stupefaction.

Hannah came with his supper but it would have been wrong to rouse him. He was clearly very ill, but she had not the strength to usher him to the bedroom. She laid the tray on the table at his arm with the glass and bottle, should he require more. Elsie brought a thick woollen blanket to spread over him, tucking it around his shoulders and under his feet. Hannah banked the coal fire and faithful Molly came to keep vigil.

Harper slept the sleep of the just. But nightmares merged with recollection of the waking day as he mumbled restlessly. His raging high temperature and wheezing cough alerted Hannah sufficiently to don her coat, stepping into the night to find help. She hurried along the street to fetch Ella Stewart to look after her bairns, then headed off to rouse Dr Foxworthy.

At first the good man presumed it was Hannah who was having the crisis, but he came without hesitation to examine Harper.

The doctor spent ten seconds taking his temperature and listening to the patient's breathing before declaring the diagnosis.

"Pneumonia!" Foxworthy went home immediately, to telephone for an ambulance for the recumbent Harper.

The girls were up all night. Ella Stewart, the landlady who lived next door indulged them, not wanting to make a drama out of a crisis. They all headed with Molly to her cat basket in the converted basement. Ella lit a fire with help from Elizabeth, while Elsie went upstairs to fetch the art satchel. Ella chain-smoked as the girls sat at the laundry table, making drawings and 'get well soon' cards for Harper.

Harper spent the next ten days in hospital recovering from the dangerous inflammation in his lungs, four of them in a critical condition, with Hannah at his bedside throughout the agreed visiting hours. A couple of days after he came off the critical list, Ali Macdonald came to visit him, with Inspector Brodie.

Having handed over the statutory bag of red grapes and dispensed with the usual pleasantries, Ali looked nervously over his shoulder at the Ward Sister, who was hovering like a bird of prey. Evidently Inspector Brodie wasn't there to invite Harper to the next charity fund-raiser at his golf club.

"The man is in a bad way," he announced, "We need a statement from you."

"Bradley? Tell me about him." Brodie looked at Ali as if to say, "He's your pal . . . you take over now."

"Andy's fine, John. They say six or eight weeks for the broken ribs tae knit. The wound is healing nicely, although he says it itches a lot. He told me to say thank you."

"Right, so who exactly is in a bad way? The joker I thumped?"

"He's had two operations. One on his skull and one on his teeth," answered Brodie impatiently. He was looking around at a nearby chair but calculated that his head height might be too low for personal dignity. Ali, who was six foot two, pulled up a chair on his side of the bed to sit on.

"Oh . . . I get it, no statement, no trial. Sorry lads. It was just one punch. I thought he had a gun in his hand. You saw what that other bastard did to Andy."

"Yeah we got him, but we still need a positive ID, when either you or Andy get out of hospital."

"Ask him about the plates," demanded Brodie.

"Did you see plates?"

"Oh, the plates! Yes, yes. They were in my coat pocket, I think."

"You think?" asked Brodie incredulously.

194

"Yes . . . well you must know what it's like Sir, in the heat of the moment. My main concern was with the casualties. Did the woman . . . what's her name – Mary Chalmers - did she return my whistle?"

"Yes," said Ali. "She's a doll. She gave us lots of background on the rogues she saw coming and going."

"Never mind about that," blustered Brodie, annoyed that Harper and Macdonald had their priorities mixed up, "Tell us about the plates! How many were there and what was on them?"

"I've no idea, I never looked at them. They were in his hand, two or three of them – the Printer that is. Wrapped in an oil cloth. I put them in my pocket but the coat was soaked in Andy's blood. I took it off . . . threw it into the paddy wagon so I could give him first aid. But it was cold, so I took it with me to the hospital. I wore it on the way home because I was foundering – but look I'm sorry . . . I was in no fit state to think about evidence." Brodie looked at Harper in dismay.

"Go on, explain yourself!"

"It was not on my mind. I was at the point of collapse. I had a high fever, with stabbing chest pains. Hannah said that I turned blue just before the lights went out."

"Yes, son and we are all glad you are on the mend now. But where the fuck are my plates? Were they in your coat pocket when you got home?" Harper blew his breath out through narrowly parted lips.

"I didn't check. I fell asleep in a chair outside the operating theatre, until McClenaghan relieved me. I honestly don't remember how I got home. You'll ha'e tae ask my wife. She took the coat."

"We already did. The coat was given away to a rag and bone man named Rooney. We interviewed him. He says there was nothing in any of the pockets," Ali informed him with concern in his voice.

"Well he would, wouldn't he, thieving little pikey bastard," railed Inspector Brodie. "The same little toe rag was collecting old woollens from my neighbour in Inverleith when he pinched the fucking hopper and downpipe off her guttering."

"Sorry gents," mumbled Harper, looking first at Ali then Brodie, "You've been thorough. Maybe it fell oot o' ma pocket in the ambulance, or at the hospital. I was just about tae put it in the evidence bag when Sergeant Chambers relieved me," Harper added as an afterthought. It sounded like an excuse. From the disdainful way Brodie turned his head away from him, Harper wished he'd kept his mouth shut.

"Don't worry Sir . . . I'll testify and the bastards will all talk, you can be sure of it."

Brodie and Ali Macdonald both saluted Harper. Then they beat a rapid retreat before the openly contemptuous Ward Sister lit on them. Harper was badly dehydrated. He felt very uneasy about the grilling he might one day expect from the counterfeiters' Defence Counsel.

"Oh well . . . what the fuck!" he grumbled to himself, reaching for the bag of grapes.

It was two more weeks after that before he began to throw off the dangerous chest infection.

Chapter Ten - *Portable Skills*

Yuletide and Hogmanay had been planned in much greater detail than in previous years. There was so much to do in respect of the house move, that this was actually unavoidable. As a consequence there was much excitement for everyone, especially the three girls. Harper had a sense of rolling forward into a new vista, with new directions and unseen barriers blocking his way. He forced himself to be alert and committed, though he was badly run down and his attenuated body craved rest. Harper knew he should make time for his erstwhile comrades but for now at least they were as pre-occupied as he was.

News of the arrests was held back successfully at first, but within a week his former colleagues' activities had begun to trickle into the national press. Now was not the time to stand in the doorway to say farewell. Harper had agreed to pay Ella Stewart, their landlady, two weeks additional rent into January '94, but he had told himself they were nevertheless obliged to have cleared the West Port house by Hogmanay, so there was no time to waste.

Ella had been invited to spend Boxing Day with them, as she had grown attached to Hannah and their bairns, becoming a friend during the heart-breaking trials and tribulations of the past year. She bought a Christmas tree and helped the girls decorate it.

Christmas, so people said, smacked of the Popish influence, ever since it had been banned as a public holiday back in 1640. From Harper's point of view, this was all the more reason to indulge his young family as he didn't care to be indoctrinated either way. If it was good enough for the rest of Christendom, it was good enough for him.

The completion date for purchase of the new house on Lillyhill Terrace was on the Friday before Christmas and despite fragile health he was determined to push for access to the property on that day. Knowing well that conveyance solicitors made their fortunes on the back of intricate search details and delays, it was almost certain that close to a national holiday season – officially recognised in Scotland or not, he would be tripped up by one of the several strands of petty requirements which made such transfers legal and binding. The very same class of pedantic bureaucrats who had abolished all the fun back in the reign of Charles the First, were precisely the ones who would be hardest to find during the latter part of December.

On asking his solicitor Bateson for a firm commitment that the matter be concluded on the twenty second, the man vacillated predictably - quoting the timing of conveyancing niceties and statistical calculations that depend on the release of funds from the lender. When Harper pressed him to expedite the matter before the holiday, the lawyer blatantly asked for an increase in his fee, amounting to a doubling of the agreed charge of five guineas.

The building contractor informed Harper that his plasterers would not put white-wash over the finish skim but he wanted to have this done before Hannah decided where to put their furniture. It was necessary to seal the walls and build two or three layers of emulsion upon dried coats, before painting the skirting. Harper intended to ask Ali Macdonald to help him, but knew his friend would be on overtime, like all of the City Constabulary.

If he could only gain access to the property and was fit for the effort, Harper decided he would spend the weekend at the new house while completing the work himself. The wagoners were due on the following Monday morning with the furniture and they had a reputation for speed. Harper's mind was on chasing the small but necessary arrangements which would ensure everyone was happy and that he himself did not go raving mad. In this intense but orderly manner the festive holiday and the house move came and went.

On the third of January 1894 Harper started his career as a Draper's Traveller – employed as a national representative for Kennington's. During the first month he worked alongside an old hand, Roger Dewhirst, who was planning to retire with his wife to Otley, in England.

Roger was the quintessential company man. He explained that there were no less than fourteen sales representatives working nationally. There were no territories as such as the management were suspicious of how that tended to work, but there was always scope to develop a particular area. Some stores required more frequent visits because they took more produce – but essentially the Accounts Department directed the work towards expanding the trade, or offering new lines to old customers.

"They keep a default check list on who has not been visited lately which can prove tiresome if a fellow doesn't keep himself busy," Roger intimated as they settled down on the train to York.

"Their way of making the slackers run around?"

"Precisely, Harper. You're learning fast. You'll do fine."

Dewhirst had devoted his life to expounding the same nuances of texture, weight, serviceability and value until they became a mantra connecting him with a higher economic reality. Roger handled bolts of cloth and sample books with respect, giving the attention of the supplicant to every invoice or bill of sale. He received cash and cheques with the innocent face of an altar boy waiting reverently for the priest to consume his wafer, then turn next to him. Customers could wait though – Dewhirst focussed on the transaction with the shopkeeper alone. He stood aloof and stately, in perhaps as fine a suit as any of them they had ever seen. Now was not the time to brook interruption, or indulge in casual conversation with lesser mortals.

As he got to know the customers, observing their requirements, Harper saw how traditional Dewhirst was in his approach and how little he did that was new. There were opportunities for adding incentives into a deal, or for pitching to the shop owner's perception of what constituted good-business.

Harper realised that if he phoned to book appointments, instead of just calling out of the blue, he could have their undivided attention. Dewhirst was too ingratiating - relying too much on *making* the sale instead of *assuming* the sale. Roger saw his clients as employers, not employees. He was an old plough-horse, dreaming of his last pasture.

Dewhirst wanted to take Harper to his retirement villa on Chevin hillside above Otley. They made an afternoon detour between York and Leeds, through the flourishing market town at the foot of the rugged Yorkshire Dales. Harper was impressed by the verdant rolling countryside as the cab climbed a steep hill along the bus route to Bradford. The driver was told to wait, while they walked round the exterior of the part rendered brick villa perched on the slope of Pool Bank. Harper made noises of approval, relishing sweeping views of the wide Wharfe Valley below but reflecting privately that he preferred what he'd seen of the nearby landscape surrounding Ilkley, a little off to the North West.

That evening Dewhirst booked them into the Black Horse Hotel, in the centre of Otley where they exceeded overnight expenses, dining on roast beef dinner with Yorkshire puddings and a decent bottle of French Cabernet. It was clear to Harper that Dewhirst liked him very much, intimating that he was 'glad to help him all he could.' Roger openly stated the view that Harper, 'would have been wasted as a policeman'. Zachariah's grounding had qualified him for an easy transition.

After their meal they both drank excessive amounts of locally produced, hoppy ale in the lounge bar. People in the Black Horse Hotel seemed warm and garrulous to Harper. The turn of conversation was quick and wide ranging, reminding him of Aberdeenshire, with the same intense social dynamic of public houses he knew there. Here was a great similarity. These were hard working people who defied presumption – who always knew more than they could say.

Everywhere Dewhirst had taken him around England so far during the handover there had been a decent pub, with good food and comfortable accommodation for their overnight stops. Tomorrow they would visit customers at Bradford, then head over to Leeds if they had time before swinging north through Harrogate, York and Durham.

Dewhirst it seemed had more lines to purvey, more clientele to service than any one old man could ever have managed. When Harper pressed him to, "put a number and a quantity to it," Roger dithered, looking down at his soft hands. The coal fire blazed in the corner of the Black Horse. Evening shadows seemed to grow deeper with the soporific effect of the frothy Tetley ale. For a moment Harper thought the old man had been struck dumb by a stroke, or that he had fallen asleep. The right side of Dewhirst's face was red from the heat of the crackling fire. A pleasant faced landlady laughed and shook his shoulder asking whether he wanted the bill now, or another round of drinks. Dewhirst 'Hmmed', drawing a masterly finger across his mouth before responding. Harper told her to bring another round.

"You know the simple fact is John . . . I really don't know. It's just not my place to do the accounts. All I can say for sure is - this is an ever expanding trade. People around the world – here in England, the Empire, Europe and the USA, want our home produce. We have a distinct niche in the market place because of our name. Kennington's and Jenner's will not be easily supplanted by rival producers.

If a garment has a label on it saying 'Made in Scotland' people anywhere will buy it. Christ alone knows why. For centuries the English rubbed our faces in the mire. They protected their own markets, waging economic warfare on everyone, including us.

Now coal is king. We can go anywhere by sea or rail. They want our raw materials and we want their lacquered tables – or tea, or Brandy, or whatever it is we think we need. Take a look around Inverleith next time you are promenading with your bairns, if you don't know who I'm referring to."

"Oh, I know. Half of the bastards who live there are English," Harper murmured, under the drone of conversation in the busy bar.

Dewhirst was drunk, but Harper let him ramble. He meshed his fingers together like an old priest at the funeral of a friend. Circumspection forbade familiarity for Harper though, in expressing his own opinions.

This old guy is almost three times my age. I need to learn all I can from him.

Now the potent ale which hampered coherence also inspired a profession of faith, which was gnostic rather than apostate, "Free trade and political liberalism blurred the distinctions between the old issues that always kept Scotland poor. As a nation we – you - the Scots I mean, or even the British if you insist – tend to live too much in the past. We think the old traditions and values are relevant, even though there was never one accepted view. If I speak too loud in here about religion, every one of these good people will lower their voices and lift their shoulders." As if to register the challenge, Harper lifted his own shoulders in anticipation.

"And . . . and . . . that's not because of religious bigotry, Harper although such a thing is prevalent in some quarters. It's because the mistakes of the past are too painful to admit to, and the present state of affairs is really no different."

Dewhirst lifted his beer glass. Piercing, light blue eyes penetrated through the random connections caused by the alcohol fighting for control of his mind.

"Yes, but what principles can you derive . . ?" Harper saw the fierce look on Roger's face and decided to shut up. He felt drunk himself, but not so drunk he was ready to let it show.

"I don't know if there is one all-embracing set of principles that I would advocate above any other Harper, one absolute certainty that is worth dying for. What I do know is that there has never been anything worth fighting for."

"Surely there are Just Causes Roger – at least from the stance of nationhood – Queen and country and all that?" Harper was baiting Dewhirst, his thin lips pursing into a gentle smile.

Dewhirst waved the thought away with an impetuous motion of his left hand, raising his glass again with his right. He leaned forward slightly to drink deeply, seeming more animated than before,

"I don't care about that. It's all deception and stupidity – all leading to economic exploitation of some shade or colour. What matters is what is agreed - who has a job. Who can marry and raise a family. Who has a roof above his head and who has a field to plant."

"So, getting back to the point, you don't wonder about the extent of the market you are currently working in?" demanded Harper, eager to bring Dewhirst back to answering his original question.

"All I know is, it makes more money than I can even begin to imagine for the family and shareholders I represent. Your interest, Harper, points to General Managers, Accountants and Bankers, who will interfere if I make any suggestions. As long as there is a slowly expanding market, I am in clover.

If it grows too fast the bubble will burst – they will bring in other reps and lower my salary, or make me work harder. Then they pressure clients to cover increased operational overheads – more expenditures and distribution costs – 'Pay more and pay on the nail.' Customers in turn start to look elsewhere for supplies."

Harper thought about what Dewhirst was saying – it was not the numinous moment of revelation he anticipated, but he knew it for the safest pathway over the mountains.

"In conclusion?"

"In conclusion, I keep my mouth shut and do my job. I make a friend of every client, so they are beholden to me. I apply gentle pressure to get payments in on time - working at my own pace - so there is always somewhere to go for repeat business."

He looked at Harper again over the rim of his pint glass, "This is the only way to survive as a traveller, Harper. Be warned - the harder you work, the more they will come to expect." Harper smiled and shook his head slowly from side to side.

An Irishmen at the bar began to sing in a resonant baritone. They turned to watch approvingly but could see another man beside him, crying profusely with tears rolling down his ruddy face, dripping even onto the full glass of stout in his hand.

Word spread that they were mourning the death of colleagues killed in a tunnel collapse on the branch line they were working on a few miles away. Dewhirst paid the bill. He and Harper retired early for their six a.m. alarm call.

The two salesmen ate breakfast in silence before setting off promptly to visit their first few customers around the budding market town, on their way up to the railway station. Harper was keen to resume the conversation of the previous evening with Dewhirst but he waited until later in the morning after Roger had taken several orders from a key client, Brown Muffs, whom he described as 'The Harrods of the North' as well as from half a dozen other major accounts around the centre of Bradford.

Not wishing to slow an already ponderous itinerary, Harper kept his impressions to himself but once they had got over their hangovers and settled onto the train back from Bradford he began to probe more.

"And what about the financial collapse?" he asked. Dewhirst seemed lost in reverie, returning his colleague's concern with a questioning look of his own, "I mean has it affected business?"

"The Panic? What about it?"

"Well, Baring Brothers almost caused a world-wide banking collapse with their speculative ventures in Argentina, didn't they? The whole rail network of the USA ground to a halt! Imagine the economic damage that caused."

"Yep, that affected everyone for a time, but now sales are up. American exporters can't compete with us. Customers look for quality because that ultimately translates back into value. In other words when times are tough, people think twice before they buy. Clients knock their margins down but ultimately they rely upon big companies like ours who will give them thirty days credit with assured re-supply. People still need clothes Harper, even in times of hardship. They will happily spend on drapes and furnishings, even if they don't own their own hovel. It satisfies a sense of achievement, provides an illusion of well-being that is visible for all – like the Edwardian wallpaper you told me about in that burnt-out house in the Highlands."

"Hmm, like the cave paintings in the Vosges."

"Come again?"

"Oh nothing . . ."

Roger looked at Harper as though he were a buyer who had just cancelled a regular order.

"Oh . . . sorry Roger," Harper smiled indulgently to cover what might have been a petulant sigh from his colleague. He laughed deeply for a moment as he tried to remember details of the story. Sitting upright on his bench in the rolling carriage as the express gathered speed through the sprawling village of Huby, Harper looked out of the window, then warmly back at Dewhirst before he spoke.

"It's just a story of parental aspirations which always amuses me Roger . . . There was an idiot boy in my old Parish High School at Huntly, name of Johnny Martin. He was the second son of a local railway engineer, who had ambitions for the boy to follow in his footsteps. His father told him it was steady employment with a good salary, so he and Johnny's mother could afford to buy their own house in the town.

Martin's passion however at the age of eleven was for drawing cartoons, also a lot of schoolboy story-telling and mimicry. He really could have been groomed for a career on the stage – he was that funny. The railway business would have survived without him at least.

When Johnny didn't have his hands shoved through a hole in his pants pocket playing with himself, they'd be in someone else's, stealing pencils to feed his raw talent. He'p me Boab! In my innocence Roger, I thought Johnny the cracked actor was the sage o' the world – he was that original. Of course all the stories of travel and adventure he told us were really his old man's. He'd been in the army in India, before joining the railway."

Roger smiled engagingly back at Harper as he listened patiently, commenting only that, "Johnny Martin sounds like someone I went to school with in Batley, where I grew up."

Harper nodded politely and continued his story, a smile playing across his lips as he spoke, "One afternoon the Art Master, Charlie Anstruther told us about cave paintings of oxen made by our early human ancestors, at Altamira in Spain you know - and in other places in France. Martin was transfixed . . . he was forever in some teacher's bad books for drawing cheeky cartoons in his day book. Paper was so precious it was rationed, but old Charlie didn't mind - he encouraged the lad to submit cryptic contributions for the annual school magazine. Mr Anstruther was something of a free thinker, if not an intellectual - although no-one around would have recognised it." Dewhirst laughed volubly as his hangover receded at last.

"The previous summer he had put on his own one-man exhibition in Elgin. Poetry and paintings essentially but he played his own corresponding music on the piano. People up there loved him for that - especially as he said he was inspired by local scenery and culture. He had a translator print his work in Gaelic, some of which he recited himself. Charlie was single but rumour had it there were offers of marriage on the back of that."

"I take it he didn't accept? I wonder if offers in kind stood, just the same." Harper smirked at images of his teacher conjured by Roger's innuendo.

"Anyway in the Art lesson, Charlie told us he had been to Paris as a student in the late 60's, seen the same exhibition of pre-historic art that supposedly inspired Manet and The Impressionists. He compared that favourably to Martin's humorous cartoons of animals - his cats and dogs and cattle, as well as familiar people. The boy visibly swelled up with pride, as we all listened attentively." Harper shook his head, smiling broadly now as he remembered the scene from childhood.

Dewhirst realised this was not the ribald anecdote he had come to expect from boys playing away from home but some deeper, more subtle question. He listened indulgently to the young man as Harper had done with him the previous evening.

"Establishment art critics said the cave paintings were 'naïve and brutal' but that just made us all laugh, when Mr Anstruther explained to us that this is exactly how children are. So this story of cave beasties struck a chord with us all - Johnny Martin especially.

Charlie, our legendary Art Teacher had us all in a dream world of trapping and fire lighting, bear fights and magic rituals. He was encouraging us to think imaginatively about our Cro-Magnon ancestors, obviously to inspire our artistic imaginations.

For a while it worked. He was flooded by suggestions. 'Collect sticks for a fire.' 'Build a cave out of straw bales.' 'Dress in rabbit skins.' 'Invent a basic language.' 'Make flint tools.' I recall the winter sun sinking over the horizon. Gas wicks were lit to supplement the poor daylight from the high windows. You could have heard a pin drop. Old Charlie gently clapped his hands, bringing back the attention of the committed troupe of cave-dwellers, ready to hang on his every word.

He proudly mentioned Charles Darwin in association with his theme. There was only one member of the class who raised a token objection, 'My mammy says we're no' tae believe in that nonsense. The Good Book says. . .'" Harper mimicked the tell-tale voice of twelve year old Ginny Murdoch, whose father happened to be a Presbyterian Minister.

"You'll get no argument from me on that," remarked Dewhirst with a snicker.

"Anyway, imagine the scene Roger. Martin at the front with his hand in the air, answering Charlie's questions, trying hard to impress us all. Mr Anstruther with his worldly experience, building up to the paper-rationed activity that would keep us all quiet for the remainder of the afternoon. We would all have preferred him to keep on talking. Every word was inspiration. I mean what did we know? We couldn't even find Paris on the map, let alone Altamira."

"Hmm, I see it. Do tell me . . . what was Johnny's gaffe?"

"Well, Charlie asked us why we thought it might be that our ancient tribal ancestors painted their caves – no doubt something to do with the origins of abstract thought and religion. Anyway, poor Johnny, the only child in the class with parents who owned their own home shot up his hand as the rest, children of tenant farmers and shopkeepers in feu to the landlord without exception, watched him, listening in awe.

'Sir, please sir, because it would increase the value of their caves . . .' Dewhirst laughed aloud over Harper's continued portrayal of the classroom scene from a time of innocence, so very long ago.

"There was a pause for several seconds as the notion swept the alert minds in the room. Charlie himself paused to let the seeming tautology sink in. Then suddenly there was uproar as they howled Martin down like the mob storming the Bastille. The story was repeated daily at school and in every home in town and the surrounding farms for weeks to come.

Johnny's reputation as a storyteller and cartoonist was actually enhanced – 'He is right of course,' people said, even if the Cro-Magnons had relatively more security than Scottish crofters, 'What an insightful lad to know human nature so well, so young,' they all agreed – in that typically introspective manner of the Highlanders.

But when he reached fifteen and got the apprenticeship on the railway, the first thing Johnny did was to find digs in Glasgow, taking his portable skills to work there."

"Hmm, the classic fart-smeller," suggested Dewhirst.

"Sorry . . . did you say smart-fella?" queried Harper.

They both laughed aloud at the bar room conceit, feeling easy comfort in each other's company, as the train pulled into Harrogate.

"Now, if you like Edinburgh Harper, you will simply love this town. You will not see evidence of the Financial Panic here . . . but watch out for the women. Wear your wedding ring at all times, or you may end up in trouble."

"Roger, I want to thank you for everything," Harper looked at his friend as he reached up to the overhead tray for their leather brief cases.

"Tssh; not a word. You have been chosen as my natural successor!" Roger placed a broad paternal hand on Harper's sharply tailored shoulder. Harper smiled confidently. All Zachariah Williams' expert teaching had come into play for him. Harper had found a naturally sustaining occupation as good as Edinburgh City Constabulary or the crofts at Ramsburn.

Chapter Eleven - *Coley's Toxins*

The accomplished Edinburgh consultant Mr Archibold Smellie explained with gentle humility that he was, "No relation to the pioneering eighteenth century obstetrician," then listened to Hannah's concerns, reading her plaintive tone of voice rather than the explicit contradictions she was querying. Those he understood only too well. How could having another baby possibly help Mrs Harper in her pain-wracked condition? The woman was desperate - imploring him only for reprieve. Anything they could do to extend her chances of seeing the girls grow up might give her some peace of mind, however far-fetched it seemed.

He tried self-consciously to reduce the impression of his large bulk upon his patient by perching on the edge of the table. Rubbing gingery fair hair on the backs of his hands and wrists alternately, Smellie watched her with interest. Hannah was sitting on a chair beside the examination couch. The gynaecologist had made time for her on a working day, between tightly scheduled operations.

Smellie was conscious of the fact that he looked undressed in his waistcoat and rolled shirt-sleeves, wishing to avoid wearing the white lab-coat that seemed to have become standard work-wear around the Royal. The pre-eminent surgeon was certain that white coats suggested the medical procedures people feared most. Wearing them served to reinforce barriers of professional interest.

He smiled at Hannah indulgently, as she leaned forward attentively in the chair, her right elbow resting on the end of the examination couch. She unselfconsciously smoothed out a crumpled newspaper article, rambling nervously about her husband and family, about Harper's investigation into the pioneering research work of George Alexander Pirie, Neils Ryberg Finsen and William B Coley.

Mr Smellie was currently more interested in the nascent discipline of Psychiatry, welcoming it in its purest biological context but with a spiritual twist. People were creatures with a divine spark of self-knowledge. They betrayed their own inner workings, as well as giving wonderful insight into the fine mechanisms of the universe by the simple understatements they laid before him. He looked for their soulful energies, the better to understand the dynamics of their ailments.

Many pessimistically accepted their fate and had no will to live. Others were stricken with terror and fought like drowning sailors until all hope was gone. On the whole Smellie noted, the majority of his cancer patients were typically perplexed but resigned to their fate. Nonetheless the process of treatment tended to distract them from worldly issues, which might otherwise destroy their morale.

Mrs Harper, sitting before him now in the examination room, was a tragedy in the making. He knew in the instant he laid eyes on her that she was the one who might bring home to roost all of the combined sorrows of hundreds of others whom he had served, while baldly accepting the logic of his own limitations. This woman was going to make him pause amid his familiar assumptions, to reflect upon the past.

At fifty-four, Smellie knew he was on the cusp of his career – tall and still handsome, with thinning fair hair curling a little wildly around his ears. He applied the same psychological dynamics to himself as a surgeon that he constantly sought to evaluate in others. He had worked consciously to refine his presentational style every moment of his qualified life. At times seemingly ingratiating in comparison to his patrician colleagues, he was in fact always assiduous and thorough. Everyone who mattered respected Smellie – except one or two of his notional superiors.

In truth his status and position in the professional hierarchy was so elevated that his detractors no longer mattered. Although some shook their heads at his flamboyant personal style, occasionally tutting at how, 'he wastes time listening to patients blethering,' they knew that all Smellie's subordinates and students revered him. Matrons and nursing sisters adored the man. He bequeathed a certain moral rectitude to those privileged to serve him. Who could utter a word against him?

This prodigious fellow had learned surgical procedure from Lister himself. Even the obvious play on his name, revived every year by a new generation of spotty acolytes, fed into the legendary status, "He is called 'Smelly' because he has the permanent odour of carbolic on his hands and arms," went the legend. Those who understood him, his closest colleagues – knew Archie to be a man typical of his generation – outwardly amenable but at heart a committed exponent of aristocratic professionalism.

At times he saw his work as part of a huge industrial cycle with himself merely providing occupation for coroners, ministers and undertakers waiting in line. He found solace in work itself, trying not to think of the dead - just the dying. He had read Freud's articles on the interpretation of dreams and understood well his own worst nightmare.

At first, half a lifetime before, vocation had seemed obvious. He was the compassionate voice in the wilderness – a modern day John the Baptist, standing to receive the sick in the Life-Giving Water. One by one he gently lowered his ailing children into the rippling, shaded pool. Some arose with joy abounding, to embrace their loved ones and resume their lives. Many surrendered to the stream however, leaving self to the World. They floated away serene, eyes closed in their eternal moment. This had been the currently accepted religious symbolism, speaking as much of childhood influences - the strong voices of school and Kirk, as of any subconscious fears.

But at times, as Smellie grew in experience to better understand the severely reduced odds of any successful outcome for patients he operated on, the dream transmuted when it recurred. Vocational calling began to feel like a trap. He was an actor in a never ending parody of initiation which led only to ultimate loss. Powerful reflexion of being the graceful agent of salvation had been supplanted at length - by a torrent of irresistible force.

The gifted surgeon found himself drowning in a river of corpses, calling out for assistance from a place of knowing he had never seen.

Now Hannah Harper's voice rang for him like a bell. Her angelic face spoke with a message from the other side. Never give up.

At times he could not separate life, death and eternity in his fertile mind. Equally, he could not help but be honest with himself - it was just a matter of time for Mrs Harper. He had discussed her fully with Foxworthy, as well as his own staff. Her husband had brought journalistic research information of possible interest to him, but it was much too late anyway.

"Finsen and Coley," repeated Smellie, writing the names on his pad, "I know Pirie and the staff at Dundee."

Hannah raced on about, 'Bacterial injection therapy,' quoting the percentage of Coley's patients in remission.

'This is the direction I have been reaching out for in my dream,' thought Smellie. The physical shock of embarrassment was running up the back of his spine, tightening the skin on top of his head, though he just smiled at Hannah with his mouth slightly open.

His anaesthetist, Patterson listened intently from the far side of the room to Hannah's description of how, "A sixteen year old boy, John Ficken, was treated successfully with Coley's toxins." She explained how, "The lad's massive abdominal tumour reduced in size gradually since last January, with vaccination directly into the growth, until it disappeared entirely during the month of August."

Patterson was there to evaluate the patient's overall prospect of enduring his witch's brew but he ought perhaps to have at least heard about toxic or photo-luminescent injections. Smellie looked across questioningly to invite comment from him, but his colleague simply shrugged. As Hannah continued her explanation, the newspaper articles waving in her trembling hands, Smellie felt the blood vessels of his cheeks beginning to flush. 'Maybe I need to go to church again,' he told himself, 'or read more of the latest theses and treatises on Psychotherapy - more perhaps about the interpretation of dreams.'

For now he reverted to his deepest intuition. He focussed upon the generality of the impression Mrs Harper was making on him. Smellie determined to discover without intrusion or controversy what this woman felt she needed from him. Then he would act accordingly. 'Surely people's best intentions amount to a kind of faith - regardless of unknown or even probable outcomes,' he told himself. If he was going to 'play God' - occasionally he overheard disappointed people accusing him of just that - then sovereignty at least lay with the patients. That was the best Smellie could offer - a kind of medical enfranchisement which substituted for actually being able to cure them - that and his earnest prayers.

When he had finished examining Hannah, she handed him the notes and articles which Harper had put together for discussion. Smellie thanked her sincerely and she left, satisfied with the outcome of their meeting.

Informing Patterson that he intended to take an early lunch break, Smellie set off hastily to the nearby University Library, his notepad and pen in hand.

The stick-like, cadaverous frame of the permanently hunched Senior Librarian, Bolton, appeared in view swiftly and silently as though he was moving on trolley wheels. Smellie imagined Bolton had been pushed firmly by some unseen hand from between the rows of mahogany shelving.

From past experience Smellie knew that Bolton continuously evaluated the requirements laid on the counter before him, seeking to establish the degree of seriousness with which he was obliged to treat them. Bolton's paramount concern was thus the amount of time it might take him to locate a particular item. When the archivist took his off-season annual leave in the early summer, the time factor for retrieval could extend to several weeks. No-one dared open mail addressed to Bolton or move items from his in-tray, no matter if urgent or long anticipated.

Smellie was in no mood to be deflected by someone he saw as having the equivalent status of an incompetent Chief Porter in a vast hotel. He placed the pad purposively on the desk between them, staring straight at Bolton like a gunfighter in a Western novel. He whacked his technically advanced forefinger onto it twice for maximum effect, while slowly stating what was written there. This was for Bolton's edification in case, as Smellie often had cause to imagine, the man could not actually read a busy doctor's handwriting. The tone Mr Smellie used made it clear this was an order, not a request.

"Write it in your own hand Bolton, if you are not clear –'The Treatment of Malignant Tumours by Repeated Inoculations of Erysipelas: With a Report of Ten Original Cases. American Journal of the Medical Sciences: Coley WB 1893," " Mr Smellie stated for the record. He waited for Bolton to read this first item, parting his lips slightly as he did so to utter his first "Hmm," which Smellie never gave him time to make.

"Priority, Mr Bolton. Most urgent if you will, likewise the next item on this list!"

Smellie waited patiently for Bolton to fail to read or understand the Danish script, "Om Lysates Indvirkninger paa Huden 1893," before pointing out the English translation in parentheses, which Smellie also read aloud, ""Professor Neils Ryberg Finsen, University of Copenhagen: On the Effects of Light on the Skin, 1893," get it translated into English and send us the bill, but have it done promptly, there's a good chap."

Bolton smiled vindictively at the surgeon, making an habitual but almost imperceptible shake of his head, before saying, "I'll see what I can do."

"No, Mr Bolton, what you really should say is, "I shall do the best I can." "

"Oh, not at all! You wouldn't want me to sound over-enthusiastic now would you Mr Smellie? Word would get round, then every undergraduate boning for an end of year examination will think they are top of my list."

"This one's a matter of life and death, Mr Bolton. I know you won't let me down."

Smellie gave Bolton the broad smile of approval he knew the man craved most of all, now that he had impressed upon him the uncompromising nature of his need. He pondered for a moment whether handing the Senior Librarian a generous tip might have helped expedite matters.

"I'm operating in half an hour, so I'll visit tomorrow for the American Journal. You can tell me then who you've found to do the translation of the Finsen paper, when it comes from Copenhagen. Then again, if you take the trouble to phone you might find that the Professor already has a copy translated into English, which he will oblige by sending us. I know that I would," Smellie called over his shoulder as he retreated. He was intentionally rationing the social graces for Bolton, "Far be it from me to tell you how to do your job Bolton! Sorry old man! Life and death though. Life and death!"

It struck Hannah as she looked out of the kitchen window to the small back yard at Lillyhill Terrace, that she had spent much of her life doing just that. Throughout her adult years she had rarely stepped out into the sun, just for the pure enjoyment of it. Life had consisted of work and more work, from the moment she shook talcum powder under her arms in the morning, until the glass of warm milk she consumed each night before bed.

For as long as she could remember Hannah had been a slave to routine. Sometimes she wondered if the back pain and bloating she'd always suffered were a consequence of exhaustion - and perhaps the cause of the cancer itself. It seemed to her that she had spent all her days since leaving school either standing or walking.

Hannah welcomed the new presence in her life. Margaret Kemp lived down the hill at Parson's Green. She came promptly every morning to walk the girls to school. The bright, pretty nurse clearly loved to play with baby Hannah. Importantly for her mother, Margaret engaged with and spoke to little Hannah in a manner befitting a much older child. Their reciprocal understanding was

216

quite astonishing to behold yet merely served to confirm what they all knew about baby Hannah - she truly was exceptional.

More to the point, Margaret was not thrown out of step by awareness of the child's precociousness. She was able to direct attention back to baby Hannah, while thinking ahead to the next strategy for occupying her interest. Margaret could sustain her charge's curiosity and maintain a conversation with other members of the family, or the frequent visitors to their house. Kemp was conscientious, professional and a natural interactor. Also she was arrestingly attractive, yet self-contained.

It occurred to Hannah that if Margaret wanted additional paid employment, the young woman could probably cope with Elsie and Elizabeth too.

Maybe she could one day cope with John Harper. Who could say?

Hannah felt angry and wistful, as she endured the endlessly miserable days until her operation, scheduled for the morning of the second Monday in February.

She had resolved, some time ago, to move back to Rotheimay with her baby. Now that she was confident in Harper's network of business connections, including many in the Highlands, she was eager to make that transition and to get settled back at home. Jessie would help look after her as she recuperated from the operation. She intended to devote as much of her time as possible to little Hannah.

What angered her most was the double-talk of the doctors. They had deterred her from the surgical procedure, 'because the cancer is too advanced.' Yet the letter scheduling the hospital stay specified the purpose of her operation was, 'to confirm diagnosis by taking tissue samples for microscopic analyses.' Despite their legalistic reservations, Hannah had, for her part, agreed to a full hysterectomy with the removal of any tumours found. Smellie warned her of, 'inflammation, internal bleeding and the prospect of a long, painful recuperation.'

She would be in hospital for a week, requiring bed rest for at least another two when she came out. Then the time would come to pack a case for herself and the bairn and buy a rail ticket for Rothiemay. Whatever else happened in the meantime, Hannah knew there was no point in settling here at Lillyhill Terrace.

She watched a solitary blue tit picking shrivelled rose hips from the hedge at the end of the garden. The dank winter gave a deceitful hint of spring, as pale blue sky appeared behind white fluffy cloud. Hannah's eyes misted with tears for the frustration of it all. Her legs ached and she had to prop herself on the edge of her Belfast sink.

I am going home, living out my Last Will and Testament. I have no other plans for the future.

"The operation was a relative success," according to the worthy Mr Smellie. Judging from the knowing smile on his face as he stood at the end of Mrs Harper's bed on Wednesday the 14th February, he must have truly meant it. Hannah's prospects of recovery were, "as good as any patient I have ever conducted such an operation on," so he told her. Hannah gazed back at him wondering why she felt so low.

Meaning: I have done my best work for you.

No-one concerned with Hannah questioned Smellie's statement, even the sagacious Great Gran, who was determined to be there to offer moral support until she came out of hospital. They were all trying too hard to be positive to allow any obvious objections to be voiced.

Margaret Kemp had taken over Hannah's role during her absence – apparently seamlessly. Harper was not looking for problem issues with the girls. Since they did not fight or complain and sounded happy, he assumed that in fact they were. Kemp seemed discreetly proficient. In turn Harper was quietly impressed by the fact that she wore a nurse's uniform to work. He had no right to ask or expect leave from his new job, so he planned to work the accounts closer to home, until he knew the outcome of the biopsy report.

Smellie told them in conference with the screens pulled round Hannah's bed that he had removed one large and two smaller surface tumours. Abdominal fluid samples had been taken from the inflamed tissues surrounding them which analysis confirmed were indeed malignant as suspected. He had also performed a full hysterectomy on Hannah. Smellie also agreed, on prompting from Harper to develop the new chemical injection therapy. He also planned to evaluate the subsequent use of radiation, after discussions with Finsen and Dr Pirie at Dundee, "But that is a long shot," he told them.

If it was possible at all to try one of the new therapies, explained Foxworthy during a home visit the day after her release from hospital, Hannah would be obliged to submit herself to these as, "Research and experimental treatments. If and when they are given the green light by the Hospital Board," he added non-committedly.

There was no way back now, but at least Harper would not have to spend the remainder of their savings in pursuing the cure in New York. In effect Foxworthy and Smellie had seized the high ground, although Harper anticipated they would drag their feet in future, now that the operation had been performed. Hannah had made up her mind however. She felt she had a duty only to her baby from now on. The rest of her little family would have to survive without her.

Harper understood this, yet his mind rebelled. The prospect of her imminent departure left him speechless. Even his tumbling thoughts were incoherent, although they had talked about this many times. Hannah's leaving had been agreed as part of a joint plan, but when it came the time his entire mind, body and soul struggled in perplexity.

Catching sight of the open suitcases packed full of Hannah's clothes, his rage finally boiled over. Supposedly there was another fortnight before her departure – why was she bringing the date forward? Was it Great Gran who had persuaded her to leave early with her? The old lady had always been his wife's closest confidante.

Harper walked out of the house on the morning of the 19th of March into silent freezing fog, slamming the front door, which bounced on its frame. So distressed was he at losing control of his feelings that he left it open. Slithering with his head down, elbows circling like a drunken skater on the Botanic Garden's pond on New Year's Day, he fumed with wild indignation. Making his way across cobbles towards the iced up wrought iron wicket gate fronting the door to the park, he ignored Hannah calling after him.

Snow had melted a couple of times, then frozen again on the enamelled frame. For weeks there had been seemingly permanent frost and fog at the top of Lillyhill. Harper kicked the gate with a grunt of bestial, livid rage. One of the vertical runners popped out of place, revealing a crystalline metallic core. He swung his leg at the framed opener again and this time it flew open, squealing on rusty hinges in the dank, cloying chill.

Storming through the tall wooden door in the stone wall behind the damaged gate, he rubbed his upper arms unselfconsciously against the cold. Without hesitation Harper ploughed on through the hollow of icy mud, swamping the thoroughfare on both sides of the wall.

His only outer garment was a cardigan. On his feet was an old pair of brown leather brogues, which he habitually looked for on a Sunday morning. Carpet slippers were for 'old coves'. They were highly polished but there were holes in the soles of both shoes. Harper never thought of personal comfort for an instant however – he had utterly lost the ability to think at all. Raging through the frosted bluebell woods up onto the Rural Road, he tried but failed to make sense of the conversation with Hannah which he replayed over and again in his teeming mind.

"You're packing?" he had asked incredulously, standing in the doorway.

"Yes Harper, I'm packing," she answered indulgently from where she knelt on the bedroom floor.

"And when are you going?"

Hannah looked up from her activity straight at him. She spoke with a level voice, adopting the gentle tone normally reserved for the bairns, "Tomorrow morning, as I think I explained to you before my operation."

"What about the girls? You'll not be here when they come home from school."

"I spent a long time explaining that to them John. It's only two weeks till the Easter holidays. You can bring them up then."

"I can't believe . . . I mean, I never thought that it would actually come to this."

The infant Hannah sat on the floor 'sorting' towels. She looked up quizzically at her father, a mirror of her mother's searching expression.

"Please don't make this any harder than it already is Harper. I have no peace of mind and no more energy for the trials of life. Allow me some dignity in my departure," she said shaking her head once only. He could see she was going to cry.

He spun away to avoid acknowledgment of her grief as it multiplied, resounding upon his own. Without Hannah there was no point in living. There would be no feeling other than depressive melancholy, or at best numbing sadness. Harper had made a habit of thinking positively for the future – now there was no future to think about, positively or otherwise.

Every assertion he had made in recent years about himself - and ultimately, though his wife had accepted them all - they had been essentially about him, led to choices bringing them ultimately to this place and time. It seemed to Harper every affirmation, denial and accommodation he had made thus far in their time together had brought them inevitably to the brink of this unnatural division. Regardless of all the sacrifices they had both made, there would have been no problem now if he'd stayed on at the farm, or the forge at Rothiemay. He knew also that Hugh Harper would give him a job tomorrow.

As Harper had turned from the bedroom door in his moment of pique, there was the John Henry Dearle wallpaper he'd spent a week's wages on, to surprise Hannah on her return from the Royal Infirmary. He paused for a moment, remembering the burned out cottage near Dornoch. Those dark blue floral patterns on light blue background - naively intended to inspire - had come to symbolise all that was unjust, vain and ridiculous about life and living. In his fortitude, during the short time since making that effort, Harper had sublimated what at the time had been a pressing need - to purchase decorating materials, then paste on the beautiful wallpaper with a professional eye during Hannah's absence. He couldn't even remember doing it now, yet at the time it had seemed important. There had been so much hard work and vain hope of precisely this nature, taken for granted and forgotten in his twenty four years.

It occurred to Harper that this effort was just another trivial example of what ordinary people wanted and what they always did. They fulfilled superficial needs, acquitting commitments with small or grand gestures of care and love each day, carrying on throughout their lives without ever thinking why or where it was all leading. But women! Women had a level of fortitude to put it all in perspective.

Walking briskly up the incline of the Rural Road with breath condensing on his eyebrows and moustache, Harper railed at what he had not admitted until now. Hannah's leaving was a fundamental question of willpower, combined with gender role.

The fact of the matter was that they had enough money to continue paying the children's nurse indefinitely. Hannah had a choice. It might be tougher for her to stay than go, but she had greater fortitude than he could begin to comprehend. In the end her leaving was a matter of pride.

She refuses to fail them! Preferring to run away, than be seen falling apart in full view. Surely Hannah must see her own golden thread in the eternal tapestry and continue to play the game here with me, where she is loved most, until the end?

Harper knew he had to prevail upon Hannah to stay, or his heart would break. He sat for a time shivering tearfully on a fallen tree trunk. This was his desperate logic, but he knew that Hannah's cancer had a logic of its own.

Finally reaching the top of Arthur's Seat, he wailed down at the invection fog surrounding his primordial Kingdom of Grief. Tears percolated through his reamy eyes in the blistering damp air. He turned to look from west to north, to ensure that he was quite alone above the sheltered city. Harper bawled raging confusion into the piercing breeze off the sea. He cursed fate; his importunate parentage – cursed every notion of tortuous moral sensibility - every teleological conceit of reason that had dawned throughout a quarter of a century into his small, guilt-ridden mind. At last 'why' had been abandoned, washed out irrevocably with self-hating curses. He was left only with hopeless tears.

Harper fell onto his knees on the rocky outcrop. His entire body was sheathed in a pocket of chilled air. Had it not been for the energetic climb, he would have died from exposure. Perspiration evaporated from his clothes. Warm breath clouded around his face as he panted with exertion and madness. Yet bright sunlight embraced the entire orbit of azure sky above.

Harper no longer knew if he believed in the deity he had been introduced to by family, school and Kirk - although like so many millions he wanted reason to believe. He pleaded for the magnificent golden stillness surrounding him to join with his mortified mind and trembling body, to experience sense beyond afflicted thinking. Without cause for faith he begged the first Maternal Thought behind the veil of delusion, to glance at him in this dilemma. All that remained to him were terms of surrender.

"Okay, so I'm a Jeremiah!" he muttered, "I can't take another step forward without a helping hand!" Then holding up his head he called out, "So what do I do now?"

As he sat shivering on a rock the answer dawned slowly, although in a sense Harper realised that he had already known it. A feeling of calm settled as he aligned meditation, Druid-like with the nothingness at the heart of all things. Laughing at himself, Harper surrendered all aspiration and wanting into peace surpassing understanding. Even biting cold ceased to hurt, as pulsating energy danced all around him in the limitless morning.

At length, as sensation rose back to self with the warming light, all that really mattered was the thought of Hannah. In honouring the commitment he had made to her unconditionally, Harper resolved to support her in every decision from now on without permitting his own hurt feelings to intrude. There had been a tremendous sense of harmony in everything they had shared in the past eight years. This harmony had to be sustained at all costs.

Harper determined to take renewed assurance with him on the journey to Rothiemay tomorrow. They would all go. The girls would have time off school with an invented illness - Measles or Chicken Pox.

He would conduct business for Kennington's in the surrounding townships – Elgin, Keith, Banff and Nairn in the ensuing days. It all seemed so simple. The plan merely required his submission to divisive Providence. It would be hard not to rail against this severance, but for Hannah's sake he would remain steadfast. He would 'shut up and get on with it,' regardless.

The sun rose above shadows cast by the mountain as the morning wore on into the hour before noon. Harper wandered back down the steep slope through a diamond encrusted snow field, into an orange glow of unimaginable radiance. Every one of a billion crystals had been reduced by sun and polished by wind into a gemmological gala of light and colours, quite unique and stunning to see. Harper had never witnessed such play of Nature's awesome beauty. He stopped to look around in awe until the breeze clamped a cold hand around his heart. But when he moved, he found himself stepping forward tentatively through a kaleidoscope of heavenly transposition.

With much of the snow above the elevation of his head now, every step he took, each slight movement brought new perspectives. As the fog slowly evaporated, hundreds more flashing combinations of luminescent fire came into view. Harper paused time and again in disbelief, holding amethyst and lemon, then bright red flashes of radiance through the moisture in his watery eyes. The face of the steep rock above burned ochre, set against deep blue sky shining with dispersing moisture. Over Fife to the north, snow clad mountains stood in glory above pools of misted forest and farmland. Frozen margins of the Forth Estuary shivered under the harr. Through it poked the rusting skeleton of the suspension bridge they would all cross tomorrow on the way north.

Harper looked around the island of fire and ice for as long as his frozen limbs could endure it, realising that he'd had a moment of inner knowing which he would try to remember for the rest of his life. In his mind's eye was the glimpse of a sacred, unifying mystery underlying all personal ambition. All around was integrated beauty, beyond words or comprehension. Dancing energy was everywhere - in all things, surpassing definition or knowledge. With awareness beyond thought, Harper knew he had been allowed to witness the dispassionate eternal eye, observing this noon day symphony of re-creation. Whether an image in his mind's eye or not, it no longer mattered. Harper was convinced he would never be alone. There was a phenomenon beyond energy. Beyond decay or mortality. Beyond doubts and questions. Harper accepted his own marginal part in all that he saw with silent amazement.

It struck him suddenly that his children needed him. They must surely have been aware of their mother's dilemma. At once he was thankful for his situation - the opportunity to recast himself as an author rather than a player.

Walking down through the gorge beneath Arthur's Seat he reviewed his strange experience with humility. Even if words could never express it – he knew that he must accept his fate with alacrity, taking something positive from it, if only the quality of forbearance.

In loneliness and isolation he would hold his head up to walk with dignity, not drag himself like a tired old duck. The sunshine and beauty of Eden had worked a change in Harper. Walking quickly back to his precious family, he looked around at all the small things that might stir imagination in such magnificent, natural parkland as if seeing them clearly for the first time.

Hurrying through the woodland above Lillyhill Terrace passers-by caught his mood, smiling back at him. A couple of dog walkers whispered, "He looks as though he's had a grand night out on the town." With trouser legs soaked up to the knees, old shoes welded to his steaming socks, hands dirty from scrambling and slipping on the steep - Harper realised that he looked more like a prisoner on the run than Moses returning from the mountain.

The girls squealed with delight when their daddy bantered with them as he stripped off down to his underclothes in the hallway. They ran upstairs to fill the bath for him.

"Just open the hot tap Elsie darling . . . don't bother with the cold. Don't forget to put in the plug!" he called after them.

Hannah smiled at him through her dismay, red eyes full of sorrow, sunk in dark pools of speechless exhaustion.

Despite Harper's trepidation the transition to Ramsburn was easy - as everyone involved had intended. There were welcoming, happy voices and gentle reassurances. According to the consensus, Hannah was to do as little as possible, whilst avoiding boredom. That was never an issue with the toddler around to keep her entertained. Within days the metronomic rhythms of the farm meshed their simple clockwork with Hannah's own needs for recuperation.

Diurnal imperatives of feeding poultry, cattle and sheep, soon became a welcome extension to looking after her own children. In truth it felt the other way round to Hannah. They were looking after her. All this farming routine was new to the girls and excitement for it transmitted easily back to their mother. They pleaded with her to let them stay and it felt a more pleasant task for her to explain why they had to return, "for Daddy's work and Elsie to attend school at home," than it would have been to say why she was leaving – had the parting taken place at Waverley Station in Edinburgh.

She was grateful to Harper for his understanding and moral support in bringing Elsie and Elizabeth to Rothiemay. This arrangement made it so much easier for Hannah - knowing the girls would think only of returning in a fortnight to visit her and Little Han at Easter. Visiting the farm would be a well-deserved holiday for them as well as stimulus for their learning. Elsie and Elizabeth were looking forward to telling Margaret Kemp and 'Aunty Marion' all about it.

Chapter Twelve - *Bastard Dogs*

The whole family ate together in the evening and for this moment there were only the sentiments of joy and good humour abounding. In the morning Harper set off with Hannah to see the specialist, Mr Mitton in Elgin. The gynaecologist would correspond with Mr Smellie in Edinburgh about her recuperation and further treatment.

They wrapped up well against the weather, taking a picnic of roast chicken and broth that Jessie had made for them that morning. As Hannah and Harper slithered along dripping lanes to the railway at Rothiemay, the bond between them felt re-affirmed again as strongly as ever.

"You know Harper . . ," Hannah began tentatively, waiting for attention, "Hmm, what's that?"

"I don't want any of this, you know, my situation, to come between us. That is my only concern," She held her face level with his, looking into his eyes. He looked away from the straight lane they were descending and his control of the two garrons trotting well within their limits, in order to turn his nose close to her cheek. He withheld a smile, waiting for her explanation, "I don't think I have any choice . . . And I think you know that I don't want this compromise. Harper, I can assure you that I am not going to be a servant to Jessie's family, or Mary Robertson's."

Harper could see and smell the faint perfume of lipstick and rouge from her face and hear the thoughtful, determined tone. He knew it was necessary for her to say this. This was not history repeating itself. At last they had an understanding. Harper waited for more he guessed was to come.

Hannah looked ahead for a moment though her hand was still linked under his arm. Her knees were pressed affectionately against his on the footboard of the rig. The horses instinctively slowed for the long hill ahead, so Harper let them establish their own comfortable pace. At last Hannah spoke with alacrity that shocked him.

"I don't want to spend my last days on my knees, hiding from commitments . . . lying in my bed like some slothful auld tart. Above all Harper - I'm not going to die in some fickin' hospital ward, eating slop for supper and being told when I can get up to go for a wee by some auld hallion of a matron."

Harper wanted to laugh out loud but waited a while, an irresistible smile spreading across his face before turning to her again, "Oh look, ye have too much lipstick on woman. What will the good Mr Mitton think?" Before she could reach into her pocket for a handkerchief, he caught her off–guard, planting a kiss square on her lips. To his surprise she responded affectionately.

"Move along now, we can lie down across the bench seat. The horses could guide themselves if ye like," suggested Harper. Hannah roared with laughter at the thought. As he tugged her gently towards him with the padded right shoulder of her splendid velvet town coat, her outrageous laughter re-doubled.

Although Smellie had ordered a full six week course of the Coley toxins from the Pathology Department at Cornell University he knew that at some point, probably in the first few days, they were certain to make Hannah so ill that she would need intensive nursing care. According to the research, treatment had been more successful when injections had been administered into clearly identified tumours. This would not apply in Mrs Harper's case although systemic treatment through injection into massive muscle tissue would suffice. Smellie was reluctant to release them for use by Mr Mitton unless his patient could be fully monitored or unless her need was otherwise deemed to be urgent.

Smellie wrote to Mitton but found it difficult to express his true intentions. He simply wanted to observe – to monitor, if not control this experimental treatment, "Ideally," he wrote, "I would like to study its efficacy under an agreed protocol. It is important to begin by evaluating the effect of the injections upon the patient and increase the dosage gradually, relative to what she can tolerate. The desired outcome is a high fever, followed by reduction of the tumour."

He went on to state the obvious – that Hannah's location prevented his direct involvement. He also advised Mitton that the Coley vaccines would, "store indefinitely if kept at a low temperature." He could wait – for a while.

Hannah recovered her strength gradually as the weeks wore on. Her relationship with her youngest daughter surprised her in its depth and harmony, yet apart from insisting on sleeping in her mother's bed during the first week at the farm, her namesake made only the lightest of demands beyond the shared focus of routines. Yet as an interlocutor of the world for her, Hannah found herself enjoying everything they did together, seeing the world anew through her child's inquisitive eyes.

When Harper came again with the girls the place seemed to spring to life. Everyone at Ramsburn seemed to talk louder and laugh longer. For his part he regaled them all with anecdotes about the people and places he had visited. The information was always novel, fresh and funny. He made time for Jessie and Great Gran.

Each time he passed Harper's sawmill on his way to the farm he attracted visitors who came later that evening for a chat. Hugh and John Harper came to visit with their respective wives, rather than expect him to ride over to Auchterless where they had their farms.

When he left at the beginning of the school summer term with Elsie and Elizabeth there was a sense of loss. The longer the intervals between Harper's return, the sweeter were Hannah's intimate moments alone with him in their room at night.

At the beginning of the summer holidays, after a long interval, he brought the girls to stay at Rothiemay on the first weekend of July. Hannah fussed over him, knowing he would have to return to work for the Monday. She talked all evening of the little adventures and precociously funny sayings of their youngest child, now advancing well into her second year.

Little Hannah had partnered up with the youngest of Jessie's brood, lonesome ten year old, Elsie Wilson with whom she made a redoubtable team. Gregarious and strikingly attractive like her mother with long blonde curls and cornflower eyes, she nevertheless needed someone to love unreservedly. The toddler was into everything, exploring the farmyard and its environs as well as every interior space of the house. Harper smiled approvingly as food and fire worked their magic. The social stroking of fourteen individuals across four generations, resident between the two crofts brought new deference to his notional status as father figure.

That night Hannah and Harper made love as purposively and gently as Mr Mitton's cautions would allow. They made love again in the morning and twice the following day, before Harper had to return to work. Despite Smellie's long term reservations and Mittons's earlier prognosis, Hannah seemed to all appearances to have returned to normal. But in her fatalistic eagerness to offer herself, she had been indifferent to the truth.

As soon as Harper was gone Hannah knew the dilemma she was in. She had felt pain at the time but had given no indication, gladly counting it part of the ecstatic pleasure they had shared after missing one another for so long. But now as yellow light of a glorious summer morning blazed through her bedroom window, Hannah felt the familiar warmth and lubrication of bleeding. It continued unabated as she coursed the carriage over ten miles of rutted lanes to the railway station at Keith, on her way to see Mitton in Elgin. By taking the carriage, she reasoned, at least she was moving. This was preferable to the two and a half hour wait for a train at Rothiemay. At all costs she needed to avoid an inquisition at home.

Hannah told the consultant, "I have nurtured my body for months, avoiding stress and over-exertion, thinking that the rest-cure was working. I even talked optimistically with Mr Harper of return to

231

Edinburgh. Now that the long school summer holidays are here, anything seemed possible. The planned arrival of my girls at Ramsburn was expected to be an acid test of how well I might cope with additional routines. All my maternal instincts were tuned in expectation. My hopes were high, Mr Mitton. But now this!"

"Bleeding is a necessary part of the healing process," Mitton explained, "As is a little discomfort, if you over exert yourself."

"Sorry, I was beginning to doubt whether my operation had worked. It's been five months. Surely it should have healed by now?"

"Well, yes. But there is extensive scar tissue inside your abdomen. These things can take a while. That's why you need complete rest."

On the journey home, Hannah tried to reassure herself with Mitton's explanation, but she knew in her heart it was deluded. The enjoyment of being outside in the glorious sunshine of an early July midday was gladdening consolation however.

She remembered with a jolt of desperation that before his departure Harper had read another article to her about Coley, the surgeon in New York. Coley's daughter had been looking for more patients for him to cure, 'with advanced, surgically inoperable cancers.'

'Who ever heard of such reassurance in treating such a devastating illness?' Harper had asked her with incredulity.

Maybe it's time to speak again to Smellie in Edinburgh.

Thankfully, Hannah's sister Jeannie was giving the girls a conducted tour of the farms when she arrived back from Elgin. She could hear the cacophony of geese over at the pond. From the direction of the noise, she guessed her daughters' location was down the hill towards the Old House.

Hannah tied the garrons, leaving them hitched. She used her handkerchief to wipe the seat of the rig, rinsing it in the water trough in the yard several times to avoid leaving traces of blood that would be noticed. She was glad to find that all the children had gone out.

Great Gran Han had been given the task of overseeing the fun and games with Jeannie's help and Jessie was preparing a late lunch.

Hannah begged her to postpone that, to "heat a cauldron of bath water." Jessie knew not to ask why, but the look on her face was full of alarm. Within minutes Jessie had the huge enamelled pot warming on the range. Ten minutes later Hannah was kneeling up to her waist in a bath of ominously discoloured water. Jessie went to fill another cauldron without being asked.

On the train back to Edinburgh Harper felt slightly guilty, looking out of the window of the carriage at the awesomely beautiful mountains and forests of the Cairngorms. He could not help the insidious feeling that he was letting everybody down - family, employer and himself included. He had consolation only in knowing that the feeling was borne of an admission that he himself could simply not cope. This was the arrangement Hannah had chosen and the girls were desperate to see her. He had no choice but to keep coming back as frequently as his guilt would permit.

His life was beginning to move in a new direction. He had sacrificed his chosen career, taking a job that amounted to a compromise but now planned to earn as much money as he could. Although he had not studied Maths since leaving school, Harper recalled the pleasure he'd derived from working out simultaneous equations at the age of ten in his first algebra lessons. Now he had begun to study at night school for examinations as a Life Assurance Actuary, easily completing a year's set work in six months.

He had also become a slave to routine. Part of every evening had to be devoted to study. Making supper, washing up then putting pots and pans away was not an option for him. There just weren't enough hours in the day. He owed a debt of gratitude to Margaret Kemp, who eagerly stood in for Hannah in this regard.

Margaret Kemp. He settled on the image he had in his mind of this reserved and efficient young woman, black hair tied back showing her impassive face and high forehead, with a beauty spot on her right cheek. In so many ways she was different from his wife yet he found her interesting, if not alluring. By any standard she was smoulderingly attractive, with penetrating sky-blue eyes, tight cheeks and fulsome, pretty lips. She was petite but well-proportioned, with voluptuously large breasts. For sophisticated Edinburgh however, Margaret was what would be termed straight laced.

Harper wondered idly why she was unattached. He could see that her quiet assertiveness might put off a young man of equivalent years. She was after all only eighteen. He decided that Margaret was too self-assured and outspoken to be taken for granted. Anyone who got involved with her on a casual basis might find it difficult to extricate themselves. Perhaps she was too young to worry about commitment. Maybe she was taking her time, until she made her mark professionally. Increasing numbers of women were doing just that. Also as single-mindedly, women were becoming ever more politically astute in their career choices.

The young woman was smart and cool and above all bloody good at what she did. Both socially and professionally she had shown unstinting commitment to his family since Hannah had been forced to retreat to Rothiemay. Harper was grateful to her and tacitly, he had been dependent upon her.

In his defensive state of mind Harper resolved to avoid all the internecine complications of Margaret Kemps' involvement in looking after him, while the rest of the family were away during the summer. She was a qualified children's nurse, not a housemaid. He felt it inappropriate to beg her to do his laundry and wash his pots.

He resolved to organise his affairs to live as much as possible on his expense account, eating hotel food and subscribing to in-house valeting and laundry services whenever a convenient overnight could be planned. In the interim he would gladly pay Margaret a retainer for doing nothing. She could occupy herself, no doubt, in the meantime.

Take a summer holiday.

He would explain all this to her in the morning when she called.

Margaret arrived at eight thirty on the dot on the morning of Monday the ninth of July. She was washed, groomed and wearing just a touch of lipstick and makeup, as if presenting herself for an internal job interview with clear likelihood of promotion. She had put on an expensive scent, no doubt reserved for special occasions. Her forget-me-not blue eyes were full of enthusiasm.

Harper made Margaret a cup of tea and they sat together self-consciously in the living room, amid soft toys and colouring books. There was evidence of a hasty meal bought from the fish and chip shop at Parson's Green after Harper's late return on Sunday evening. His disarming excuses met with a knowing smile. The sudden unspoken awkwardness between them melted with Margaret's discovery of a bendy rubber clown, shoved down the back of her cushion on the sofa.

They both smiled and laughed about Elsie's perennial favourite, repeating some of the circus dialogue she had with 'Mr Bendy'. Margaret folded her legs to one side, unselfconsciously drawing attention to the tight contours of her neat hips. As she sipped her tea she looked over her cup into Mr Harper's inscrutable grey eyes.

As Harper explained all of his neat running-man deliberations to Margaret her angelic face instantly became distant and disapproving, as though a cloud had passed over the brilliance of the sun on the finest day of summer. But her head did not go down.

What was not apparent was the fact that she was hurt by the implication that Harper did not need her. It occurred to the girl that he may even have decided to avoid her. There was a greater social dimension to this, Margaret felt which John Harper just could not see.

Hannah had taken a lot of trouble to find out about Margaret, befriending her family who lived at nearby Northfield. For the past year there had been a sense of a growing contract between the two women. Margaret thought the world of Hannah and her bairns, and fully understood the heart-rending crisis the family were undergoing. But she could have been earning more at the Royal Children's Hospital on Sciennes' Road.

Margaret Kemp openly admired John Harper. Everyone she mentioned him to thought he was as wonderful as she did. Now all that history seemed to amount to nothing. Hannah and the girls were gone for the summer and it transpired Harper was actually prepared to pay to keep her out of his way.

She wanted to ask when Elsie and Elizabeth would return but even that might seem presumptuous now. She was being dismissed. All that was left to her was to leave immediately with her dignity intact. Harper found it curious that Margaret did not ask the obvious questions and was a little perplexed at the flash of heat that she left behind, as she stood up and promptly strode away, "Well, if there's nothing more I can do for you, I'll be on my way," she stated in a clipped tone without looking at him. She deftly latched the wrought iron gate at the end of the short pathway, without a backward glance or a smile.

"Jesus!" whispered Harper, standing in the doorway with his mouth open, as Margaret's pace quickened. Her low heels resounded briskly on the pavement, despite the steep downward gradient of the hill, "What have I done now?" Harper groaned to himself, "I can't be right for being wrong. I'll have to sit down and figure this one out too!"

The pretty children's nurse returned in a day or two, or maybe it was three - Harper wasn't sure of the passage of time so pre-occupied was he with work and study. She took off her coat without comment and went straight into the kitchen where she immediately began to wash dishes that he had allowed to pile up in the sink.

"No, don't say it! You're still paying me for God's sake," she answered vigorously when he objected, "I should be here ironing your shirts and making your supper, or at the very least laying in your supplies for the weekends." He leant against the door-frame, looking mildly confused.

"You're making me feel guilty!" she added, turning her sweet face up to look at him, like a flower following the track of the sun, "And I'm not about to resign."

In that instant Harper was struck by Margaret Kemp's forthrightness. She was countermanding him. There was nothing else to do but dismiss her on the pretext of neighbourhood gossip about sexual proclivities, or magnanimously accept her point of view.

"Hmm, oh very well," came the reply that let Margaret back into Harper's Spartan scene.

"Seriously now, what can I be doing to justify this arrangement? I may as well go back to nursing if you don't occupy my time," Margaret demanded, looking over her shoulder with a challenging tone. Molly the cat searched the young woman's face from where she waited next to her empty food bowl, "You know, I think those girls will never forgive you if this beautiful cat runs away, due to your not being here to feed her!"

Harper had been thinking very clearly about Margaret in her absence and concluded that there was much that needed to be left unsaid. Not least that she had earned his respect and that he had genuinely missed her as a friend. She was very special and clearly there was electricity flowing between them but to even tacitly recognise it, would be to kill it where it stood. Let it be what it would. Harper would never admit his attraction to Margaret to anyone, nor ever overtly encourage it.

Harper had grown World-weary and grim. He longed for that quality of simple happiness which children have when they are secure and don't need to worry. He wished Margaret would find a boyfriend. Conscious of the need to put up mental barriers, he fully accepted that he found the young woman intensely attractive.

Other than that, like many other more mature women he knew, she meant nothing to him, compared to his love for Hannah. Each of them had evidently rehearsed a rapprochement however and his reply was as ready and as easy as hers, "Well, look, the simplest thing would be for me to leave a list of jobs for you to do. I'll have to think about what precisely I might need and on which days. My routines vary so much, depending upon where I travel. The first thing you should do is get a key cut. I happen to agree with you about Molly. You have actually touched upon my worst nightmare."

He smiled, reaching into his pocket for his front door key. He slid it across the kitchen table from where he now sat.

"Well if you need to make a list, you could do it now while I go and get the key," suggested Margaret, leaving immediately with an irrepressible smile on her neat little face.

The first thing Harper had done when the girls went to Rothiemay was to plan a working itinerary that might take him to the north of Scotland as frequently as possible, without it becoming obvious to Marlene in Accounts who authorised his travel expenses.

Marlene was a working class girl whose quite stunning beauty and fine character had brought her marriage with family commitments at an unwarranted early age. Now she was a single woman with only one son, still in his late teens, to worry about. High intelligence and opportunity had brought her a safe career in her late thirties. At one point Marlene had worked in the staff canteen at Kennington's. She was always noted for her friendliness and efficiency, tempered by discriminating, maternal generosity. Everyone who saw her smart respectful manner approved of it - that and her dancer's legs and magnificent chest. When the time was right, Marlene Gibson, formerly Baxter, gave up her bangers and mash to sign up for a sandwich course at St Margaret's Women's College. Kennington's had been only too glad to allow paid leave and talk to her prospectively of advancement.

Now she had a degree in Financial Accounting and was learning daily on the job. Compared to 'The Old Tay Bridge' as some of the younger reps rudely styled Maia Stratton, the Accounts Department Supervisor who made every period-end a time of crisis - Marlene was a breath of fresh air. Instinctively Harper would have liked to have chatted more with Marlene, even though she was fifteen years his senior. She was still strikingly attractive yet down to earth and amenable. She was open and garrulous – happy to exchange personal stories although Harper sought to avoid divulging too much about his own situation to her.

What he did do however was seek official approval from the bosses making it clear to Marlene also that his intention was to work the homespun suppliers in the North and West of Scotland. Purportedly his ambit was to see what variety or additions might be added to perennially popular lines of linens, plaids and knitwear. It might offer cover for visiting Hannah - if he was in Inverness or Aberdeen, Caithness or Fort William for concurrent business purposes.

He planned to pay the additional rail fares to Huntly, Elgin, Keith or Rothiemay out of his own pocket to avoid suspicion, or simply break his journey in any of these places accessible to Ramsburn for a favoured stop-over. He would make a point of booking into the Station Hotels in each town to get receipts, even if he did not actually spend the night there.

Harper spent a weekend mapping out his annual rolling plan for visiting Hannah, while spotting lucrative or neglected accounts from perusal of the monthly ledgers. At all costs he intended to keep his end up, if necessary by happily 'stuffing-up' his account clients with goods they might take a year to sell.

Stratton was superficially pleased with his apparently analytical approach and Marlene began to anticipate the locations he would frequent. It was all beneficial to the home economy and less travelling than visits to some of the English customers. The bosses told Harper they were happy with his focus on traditional suppliers and retailers. Above all Harper decided he just needed to outscore Roger Dewhirst in terms of new business generated over the fiscal year. Roger had now retired to Yorkshire so Marlene was happy to give Harper a listing of all his former clients.

When Harper was ready to visit Hannah again, he borrowed the Strong-room key from Marlene, at the beginning of a new accounting month. He knew she would have completed her balances and not be inclined to throw him out, so he devoted an entire morning to the books, confirming what he had gleaned so far. The plan was to apply his combined Police and Actuarial training to get an overall picture of Purchasing and Sales activity for the entire company – not just the North of Scotland. There would come a time when he had to compensate for low level activity.

He made notes for future scheduling of his own itinerary, with an eye to neglected suppliers or sales outlets anywhere near Rothiemay. He made reference to a fold-away map of Great Britain, noting railway stations and addresses. The Accounts Department staff all thought he was as keen as mustard which indirectly he was.

When one of the Partners, Mr Soutar met Harper in the sanctum sanctorum, sitting at his very own work table, Harper smiled and chatted with him affably. Soutar looked at Harper inquisitively over his reading glasses.

The Finance Director was cradling a high quality paper file in his arms, as lovingly as any mother with her firstborn. Harper thought Soutar looked like a taciturn waiter from a third class hotel restaurant but immediately shunned this illusion as dangerously misleading.

For some strange reason Harper thought instead of the strangely emasculating ritual Chambers had talked him into at the Masonic Hall a year ago, of the ridiculous apron and blindfold he had been obliged to wear when the time came for his initiation. Harper tried hard not to smile as this might have betrayed his humorous impression of the old man.

Soutar continued to look at him questioningly. In that moment of scrutiny as their eyes locked, Harper imagined the mechanical whirring of Babbage's Difference Engine. He could sense in Mr Soutar's massive, furrowed head and musty suit a hint of the magic of Merlin. He felt obliged to offer some explanation beyond the mundane as to his presence in the Period End lock-up. Harper needed to do this without making it obvious to Mr Soutar that he was planning to cover his tracks.

Judging from the unsmiling scrutiny of the old man's watery grey eyes, magnified through thick bifocals, Mr Soutar probably already suspected Harper of fraudulent activity. In anticipation of such rightful distrust Harper genially asserted, "I have an open duality of interest, Sir," which seemed to meet Soutar's suspicion half way, "Prompting me to understand the inner workings of the business - for personal reasons, as, like Mrs Gibson in Accounts, I too am studying at night school."

"Well it's certainly very nice to meet you, Harper. We don't often get visitors up here," Soutar intimated with Benedictine warmth and a tinge of sorrow. He lowered his right forearm with hydraulic precision, still clutching the secret numbers to his chest. They exchanged Masonic hand-shakes as Harper tried to sound as ingenuous as possible, "You're very kind sir. I will come and ask Marlene for the key again, if I may. Although never, I assure you, near the end of the month, or the fiscal year. I've heard there are huge seasonal fluctuations in the clothing and drapery industries. I want to be in the right place at the right time." Soutar seemed appeased but he merely grunted, before sloping off to his rosewood panelled office with the top-secret information.

Harper wondered idly what was in the slim file, reflecting that men like Soutar only ever think in terms of perspectives and probability, like a biologist studying Gannets on a cliff face.

No matter how hard I work to impress them or be noticed as a worthy employee, they will still take me for granted, like all the others.

Harper knew that he would always be a cipher, representing a very small quotient in the definitive algebra of Jenner's vast commerce. He concluded with a wry smile that the file was most likely Soutar's personal expense account. Harper decided to beat a retreat.

As he emerged from the Ledger Room, he could hear Marlene's voice raised in rapturous tones from within Soutar's office. Harper thought he heard Marlene say, "Oo-oh yes . . . she will love that!" She had just taken Mr Soutar a cup of his favourite Earl Grey. He had no secretary as he was never available to outsiders, although the other Directors knew where to find him. Mostly they too avoided the Finance Director, as they generally didn't want to hear what he had to say about stringencies.

Marlene emerged with a smile on her Hellenic face, gently clicking the elegantly figured door shut behind her. Harper looked at her quizzically across the red and gold Indian rug between them. The hotel impression resurfaced, this time with different, more appropriate connotations in which Mr Soutar was the philanthropic owner-manager.

"Anniversary present for his wife," Marlene whispered huskily, shaking her hand as if it were injured. Harper felt an involuntary sexual frisson shout in his abdomen. Marlene Gibson was very like Hannah he realised. He shook his head as though to say, "I have no idea what you are talking about."

Marlene walked over to him with a smile of voluptuous intrigue on her lovely face. Her indigo eyes momentarily searched Harper's, then she whispered warmly into his ear, "The old bugger is buying her a three carat diamond ring. That was the jeweller's report for his insurer. You can't really tell much from a photograph but I'll bet it will put a smile on her face."

Harper was about to say, "His too I imagine," but remembered the need to maintain formality with Marlene. He just gazed at her instead. One of the accounting clerks looked up from his invoicing and Marlene turned her back on him. Looking at Harper she put a finger up to her mouth.

"Hmm, no, I won't say a word." Harper winked at Marlene and gave her a warm smile, which meant a lot more than he could say. Marlene's eyes followed Harper with delight as he walked purposively to the lift.

In the early morning following Hannah's trip to see Mitton, her fourteen year old step-sister Jeannie Wilson had been given respite from normal chores and duties of care for her three nieces. She was sent by her mother Jessie post haste to, "Fetch Dr Payton. Try to get him before he sets off on his rounds." Her younger sisters Betsy and Elsie Wilson watched Jeannie running down the lane. All of them loved their step-sister and they realised she was seriously ill. Jessie sat down with little Hannah to read to her and keep her distracted from the mounting concern for her mother. Who knew where Payton would be if there had not been a queue of locals in his surgery? He had given express instructions to Jessie Wilson to, "Come and get me if Hannah needs urgent attention." But his rounds covered a vast area, and Payton was always in demand. Jeannie might not be back for some time.

Great Gran had taken the two older Harper girls as she did each morning, to feed the geese and hens and to collect any eggs laid overnight. Sometimes the sheep dogs, Sally and Tex would come along to round up any lambs marked for slaughter. Elsie and Elizabeth marvelled at how Great Gran could work the dogs so efficiently with her whistles and throaty calls. The dogs understood routine better than the children did. If one was left behind in the kennel, it would whine and yap until released to join in with the other. The collies were enthusiastic and vital in all their working. Strict discipline made them consistent and obedient.

Great Gran showed Elsie and Elizabeth trophies she had won from many years of breeding sheep and also from exhibiting the skills of her dogs in round-up competitions. All four walls of the sheep-shed were covered in plaques above head height. There was always a pile of clean bedding-straw ready for a sick or pregnant ewe, or unexpected bad weather that could come at virtually any time of the year. The Harper girls were quietly amazed by the old lady in her corduroy pants and trilby as she pointed out these essential features. She always wore a sleeveless sheepskin, over an Arran wool seaman's pullover. A glimpse of Great Gran Han approaching from the house carried the feeling of happiness itself.

Great Gran Han was handsome, redoubtable and proud in her life-long pastoral element. Any of the eight children would flock around her in joy, with their requests for advice and offers of assistance. She was the most natural teacher there ever could be, never once having to scold or raise her voice. The summer days of '94 sang with enthusiasm, echoing with the ecstatic voices of happy bairns.

In the way of children everywhere her seven granddaughters and grandson bombarded her with a thousand questions. If they were ill-expressed or too complex to answer without tiresome qualification, Great Gran Han condensed problems for them in a simple way.

"Great Gran . . . why do the sheep run from the dogs?" asked Elsie, her permanently smiling, dark eyes for once positing a notion of doubt.

"Oh, it's in a dog's nature to kill sheep my dear. But these dogs have it in them to always be obedient to human masters, which is a stronger, learned behaviour."

"So they just round them up?"

"Yes, Elsie dear."

Great Gran was always moving, and fair haired, green-eyed Elizabeth, usually traipsing far behind, was now running to keep up.

"Why?" Elizabeth was on a quest to know everything and 'why?' was the foremost of her six friends. She had realised early on that questions held the key to the world of adults. 'Why?' always met with a response – usually a smile and an explanation. Elizabeth had Great Gran Han on the hook.

"Why do roosters fight each other?" demanded Elizabeth as they approached the wired-off run.

"Hmm, to hold onto their share, like all of mankind," expounded Great Gran as she bent down to fill a feeding pail from the seed bin,

"You mean their share of the grains?" ventured Elsie, picking up the theme.

"Yes, and their territory. Their roost and their favourite place in the sun . . . they fight to be the proudest cock, with the pick o' the hens."

"They're too busy fighting to eat!" observed Elsie.

"Yeah. They're too busy fighting to eat!" echoed Elizabeth.

"Hmm. I suppose they're not unlike men everywhere dears, they live for their pride."

"You mean like Frank?" asked Elizabeth. Elsie and Elizabeth both had an unspeakable crush on fourteen year old Frank, so this time there was no need for the echo.

"Oh Frank is still a boy, but fighting for his pride may soon come to him too." The girls were not entirely sure what Great Gran was talking about but assumed it was the purest wisdom. Later that day the girls would conspire with Elsie Wilson to make a point of warning off Frank for, "being too proud and starting fights with Jeannie and Betsy." They'd all heard him bossing his sisters to, "keep away from the trucks," when he and Ewan Harper had started the timber yard in the old quarry.

In the meantime they mused for a while in the pure morning chill, looking with satisfaction one to the other as they drank in the living energy of the moisture laden air. The first warmth of the fat summer sun caressed their bonny cheeks as its rays peeked through the canopy of the Rookery. Elsie and Elizabeth ran after Great Gran Han to delve in her pail for handfuls of grain to scatter for the poultry and geese.

"Come on now ladies, keep up wi' me . . . there's work to be done around here!" shouted Great Gran to the hens still inside the hut. The girls squealed with delight, repeating her call to the roosting hens. They knew to stand far enough away from the door to allow the hens to run through from their hut into the grassy compound. Today it was Elizabeth's turn to carry the egg basket. She raced back to the gate where she had put it down.

"Why are the dog kennels next to the hen's house, Great Gran?" resumed Elsie with a thoughtful tone.

"Oh, now there's a good one. You'll make a fine farmer's wife one day. But I'll not tell ye straight out. See if you can find a reason –

245

maybe you ask your little sister if she knows. Now be gentle as you approach the creatures. You never want to frighten them." Great Gran nodded towards the place where the Ram's Burn languished in a hollow to form a shallow pond. She handed the grain pail to Elsie as she opened the gate for them.

As Elsie and Elizabeth moved on to feed the geese their debate about the dogs could be heard from the hen compound where Great Gran had held back, wishing to avoid close observation by the girls. She turned into the corner to hide her movement, swiftly despatching the bird she had selected for supper. She muttered thanks to the Almighty as she emerged from the hut with the lifeless hen swinging from her right hand. In that instant the old lady saw that little Hannah had wandered down from the farmhouse with Jessie to join them in their rounds. The child had been with her in the hen house as she had wrung the hen's neck. She had been invisible to Great Gran, doubled over gently stroking a laying hen by the door of the shed. Great Gran tried to act naturally but had a momentary sense of being trapped in time. The old lady's heart leaped into her mouth as the bairn gazed at her.

"Why did you kill it Great Gran? Was it bad?" enquired the innocent.

"Oh no, child. Its goodness was the death of it!"

The girls walked in silence up the lane ahead of Great Gran and Jessie. The geese had taken over the conversation, with their objections to all things human. No-one could overhear as Jessie explained Hannah's relapse to her mother. The annoyance of the gaggle had been sparked by the livestock man Alex Harper, now working among the sheep in an adjacent field with the collies, Tex and Sally. When the chores with the geese were completed and all the fresh eggs retrieved, the girls turned back along the lane in time to witness the completion of the cut out.

Well rounded and vigorous sisters Kate and Fiona Robertson stood by the tail board of the covered wagon like Russian dolls, as half a dozen sheep raced up onto the bed of the steam-driven truck.

Respectful pleasantries were exchanged between the young ladies and the drover, who had a sparkle in his eye for adolescent Kate.

Then Little Hannah spoke up, "Them's bastard dogs Great Gran, biting they poor wee sheep!" She pointed accusingly with the middle finger of her right hand at the culprits. The dogs actually looked mortified, their tongues lolling as they looked back at the toddler, seemingly in dismay at her disapproval of their technique with the sheep. The drover, Jimmy Murdoch, was deeply impressed. A smile played across his leathered face as he kicked home the bolts, suppressing a belly laugh. Eyes aglow with humour, Murdoch pursed his lips to speak but thought better of it. Instead he reached into his pocket for his pipe and tobacco.

Frank Wilson laughed raucously though, at Little Hannah's bald profanity. Tall and loose limbed like his father had been, Frank was at an age now when he felt he could challenge everyone and everything. The girls who loved him laughed because he laughed. In fact with the exception of the earnest Little Han, they all laughed for over a minute, though Great Gran Han cautioned them not to repeat the bad word. They were all equally relieved that Jessie who'd hurried back to her charge at the farmhouse had not heard it because they had known instantly there would be an inquisition about Little Hannah's use of playground language, given that she'd not yet had an opportunity to learn it on the playground.

As ever Great Gran saved everyone's embarrassment, speaking warmly through a swell of delight at the innocent's singular view of the world, "Oh don't worry dear. The dogs are only nipping the sheep's ankles to make them behave."

"Oh, but it just hurts so much!" insisted the tiny, empathetic observer. They all stared at her – people and dogs and sheep as the sun climbed gallantly into his reclaimed sky. The old hen's opaque eyes saw nothing, as the creature swung upside down above the dusty lane in the hiatus.

Only Great Gran Han registered the true depth of concern in the child's words. As if to confirm her concerns, Dr Payton arrived with

Jeannie just as they got back to the farmhouse with the hen and the fresh eggs. Seeing the women were busy with their chores he went straight in to see his patient. Great Gran Han took Jessie to one side, to intimate her worry about the youngest child's evident exposure to her mother's voiced suffering.

Well established now as the family mascot, Hannah was the little one who watched her elders, young and old from the cobbled yard or the market-garden where she would dig with her trowel. Jessie looked over her shoulder to ensure they were not overheard before speaking, "Ma, I feel it would be wise to begin to wean Little Hannah away from her mother's side. From now on we must plan to distract, or occupy the bairn as much as possible. I will try to help you."

"Maybe we can ask Jeannie, now that she's left school?"

"I agree, if we can swear her to secrecy. It's essential the child should no' witness scenes o' distress like this morning! She needs as many attachments, additional tae her mother, as possible."

"Oh, dear Lord. You're right Jessie, soon she may need them all." The adults continued speaking in their dispassionate code, relaxing at night when the bairns had all gone to bed. Jeannie Wilson had become a problem though. Although not part of the adult circle, she already knew too much - which tended then to be passed on in secret to eleven year old Betsy, who in turn tended to repeat things she'd overheard to Kate and Fiona Robertson as well as their eight year old half-sister Elsie. Elsie in turn briefed the Harpers about their mother's medical dilemma and long term prognosis. All were sworn to secrecy yet everyone knew – apart from Frank.

So Jessie and Great Gran Han paraphrased their conversation, skipping past the unthinkable as only women can do. Their topic for tonight, "Where did she get it from?" Little Hannah was learning so fast, they must not take her innocence for granted. Their planned strategies for distracting the bairn were unequivocal, though they laughed heartily at her condemnation of poor Tex and Sally.

Harper came the following weekend bearing gifts for all. Colouring books and crayons for his three girls. Large boxes of Edinburgh Rock for their five aunties and one uncle – Hannah's adoptive sisters and brother. At night the adults had an open, garrulous family conference and the children listened from their bedrooms as all children do when three generations of adults are discussing important matters into the small hours of the morning. Without knowing the precise details they sublimated the quality of concerned adult voices overheard in conference, with pleading objections in response from their mother. All the Wilson, Robertson and Harper children knew that there was something seriously wrong with Hannah's health. They got out of bed each night to listen from the top three steps of the stairs. Surprisingly they were never discovered although little Hannah joined them, laughing at what she thought was a great game and talking too loud in her excitement.

Encouraged by her young aunties to 'do something naughty for once in yer life', Elsie Harper sneaked two pieces of shortbread from the kitchen which took all Jeannie's maternal skill to divide equally. Elizabeth, the natural magpie, brought chocolate and Edinburgh Rock which she secreted under her pillow until it was assumed everyone was fast asleep. Jeannie Wilson, a youthful model of her dark, comely mother daily assumed the credibility of a young adult. When she declared Elizabeth to have, "An appetite like a horse," everyone laughed but it fit with the growing legend of her niece's prolific energy and eagerness at meal times.

Elsie Wilson taught the Harpers how to tell the time in order to gauge when the adults might retire. Elsie knew when there was an increased danger of getting caught and more crucially when to distribute the smuggled treats for a midnight feast. Betsy brought her own special home-made lemonade which had to be drunk from the bottle with great care, "so it disnae shoot up yer nose," she told them.

All six of the young aunties, allowed to sleep over with their nieces on special occasions if they chose to, waited on the landing and stairs with board school discipline for the stroke of twelve. Then they shared out the goodies with earnest whispers while still eavesdropping. The adults talked so loud and drank so much tea and whisky that they never once suspected being overheard.

The children heard snippets of a worrying discussion about lack of money. There was talk of a possible trip to New York. Everyone but Harper said this was 'too much to afford and pointless if the same treatment can be done here.' Harper argued the case in favour of, 'the brilliant American doctor' but their ma was overheard saying very clearly, "I would rather die in my own home."

There it was, Hannah was dying! All eight of them were shocked to the core. Elsie Harper said her dad reported to them that New York was in England – he had been there with Roger Dewhirst, but Betsy Wilson who was nearly twelve, insisted, "I've seen it on a map and it's definitely in America."

Profound secret worries translated into the girl's play, their diaries and pictures. The last option open to them was to admit to the adults that they knew, so instead they whispered in corners or out in the lawned garden behind the house. Asking Great Gran Han directly would invite probing questions, to possibly give away the nightly midnight feast on the stairs. Instead they discussed ways of helping Hannah and Harper by setting up bric-a-brac market-stall at the end of the lane where there was always commercial traffic, as well as people young and old walking to and from the farm worker's cottages up the road on the right.

Eventually they voted democratically on involving Great Gran Han who Betsy said, 'would never give a secret away'. As an honorary 'grown up bairn,' she was sworn to secrecy with earnest whispers in her ear from Elsie Harper, as the old lady brushed out her long hair, platting and tying it into a neat circle like a medieval Queen. In the gravity of a desperate attempt to save Hannah, Elsie Wilson invited

Great Gran to surrender her antique Grandfather clock, which no longer kept time. The classic timepiece had been an anniversary gift from her 'Dear Old Drummond' but Jessie often said it was 'a waste of space.' Great Gran Han decided to keep the clock but managed a guffaw promising the girls, "Your secret is safe with me." She indulged them in helping to find unwanted items for the stall, telling herself that at least it was a constructive way of involving them in the harsh reality, "without pestering their mother."

In turn Great Gran Han bound them to the agreement that secrecy must work both ways, "You must not talk about these worrying matters – that's the best way to help your mammy to get well," she insisted. With help from little Hannah in rooting through the kitchen and dining room cupboards she quickly found a chipped Staffordshire sugar bowl for them, with a silver plated 'Man Spoon' that had begun to tarnish. She lent them an old sewing table with an embroidered cloth to present their clearance sale on for passers-by.

Betsy Wilson suspected that for once her Grandmother's heart was not in the game. From Jeannie's more mature perspective the old girl had clearly begun to lose her fabled canniness where the Harper girls were concerned. Maybe she was compensating for an underlying sense of guilt in respect to Frank's inheritance.

Hannah meanwhile had taken to her room. Even Little Hannah was diverted away from visiting her during the latest crisis although to all appearances she seemed perfectly normal – sitting up in bed reading or crocheting. Jessie's sighs at the washing tub gave the lie however. Occasionally the captivating phrases of a bright mazurka or *l' Heroique* would echo from the sitting room across the summer fields. The girls would come running, "Mammy's up! Mammy's up!" they cried, running round the end of the cobbled yard, only to be intercepted and shushed by Granny Jessie.

But every evening an hour before their bedtime Hannah would emerge from her convalescence to sit and read a story with all three of her bairns around her on the sofa. They would be obliged to give an account of all they had seen and done that day. Great Gran Han knew it was only a matter of time before one of them would slip onto the topic of charitable fund raising.

Some of the younger children from the farm cottages up the road, who were allowed an hour or two away from routines which they would not normally be available for during school days, came to join in the clearance sale. They took it just as seriously as the Wilsons, Robertsons and Harpers.

Mrs Grant used it as an opportunity to have a good clear out of clutter although she ended up with unwanted items bought by her unwitting husband and son. She had sent her daughter Maggie with a sensational box of ornaments.

Passing traders and delivery men all expressed indulgent interest in the novelties displayed at the end of the lane. When the girls had sworn them in on the Holy Bible before explaining what it was all in aid of, they reached into their pockets to a man. One or two made a mental note to sweep straight past the gate without slowing down the next time they were passing. But once word got round the nearby farms and villages, most stopped again nonetheless - with items of chipped porcelain, unwanted vases, home-made jam or knitwear.

Several of them fell for the embarrassingly poignant hard luck story. Though all vowed to keep the secret, word spread into the local community of Milltown of Rothiemay. Most of the working men were interested in purchasing a slice of GGH's outstanding Victoria sponge cake or a butterfly bun, washed down with lemonade or Ginger beer which Betsy produced over at the Old House, with security arrangements rivalling a supplier for the Royal Mint.

Even the most parsimonious of the delivery and collection waggoners delved into their breechs for a farthing, feeling obliged to select some little item in exchange.

"I think I micht tak' this," decided Fraser Campbell, the Barley man, holding up a flouncing porcelain figure with a glued on foot,

"Fer the wife, ken. Aw, she'll lo' that, so she will lassies. Many thanks noo!" he said dropping a ha'penny into their bowl.

In retrospect it was no surprise that Jessie didn't notice and promptly intervene. As ever, there was just too much activity around the farm for her to pay attention to anything additional. For her part she had not the faintest idea what the girls were up to. Their mother Hannah, had she known, would have been mortified.

The Minister, Reverend Blair got word of the local children's need for an extension of the Third Love. He decided to raise the matter discreetly with the Standing Church Committee of his dutiful Parish Assembly, to make ready for concerted intervention.

On the third day of the girl's secret fund raising activity a tall hugely powerful man wearing a bowler hat, came walking from the direction of the crossroads at Rothiemay. Challenged by the zealous Betsy he immediately assented to the secret accord, swearing on King James' Bible like he was used to giving evidence in court. The man bought lemonade and three buns. Quenching his thirst while sitting on the fence observing, he soaked up Elizabeth and Elsie's explanation. He asked discreet, open questions in a polite manner which encouraged them to talk about their dad's best intentions. Looking around in all directions, to see if they were observed he went on to promise further financial assistance if they in turn told him everything. He asked lots of questions about why they were selling off their possessions but seemed a little doubtful in respect to the quality of their home-made attire, venturing to suggest, "None of you girls look poor." He pressed Elizabeth for details of their trip to America and how soon it would be.

"My daddy wants us all to go. But they're no' coming," she said, pointing to Betsy and Elsie Wilson and her half-sisters Kate and Fiona, "It's desperately urgent." She intimated with the gravity of four going on forty. If we don't go to New York now, we may never get another chance!" she added, by way of a formal quotation.

"And where is your daddy now?"

253

"Oh, he's working the accounts up here in the north, so he can get here quick if there's an emergency! But Kennington's might sack him if they find out."

Curiously the big man, who was certainly not from round Milltown, didn't smile with benign embarrassment at that point, like all the others had done. His eyes seemed to darken with an inner secret of his own. The charity-stall sales team watched the man walk off, concluding, "He's a stranger in the area." He stopped at the end of the row of cottages where the Grants lived, to take a notepad and pencil out of his pocket and stand for a time looking away from them at the hills flanking the river Deveron. Elsie said he was sketching and she would have given him one of hers, "if only he'd asked." Eventually the girls lost interest in the big man, Kate Robertson deciding in conclusion, "He must be a burglar, because he's English. Alex Harper says they steal everything."

As the days wore on the remarkable bond between Great Gran Han and Little Han began to grow. It became a topic of interest for all. The older children, including nominal aunties and uncles Jeannie, Betsy, Kate, Fiona, Elsie and Frank, began to make their own inferences about this relationship - generally magnanimous rather than unfavourable.

Like all children, the girls were very observant, and at times intensely competitive and jealous. Ramsburn in the summer of 1894 was a melting pot of female-oriented social learning – always tolerant and synchronous, even when any of the bairns slipped out of the mould of being a good little girl. So it came as no surprise that the toddler got special treatment.

When Little Han cried, Great Gran picked her up. When she unearthed some of the potatoes instead of burying them deeper as everyone knows, much to Frank's chagrin as it was his job to manage the market garden, Great Gran explained to the mite about seasons - rain, sun and harvest.

Equally attentive when she cried with toothache as when she frequently skinned her knees, Great Gran Han soothed Little Han with cool drinks in the night and consoled her with emollient cream and hugs in the day. She was the one who ran to 'kiss it better' and to carry her wounded princess back to the house whenever she came to grief. Sitting with her on the wall when Little Han was too tired to walk up to the sheep pasture, she supported her, although it was the child who had insisted on following the dogs. In essence Little Han was copying her mum - exploring what Great Gran might do to help if a body was too tired to walk for themselves. Great Gran was humiliated by Little Han's mimicry and insight.

"Ohoof! My back is breaking!" she pleaded, rubbing her hand on her forehead, placing the other on her tiny hip – this after helping to carry a small basket of eggs into the kitchen from the hen yard. She placed them signally on the kitchen floor, ready to be checked prior to collection by the egg man. Sorrow had impinged so greatly Great Gran Han did not even laugh, though her first reaction was to split her sides.

Jessie turned from the sink in awe of the toddler, her mouth agape as she looked at the old lady removing her boots in the doorway. Great Gran put a characteristic hand to her mouth as tears welled in her eyes for the child's precocious wisdom and ability to act out her concerns. The old lady's throat tightened. She waved her hand at her daughter to be silent, feeling a complex and beautiful kind of distress welling up inside.

"Here Granny, wash this one now, it's no' cracked." Little Han passed the first of the eggs up to Jessie for inspection. In that moment, Great Gran Han was startled to glance over her shoulder to the half door, open at the top. There waiting for welcome was the beatific visage of 'The Man in Black' – none other than Reverend Jim Blair. To Great Gran Hannah he looked every inch the model of Correggio's *Ecce Homo,* without of course the crown of thorns.

"Good morning ladies. I trust I find you all in good spirits?" asked Jim, by way of announcing his presence. Turning to greet him with a warm smile, the old lady had a sudden nervous feeling that the game was up for her little fund raisers.

When Harper visited the following weekend Hannah's condition had stabilised. Great Gran instigated trips: to Dufftown to Wood and Henry the photographers, for the Harper's to have family images taken at her expense and then the following day to Elgin – purportedly to see ruins of the fine cathedral there, 'The Lantern of The North'. She even prevailed upon Jessie to take a day off.

As always Jessie needed to make herself busy around the farm so she said, but Harper insisted that the girls were too much for Great Gran and fourteen year old Jeannie Wilson to handle. Harper gave Great Gran the money for the rail fares. Taking the hint that the couple needed time together to discuss the future, Jessie agreed to go along too.

On a fine summer day the girls drew coloured pictures, made brass rubbings and picnicked by the river Lossie. In truth Great Gran's motive for the trip to Elgin had not been merely to entertain the children, but to relieve pressure on the couple. To let them walk together around the lanes and woodlands of Rothiemay, talking intimately without opinions offered by others.

The old lady had known all along that Harper was sensitive to this kind of intrusion. She knew that all views, welcome or otherwise had been freely expressed and well received recently. Now it was time to back off. Harper had grown up a lot. He was much less possessive of Hannah than a year ago. Great Gran Han was pleased to see such harmony in her family at a time of crisis.

Hannah walked with Harper through the forest and sat on a fallen tree where they had first made love, in a golden time which seemed a lifetime ago. They talked about Great Gran and Jessie, Frank, Jeannie and Betsy Wilson - in fact all the bairns, including Kate, Fiona and Elsie - their plans, their uncertain futures. They talked earnestly but distractedly about their own fine girls too, laughing in celebration of their innocence.

Hannah reasserted many kind thoughts about the Minister and local people – especially Dr Payton and his wife. Harper was concerned to find ways of reimbursing those who had been embarrassed into giving money to the girls but Hannah felt that it didn't matter. They decided not to caution them in a heavy handed manner in view of their good intentions. That would have been abhorrent to Hannah. Both sides of their street-sale transactions had been charitable, so no harm was done.

Cautiously Harper expressed gentle concern over Hannah's condition which for the most part she had avoided talking about. She had a persistent cough – 'bronchitis' supposedly, even though it was the warmest part of the summer.

"I'm fine Harper – fine. I was ill for a few days but now it is definitely breaking up."

Then there was a silence of a kind which often arose between them as each followed their own thoughts. Even in time of doubt they never argued and were invariably easy in one another's company. Unlike some married couples, Hannah and Harper realised that in fact there was no tension between them or need for either to fill the spaces in a conversation. They simply smiled as they gazed at one another in the place they had first fallen in love. Hannah's eyes clouded over, following her own trepidation. At length Harper asked her to voice her concern.

"Oh, you know I was just thinking. I really miss you Harper. This is going to drag on, whether I live or die," She picked up a stick and poked it into the dry soil. A wren landed horizontal to the trunk above her head, pecked out an insect and flitted away, "There's a cottage for sale down by the crossroads. It's small but it could be built onto. It has huge gardens and an outbuilding at the back. Maybe you could work at the saw mill if you are not interested in farming. Hugh would let you manage it for sure. It makes a fortune, even if they never spend any money on improvements. You could ask for a decent salary, whether he gives it to you or not. The girls would love it here."

Harper was silent for five minutes or more, he even shut his eyes to let the warm fragrant air of the forest soak into his lungs and brain. In his mind he saw Edinburgh where he re-ran the excitement of his first arrest. Then came a dozen other fleeting images in random sequence – the streets and the people, the laughable Masonic initiation with vows of charitable brotherhood and secrecy, the weekend at Portobello when he was shocked to discover Hannah's opium dependency – then a hundred lonely railway stop-overs, all set within the constant pressures of most precious time.

"Sentiment," he intoned flatly, thinking aloud. He opened his eyes to look at Hannah, before expressing himself more emphatically, "Sentiment rules everything. You know - what people do and why they do it. If you like, it's 'the appropriateness of feeling' - however that is communicated, which determines what happens to individual people."

He pondered for a moment before completing his thought, "Ken, woman I've been studying this. I often read about it in the papers. *Sentiment* – governs market forces and grand economic designs. When the sun shines, like today, the Co-op manager has tae have already stocked up on bread rolls, boiled ham and cream soda. Next day it rains and they aw want mince and tatties. If he disnae anticipate the weather and provide for their unmade choices afore they even look out of the window first thing in the morning, mind – they'll complain. He keeps getting it wrong – he'll be out of a job."

"That's interesting. I'm sure you're right," Hannah removed her shoe to drop out a flake of tree bark, "But how does that relate to my question though Harper?" She placed her shoe over her toes, wagging it tentatively.

Harper wished to avoid offending Hannah with an evasion. He did not intend to patronise her but felt their lives had been compromised enough by both family and her progressive illness. As so often before he tried to imagine the course of their lives without those compromises but where once he could speculate, now he felt bound by a host of impenetrable pre-conditions. All he knew was that he loved Hannah and their bairns. He thought for a moment before speaking dryly.

"We are all exploited to a greater or lesser degree, including the wealthy. You can't run away from it Hannah – its part of living. Look at Hugh and John, sitting back piling in the dough from their saw mill. They just cannae stop working. Neither of them have ever had a holiday, not even a week in Nairn. Money is just a function of their existence – like corn feed for the chickens. They'd rather spend it on new cutting discs, or a paddle wheel, than on themselves or any member of the family."

Bracing his arms behind his head, Harper looked at her for comment. He scowled as the blazing sun penetrated the uneven canopy of the conifers, slanting onto his tanned forehead. An unrelenting buzz from the 24inch log trimmer a quarter of a mile away down the lane argued his case for him. Its howling echo fell down through the deadening trunks of the forest, reminding them of the perennial human clockwork of destructive acquisition. He earnestly searched Hannah's eyes, breathing shallowly as though under great stress to avoid saying what might hurt her, "I just don't want to be exploited so much that I can't make choices. Here the choices are limited Hannah – that's all."

She knew that the force of his argument was irresistible. What else could she say that had not been said before? Hannah twisted her knees sideways, levering her foot into the shoe and stood up. Harper took her hand and they walked back to the track.

"You love this place don't you?" pronounced Harper.

"It's my home. I feel privileged to have lived most of my life here." Harper was silent for a few moments before he resumed, "Hannah, I don't see the whole picture. I work so hard I barely get time to read anything of interest, let alone think for myself. But look, the world is changing faster all the time. There are women's political groups springing up all over. There is a growing labour movement in the big

259

cities and coal fields. Without a decent education or patronage, affiliations such as these are the only chance for any voice in this world."

"What's your point, I thought you were more interested in the Masons? Inspector Brodie wanted you to play golf with him, until you lost his damned plates."

"My point is we have three darling daughters. What prospects have they for any kind of future choices living in Rotheimay? Women have no inheritance rights. No voting rights. No proper access to higher education." They stopped in the lane and looked at one another contemplatively, "Here we have one foot in the past Hannah. In Edinburgh we have one foot in the future." He paused and added, "Whatever that might hold," self-conscious for having laboured his 'one foot in the . . .' analogy. He hoped he'd not offended her but she just smiled and hugged him.

"Oh, I do miss you," Hannah declared warmly, "and I don't think any of us get to see 'the whole picture.' Surely if there is a meaningful purpose to living it must have something to do with making choices, sentimental or otherwise. I believe it is so. Living freely in your mind really is all about choices. It's more than that in fact – it's about conscious reconciliation and acceptance. That's why I still pray and I still go to the Kirk, Harper."

"Hmm, suitably rebuked. But in the final analysis, the Kirk did fuck all for the Scots except stir up centuries of the worst kind of political division, then preach forbearance to the homeless. Maybe that's all part of the Grand Design too," he added with a twist of irony around his mouth.

Walking down past the Sawmill in the direction of the Milltown, where Harper agreed to at least look at the farm cottage, they linked arms affectionately. After a few minutes of pondering he spoke again.

"Maybe I am too ambitious. I should just stay here and slave for Great Gran, until Frank is old enough to take his inheritance – or work unquestioningly for my two uncle-dads." She laughed aloud at his mocking tone.

"No, I'm joking of course . . . I'd get drunk one night and kill the tight old bastards!" They walked on arm in arm down the lane, affably waving and greeting the men at the saw mill as they passed by.

When the girls returned from visiting the ruins of Elgin Cathedral they showered their ma and pa with coloured pictures from their sketch pads. Wide-eyed Elizabeth asked Harper if he wanted some of her money but he declined graciously saying, "Oh no darling, Daddy has lots of money! Look," he said lifting her onto his knee, "I have this leather wallet for notes. And there are coins in my pocket." Unfurling the folded notes to explain the denominations in the received English reserved for his clients, he gave Elizabeth a florin to keep in her piggy bank, then one each to Elsie and Little Hannah.

"I also have this look, if I spend all my notes," he said, wafting his thick cheque book with an exaggerated smile, "I just have to write my name here - then tear off the cheque, give it to the train people or the shop people, or hotel people. They give my cheque to their bank. Then my bank gives them some of my money. So you don't have to worry about me!"

"Well Daddy, I can make some notes if you don't have enough. You can take my money. Then mammy can go to York," Elizabeth commended with fierce innocence.

"Well, you know I think you're right. I have a friend named Roger who lives not far from York, Elizabeth. I like him very much. He gave me something for which I will always be grateful."

"Was it money daddy, or jewellery like Great Gran's?"

"No darling, it was peace of mind. Roger lives in a beautiful house. I think when mummy has had her treatment and is feeling a bit better I will take her to see Roger and his wife. There is a big hill there, just like Salisbury Crags. They call it 'The Cow and Calf.' And there is a hill like Arthur's seat, which they call 'The Chevin.'"

"Daddy, we want to come too," Elizabeth looked to bright-eyed Elsie for support as she listened eagerly, towering above her sister in a green satin dress with her regal platted bun, "I'll give you my money," persisted Elizabeth.

"Yeah and me too," agreed Elsie enthusiastically.

"Me too!" echoed Little Hannah, who stood with a hand on Harper's knee, watching his face for affirmation that the deal would be done.

"Well, I think it's all up to Roger but there is a nice hotel in Otley, called the Black Horse. Maybe we will stay there. We'll just have to see."

Crestfallen, Elizabeth went away with her 'money' dubious about the coin Harper had given her, the mystery of exchange deepened but not dispelled. Grown-ups generally knew most things. Harper clearly knew everything.

Elsie was wrong about the money. So were Jeannie and Betsy about America. They are not grown up at all. Roger wasn't even a doctor.

Money was clearly an adult domain. All the grown-ups needed was a little help manufacturing it because they didn't have time to do it for themselves. Elizabeth decided to make a cheque book and then they wouldn't need to make any money. First she had to learn how to print and sign her name though, which was a skill she needed to develop. She chose Great Gran as her tutor, catching her just at the right moment as she was finishing the accounts. Elizabeth climbed up onto her lap to spend an hour normally devoted to reading, learning how to write the letters of her full name: Elizabeth Drummond Wilson Harper. The old lady explained that these were all relatives of the family – "Grandparents who are long gone."

The child held the pen naturally. She shaped the letters carefully, subliminally impressing the characters of her ancestry upon recollection although she was too young to question the implications. When Elizabeth had gone satisfied to her bed with craft work planned for after the morning rounds, Jessie stared at her mother without a word. Great Gran answered her unspoken question.

"Who's going to tell them the truth if I don't?" Jessie went about her business without comment.

Dr Payton knew there was nothing he could do to save Hannah in the longer run, but he insisted upon her having complete bed rest with a course of Blaud's Pills to balance anaemia. Discomfort and diarrhoea followed, but at least the bleeding stopped.

Hannah was going quietly out of her mind. There was only so much she could derive from *The Memoires of Sherlock Holmes*, or waiting for the next episode of George du Maurier's *Trilby,* to be published in Harper's Bazaar. She'd had enough of crocheting in the half light of a cool interior while her beloved bairns were out playing in the sun. Hannah felt as though time was repeating itself - the only difference being the fact that she wasn't standing in the kitchen watching her step-sisters through the window.

Despite playing down her ailments to Harper, she had developed a cough and was running a high temperature. Whenever she rose to play her piano, she felt dizzy and quickly became fatigued. The rest-cure was killing her.

For his part, Payton was assiduous in making a visit to Hannah part of his daily rounds before evening surgery. He told her he would come each day until he was sure her energy levels were restored, with no contra-indications.

His wife called with a bottle of Burgundy, flowers and a pile of music scores. Hannah brightened immediately when she heard the voice of Judith Payton. She spent an hour telling her piano teacher all about Harper taking her to see Paderewski in Glasgow. This refined, mutual interest naturally spilled over into wide ranging anecdotes which both women felt free to throw into the mix. They knew one another well enough to begin supplementing a shared history that went beyond music. But Judith did not outstay her welcome. She hoped Hannah might find the sheet music selections from the popular German pianist, Moritz Moszkowski, "a suitable distraction, once your condition is stable again. Also I think you should follow

263

your instincts, Hannah - get out in the sun. Put up a hammock in the garden, or sit in a deck chair. Drink some red wine for your anaemia – that is full of iron. At certain times I think it's best to ignore doctor's orders – but don't tell Joseph I said that!"

"Don't worry . . . I won't breathe a word. But I will take your advice – all of it – regardless of doctor's orders. Thank you so much Judith."

When the iron tonic began to take effect, which it did within a day or so, Hannah went to the piano and played as never before.

On his third visit within as many days, Payton listened carefully to all Hannah had to say about her treatment and operation in Edinburgh. He knew Mitton and had heard of Smellie. Above all Payton was keen to know all about Coley's pioneering treatment, with all the research information from the USA.

"Would you like to try it once your chest infection has cleared up?"

There was a hint of urgency in his voice which told Hannah the alternative was grim. She also caught a look of fire in Payton's eyes, which she had not seen with any of the other three doctors who had treated her thus far.

"Yes of course . . . If you can convince Smellie and Mitton to climb down off their high horses. They are like two gunslingers armed to the teeth, staring one another out at the O.K. Corral. I understand Mitton now has the dope in his fridge at Elgin, Dr Payton. If it works I want it! But I'm not spending six weeks in hospital."

Hannah remembered Foxworthy and how he had expressed concern about her long-term prospects of recovery. Foxworthy was a good man but Payton was different somehow. He knew Hannah and truly cared about her as an individual, not just as a patient. She agreed to his request, to get formal agreement for the Coley Fever Therapy.

She asked him if he needed to examine her more fully, or sound her chest. Payton declined, saying he was afraid that he 'already knew what he would find.'

"Actually Hannah, I don't want to waste any more time. But I would prefer to wait until the bleeding has been stopped for several days and any traces of anaemia are gone. I will return in a couple of days to take blood samples for testing. In the meantime, I will speak to Mitton and if necessary to Smellie, about use of the Coley vaccines, or a capsule form of the same treatment. I've seen it discussed in the medical journals. In the meantime you absolutely have to remain in bed, even if you feel fit."

"Okay Dr Payton!" remembering what Judith had said, Hannah had no intention of staying in bed.

"But maybe drink the wine Judith brought you," He added with a smile.

Payton went to the Forbes Arms Hotel in Milltown of Rothiemay to phone Mitton. Mitton agreed to give Payton both the capsules and the vaccines for use under his direction, provided that twenty four hour nursing care could be arranged for Mrs Harper. He also agreed with Dr Payton, that a phone call to Smellie in Edinburgh would not go amiss.

Mitton stated for the record that his advice was that, "Treatment would be best conducted in a hospital, as ideally injections have to be administered directly into a tumour for greatest effect." He suggested Dr Grey's Hospital in Elgin, although strictly speaking Hannah was resident in the county of Banff and should therefore attend the Chalmers. He expressed regret at her unwillingness to return to Edinburgh. Mitton stressed that, "Professional medical supervision with appropriate record keeping, is required to monitor dosages of the Coley toxins and their effects."

Payton was essentially given the green light to put his own reputation and career on the line.

"Ah well, I'm near to retirement," Payton mused, as he walked back through the Milltown to his surgery.

Jessie sent a telegram to Harper, advising him of Payton's proposed intervention and he agreed to come the following day to fetch the girls. It was late on Friday evening when he arrived. There was nothing he could say to explain the situation to them without making it worse, except to lamely state, "This is the same *new* treatment your mammy would have got in *New York*. Only she wants Dr Payton to do it for her at home."

It was a long weekend of tense optimism with hushed conversations about Coley's incredible reduction of enormous tumours and the precise requirements of 'intensive nursing care.' Jessie and Harper took turns to check the stairs to ensure that the girls were not listening. The vacation in Rothiemay ended abruptly for Elsie and Elizabeth, on the bank holiday Monday, August 6th.

On the first part of the journey back to Edinburgh they had the railway carriage to themselves. Yet there was an invisible barrier between Harper and his two daughters. They felt he was discriminating against them, whereas in fact he empathised with them fully. He couldn't rationalise his decision to bring them home – so he put that down to 'sentiment.'

"Why did Little Hannah get to stay with mammy and we have to go home?" they demanded. He had the perfect answer, but just could not explain it graphically enough to buy them off to their complete satisfaction.

"Mammy needs a nurse for six weeks. Whoever Dr Mitton agrees to will have to sleep in your bedroom." It sounded like a lame excuse and Elsie was smart enough to know it for a lie. She turned her proud, beautiful countenance away and folded her arms. Elsie had let her hair down out of 'Berengaria's bun' as Great Gran Han had jokingly named the tight circle of plats. She no longer needed to keep her hair safe from the hazards of daily life on the farm.

The girls refused to look out of the window at the rolling hillsides, simply because Harper had suggested it. Close to home they chorused dismissively, "We've seen the Forth Bridge before," rating the remarkable new construction and the view beyond it out to sea, with equal disdain.

Only when they saw Margaret Kemp at Waverley did the tension release. Harper had forgotten that the girl had agreed to meet them 'to help carry their bags'. He remembered suddenly that they had both anticipated difficulty with the necessary separation of the girls from their mother, especially as they had expected to spend the whole of August at Ramsburn. Perhaps because of his dismal mood, Harper felt an unexpected bolt of pleasure, seeing his children run to Margaret. He noticed how she embraced them, reciprocating their open affection. He wasn't torn, he was glad. Without Margaret Kemp he might have considered throwing himself off the Black Wall at Salisbury Crags.

Suddenly it was all too much for Harper to take. He felt the need to run for cover. Everything he did was an unwelcome compromise. He was incapable of autonomous action. Even his most private thoughts were exposed to the scrutiny of the World. There was no certainty in his situation, just conditions which led to reactions.

There is no right and wrong, only what seems possible, or justifiable given the prevailing circumstances.

Even suicide was an action he could now understand. Not for him in that moment, yet possibly for someone in deep despair.

The following morning, another hard working day, Harper headed for Waverley via the University Library. There had been many authors mentioned by his tutor, Jim Reid at night school who were not on a specific reading list, yet deemed appropriate for wider enquiry. Some names kept cropping up time after time in Professor Reid's lectures.

Harper borrowed a compilation of David Hume's philosophical treatises, which he remembered Zachariah Williams had also once commended to him. When the pretty librarian had stamped the fly

267

leaf with a return date he placed a reserve on two of Adam Smith's works, which were also perennially popular.

Harper bought a ticket south, deciding to break his journey at Peterborough. He could idle for an evening and get up late the following morning. He had no plan but to read, rest and hopefully avoid taxing interaction. He could not get his mind off Hannah's terrible dilemma. Harper was frightened rigid at the thought he might never see her again alive.

Even then he found he was the subject of interest from another man, sitting thirty feet away from him in the open carriage. There was something familiar about the fellow, although he did not appear to be a travelling salesman or buyer. Even idle curiosity made Harper feel paranoiac. When he saw the man glance at him once again with what he took for prying interest, Harper stared back with naked animosity - such was the rawness of his nervous state.

Arriving in the expanding market town with its pall of boiling sugar and profusion of wasps in the middle of the afternoon, within fifteen minutes Harper dropped off his overnight bag at the Great Northern Hotel and walked unannounced into Shelton's Furniture and Drapery store on Lincoln Road. There he asked for and was pleased to be able to meet the proprietor. Shelton invited him into his office where he offered refreshment. Harper asked for tea.

Shelton chatted casually about the demand for red bricks in the northern industrial towns and how, "The future of this historic city will be assured for years to come, thanks to the clay pits to the south of the town."

Picking up Shelton's theme, Harper speculated, "There will surely be an influx of labour from far and wide, to sustain such a crucial industry." He explained how the experience of his company, Kenningtons, and Jenners behind it, with their foremost place in the retail market could benefit Mr Shelton, "In helping to predict your customer's requirements."

The gentleman told Harper, "I fully agree. It's my business to always be on the look-out for new trends and new products. I have nothing but high praise for both Kenningtons and Jenners. There is mutual interest here young man, with no direct competition for market share." The managing director took Harper's card and shook his hand warmly, assuring him of future business.

Harper spent the remainder of the afternoon reading in his room at the Great Northern. He ate early in the dining room, looking out with curiosity onto the railway station. In the fine, traditional restaurant he ordered fillet steak with battered onions, petit pois, mushrooms and sautéed potatoes. Feeling a deep need to compensate for missing home cooking, he savoured every bite. Falling under the gentle spell of a bottle of Merlot, he watched the other diners – mostly local businessmen and travellers like himself. These patrons laughed and talked confidently, in striking contrast with railway and agricultural workers he'd seen in the public bar on the other side of the building before dinner.

Less well-off customers mumbled together with their East Anglian drawl, sipping thick local ale in uninviting corners. Harper noted that one or two of them stared as he walked through, as though challenging him to sit down and account for himself or move on. Now he looked around the restaurant, half expecting to see the enormous fellow who had stared at him on the train. He had definitely risen to get off as Harper stepped onto the platform.

On the whole Peterborough seems a strangely territorial, unfriendly place, with a shoulder turned against itinerants it thrives on.

Replete and slightly drunk after his meal, Harper strolled casually into the centre of the old city, staring up at soft blue evening light as it shrouded magnificent spires and the stained glass West portico of Saints Peter, Paul and Andrew's Cathedral. Candle light and plainsong coming from within ran a cold tingling of awe up Harper's spine.

How could such a glorious construction be an act of complete folly?

It had a convincing presence in itself, but Hume would have considered that perception entirely misleading. Harper thought of the little Free Church kirk at Rothiemay, which had no doubt been torched by the Whigs.

Who can really make sense of the World? No doubt this magnificent cathedral was lucky to be spared King Henry's wrath.

Words without meaning clashed in Harper's dizzy mind: scepticism; compassion; rationalism, humanity. The more he pondered the less he felt sure about anything.

An attractive, well-dressed woman whom he'd noticed earlier dining alone in the hotel, approached with an inviting smile. Harper noticed she was wearing a blood red dress under her fashionable cape. She asked for a light for her machine rolled cigarette, inserted in a gold inlaid, ebony holder. The woman gently touched the back of Harper's hand with her fingers as he held up the match for her. The touch told him everything he needed to know about her. Harper tipped his hat, smiling back. She was on the game and he looked like a prospective punter. For no obvious reason he thought again of the favourite places for suicides in Edinburgh.

Perhaps hers is a kind of moral suicide - if there is indeed any such thing as 'morality.'

Dismissing her with a knowing tilt of his head, Harper strolled back to the hotel where he bought another bottle of red wine from the bar. So deep was the desire for release, he was glad to pay excess for corkage. He took the St Emilion up to his room with a large glass borrowed from the restaurant.

There he read for three hours, smoking his pipe as he challenged himself to derive some kind of meaning from the Universe. Lifting the window sash to watch the London express race through the nearby station he wondered if it were possible to rationalise the connectedness of all things as one integrated dimensionality – even imagine what was outside of himself in any consistent way. Orange light seeped past the blinds of the rear carriage. He wondered idly about the people resting in the sleeping car.

They might as well occupy a different universe, for I will never know them. Yet they are most likely as familiar and turgid as I, in their daily grind and hopeless thoughts.

Perhaps because of the alcohol relaxing his brain the words Harper read seemed to defy logic. He understood them individually yet their context seemed to evade perception. Rivers appeared between the letters. He found himself repeating sentences, reading the same lines twice or even three times in his determination. Forcing himself to continue as though on some mission following the footsteps of a brave pioneer into an unknown territory of the soul - the more confused and drunk he became, the more Harper waxed in sympathy for the tempestuous soul of the brilliant author, David Hume. Harper's mind was a bundle of primitive sensations yet all conjunctions of his personal desires were blunted by reason.

At around one o'clock in the morning he lay face down onto a bed that had been softened by a thousand travellers. Listening to the lonely hiss of gas lamps outside on the street and a night watchman whistling on the station platform, images began to tumble rapidly through his mind, until one jumped out - like a Lumiere brothers projection.

Hannah was sheathed in pain, restless under the watchful trees of Ramsburn. He felt his lonely children at home in their beds, pining in confusion and observed attendant Margaret with her young adult's self-assurance, unworried by the life ahead of her. He saw the sleeping souls of an entire city as he walked the beat once again in his imagination.

The skin on his face became stretched with tiredness but in his mind Harper embraced all the souls he felt responsible for, with arms wide in recognition of their pain. Before losing consciousness he whispered a very short drunken prayer, for Hannah and his family; for Zach who had inspired him to erudition and for the defiant, naturalistic soul of David Hume, the long dead savant. As a lonely tear rolled across the bridge of his nose Harper muttered the conclusion to all his pain aloud so he might remember it in the morning, "Existence may have no apparent meaning, so let it have whatever meaning I wish to imbue it with. And bollocks to all the rest!" Harper finally fell asleep in the hard blue gaslight, with his clothes still on.

Hannah could not resist a smile as she watched Dr Payton fussing over her treatment protocol. He read the accompanying information aloud, as if he had never heard it before. She was delighted to think that this effort was not exclusively for her benefit. It served to underscore the reality that this breakthrough was as momentous for Payton as it was for his patient. In truth she was bursting both with pain as with edginess yet Joseph Payton charmed her soul. Hannah felt she had made the right decision by returning home.

In her disjointed imaginings the country doctor was St Luke, or maybe James the brother of Jesus. Payton was assiduous to the point of fussiness. Although he was slightly built, there was iron strength in his lithe, stick-like frame. Curiously the doctor seemed to do all his thinking aloud, "I have a choice – hypodermic, or capsules for you to ingest."

After pondering long, he stood to approach her, to administer the injection of fluid. In that cat-like, dynamic movement some essential quality of Payton's quiet energy was carried. It made Hannah flush suddenly with the certainty Harper had first brought her on the back of the New York Times article about John Ficken's remission, eighteen months previously.

Payton's dark eyes seemed to communicate sacred knowledge – a quality of benign assurance which brought calm to his patients. The fact that Payton was a Jew gave him celebrity status in a community imbued with ideological Christianity in all its contrasting hues. For Hannah he represented the anointed amid a divided community watching a distant world, while it tried hard to forget the hateful crimes of its own recent past.

Meanwhile municipal Scotland slips quietly into deepening scepticism.

Dr Payton knew that actions spoke louder than words in his burgeoning agrarian community. He cared what people thought, and worked hard to sustain their good opinion of him. Unemployment and social dependency were alien to the parsimonious Aberdonians but sickness was unavoidable. Payton could repair people, putting them back into the swim, where ownership or enfranchisement, stock yields and harvest crystallised their individual status in time before the Almighty. Payton gave them time – the only currency that really mattered to them.

In turn the locals revered his personage more than any elusive, spoilt nobility. They respected the man's gracious authority beyond that of local empty-handed ministers, or garrulous priests. All the women talked of Payton favourably and all their men agreed. His only known weakness was for superior Burgundy.

"On the other hand," according to foul-mouthed but incontrovertible Donald McIntyre, resident pub philosopher at the Forbes as he qualified general approval the last time they'd listened in on Payton using the phone to Mitton, "The 'Good Doctor's' shite does smell a bit." The belligerent townsman articulated this view with certainty through the froth sucked from the top of his fifth pint. None of McIntyre's usual circle of boozy associates laughed too much at the mad butcher's irony. Equally no-one, even local Bobby, Bill Stevenson dared to challenge Donald as to how he had come by this information. As always the gigantic, scowling McIntyre seemed misanthropic in the extreme as he held court in the bar with his pals Stevenson, Hendry, Lorimer and Murdoch.

Peyton himself had sat with them for half an hour earlier that evening, standing his round as always as they pumped him for news from civilization. As a consequence the regulars were wary of blackening the good doctor's reputation though they all kept a secret shine for his petite, comely wife.

Perhaps as Billy Stevenson et al, the butcher's pals unanimously concluded about McIntyre years ago but needed to keep reminding themselves whenever he embarrassed them by stepping over the line, as he frequently did, 'Don's black moods come from chopping up too many animal carcasses.' As always McIntyre had drunk too much and was ready for an argument with anyone he knew, or preferably a fist fight with someone he didn't know. But everyone, even McIntyre owned a piece of Dr Payton's celebrity.

Each of them added betimes to the living legend. In a simple sense Dr Payton's life in the locale of The Milltown was a poetic analogy to The Greatest Story, told over and again: The Word was made flesh and dwelt among us.

Chapter Fourteen - *Fever Therapy*

Dr Payton asked Hannah's permission to move her things. She smiled, shaking her head at his unnecessary diplomacy, "Of course Dr Payton, just brush them all to one side. When you've finished I'll ask Jessie to throw them all in the blanket-chest out in the hallway. We'll make a little work station for you."

Payton smiled back at Hannah across the room as he carefully re-arranged her perfumes, powders, hand-mirror and combs to the left side of the dressing table as if they were as delicate as the Coley vaccines.

"Thank you," he replied, working with his hands and his mind at the same time.

Hannah had the distinct impression that there was an energetic light around Dr Payton – an aureole reminiscent of the halo surrounding Celtic iconography of the saints. He reminded Hannah of nothing so much as Carus's *Gospel of Buddha* - a copy of which Harper had given her as a birthday gift. For Hannah, unwilling in the practice of her faith to discriminate so much as conflate, Payton was an Eastern ascetic – a selfless Buddhist monk living constantly in the moment, like a child. Even the manner of his reaching into the cracked and worn physician's bag, held more charming mystery for Hannah Harper than the items he withdrew from it. What delighted her most was the impression that Payton wore the constant smile of Padmasambhavara.

Dr Payton called for Jessie and gave her a thermometer with directions for use. He confirmed the location of additional blankets; told her to prepare the small hearth with paper, logs and coal ready to burn. He recommended bed socks, with a hot water bottle for the chills that always follow a fever.

There was bright laughter of excited anticipation from the two women which drew the attention of Great Gran and Little Hannah. After five minutes of levity during which the bairn climbed into bed with her mother, Payton gave the cue for their visit to end with a glance at Jessie.

"Okay darling, Mammy wants to have a long sleep now, so we'll let Dr Payton finish his job here!"

"Come on angel. You and I need to keep Ramsburn working while Gran looks after mum," confirmed Great Gran. Little Han and Great Gran kissed Hannah, wishing her good luck. Even the child acted as though her mother was going off on a journey into the unknown. Hannah joked about feeling like a space traveller in Jules Verne's *De la Terre a la Lune*.

The injection deep into her left buttock was unexpectedly painful but otherwise seemed an anti-climax to Hannah, after the entire 'confab' about Coley.

How can tertiary stage cancer be cured with such ease? If Anton Chekhov and Louis Pasteur knew what Coley knows, why is the same treatment not carried out everywhere as standard procedure?

Dr Payton promised Hannah he would return as soon as possible to check on her, then went off on his rounds. Jessie brought tea, assuring Hannah of her prompt return, to watch for the onset of the expected fever.

Alone at last, facing the onset of her ultimate earthly trial, Hannah folded icy cold legs under the blanket. She let her imagination wander gently through the window beyond the end of her bed, seeing in her mind's eye the red climbing roses filling the room with scent through the open sash.

She slept for two hours but time dragged when she woke. Her pain abated marginally as she relaxed, breathing easily in preparation for the ordeal ahead. Hannah read for hours, in an attempt to restrict the focus of her apprehension but chthonic excitement followed with moderate, self-generated tachycardia. She could not rest. Her body itched and her fingers began to swell. She had to elevate first her right arm, then the left to gradually restore feeling.

Rising to get up and walk around the room, she decided to dress in day clothes then went to play her piano. At first it was impossible for her to concentrate enough to play even familiar pieces but the easy keyboard and loose muscle tone of her upper body lent itself to practice. Joy returned quickly with her rediscovered skill.

Unexpectedly, Hannah felt a wave of sleep stinging her forehead and eyes. In her state of high anxiety she welcomed the release of tension that tiredness brought with all her heart.

She woke in the night to see ministering angels: lamps, food and drink brought into her range by Jessie with cautious good humour.

Day came and with it Payton who supplemented the dose, injecting it on the other side for good measure. Again nothing happened. The pain in her abdomen, legs and lower back reduced as it tended to do on occasion, replaced by the puffiness that usually presaged more bleeding. Jessie remarked that the black orbs under Hannah's eyes had lightened.

"The product of much needed bed-rest," commented Payton.

"Hannah never could relax. It's not in her nature," Jessie confirmed, guiltless in ascribing a living epitaph.

"Well, at least now she'll have to follow Doctor's orders!" Great Gran added, with kindly humour.

"Yes, we could all do with some o' that, Dr Payton," Jessie agreed with a sighing tone.

"A woman's work is never done," complained Great Gran, "Look at me at nearly eighty, Joseph . . . I'm the living proof!"

"I know this well, madam," answered Payton, shrinking in stature before her gloomy aphorism, "I see dedication everywhere I go. My only hope is that I may advance in years as gracefully as you have, Great Gran Han!" The old lady seemed to glow with the restrained pleasure of a prominent Royal, charmed by a subject Head of State.

With nothing more to do there Payton left to continue his rounds. Jessie followed him outside, to the door of his carriage.

"It doesn't look like it's going to work, Doctor." Jessie's remark was more of a question than a statement.

"Oh, I imagine it's much too early to say."

"But you expected a fever and nothing has happened."

"Oh, but it will happen and soon. If the fever comes you must be quick. Get Alex Harper, failing that Frank or Jeannie or leave Great Gran with Hannah and come yourself. But send for me immediately, regardless of the hour. I will leave a schedule of my rounds with Judith. Be ready Jessie. You have to keep her warm, and the room well ventilated. Use the thermometer, like I showed you. Sterilise it with the surgical spirit after each use.

If her body temperature goes above 102 degrees, have cool water ready to sponge her down – especially her face, neck and head if she is delirious. This is critical Jessie – make regular use of the thermometer but do not overdo the attempts at cooling. Remember . . . the high temperature is desirable so no cold baths! Keep her wrapped in lightweight, absorbent night clothes and get her back into bed if her core temperature drops suddenly, as at some point it may. You will know if she starts to shiver.

For my part, I must keep a constant check for swellings, or fluid that may build up. I may have to tap necrotic fluid off. The first week will be critical. There is a chance that we might lose her, Jessie! I have never deliberately given a patient a fever before, let alone tried to maintain it at a dangerously high level for several weeks." Payton searched Jessie Wilson's eyes with benevolent concern.

"You're a good man, Joseph Payton. I know you are doing the right thing for my daughter, even if nobody really understands why it works," she affirmed quietly. A broad smile suddenly spread across Jessie's strained face as a chorus of summer evening blackbirds echoed her heartfelt sentiments.

"And you are a good woman, Jessie Wilson. It is my privilege to do this for your daughter."

As she watched Payton's carriage disappear round the corner of the farmhouse into the lane, tears ran freely down Jessie Wilson's stoical face.

On the evening of the fourth day there was a sudden coldness on Hannah's forehead. It struck her that there was a curious difference in temperature between opposite sides of her nose. Although she was hot and perspiring, her nostrils felt chilled and damp. The touch paper was lit - and within a few short hours, Hannah's body was ablaze.

By midnight her mouth and throat no longer held sensation other than a painful, arid hollowness. Drinks could no longer assuage thirst, so swollen was her epiglottis. Her eyebrows percolated moisture between downy hairs and her eyes puffed up, so that she could barely see. Hannah's lower back ached, while her internal organs floated in a bath of fire.

Annoying, unreachable sweat dripped down the cut quill of sinew at the base of her spine, backwards from her buttocks. After hours of restlessness with increasing inflammation in all her muscles, Hannah was now unable to move yet was alert enough to dread soiling herself. In her vigilant, dreaming mind she was still active yet her body was a dead stranger, unmoving. She had to plan each tortuous movement of wracked muscles according to wherever the cold, gripping pain seemed to register deepest discomfort.

Hannah groaned as loudly as she could to alert Jessie for help and when she opened her eyes, a she-wolf stood four-square lolling her tongue and teeth at head height next to the bed. The shock of its sudden appearance was frightening. Hannah recoiled. Perhaps this was a visitation from the Angel of Death, in a more tolerable guise? The fear of it shook Hannah awake suddenly, weak as a new-born lamb. She attempted to cry out for Jessie again but her voice was no more than a croak. If she stayed in her broiling sick-bed any longer her heart would fold in upon itself. Mustering all her determination, Hannah swivelled her feet to the floor and stood up, shaking at the side of her bed, unsure what to do but knowing something needed to be done. Jessie came quickly, ushering her to lie back down.

"Oh my," Jessie droned, feeling warm perspiration that had soaked through Hannah's nightgown and onto the sheets.

Recalling what Dr Payton had said she diverted her patient to a chair beside the fire. Quickly throwing off sweat-soaked sheets to replace them with a light woollen blanket – one of several stacked on the dressing table, Jessie laid Hannah on top. She folded two more in readiness in a triangle at the bottom corner of the double bed.

Jessie rolled Hannah over onto her side to take her temperature as Payton had instructed. She wrote time and number down on the card provided by Sloane Kettering Hospital in New York – 1.30 am - 102 degrees; then swabbed the thermometer with surgical spirit. She woke Alex Harper, who had agreed to stay for the duration and the lad went silently to prepare a horse and hitch up the carriage.

Jessie sat silently in the darkened room, trying to think what little else she might do to for poor Hannah. Feeling utterly helpless she watched Alex's shadow passing behind the curtains as he walked with a lantern towards the stable. Hannah began to mutter and groan again, then cried out in terror as Jessie placed a blanket on top of her.

The she-wolf had mounted Hannah's recumbent frame, crushing her limbs, wrestling with her to tear out her throat. Jessie moved to her daughter's side to console her.

Mindful of advice about cooling and re-hydrating Hannah's body, she was alert to the emphasis Payton placed upon not overdoing this. Jessie kept telling herself, 'the fever is the cure.' All the help she could really offer lay in speaking softly, consoling Hannah while mopping her brow.

Great Gran came to Jessie's side, silently taking in the scene. Without a word she went to bank up the coal fire.

"I'll keep taking her temperature every half hour," Jessie suggested, "I think just one blanket will be enough. I will add or take away a layer according to how high it soars."

Payton came within the hour. He made Hannah sit up to drink half a pint of water with dissolved liver salts and glucose added. He ordered Jessie to fetch a pitcher and to ensure Hannah was made to drink every hour, on the hour. Alex brought two more armchairs from the lounge for them to keep the night-watch in comfort. Payton did not need to make use of the thermometer. He could tell Hannah's state with a look and a touch although he cautioned Jessie not to attempt this. Finally Jessie fell asleep, snoring softly in exhaustion for three hours after the sun had risen. Payton waited until he saw that Hannah's life signs were stable before setting off to his morning surgery.

Dr Payton returned after midnight the following day – knowing that the struggle would become more critical as his patient weakened. They worked through the night in the same way as before, monitoring Hannah's body temperature and fluid intake. Her fever fluctuated between 102 -105 degrees. Even Payton was deeply concerned. He was mounted on a bolting horse.

As soon as the fever broke on the second afternoon the patient was moved to the armchair by the fire, where her status could be monitored as she chattered and trembled for half an hour before falling into a deep sleep. Payton left for his rounds and Jessie changed Hannah's damp bedding again while the fire grate was shovelled out by a laconic Great Gran Han, gasping on her knees.

Two hours later, Hannah was sitting at the kitchen table with a bowl of Cullen Skink, a blanket wrapped tightly around her shoulders. Payton returned with his wrinkled bag and shining, keen eyes, relief written all over his face. Jessie was sitting opposite her daughter with feed bills and her cash tin, a broad-nibbed fountain pen in her hand as the doctor knocked and entered in one movement.

"I can see why this hasn't caught on world-wide like it ought to have done," he muttered with disarming irony, "No-one has the guts to do it! Don't get up, don't get up! We all have work to do ladies, lives to lead. I'll be in and out over the next month or so. Please don't let me break your concentration."

"As you wish doctor," Jessie agreed, exhaustion etched on her face.

Hannah mumbled a greeting through the thick soup in her mouth as Payton sat down where he could observe her without intruding. He placed his bag on the table and slowly took off his riding gloves, allowing Hannah a moment to regain her poise. He noticed that her hand shook slightly as she brought the spoon up to her lips.

"That's good Mrs Harper," Payton observed thoughtfully, looking at the bowl of fish soup, "Replace the salts. Try some scrambled eggs. Maybe eat a small portion of boiled potatoes with butter or some cabbage. Fruit also. Maybe a spoonful of honey each morning for your tummy. Small amounts of each . . . but look for variety," he peered across at Jessie sitting at her accounts. A glance over her spectacles showed that she had registered the advice.

"Eat with a purpose Dear, for I fear we have a long way to go! When you are strong, we have to repeat the ordeal. And water, drink plenty of water. Not tea mind, or milk . . . just water."

When she had finished her meal, Hannah returned to bed, utterly exhausted. Payton examined her cursorily, taking her blood pressure and temperature, both of which were low.

"It is too early to judge if the tumours in your abdomen have reduced in size. But there is a predictable distension with some lessening of surface pressure. There is clearly a build-up of fluid, which is excellent. Coley is right. He *has* actually found the cure for cancer! You can expect a fair amount of bleeding." Hannah looked alarmed.

"In this instance that's a good thing Mrs Harper. Just be ready for it."

"Oh, women are always ready for that Dr Payton. I don't think I'll ever get used to it though!"

"And you feel no pain?"

"None."

"Remarkable. And stiffness?"

"Much less than before the fever"

"Oh and you must be exhausted?"

"Well, yes but I think I'll feel better after a proper sleep."

"You will, for sure. Sleep when you feel like it, but try to maintain the pattern of diurnal routine. Do you understand that?"

"I think so. You want me to be active if I feel like it, during the day."

"Precisely - tire yourself out so you will sleep normally at night. I will return after surgery tomorrow to give you the next injection. From now on it will be just one at a time. The fever may not be as bad, but we don't know for certain . . . so you must get Jessie to monitor it – or do it yourself at first. Alert her immediately if the thermometer reading goes above a hundred degrees."

Payton paused and looked at her long. There was professional rigour in his words but his voice betrayed tenderness and affection, "How was it Hannah; the fever I mean?"

"I didn't know anyone. I thought I was Little Red Riding Hood and my ma was the Big Bad Wolf. Evidently I tried to escape from her a couple of times." They both laughed knowingly, but for Hannah it had been all too real. Dr Payton watched her benevolently as she continued to portray her sparse recollection of the fever. When Hannah finished speaking he sat at her bedside pondering, unable to speak. He could not truly participate in her individual suffering though he had often wondered what part sheer willpower might play in creating or reducing sickness.

Hannah spoke up again, as though reading his wish to empathise with and cure every patient.

"I'm not a child anymore. I'm not afraid of the dark. Darkness is where we all come from . . . and where we will return, Doctor." She took his hand. There was a connection between them that went beyond words.

"Everything else is just a dream Joseph, everything!" she told him with a smile.

Payton left without breaking Hannah's train of thought or his own, climbing onto his carriage without a word. After completing the remainder of his rounds, lunching at the hotel in the Milltown and making love to his wife in the warm summer afternoon with the bedroom window open – the doctor could still not get past what Hannah had said to him. He carried on with routines for the rest of the day but his mind came back to that scene. Finally he attempted to explain it to his wife.

"I think I may be losing my grip on reality," he began.

"Truly, you've been reading Dr Freud again?"

"No, no. I'm not sure that would cover it entirely, although Freud is onto something bigger than any of us."

Joseph Payton spoke sincerely about the way Hannah's words had struck him. He even tried to express the non-sexual, loving connection between them. Judith studied his face with an indulgent smile. Then she hugged her man generously.

"I don't mind if you have a crush on one of your patients. I think the Christian Greeks called it 'agape'."

"And I don't mind if half of my patients have a crush on you," retorted Joseph, "Hume thought our best intentions were entirely the product of our natural desires," he added pensively.

"Just don't let me catch you falling for some old granny with a fortune in Chinese porcelain," Judith replied, an acid warning in her voluptuous laughter.

The Paytons sat at a white enamelled table in the back garden of their watchful, hedged villa. Judith brought a bottle of vintage Barolo with two large wine glasses from the cellar. They sat in silence for a while, listening to blackbirds singing their hearts out under the joyous canopy of their mature garden.

"I love this country. This is my home," declared Joseph Payton, without a hint of sentiment in his voice.

It was a cold morning in early October when Hannah emerged into the sunlight to discover the cause of excitement amongst the yearling cattle. A breath of morning dew lay on the wooded hollow cradling the farmhouse and its outbuildings, yet the slanting rays held a false promise. She ran into the lane shouting for the dogs to help. Someone had left the gate to the pasture open. The cattle eyed Sally the sheepdog warily as they chewed. The shrewd Border Collie paused judiciously in the lane with her head down, looking at the herd with ears pricked forward, awaiting further instruction. The bullocks formed a predictable tight alliance against her, standing their ground. Tex ran in circles behind Sally with his tongue lolling, his listening posture all excitement.

Hannah realised her folly as she approached the open gate but was also conscious of running for the sheer pleasure of it. Moving lightly over the ground with muscles working properly for the first time in seven years, she wasn't inclined to slow her pace. It struck Hannah again that the collies knew every aspect of farming life, including human expectations. Great Gran shared in Hannah's laughter as she arrived from the house with the key for the padlock on the gate.

"One of the cows has got back in with the boys," Hannah explained, "Some of them are due for slaughter." Hannah explained that she wished to avoid complications when the drover arrived. She told Great Gran she would make the transfer to a vacant field, 'Where the poor girl can calm down.'

The 'poor girl' in question, a two year old heifer the girls had named Abbie, was quickly extracted under loud protest. The dogs waited near the gate, eager to be summoned for the cut-out and the bullocks parted like the Red Sea when Hannah singled the heifer out with a switch. The cow ran straight across the lane into the lush, vacant pasture. The collies stood tall and watchful at a cricket fielder's distance, ready to run ahead of the cow if she tried to escape along the lane or back into the field with the bullocks. Hannah came striding down the slope to shut the gate before any of 'the boys' followed. The heifer lowed at them repeatedly – calling them to join her. Tex leaped over the gate with a running bound.

Later that day Hannah ran when Little Hannah threw her the ball. She ran when two of the hens escaped through the wire of their pen, into the woods around the Ram's Burn. Best of all she ran when Harper arrived, walking up the lane after he had bumped into Hugh Drummond in Elgin. His old friend had dropped him off at the road side. Hannah had never felt so vigorous in her entire life. Coley's Fever Therapy had worked. The cancer that would certainly have killed her by now was gone.

Wearing a look of incongruous confusion on his face as he glowered in the afternoon sunlight, Harper smelled of soapy ale. He was burdened with trade samples under his arm and in his hand was a brief case. A bowler hat sat askew, tipped back on his head. Mud from the lane covered the vamps of his town shoes and he felt the self-conscious inebriation of a man who has drunk too much at lunchtime on an empty stomach. But Hannah's delight at seeing Harper penetrated through all his awkwardness as she planted her firm body in his way. She hugged him with his hands full, scattering his alcoholic fugue with her whirlwind of warmth and good news.

"Harper, it has worked! I'm officially in the clear! There is no pain and no inflammation. No stiffness and no bleeding – for the first time since before Elizabeth was born. Did you get my telegram and my letters?"

"Yes, yes. I'm sorry for not writing back. I thought it would be best to just come straight up." She took his heavy sample-book and swung it up into her arms. He noticed that her once voluminous chest was beginning to fill out again under Jessie's regimen. Harper thought she looked stunning as they walked slowly side by side along the lane.

"Marlene in Accounts, Hannah, and Mr Soutar . . . they know. I don't know why but I think they suspect me of fraud. I think they have had a private detective following me. Someone has been talking behind my back." He began justifying his recent absence but the explanation tailed off. Hannah ignored his excuses. It was her moment.

"Oh it's alright," she assured him with a smile, "I know that you are always on the run. I suppose you expected to find a corpse when you arrived. I couldn't write when I was ill. They had to test my reaction to the doses. They increased them every other day until I got the fever. Payton warned me that two of Coley's patients died. They are more concerned by that than the one hundred and ninety eight he has saved. Apparently he has come in for a lot of criticism from another doctor – his superior, a man named Ewing who sounds like a real blockhead. Mitton and Payton had to be careful, to follow Coley's instructions to the letter."

Harper wanted to say, 'The more so because you were too stubborn to go into hospital' but felt the creeping cold of alcohol on his numbed senses and decided to hold his tongue. Now was not the time for controversy. He listened as Hannah rambled on, a tremulous note of relief in her voice. She turned to look into his eyes as they halted half way along the lane. They were hidden by the quarry enclosure which Ewan Harper and Frank had cleared for their flooring and roofing timbers, below a wooded outcrop sheltering the farmhouse from westerly gales.

"At first I thought I was gone for sure Harper. Payton said my temperature hit 105 degrees. I didn't know what day it was, or where I was! Thank goodness for poor Jessie. She changed my bedding and wiped me down two dozen times. Fluid came through every pore of my body and afterwards I bled for days. I was as weak as a lamb and sick as could be. Each time the fever broke they let me rest for a few days, then started it again. In the end I was so frightened that I couldn't face it any more. I was set to tell Dr Payton to just let me die. I just wanted you to be there!"

"I thought it was just a course of injections. That it was all under control?" he offered weakly.

Hannah wept for the first time since her treatment began. They leaned their heads against one another pathetically, still holding the accoutrements of Harper's precious work between them. He kissed her cheeks and tasted her tears. She immediately shook her head, ignoring past sorrows and sniffing smilingly at his roguish, sensuous touch, still rattling on like a teenager.

"But the thing of it was - the pain started to reduce immediately! When the fever broke after the second treatment, Payton examined me. He was astounded to feel the biggest lump had halved in size. He carried on the injections and they got smaller still."

"Yes, of course. I can't believe it. I just assumed from your letters it was all straightforward. If I hadn't had my hands full - with the girls, my studying, work an' all . . . I would have come . . . I have no holiday entitlement left but they would have allowed me compassionate leave."

She balanced the sample book on the top of the gate post to the farmyard and blew her nose.

"Anyway, now it's alright Harper and it's over. I only had the fever really bad that one time. The rest of the time they kept it below 103. And now the fluid and bleeding have stopped," she repeated, in the disbelief of such an incredible reprieve, "The lumps are gone completely. Now I'm cured Harper!" she said again with matter of fact lightness. Hannah's alacrity gave the lie to her true feelings. In her eyes Harper saw the abyss she had crawled out of by her fingernails.

"And no pain?"

"And no pain! They are to keep me under review because as we know and as they keep telling us – they always hate to lose a patient! "

"So when . . ." began Harper, about to ask the obvious question.

"No, I can't say when I will come home. I'll stay here until Dr Payton gives the word." She reflected for a moment, slowly shaking her head with a difficult recollection.

"You know, that little man has the gift of Saint Luke. It would be an insult to him for me to change my mind now. I placed myself in his care and he's brought me through this. It's only fair to let him be the judge of my fitness."

"Well, it's nice to see that you're running around and getting plenty of fresh air. You know the suffrage movement in Australia are encouraging women athletes. I like the way you move! I think we'll enter you in next year's Edinburgh Games." Hannah punched him on the arm and he laughed aloud.

"Hannah you really are back to your old self. I can't recall the last time you punched me so hard on the arm!"

"The first thing we should do – is have an open house. Invite your family over."

"Zach and Annie – we should go over and see them tomorrow, if you're up to it".

"And the Paytons, I want to hear her play my piano again." They swapped burdens so each could put their free arm around the back of the other as they strolled along the lane, laughing and reminiscing.

Payton was pre-occupied by an outbreak of Tuberculosis in the last weeks of November. This always frightened him as it seemed to spread so quickly from the forges to the farms – or perhaps it was the other way – he was never really sure. It was approaching the Christmas period when he finally telephoned Smellie to ask him if he wanted to see his recovered cancer patient.

Payton told him that she was well enough to travel and that her recovery was, "nothing short of a miracle." Rather than express enthusiasm, Smellie asked detailed questions about the induced fevers and how long the treatment protocol had lasted.

"What were the dosages and the details of precisely where injections were placed?" Payton promised him a full, detailed report. "How many Coley vaccines are left?" Payton assured him they had sufficient to treat several patients – they had been so effective. Smellie politely requested that Payton give time and attention now that his patient was in remission, to compiling detailed notes of his treatment regime. Payton was slightly abashed because he thought he had already agreed to that but he listened without interrupting the fine mind at work on the other end of the line. He was struck by the contrast in their locations and thrilled by the mental image of the busy hospital in Edinburgh. Smellie had run on in his inquiry to ask about suitable refrigeration for reserves of the Coley toxins.

"Oh yes, yes," answered Payton with a flash of natural pride, "We have a storage facility in Elgin," then slowed thoughtfully, "But as a matter of fact, I could do with a proper gas refrigeration unit at my surgery. I have to rely on regular deliveries from a local ice house at Banff. We are also well stationed here for fisheries and breweries. They always have supplies of ice. The two big hospitals of course have cold rooms in their pathology labs." Smellie listened in silence, pleased to note that he wasn't talking to a man from a previous century.

"The Italian hokey-pokey men in Elgin actually have a sideline, delivering blocks of ice. They are as regular as clockwork Mr Smellie, dependable as the sunrise in the morning."

"Hmm, you wouldn't say that if you lived here in the capital Dr Payton!" Payton laughed before he continued, affable but determined to make his request on the back of, 'research done in the field.' A small audience, listening to his half of the conversation from the saloon bar at the Forbes Arms Hotel tilted their heads silently to pick up the line of humour.

"But you have hit on a small problem Mr Smellie. It is not easy to regulate the precise temperature for storage of the toxins."

"Right, well you order a thermostatically controlled medical unit and tell them to send me the bill. Assuming that is you may have room for it?"

"Oh yes, I have been considering this acquisition for some time and I do indeed have plenty of space, thank you. What of your prognosis sir?" There was a long pause before Smellie answered. Payton could hear the whistle of air running past the hairs in the man's nose at the other end of the telephone line.

"I have the deepest reservations about this. I will be honest and say I did not expect her to survive long after I operated," he paused again, as though making a decision whether to make a full confession, "There were metastases and ascites, Dr Payton - malignant growths, spreading from the larger ones, with inflammation and necrotic fluid, which had to be tapped off following the operation. Who could say where it might have spread in the meantime?"

"I understand Mr Smellie. Mr Mitton told me as much also. If I may make so bold he intimated that he would not have attempted the operation, the cancer sounded too far advanced."

"No, and that is precisely my point Dr Payton," Smellie took a deep breath as though making a reluctant judgement, "Let her come here for examination if she will, if she can afford to. I would very much like to see Mrs Harper again. But advise her strongly on my behalf - and I think you should make it clear that we are of one mind here – there may well be a recurrence of her cancer. I cannot evaluate the effectiveness of this new treatment. All I can do is examine her and perform more tests. Then I will send her back to you. In a year or two we will have the new X-ray machines installed which will at least let us know what we are up against. I would not hold out too much hope for that schedule either. I find that the more enthusiastic people are the greater their disappointment tends to be. I've seen too much of what cancer can do, Dr Payton."

"Yes and of course any operation is traumatic."

"I believe Mrs Harper should continue this treatment locally. That at least will allow Mr Mitton and yourself the experience of seeing it through."

"Well, I suppose I should be flattered that you place such trust in me, Mr Smellie. People here have plenty of experience in offering medical care at home. Her mother is very supportive. She kept her hydrated and well supplied with hot and cold palliatives for her fluctuating fever. I didn't even have to ask, she knew what to do."

"Well exactly, I'm sure they are wonderful. No doubt it's second nature to people up where you are. Makes you wonder how many new-born lambs the woman has saved from the snow, no?"

"Well I think you've hit the nail on the head. They often see the veterinarian working up close. Sadly doctors too, more often than I'd like."

"Yes, well I wish some of our nurses at the Royal were as proficient."

"Well sir, I will tell her precisely what you said – in terms of the advice that is. She chose to come here, so there will be no difficulty persuading her to stay."

"Good man Payton! But tell Mrs Harper she may call at my morning clinic next Monday at ten, or Wednesday afternoon after two thirty. She will not have to wait - and congratulations again, to both of you!"

"Thank you Mr Smellie, you are most gracious!"

"Oh by the way . . . hello, Payton, you still there?" Payton spun back with the cord wrapped around his arm. The men at the bar smiled in anticipation. One or two craned their necks over to see and hear the telephone conversation better.

"Yes, yes . . . Go ahead man!"

"Do you know of a Russian doctor named Chekhov?"

"Anton Chekhov, the young Russian playwright? Yes, who doesn't? Marvellous stuff!"

"Indeed. Well, he discovered this effect before Coley published."

"What, you mean the fever therapy?"

"Not the therapy but the effect. Chekhov noted that erysipelas infection reduces cancerous cells. Louis Pasteur, who is of course a favourite adoptive son of this great city of Edinburgh, has made similar observations. Ha! Local brewers and City Fathers love him - not to mention those who regularly drink his health with homogenised produce - whether beer or milk."

Payton laughed, "Well, I assume this new medical insight will be well received in Lothian then?" Smellie was silent for a moment but decided not to divulge what he knew, "Hmm, well I'm not sure about that Dr Payton. If there was a way of controlling the fever, or of stopping it if it rises too high, then it stands to reason that the Coley toxins would become the simplest intervention for cancer patients. We will see."

"Indeed sir, we will. I will order the refrigerator for my surgery and send you the bill, Mr Smellie, along with my report. Many thanks sir."

Smellie said goodbye to Payton. As he replaced the receiver on its cradle, he glanced despondently at an article in the December issue of the American Journal of Medical Science offering readership unequivocal evidence that Coley's cancer treatment did not actually work - despite three hundred or so patients that it had saved to date.

He knew himself to be a busy and pragmatic man who had seen every variety of career ambition and vested interest played out in the most forceful and vicious manner. Normally he could step around them without getting involved but he had a very bad feeling about this entire matter.

Financial puppet masters brazenly traded in people's lives in every sphere of economic exchange. Medicine, like illness itself, was a lucrative industry and no exception. Scientific interest should never extend to the blatant manipulation of evidence or indeed character assassination, but Smellie had been around long enough to know that it frequently did. The higher the stakes, the more creditable would be Coley's executioners. He tossed the article onto the right hand corner of his desk, glancing as he did so towards his colleague Patterson.

"The pharmaceutical industry cannot patent killed bacteria of Erysipelas or Streptococcus, Martin. Any hospital lab can generate this remedy and mount a retrospective legal case to break the Parke-Davis patent, especially as the treatment protocol must be tailored to the size and weight, as well as condition of the patient. If they all did, which they will and the treatment becomes commonplace, who will spend millions developing X-ray equipment to locate and bombard tumours? That's where the money is and that's where investors will see the future because it chimes with the future of all scientific research."

Payton's enthusiastic voice was still resounding in Smellie's mind. By now there were dozens, if not hundreds of others around the World, like the GP in Morayshire, who had tried fever therapy for themselves and found it a cinch.

"Poor old Coley," Smellie looked across the room to his laconic anaesthetist, "It looks like someone at Sloane Kettering doesn't like him. Either way the bastards are lining up to destroy him now. No doubt without any good reason at all."

"Really, is that what you have been reading? Do tell," re-joined Patterson with barely casual interest, as he cowboyed his wheeled swivel chair across the surgery floor to lift the article without standing up. Smellie looked across at him indulgently, perhaps offering more respect than his colleague deserved.

"His treatment is too simple and too effective. Literally a magic bullet." Patterson spent a minute silently flicking through the journal, then stood up. He looked at Smellie indulgently, arms at his sides waiting for his colleague to scrub-in for their next procedure.

"A magic bullet indeed Archie, except for the fact that it is the pharmaceutical industry that has the pact with the devil, not the young bone surgeon."

"Medical science has stumbled upon a simple and effective key to curing cancer which it will choose not to make use of until it first dismantles the lock that it fits," Smellie looked at Patterson thoughtfully for an instant before shaking his head slightly. Patterson slid the academic extract into the out-tray.

"Hmm, that could take another hundred years Archie," grumbled Patterson. He hadn't bothered to read the article – after all it wasn't his specialism.

Payton unravelled the tangled cord by letting the receiver hang down by his knees. As it spun in circles he wondered why there was a sudden hubbub behind him from men scattered around the lounge. When he had put it back on the cradle he turned around to applause and shouts.

"Bravo, Dr Payton!"

"Champion, Joseph, champion!"

"Well played that man! Did yis hear boys – a refrigerator? Order one fer ma butcher's shop while yer aboot it, Joe. Send his worship a bill fer that too! Willie, Willie, a dram fer the man!" Donald McIntyre the butcher called to the barman, wagging his finger toward the good bottles below the counter. Will Hendry the barman put out whisky glasses for all present for a toast.

Payton was speechless. He knew every one of them as well as they knew him. In the best sense of the word they were all *his* patients. Of course he realised this was as much about Hannah Harper and her family as himself. Delighted at this effusive social recognition but not knowing what to say, the doctor smiled self-consciously and took a bow. As if to save his embarrassment, Henderson picked up his accordion and started to play, in time with a wave of warm banter. By some unseen magical process, word of the miracle cure seemed to have radiated along the streets and lanes of Milltown. Judging from the numbers already in the pub just after opening time, it was cue for an instant party.

The lounge of the Forbes began to gradually fill up and within two hours Payton was as drunk as an Edinburgh advocate at a debating society evening. When he finally made it back to his surgery at eight pm. Mrs Payton had got wind of the cause celebre. She had decided to put a handwritten notice on the surgery door:

CLOSED FOR THE EVENING.

Before taking off his shoes and settling by the fireside for the evening, Payton took the artist's brush out of the drawer beside the Belfast sink and daubed a footnote on Judith's thoughtful notice:

Due to cancer cure.

Little Hannah sat on stairs in her pyjamas with Great Gran who was pandering to her defencelessly. The toddler cried inconsolably for over an hour watching the front door, then still refused to go to bed. The bairn had long ago embarked on a spiritual vigil for her mammy which a glass of warm milk and a teddy bear could not help her make. Great Gran explained that, "Daddy has gone with Mummy to see Mr Smellie in Edinburgh," but the words simply registered uncertainty and confusion for the child. She had decided to set her stall against the vaunted Edinburgh specialist because Betsy Wilson made a joke about his name, referring to the pre-eminent surgeon as 'Smelly bo-bo' which in the relief surrounding her mother's recovery was played to exhaustion despite Jessie's disapproval.

In their elevated mood of relief and fond attention to one another Hannah and Harper had been too busy to explain their departure to Little Han. Amid all the talk and excitement they overlooked an essential communication which momentarily broke her heart, pitching her into a chasm of isolation.

In her childish perception she accepted Great Gran's explanation that this was, "best for mammy" but it still reduced to a feeling of separation she had come to dread, sitting on the stairs with her sisters months before. Elsie and Elizabeth had talked about her imminent departure with Daddy when they had all listened together. Now they had gone to Edinburgh also, and neither of them had come back since.

Little Hannah was left behind with her own burden of care for Great Gran and Jessie, who everyone knew worked too hard. The younger Wilsons, Betsy and Elsie and the Robertsons, Kate and Fiona lifted and laid Little Hannah like a living doll. But she had issues of attachment as well as abandonment. All she had wished for during the long months of her mother's recuperation was for *her* company, not someone else's. Lately this had been restored but now without a word her mother was gone. Although there was a deep bond of love between them Great Gran Han realised that her namesake was inconsolable, suffering a tragic and inexplicable sense of loss akin to bereavement. All she could do was hug the child as she sat with her on the bottom step of the stairs, ostensibly awaiting her mother's return.

Loneliness is the sharp soil into which every child's soul spreads its roots.

Great Gran banked the smouldering evening fire with more coal and wood and put the kettle on to boil, calling to Little Hannah, "Come and help me make some tea." The door opened immediately and she ran in from the cold, deserted hallway. The toddler helped her to find biscuits, so Great Gran did not have to bend over to the bottom cupboard. Great Gran brought a blanket to wrap round them both. They decided to select a story book to read, which was easy, "Mowgli, Great Gran," little Han suggested, pointing with the second finger of her right hand to a blue covered hard back book with gold elephants embossed on the cover.

"Oh yes, *The Jungle Book*. How delightful. I've been looking forward to hearing the rest of Mr Kipling's short stories," Great Gran pulled the huge armchair up to the roaring fire, "What fun!" she said conspiratorially, looking down at the worried little tot, "You and I will read them together until we get our fill."

At last the key question burning in Little Hannah's mind came.

"Great Gran – where does a body go to when they die?"

"Oh well, now," began Great Gran, her voice rising with a tone of forced enthusiasm as she struggled to think of a reply, "The person goes up to Heaven to be with the Lord Jesus Christ and all their departed relatives."

"Great Gran, what's Heaven like?"

"Let me think, Darling . . . It's a beautiful place, full of gardens, with fountains and flowers, bright lights and beautiful buildings."

"Is Heaven like Edinburgh, or like New York? Or is it like our farm with Tex and Sally and the sheep and coos?"

"Well, yes and no. It's more like a sea of good dreams where everyone meets together and can learn about God's wonderful plan for the world. Everyone is happy together in heaven. There is no illness or death."

"And no cancer?" asked the innocent, looking up at Great Gran.

"No darling, no cancer," Great Gran replied with a lump in her throat the size of Alaska and her face as limp as a torn cloth.

It was three am when fatigue supplanted sorrow and the child finally fell asleep in the old woman's arms. Great Gran decided not to disturb her by carrying her to cold sheets. Within minutes she too drifted into slumber. They slept together in the big armchair until the cows came to wake them - snorting and lowing softly for attention as they ripped the lush grass below the window.

The working day on the farm was half over as Great Gran shifted her weary limbs, to rise and make breakfast for the workers. Pulling the back of Jessie's apron to reassure her, Little Han announced to all and sundry in the kitchen with great confidence, "I've been to Heaven and the Sea of Dreams but my Mammy isnae there. That's good though in't it? . . . because we'd all be sad an' miss her. She must still be at the Royal 'firmary with Mr Smellie and Harper."

"Oh, that's very good," Frank agreed, as he stirred fresh milk onto his porridge, "That means she's definitely alright. D'you hear that eh, Great Gran?" The old lady turned from her frying bacon to wink at the boy. His face was full of suppressed glee at the child's innocent logic, "Sea o' Dreams, eh? Boy that's precious, Great Gran. I love that. I'nt she a wee, charmer, eh?"

Great Gran looked across at Jessie, cautious about sharing her glee but the light of love shone on the children chatting at her table.

"It's amazing the difference a few years can make to the wisdom of a wee man," Jessie murmured to her mother, "One day soon he'll be the boss for sure."

Little Hannah got down from her stool and climbed up next to Frank. She kissed him square on his mouth with a moist, fresh-milky kiss which left a ring around his mouth. Frank smiled broadly, showing his teeth as he wiped the moisture from Little Hannah's kiss away with the back of his hand.

Another year turned slowly and another family reunion came at Easter. There were bluebells in the woods, hope in the soft sunshine. Watchful birds and eager foxes asserted the beginning of a new life cycle. The girls were keen to learn more about life on the farm. Elsie told great Gran what her friend Maggie had said, "Mr Grant would like tae shoot the foxes but they are no' on his land."

Great Gran replied contentiously, "The foxes keep things in balance, Elsie. They could ne'er get to the hens because of Sally and Tex." Elsie and Elizabeth probed her to tell more about 'the balance.'

Great Gran Han explained about her market garden - cabbages and potatoes that rabbits from the woods liked to eat, given a chance. They were her rivals. She told them that the foxes lived right behind the house in a hollow on top of the wooded outcrop. Their presence was a natural barrier to rabbits venturing through the copse into her vegetable patch, "That's why the warren is over by the edge of the road, in the cow pasture. The foxes are wary of the cattle. One kick and they'd be out of business. But the rabbits would be taking a big risk passing the foxes den to the farmyard to get to my vegetables. The foxes are clever like the dogs," she explained, "They know that I tolerate them . . . As a matter o' fact I'd sooner shoot one of they fucking deer," she snapped irately, pointing to a group of twenty that had wandered down off the fells onto a neighbour's land. She turned on her heel to walk back into the farmhouse.

The girls were aghast, eager to know why the deer presented such a challenge but that question would have to wait. Great Gran self-consciously slammed the kitchen door. Inside, she listened with a guilty smile for the gale of high pitched laughter she knew would follow her inappropriate cursing.

Their mother Hannah could not resist working. It began invisibly with household chores. Then she went on shopping errands to the Milltown, ostensibly for exercise. Working soon became an elective routine that grew incrementally. Everyone agreed she had natural ability with the cows and it saved time if Hannah took over daily routines of moving and milking. The cattle sensed her gentle authority and most of them would come to her on sight, welcoming her as a friend.

Jeannie was happy to defer to Hannah's experience as a farmer so she took a job at the local woollen mill to bring in regular cash wages that were always welcome. The same logic extended to the four younger children – Betsy Wilson, Kate, Fiona and Elsie Wilson. They gravitated to Hannah for advice about everything. Dress; rude boys; affairs of the heart; difficult school work, the tristesse of rising each day to boring routines and the resolution of jealousies or petty conflict with peers and siblings. The fact that she was their sister, or step sister, meant that they not only loved and revered Hannah – they owned her outright. She was their celebrity.

Reverend Blair referred to Hannah Harper regularly in church services, as though she was a female Lazarus, living testimony to the miraculous power of faith. Through thick and thin she had always been a member of his assembly, now he pressed her to join the Church Committee. She had, "respect and influence in the local community," so he told her.

There were whispers among the young ones of his having fallen in love with her. Blair was a handsome man of mature years, well-educated and gracious in his manner. Despite the surname he seemed characteristically English in his expressions, although he hailed from the coastal village of Tighnabruaich in Argyllshire. Blair was tall and pallid, in Hannah's opinion quintessentially benign and approachable.

"Like the Paytons," she intimated to Harper, "I think Jim is a very special individual, in a very special place. We are lucky to have him here."

Blair was what the Church saw as the ideal minister for an outlying parish, which may not have entirely healed the deepest wounds of historical memory. Reconciliation was the priority.

"Yer no in Glesgae now laddie," had become the paradoxical catch-phrase of a community moving on from asinine sectarianism, still prevalent in Scotland's larger industrial communities.

Blair announced to his flock, "My 'notional Church' is a place of refuge – sanctified and hallowed in the name of the Lord – like any church of mediaeval times. All are welcome, whether sinners, or saved."

Not long after his arrival, Blair had taken down the old Church of Scotland sign and refused to put it back up. He announced that he would never lock the door. Blair became a local hero, consciously trying to undo the prejudices of the past. Religious affiliates of three other prevalent Christian communities read or heard about him and beat a path to his door, speaking of their Episcopalian counterpart from the pulpit with warmth, if not complete approval.

When Rangers played Celtic in the Scottish Cup Final Blair conducted the Sunday service in a green and white hooped jersey, with a blue rosette pinned to his breast.

"The spiritual message," he told them, "is about recognising the achievement of others – while celebrating life with energy and endeavour."

Harper came once again and tried once more to draw from Hannah a commitment to return home to Edinburgh. Her wide eyes warned him there was much she simply could not say. She was in pain again. Each time she engaged in a lengthy conversation, an irresistible cough would get in the way. Once or twice when she stood up suddenly, she felt dizzy. Harper noticed one morning as Hannah got out of bed that she immediately collapsed back onto it. He had more than once seen a Saturday night drunk stumbling out onto the pavement, suddenly poleaxed by the fresh air but Hannah hadn't been on the bevvy.

In the autumn of '95 Harper insisted on taking her to see Mitton at Elgin. The consultant mumbled contentiously about the treatment perhaps not being as effective as first assumed, "Coley's research methods have been called into question by some notable people in the field over the past year," he declared tersely, "Two of his patients died of fever."

"I know. I told you that Mr Mitton," Harper replied disdainfully.

"Well that's as may be. My point is there are new and better techniques on the brink of mass production. There is ground breaking research into X-rays, being conducted by Dr G A Pirie over in Dundee, with similar initiatives at the University of Glasgow."

But Harper already had a smart Bobbie's perspective on the evidence, not only regarding the significance of Coley's fundamental breakthrough for immunological science but the prognosis for tertiary stage cancers of any origin, however treated.

He was now also something of an expert on the interpretation of statistical information and the actuarial basis for decision making where investments were concerned. Harper challenged Mitton with biting irony, barely managing to hold his temper.

"If I was in your shoes Mitton, I'd be throwing my entire budget behind the 99 per cent success rate!"

"But you're not in my shoes, Mr Harper – and you don't have the burden of responsibility."

"Look, Mr Mitton, with all due respect, why don't you leave the cutting edge atomic physics to the theorists? How many cancer patients have they cured?"

Mitton made no response other than to stare at Harper in exasperation. With reluctance he agreed to order a new batch of the Coley's toxins for Hannah from Parke Davis, the drug company in Detroit.

As they walked out of the hospital entrance into the late October rain, in the name of scientific realism Harper fulminated about such biased interpretation of the statistics, "They think they are comparing apples with oranges – but they're both still fruit! Why would they count deaths from intervention and not count deaths from lack of intervention, ignoring the predicted outcome if nothing is done? And what status do pointless surgical procedures have in that overall picture? How completely ludicrous! Stupid fucking self-serving bastards, all of them! *Two deaths out of two hundred,* Hannah! Coley has discovered a cure for cancer but they are stopping him from using it on a technicality!"

"Will you please stop cursing like a coal heaver! I think you made your point eloquently enough. Mitton is offering me the treatment!" Harper sullenly hailed a cab.

Once inside, Hannah smiled serenely and shut her eyes. Her head rolled from side to side as the taxi rig bounced along the cobbled street fronting the railway station. Her head was swimming and her stomach felt like it was about to turn inside out.

Eventually more of the Coley toxins arrived at Payton's surgery for Mrs Harper's treatment but the vaccines were greatly reduced in strength and seemed to be less effective when applied. Hannah bluntly refused to go into hospital, where her tumorous lungs might be tapped when the desired immune reaction kicked in.

For the next ten weeks Payton subjected her to a controlled fever, with careful use of thoracocentesis when she twice showed danger signs of pneumonia. Hannah quickly stabilised again and within a month of Hogmanay resumed her daily routines with a light heart, as though nothing was different.

"It's like the injuries you used to get from playing football," she told Harper one night when they were in bed, "Only on the inside. The lumps disappear just as quickly as a bruise, when I have the injections. Obviously I am prone to it for some reason. I'm just so glad they have found a way of treating it. One day soon Coley will be vindicated." Harper held her in his arms until they both fell asleep.

To Dr Payton's chagrin the unseen malignancy had receded but not vanished and in the winter months it came again. Hannah found that her head was often light, and she could feel stabbing pains of exhaustion across her heart, though she said nothing. When she coughed as she did daily, there was wracking discomfort and the taste of blood in her mouth. When she vomited as she also did daily, there was dark brown bile which she urgently sluiced away. She slept long without finding rest, glad only that the awful, gnawing ache in her abdomen and thighs was no longer the primary cause of her distress. She tried to counter it bravely by walking it off, breathing deeply to use all of her lungs.

When the vernal equinox came during the fourth week of March she dressed Little Hannah for the invigorating cold to walk hand-in-hand under a clear sky through the gloaming, to see the Northern Lights. They took soup and buttered bread in a knapsack. Heading down through the Milltown they walked past the ancient stone circle, eerie in the diffident frost and up onto Gallow Hill to the highest point above Deveron Valley within half an hour's distance.

Sitting on a fallen tree together they watched, huddling for warmth as the horizon to the north began to shimmer with curtains of undulating green and pink light.

"What is it mummy? Is it really angels dancing?" asked the innocent.

"Yes of course, angels dance wherever they like but it's not just that."

"What else is it then mammy?"

"It's the hand of The Creator, reaching out across eternity."

"You mean God. What's he cratoring mammy?"

"Oh, everything there is - all the stars. Worlds like Earth with all its hills and forests. Creatures and people like us."

"Mammy, mammy! I think that's the Sea of Dreams," breathed Little Han sensationally, looking along her raised arm as she pointed with her middle finger to a curtain of green light descending beyond Knock Hill to the north – giving assurance to her own assertion and enchantment to her mother, "*That's* where we all go when we die!"

When the girls came at Easter she cautioned Harper against probing too deeply into the delay in resumption of her treatment. Outwardly she seemed self-assured, almost complacent, yet inwardly Hannah was in turmoil. They had a day out at the seaside and on the way took a detour to the photographer's in Dufftown.

Kind and sensible, Elsie played her mother's game, acting as though everything was normal but try as she did Elizabeth could not get her younger sister to look anything but glum. Little Hannah wore her concern with a downturned mouth, refusing to smile for Mr Henry behind the camera. She was the barometer for her mother's fatalism.

In the second week of the holiday Harper forced the issue. Hannah conceded to another expensive and tiring day trip to Edinburgh to see Smellie.

"I am concerned that you may have fallen between two stools Mrs Harper. If you were here in Edinburgh I would be more than happy to stake my reputation on Dr Coley's treatment regime. Why don't you return here where Mr Harper may visit you in hospital as he frequently as he chooses?"

Hannah pondered Smellie's suggestion, speaking genially when she replied, "Oh, I don't think much has changed in my situation. To return now before I am cured would be to admit I was wrong in the first place. The fact that I am still here is entirely due to William B Coley. Let's be honest Mr Smellie . . . we all know this."

"Are you telling us that Mitton has given up on this?" demanded Harper.

"I cannot speak for another physician, Mr Harper but the tide is certainly turning for Coley. A patient who refuses to go into hospital for treatment merely augments the potential for his detractors to say, "I told you so!"

"But Dr Payton is willing to try again. Surely his experience counts for something in all of this?" pleaded Hannah.

"Yes, indeed it does. And as long as you have that support, Mitton will play his part. He is a fine fellow. I won't hear a word said against him," said Smellie firmly as he looked at Harper, clearly aware of his view.

"The fact is that the Americans are killing this remedy, not us. In any event, Mitton has ordered more of the medication."

Trying to act normally, Hannah occupied herself with chores throughout the lengthening days. Taking buckets of feed up to the poultry one morning in the third week of May, she fainted twice although initially no-one witnessed the event. She fell in the lane and again twenty minutes later on the uneven ground on the top pasture, toppling over backwards like a baby that had not yet learned to walk. Hannah knew the cancer was in her brain. The cows halted their shredding to watch her benignly.

When she sat up on the grass bank looking back at the pretty farmstead with its two houses, its scattering of barns and sheds, she found herself pre-occupied in listening to its gentle, humming sounds. Everything that existed was constant, interacting movement and sound. This time she saw the introspected vision without the Tincture of Opium she had once been dependant on. Hannah felt peacefully resigned. In that moment she felt there was nothing she absolutely needed to do that she had not already done. She was completely relaxed, completely absorbed in being.

Harper was catching up on neglected accounts in the Midlands. Elsie and Elizabeth had another month at school before the summer break. Payton had taken a long overdue holiday at a time of year when demand on his services was typically at its lowest. Hannah knew that if she alerted Jessie to her failing condition her mother would flap, insisting that she go into Dr Gray's Hospital in Elgin. That prospect frightened her more than facing the end.

In her heart Hannah felt overwhelmed with gratitude by the impression her living had made on others and the recognition they in turn had given her. She sat on the bank of the high pasture with her hands flat on the warm grass, watching the sun burn off haze on the magnificent high valley all around, knowing now that she would have no life beyond Ramsburn other than the romantic time of promise she'd already spent in brave Edinburgh.

Little Han alerted Great Gran Han to the damning reality, "Mammy's not well. Look, she's sitting down because she's tired. She's spilled the seeds!"

That evening her mother and grandmother wrung a promise from Hannah that she would go up to see Mitton the following day. He could give her the injection to begin another course of fever therapy and the locum, Dr Campbell could come out in a couple of days, to keep it going until Payton returned. There was no argument.

As the sun rose above the rookery the following morning, Deveron Valley resounded to the brisk harmony of Spring-time and the carnival of all living things. An hour after dawn, brave morning sunshine was warming even the darkest places constructed by men when the hands on the clock ceased their movement for Hannah Harper.

When she went to rouse her, Jessie's single cry of sharp anguish was lost to all but the dogs, amid the morning exultations of cockerels, cattle and sheep.

The end had come unexpectedly, if not suddenly. It was a little after five o'clock in the morning, on the twenty sixth of May, 1896, when her kind heart stopped beating. Hannah Drummond Wilson Harper had experienced just thirty three years and three months of earnest hope, in her daunting, exquisitely harmonious world.

Chapter Sixteen - *A Benediction Forbidding Mourning*

Following the shock of the unjust and deeply tragic event, there was mutual if somewhat shaky consolation in talking about what had happened – a confluence of versions allaying guilt which reinforced sentiment.

"That locum Dr Campbell was a greenhorn. He clearly had nae idea what tae do. Hannah had nae faith in him," Great Gran cried sharply to her daughter, wiping her eyes on a corner of her apron. Jessie was more sanguine when she finally steadied her breathing but could only venture a lame aphorism.

"Ma, no-one can cheat their fate. When it's your time tae be ca'ed, you go to meet the Lord . . . none of us knows that time. She had suffered so much!" Jessie added, as if to draw a line under the medical deliberations. She had done all she could and was not happy to attribute guilt to others.

"But he might ha'e sent her into the hospital if he was not sure what tae do. They could have given her the fever therapy and tapped the fluid off from her lungs. She would have been home in a couple of weeks. He said as much, so why did he wait, the stupid man?"

"Yes ma, but Mitton had to order more Coley Toxins. The refrigerator didn't come for two months remember. Dr Payton said the last lot went bad. And the second batch didn't work like the first lot. There is no-one to blame. They all did what they could."

"She ne'er went tae see Dr Pirie for the X-ray," re-joined the old lady, unwilling to let it go.

"What's that Great Gran?" asked Harper, his voice croaking from the length of time his mouth had been welded shut. Harper had known from eight am the previous day when the telegram had come that, "Please come to Ramsburn immediately. STOP," meant the tolling of the bell for Hannah. He had been spared witnessing of the final thrust, only to be burdened by dread of the Grim Reaper for the implication of those five words. From that moment, each time he tried to speak his chest and throat immediately clenched in anguish.

Jessie answered for the old lady, as Great Gran wiped away a fresh overflow of forlorn tears.

"Oh John, Mr Smellie told Dr Payton they could locate the lung cancer, so they could inject directly into it. Payton phoned Dundee. They said that if Hannah went over on the train they would send back an X-ray image in a couple of days. Joseph said he had read up about Coley's work. He told us that he was completely certain that it would work. He was just waiting for the letter of confirmation to come from Dundee. Dr Campbell says it came yesterday," Jessie looked at Harper, lowering her voice as she noticed his heartbroken expression.

"She had a persistent cough - but that is all! She had her things packed and was ready to go into hospital for them to inject into her lungs," put in Great Gran, combative as ever, "She ne'er gave up. She would ha'e soon been on the mend again!" she added defiantly.

Finally Harper smiled and got up to hug each of the women in turn, "I love you two!" There was nothing more to be said.

Where she lay with her eyes closed in her bedroom, one after the other they took their leave of Hannah. Elizabeth said she was sure that her mammy was, "Still in there."

Elsie was uncomprehending, "Her face looks as though she might wake up and speak again," she pronounced.

Little Hannah had the last word, "Don't worry, Ma's just crossing the Sea of Dreams to Jesus in Heaven." She climbed across Harper's knee to kiss her ma, waving goodbye as she ran out of the room after her sisters. That was the final pathetic coup for him. Harper asked Jeannie if she would follow them, "Take them off my hands for an hour or two will you? They could feed the hens or something."

"Sure Harper, that's fine." Jeannie hugged him, then left quickly to organise the bairns.

Harper felt that he was about to fold like wet paper. He closed his eyes, letting go of Hannah's cold hand. His head fell onto her unmoving chest and he slumped onto the floor, kneeling not in

310

solicitation but mental and emotional collapse. Their desperate tribulations were over at last but what they'd shared had been magnificent, the more so for their mutual concerns. Every minute spent in her company had been the deepest joy.

Sorrow slowly transported Harper into a universe of reversed feelings. He had spent so long expecting his beloved Hannah to die, that recent hours of grief on his journey from Birmingham via Edinburgh simply merged with previous years of sadness gone before. Now he was experiencing a tangible sense of relief that her suffering was ended, after so many years of frustration and pain.

Harper felt certain there was a presence observing him in the room as he knelt on the floor by her bed. Light and hope filled his senses. Images of every exuberant moment they had shared over the previous ten years came back in a torrent of fulfilment. He put his left hand over his eyelids to keep them sealed, in order to prolong the perception of joy sustained. With cupped fingers he held Hannah's tight hand. Before time intruded he stood up to kiss the forehead of his far-seeing soul mate and whispered, "Hey, Woolly Bird! I'm here now. No more worry. I know you are still with me. I can still hear your voice!"

Harper felt his heart well with love from a dimension beyond pain and knew he was beginning to understand the necessity of sacrifice and sorrow. He had come to terms with loneliness too, having felt so much of it over recent years – although he knew it for what it was – an untamed animal that fed on sorrow.

His mind went back to a vaguely remembered, hopelessly drunken evening spent two years before, alone in the mire of natural philosophy. He'd decided then that compassion is the eternal touchstone. Harper was inspired by the love he had shared with Hannah. Misery would not break him.

"We will always be together . . ." He heard his own cracked voice, then caught sight of the gaunt face looking back from the mirror above the dresser.

The girls will think I'm a sight.

Rinsing tired eyes, he changed out of the creased business suit he'd been wearing since the previous day in Birmingham into another of fine quality. He imagined he heard Hannah say, "Come on Harper, it is time for us to walk in the woods."

Harper walked for miles in a loop along Glen Barry then back along pastures flanking the Deveron. Although his heart was heavy with loss, her love had healed him many years ago. He felt as though she was walking by his side. Harper vowed that nothing he knew or wanted, or might lose – nothing under the sun would make him cry again.

"I will always love you, Hannah!" he called feverishly into the breeze rippling almond blossom in the lane below Marnoch.

Without a clear purpose he walked aimlessly in a circle, impulsively calling into the church in Rothiemay for the first time in five years. Admitting his exocentric nature at last, Harper accepted a motive to relate to others beyond family for once. He spoke easily, if a little distractedly to the minister about his loss. In turn Hannah's friend tried to console Harper with honest words. Reverend Blair assured Harper of his good offices and that he would speak to the undertaker on his behalf. Harper thanked him and walked towards Auchterless, with the intention of visiting his adoptive parents.

He ate supper with them, for once basking in genuine love and concern. Explaining briefly what else he had to do, Harper borrowed a rig from his Uncle Hugh. He headed off towards a magnificent daytime moon waning low on the horizon, to take the sad news to Zach and Annie.

When he arrived at Elgin two hours later the soft evening had faded into resplendent, star strewn darkness. Harper pulled the pony up outside a large detached villa set in fragrant spring gardens and surrounded by mature trees.

He planned to spend the evening with Zachariah Williams, whom as a child he had felt to be the most dispassionately thoughtful and kind man in the world. Harper needed to bare his soul to the only person he completely respected and trusted, now that his true friend was gone.

For years Harper had neglected his childhood mentor and at first there was a natural reserve between them, with careful propriety shown by both men. They reminisced, mainly about distant memories, but Harper was careful to step around the painfully guarded subject of his father. Zachariah obliged him gracefully - in his eyes Harper could read the benign caution of the life-long diplomat.

Zachariah had married a widow twenty years his junior, who worked for him first as a seamstress, but now managed his bespoke tailoring business. Annie Williams fed and watered them, producing sandwiches and salad although Harper insisted he had eaten earlier.

Having drunk more wine than she was used to, Annie took her leave at ten thirty after hugging Harper firmly with wet eyed condolences. Tomorrow was nominally a working day but Zachariah had no need to tax himself. People always had to wait for the very best quality suits.

Harper relaxed in front of the stoked fire, as Zachariah moved to the sideboard. His silent question with raised brows, bottle in hand, and Harper's thoughtful nod of approval was the only ceremonial. Zachariah placed his finest malt and glasses on the table between them, assuming that John would reach for it without being invited.

"I don't want to keep you up too late, Uncle Zach," Harper stated tentatively.

"Tomorrow I will rise when I feel like it, John. I will work when I want . . . after first walking by the river to clear my head," Zach smiled self-assuredly, lifting his glass to his lips with poise.

"Slaintje!"

"Good health!" Harper echoed, lifting his glass in acceptance.

They talked about life, love and disaffection. About God's plan and how it might be discerned – "to inform purpose, thought, or feeling."

They questioned appearances and change, speaking lightly of
Jacobites and Clearances. They moved on to colonies and economic
systems – dependency, autarky and empire.

 "But the fuckin' English?" declared Zachariah, laughingly, shaking
his head in confusion.

 "Aye, the fuckin' English!" echoed Harper, shaking his in
bewilderment.

To avoid unresolved contention they skated round the 'fuckin'
English,' bracketed Napoleon and the Boers then agreed how quickly
the succession of desperate conflicts had been forgotten, along with
the struggle and pain of millions.

As they drank and chattered they shook their heads at disregarded
horrors, quickly replenishing their drinks for fear the reality might
impinge too greatly. Raising glasses again to toast friends and family,
Harper found himself laughing, for Zachariah was such easy
company.

 Zachariah was from Gateshead but his forebears were Welsh, so
that made him an honorary Scotsman. The fact that he had lived
most of his adult life in the Highlands gave him a different view of
the privilege of being part of that community.

"You love it here don't you Zach?" Harper remarked.

"Yes, unhesitatingly I would say that I do love it here," answered
Zach, his bright eyes conveying the hint of a hundred stories, "You
know John, you should come back . . . seriously man," he intoned,
with his head and Caithness crystal glass tilting forward at a
reassuringly parallel angle of about twenty degrees. It meant if Zach
fell asleep in the armchair, he would probably manage not to spill his
drink.

"Hmm, I think you know why I left Zach?"

"Yes, of course, but here there is balance John. We don't experience
the same rate of change as the rest of the world - although mark you,
change when it catches up can be devastating. But there is a kind of
magic here in the Highlands in all that your eyes behold. And . . .
and it transmits to everybody, young or old in some indiscernible

way, I am certain of it. Hutcheson was on to something not properly perceived. People have a natural tendency towards good. And good places create their own history, by working some invisible force on them. I don't know anywhere quite like this region and I have travelled all over Europe and the Americas, sourcing the finest wool. Look at me John – I'm seventy six and people think I'm still in my late fifties. Here people don't really live any longer, I know that . . . but it sure as hell feels like it."

"Dear Uncle Zach, I know you are right! Hannah always says that! – coming here actually gives her more time with her family overall, than if she's in Edinburgh."

Harper's voice tailed off into the appalling shock of remembrance. The alcohol had done its job of taking his mind out of time. He put down his tumbler of whisky, spreading fingers over his brow to shut out anguish suddenly twisting his face. Eventually he looked up at Zach, the person he would have chosen as a father if life had ever been that simple, in any respect.

"I always knew I'd not be with her at the end," Harper told him, with a plaintive gasp of regret.

Zachariah watched Harper sympathetically without moving or speaking. He was poignantly glad to have shared the young man's grief, whilst abhorring its cruel circumstances. It had brought John back to him this day, affirming everything Zachariah had taught him as a child. That respect resonated with the old tailor, more than he could say.

In that moment, Zach wished with all his heart that his old friend in Bristol, John Harper Senior, had admitted his mistake. In his place Zach would have openly adopted his illegitimate son, especially as the child's mother was never in the scene. Ironically it was Zachariah who had come to know this fine boy - loving him like a son.

Harper was clearly in shock as he resumed his assault on the Glenlivet with nervous appetency, as if the most urgent need was to obliterate feeling. Zachariah reached into the cabinet to confirm he had another ready if needed. It was needed. Harper had to talk and Zachariah wanted to listen.

"The doctors in Edinburgh never had the time for her Zach. Not at first when it mattered, when they might have done something for her. Doctors in big cities generally don't listen nowadays. Here you have the farriers and cowmen with tuberculosis. Occasionally grandma boiling water to deliver a baby . . . ," he shook his head slowly, struggling to make his point as the sumptuous aroma of whisky flooded his senses, "But yes, I think a body's chances are better here. At least the doctor will see you straight away, or come out. The queues man! Have you ever seen the queues in Edinburgh?" Zachariah shook his head slowly, smiling as if vindicated.

"Man, you can't imagine! Dr Foxworthy has a plaster of Paris skeleton in his surgery. Last time we were there in February, when Hannah's cough started, some old hallion in the waiting room had missed her turn. There must have been twenty or more sitting examining the floor tiles, all wheezing an' spluttering. Just then the Member of Parliament, Willie McEwan, walks through accompanied by his nephew, Younger. They were ushered straight in to see the doctor without even sitting."

"Oh now, this I can imagine John. Rank has its privileges, nay? I would gladly defer to such a great man!" Harper nearly choked on his whisky. He had to hold his hand up to his mouth to deal with the snort of laughter Zach's caustic insincerity produced.

"Boys, oh boys, was she angry! She got up to bustle across the waiting room, with a face like the Gorgon. She hammered on the door, posting her intentions if the MP dared to open it. She scolded all three of them up and down in full view of the people waiting. 'Some of us have been there for an hour and a half," she told them. Then she pointed at the skeleton and yelled, 'Sure, there's a man died waiting and you just propped him up in the fickin' corner!' No one dared to laugh but it was the funniest thing, Zach. She railed on at the receptionist until she got bumped up the line to see the doctor next. As she left everybody snickered, Some young lad even whistled and clapped."

Just before the midsummer dawn Zachariah prevailed upon Harper to have breakfast, though it was essentially still the middle of the night. He made them each a plateful of gammon, eggs and fried tomatoes with potato scones and oatcakes. Harper made tea to wash it down. They ate slowly in dyspeptic silence, as the savoury flavours merged with floral refulgences of the whisky they had drained to the last dram.

At length Harper broke the pre-dawn silence of the listening house, with wistful reluctance, "If you ever see him thank him for me, for the money, Zach. I know he was concerned about our predicament. In all, the treatment was not so expensive. She refused to travel to New York, although," Harper paused to swallow a mouthful of tea before he finished the admission, "your cheques – his money I should say, could have made that possible. If she had done it, I know that she would be alive this day." Harper looked straight at Zachariah, speaking with quiet, flinty honesty though his eyes were moist with tears.

"He gave us an opportunity Zach, when we needed it most. I won't ever forget that. Tell him so. He has earned my deepest gratitude - if not my forgiveness, or my genuine respect. Money isn't everything."

"No indeed, money isn't everything. Far from it!"

They stood in the whispering scent of a velvet morning, lowering their voices with respect to those who were only sleeping.

"I've spent three years thinking about nothing else, Uncle Zach. The seasons came and went and we just kept soldiering on in hope. It wasn't all bad but I honestly don't know how we managed. I would not wish such uncertainty and frustration upon an enemy. I couldn't ever talk about it in detail because even a straight telling would put the cold hand on a man's heart. It was like walking on egg shells. I was afraid of upsetting my bairns. I consistently lied to my employer. D'ye ken, I made that rail journey fourteen times in twenty four months? I often came through Elgin but never had time to spend an hour with you and Annie or bring my girls to get to know you properly until after the first Coley treatment." Harper's voice thickened at the injustice of unremitting providence until he could speak no more.

"Look, John, we understand. It has been good just to see your face. In future we will have time for all that." Harper shuffled his feet pensively, looking down the street towards the town, before clearing his throat and finding his voice again, "Now they tell me that the master from the academy, Bell is the man behind the telephones?"

"Oh yes, he was always 'well connected' - you'll pardon an old fool's a stab at humour!" Harper laughed gently and smiled, "Did you know that Hannah was offered his old job as music teacher at the academy but she turned it down? When you step out over the threshold Zach, you never know where the road will lead you, eh?"

"No you don't son, that's for sure. But the best thing is always the homecoming, nay?"

The two men looked at each other long in silence. In his drunken fugue Harper imagined that he could see an aura of white golden light, emerging to meet over their heads under the star strewn sky.

Have I drunk so much whisky I'm beginning to hallucinate?

"I can't believe it's finally over, Zach. I just can't stop thinking about her."

"No, nor should you."

The two good friends shook hands firmly, and parted without wasted words, each determined not to say goodbye.

Harper spoke softly to the tethered horse, stroking its neck to wake it gently from slumber. He intended to head home to Ramsburn with the rig, but the old garron made the turns without need for direction until he came to Hugh's farm. By then Harper was half asleep. He had to rouse himself to get the horse to walk on. When the long miles had passed as quickly as a short lifetime, Harper lay loaded in the half light of dawn next to his darling Hannah with his clothes still on. He was afraid to touch her in her intermediate state.

She has always been nearer to perfection than me. I must let her go.

In his intoxicated, reeling sleep they were together in paradise. She spoke to him from a place of eternal benediction where all mourning was forbidden and every contention resolved. In that all-enveloping oneness of shared love there was only resonating light out of which the totality of things that are, become manifest, if only for a time. All loss and all pain were transmuted back into peace, surpassing understanding.

As he regained wakefulness Harper broke his vow of the previous day, to let tears well up one final time. Still drunk and with a throbbing headache he no longer cared about tribulations. His eyes were flooded with the summer dawn light which had inspired his other worldly dreaming.

Thinking of Zachariah's commendation to return to live in the Highlands Harper imagined himself the war hardened Jacobite, recollecting a compounded folly. The romance had been brief but exuberant. Now all that was left was the dejected homecoming. He spurned the romantic image with a scornful laugh, ready to face the future with surety.

In the old habit of piling himself with thoughtless guilt, he let his mind roll momentarily over some of the petulant misgivings of the past but knew in an instant there was no luckier man alive. He decided that he must forgive everything: himself; the impossibly avaricious world of men; Almighty God even - for creating inconceivable absolutes and dualistic, unavoidable suffering and for taking the unbounded love he had come to know away from his senses, to distil it within his bursting heart.

He caressed Hannah's face with trembling fingers then kissed her sweetly for the last time ever, dreading the awesome weight of her permanent loss upon his weak shoulders.

How can so much love leave so much pain? Goodbye Hannah dear. Watch over us please.

Rising nervously to greet his future like a schoolboy on his first day, he staggered slightly under the effects of the malt and the shocking fatigue of bereavement. But Harper carried in stark wakefulness a new caution and a new resolve.

I must never forget I am living for Hannah too. From now on I must try always to see events through her compassionate eyes.

Stepping out into the cobbled farmyard he stood for a while in the glistening mizzle of a summer morning, unsure whether the sun might rebound in glory or curl up longer in slumber.

Feeling out of place in his smart grey suit he looked down at the unavoidable ordure on his polished leather shoes as he shivered in the shadows. Walking briskly up and down the lane bisecting his old territory to warm aching limbs, Harper listened to the wild sounds of the farmstead. A Cockerel gave vent with savage bravura to territorial sexual pretensions, contemptible of his sorrow. Snorting cows munched up close to the house, reminding sleepy patrons of their good service contract. His old friend, Tex sniffed fiercely through the gap below the door of his kennel then whined and scrabbled at the latch.

The modern man of sorrows stood in the place where the World had begun turning for him ten years before, where he'd ceased to be a boy. Stealing a few minutes before this day's dreadful accounting began, he reflected a little on his past. Sentimental feelings flowed unashamedly as Harper looked around at the buildings; the woodlands, the hills and fields that once he wanted to run as far away as possible from. Now his heart would be buried here in this place which could never be home. He loved Ramsburn all the more poignantly for knowing he would soon have to leave it for good.

Although the world of men had offered her nothing beyond the assumed protection of a good husband, Harper had grown used to seeing the trials of life predominantly through Hannah's eyes. He had been self-absorbed and morose when he found her and fell in love. Enlightened, benevolent and brave, she had first tamed then civilized him. He had known from that first moment that her voice, her sensibility, would forever resound in his head. Hannah's generous love had filled his heart, carrying him forward to become the man he was now. He would make decisions for himself from now on - but he would live also for her. She was gone from the realm of human experience but would remain his soul mate through the future's golden days.

"Now, think of the girls!" he heard her say.

Stabbing thumbs into his aching eyes, Harper massaged his forehead and face. He composed himself slowly, gulping in the fragrant blend of country air with its subtle reportage of fecundity and decay – its millennial reassurances of tomorrow's routine. The morning breeze acted as a salve to the fruity reflux of whisky in his mouth and the narrowed capillaries of a well-earned hangover.

Harper thought of his dear friend Zachariah, how it was he who had helped him so far in everything – the apprenticeship he'd spurned; the references that got him into Edinburgh City Police force, then the vital transition of becoming one of Kennington's national sales team. Even people at his local Lodge in Edinburgh knew of Zachariah and his aristocratic connections.

Harper thought also of dear old Great Gran Han and golden hearted Jessie. They were his family now, much more so than his taciturn Uncles. Harper knew he'd been blessed by angels. At last he let out a long, audible sigh rising to a stifled groan. Affecting a dispassionate brow and paternal smile across his lips he went back to the grey farmhouse, to console them all as best he could. Stepping silently through the kitchen door he could hear the family emerging from their slumbers as he took off his coat and jacket.

Knowing that he had to keep fully occupied, Harper rolled up his sleeves and washed his hands. He reached up for the frying pan - found eggs, ham and potato scones, although his stomach felt like a hearth full of soot. He boiled the kettle for tea, working swiftly and efficiently as he distributed plates and cups for all. He was doing something with his hands, if not his mind. That was enough to put him back in control. The aroma of frying bacon made him salivate again. Even though he didn't feel hungry, a little breakfast with hot tea might suppress his raging hangover. Voices came from behind him as he worked.

So the world has not stopped turning.

The girls were speaking to Grandma. Noticing that his hand shook with delirium tremens as he slipped a fried egg out of the pan, Harper turned to meet Jessie's swollen eyes. Neither of them could think what to say. Their silent looking acknowledged the presence of one absolute malediction - death.

"We have no choice but to embarrass our man," Somers mumbled, as though talking pensively to the furniture, "It's a horrible thing to do, but we just cannot allow him the opportunity to run, now that we know his intention. We'll take him immediately after the funeral service. That in itself will deliver the equivalent pressure of a day or two of intensive softening up."

Ignoring Wilson's squeaky guffaw, he paced slowly up and down the room, hands clasped behind his back as he spoke softly. Garner thought of his creditable chief as Napoleon in his hey-day, revealing plans for the Tsar.

Garner and Wilson glanced at one another, intimating unspoken surprise, something rare for both men, "Interesting!" whispered Wilson, giggling at his own informal characterisation of Somer's legendary cool.

"What did you say lad?" snapped Somers.

"Oh, that what you said is 'interesting' sir. I can test out my new theory about guilt."

"Explain!" demanded Somers.

"Well sir, according to the Psychoanalysts, if a man is guilty he bluffs it off, relaxes and has a good night's kip in custody," He explained briskly in his convincing Yorkshire drawl.

"Go on, Wilson."

"Yeah right . . . But if he's not guilty he gets agitated. He paces up and down. He can't get it off his mind. Won't let it go."

Garner had the set and garrulous outspokenness of a French international prop forward. Wilson the pug nose and swift feet of a heavyweight prize fighter. Anyone seeing them paired as part of a surveillance or arrest team could not resist the idle temptation to imagine a bare knuckle contest between the two men. It was far from clear who would be the favourite but the notion itself was frightening. There were of course many larger men but few with their cold self-assurance when it came to taking down a quarry. Garner and Wilson were hounds of hell hanging on their master's every word.

Somers ignored Wilson's insubordination – taking it for what it was – superficial approbation of his own acknowledged insight into the criminal mind.

"What if he reacts violently sir? I mean, I would, regardless. I mean, if it was my wife's funeral."

"Good point Garner. I'm sure you can deal with that. That is why I picked you. Either way, I expect a positive outcome. Under the circumstances I anticipate that he will either make a full confession, or try to leg it on his tod. The local Police will support us. If we ask nicely they may even provide us with an interview room." Somers continued to look straight at Garner, his head held back with an air of expectation.

"Alright, Sir. I take your meaning . . . I'll speak to them."

"Tell the local Constabulary nothing about our target until immediately before moving in on him. Make it clear they are not to discuss our presence or purpose with any outsiders, on pain of immediate disciplinary action. Tell them you have that direct from their Chief Superintendent. If they pump you for information as any good Bobby would, tell them we are investigating burglaries in stately homes and large country residences. Ask them to provide detailed information on any known locals with form. That will shut them up for a day at least. That is all we need to make our arrest. Remember we represent 'Home Office interests', but do not mention any Treasury investigation at this stage. Is that absolutely clear?"

"Yes sir!" The two men spoke as one. Garner and Wilson had military enthusiasm – both had the worn pride of the Colour Sergeant. Somers knew they would not let him down. He slowly paced another two lengths of the room before resuming his briefing. Garner and Wilson watched attentively with ears pricked, like salivating dogs waiting for the next morsel to be tossed into their mouths.

"We know he's well respected in the community although he clearly thinks he s a cut above the rest. This will not go down well," Somers advised them, stopping his pacing to look at his men for emphasis, "So the element of surprise is essential. We need the local Police as back up. Remember our man is a former Bobby.

If Ted's little chat with our quarry's children bears out, then presume the man must know we are on to him. Word is he would have flitted sooner, but the wife was too ill to travel. I think he may have spotted one of you watching him. That's why he has stayed away from the network principal – the mechanic who designs the plates." Garner put his fist up to his mouth and coughed self-consciously.

"I'm sure of it sir," he stated, "I did mention it in my report, sir. We could have done with another man on him," Garner reflected wistfully, "Or a Travelling Rep cover story, so I could have made contact."

"Yes, you don't need to tell me." Somers stopped pacing. He sat down on the arm of a leather studded chair by the crackling fire.

At that moment there was a knock on the door. Harrison the waiter, who hailed from London, entered with the trolley of food, "Soup and mushroom soufflé, with locally cured bacon, times three. I will return with your sweets. Enjoy gentlemen!"

Wilson, the epicure, had ordered for them all. He let out a soft 'wow' of enthusiasm when the man spread the food in front of him.

Harrison had the benign air of a successful but over-enthusiastic prelate. He never ceased smiling and talking. The hotel factotum – bell-hop, barman and chef, had escaped from the smog and bustle of the Empire's hub. Now he had found both his true home and his true love. He felt it was his duty to tell the world how much he enjoyed cooking.

The Special Investigators encouraged Harrison to engage with them and chat, ever keen to try out strategies for the practised deceitfulness of deep cover and open questioning. They'd probed the enthusiastic lad about the travellers using the hotel, yet he had no idea who they were.

When the waiter left, they ate in silence. All three of the Treasury men finished at almost the same time. They casually piled up the plates on the trolley then moved apart again, as though subconsciously needing a safer distance from one another.

Garner went to the window where he smoked. Somers dominated the room with more Napoleonic perambulations. He was a neat little package – this was his way of taking up more space – of saying, "Shut up and listen. I'm the boss." Wilson lay back on the double bed, stretching like a bear waking from hibernation. He released a throaty growl of pleasure as the muscles of his broad back tightened, then relaxed.

Garner watched what he took as Wilson's casual insolence disapprovingly, not because he was giving front to the 'Old Man' – no one would do that - but because it presented a challenge to him as 'Top Viking.' Garner with a few pints inside him could be rudely outspoken, rough and profane but on duty he was invariably disciplined and calm. He was a man who would follow orders, yet still proud of being the rudest bastard on the force.

Wilson smirked at Garner, patting the neat surface of the double bed invitingly. Garner stared at the clown with the eyes of the basilisk. Not one muscle of his architectonic head and shoulders so much as twitched involuntarily, in response to the provocation. Wilson chortled gleefully at the thought of his own casual brinkmanship.

Somers resumed his train of thought as though nothing had interrupted it, "The thing of it is - Harper might recognise anyone who's worked alongside him when we were in Edinburgh. We can't afford to train more people just for him, so I will need to hang back out of sight until you cuff him."

"How exactly do you want him taken sir?" asked Garner.

"Hmm. Just stay back until the burial is finished and people are departing, Garner. Then move alongside him and ask him for an hour of his time," Somers proposed with disarming optimism.

Wilson laughed his characteristic high-pitched, piggy laugh. He seemed to relish all aspects of cruelty whenever it was in conflict with natural justice, which Somers found alarming. Wilson was as dependable in a tight corner as a Staffordshire Bull-Terrier, yet Somers privately doubted his sanity.

Somers superior, Reginald Chatwin had recommended Sergeant Edward Wilson. He usually laughed benignly about the detective's notorious exploits, typically involving incredible feats of strength in which he prevailed over unfavourable odds without a scratch. Chatwin had once described Wilson as, "a one man battering ram – useful to have around when a door needs kicking in at five o'clock in the morning."

"Do we actually hand-cuff Harper in front of all the mourners, or just tell him we need to ask a few questions?" Garner asked thoughtfully.

"No, no. Just tell him, 'there was an Edinburgh City Police matter he was involved with which requires clarification.' Advise him of the fact that certain crucial evidence is deemed to have gone missing and we need his version of events to help us secure a conviction. Tell him that you realise it is very inconvenient, but you came a long way to interview him without being aware of his loss. It is imperative that you speak to him, right now. Make sure you apologise. Act disingenuous. This is really important Garner, d'you understand man? Treat him like a civilian rather than a soldier, otherwise he'll read you like a book."

"Disingenuous . . . 'the fuck's that mean?" demanded Wilson. This time the grown-ups ignored him.

But Garner was nobody's fool. He was hard as nails in every respect and smart with it. He looked straight at Somers, "And when he tells us to go fuck ourselves?" Wilson's squealing laugh raised a semi-tone, as the exchange became more interesting.

'Interesting' for Wilson denoted the potential for 'trouble' which he was employed to 'sort out' - Wilson was a simple soul who was extremely happy in his work.

"Make the invitation, but give him no alternative," advised Somers, "Be ready, and be quick. If he bates, cuff him and take him. I'll be there as back up with the artillery piece." Wilson looked at Garner and his thin lips curled in an unspoken sneer. Somers drew a deep breath and let it out between parted lips. He had studied this quarry well from a safe distance.

Harrison's polite knock on the door prompted Wilson to skip over with the trolley, which he lifted with one hand. The other two men went to sit down as Sergeant Wilson came back with three bowls of Spotted Dick and custard.

"This is you, ya silly cunt, on that Peterborough train . . . Spotted Dick!" Wilson whispered to Garner. Somers seemed to be pondering deeply.

Absolutely no one can be trusted where large amounts of cash are concerned – whether real of fake. That includes policemen.

Somers felt this mantra pointed to the ultimate raison d'etre of his specialist Treasury Investigation unit. John Harper had turned at some point, so he told himself. Like many of his counterparts the Edinburgh Bobby had been obliged, due to lack of trained manpower, to work for some time gathering information on the inside, beyond the normal requirements of uniformed police.

His involvement in Operation Purse Seine - the swooping raids across Lothian in '93, had been all too convenient for the criminal organization behind the forgeries. Probably Harper had been paid well for a tip-off, at some point before the raids. Then he'd simply hung back when the forgers had legged it, feigning illness. He'd picked up the invaluable counterfeit plates and hidden them for future use. Although he had not bolted yet, he was clearly planning to do so.

Yet somehow Somer's experience told him, there was potential for disaster here. He would allow Garner and Wilson the chance to get it right on the day, while also preparing for the worst. If Harper escaped into the surrounding countryside he **might easily** make it to one of a number of railway stations or seaports in the region, from which he could easily disappear for good. Failing that he could hide like a fox for months without detection. Covering all combinations of the suspect's options in that event would be impossible.

Harper was the discreet connection Somers and Chatwin had craved for years. The man was smart. He was attending night school classes in Financial Law, with the intention of becoming an insurance company actuary. Some unknown businessman down in the south of England was financing his progression. Chatwin and Somers agreed that Harper was a sleeper – an insignificant parasite, worming into a career where he would become the connection for bent bankers and money launderers for decades to come.

If he completed his studies, the former cop might one day soon be in a position to legitimise the wealth of any number of influential fraudsters in Scotland's capital. This was the pattern – this was how it always worked. It was Somer's plan to seize Harper and break him, before the memory of his deceased wife began to slip from his mind. Guilt was a wonderful tool in the hands of a skilled interrogator. Harper had three beautiful daughters – he could not possibly abandon them in exchange for a life on the tough streets of New York – no matter what the monetary incentives. This was going to be the breakthrough that would set the seal on Chatwin and Somer's careers.

Somer's palms sweated as he succumbed again to an unspoken temptation. Feeling for the cold, oily metal nestling in the pocket of his tweed jacket, he confirmed the timings once again before dismissing the dogs of war. The three men wished the others success as they left the room. As a good Churchman, Somers blessed himself before petitioning the Almighty for forgiveness for the radical action he was about to take. He felt with a reasonable degree of certainty that the man was guilty however.

A bevy of small children emerged from the gate at the side of primary school in Milltown of Rothiemay. They ran like hooligans up the street for it was the half term holiday and they were jubilant, if only for a few moments. They slowed their pace suddenly and were respectfully silent, even though the rough calls of a boy walking towards the river invited them to look back at him, to confirm an arrangement for tomorrow.

Salmon fishermen hurried awkwardly in their waders across the street, in the direction of the low water downstream of the bridge. Like the school kids, they too had spied the dressed black horses of the funeral cortege with their nodding plumage. The anglers looked guiltily along the lane, unconsciously trimming their wafting rods as though any kind of fun might offend the locals.

The gentle tones of a Highland lament rose into the surrounding forest canopy, drawing the idle consideration of juvenile crows. The birds leant forward like delegates to the Assembly of Churches, eagerly awaiting the arrival of the Moderator. Large, rangy fledglings peered in curiosity at the passers-by, hoping for some sort of unexpected opportunity. They scrutinised the white handkerchiefs which looked so like paper bags, maybe containing food litter.

Jack Garner and Ted Wilson sat nursing their drinks at the roadside window of the Forbes Arms under the watchful gaze of Rona Hendry, the strikingly beautiful bar girl. At first she had taken them for outdoor types, wrongly assuming that they were up for the fishing. Rona's curiosity had been aroused not so much by their predictable line of questioning as the fact that they had nothing to say about themselves. She shook her head resignedly, watching them with contempt as they peered out of the window at the approaching funeral cortege.

They're English and the English have nothing to say unless they are drunk. Aye, an' then you cannae shut them up! Donald McIntyre can shut them up but they tend never to come back. Donald is bad for business. Maybe they are Petermen, planning to kill the fish with dynamite late at night.

330

Rona had heard this mantra about the reserved, self-seeking English from her father many a time. She smiled at the men to give them a last chance to engage with her politely but they pretended not to see her.

Game fishermen came from all over the world at this time each year to rent rooms in the hotel or estate owned cottages along the river bank. Above the bridge was a steep fall in the winding Deveron. On the inside of the river bend a woollen mill had been built above concrete paddle wheel culverts, to the south and north of the bridge spanning the river. A hundred yards below the white water torrent, the mill and the bridge, was a normally broad-flat section of river bed where returning salmon rallied and rested at easy wader depth.

Now the sun shone as though all was hope in the world. Fat elderly fish flashed silver as they casually snatched browsing insects. But these men seemed oblivious to that. They were not talking about what they had taken earlier that morning. Nor were they interested in the enticing views through the windows on the river side of the lounge.

Rona Hendry's world was framed in those windows. Each momentous event of the passing years had been seen or could be imagined unravelling against that wondrous backdrop. Deveron was murmuring music to Rona – mystery and passion of the soul. There were wooded banks where lovers walked in the sunset. All the water in the glowering skies and crouching mountains had passed by Rona's windows at some point in her twenty three years. She knew as she gazed, that although she would forever be inspired to longing there would always be comfort in homecoming. No sage had ever taught a finer or more profound lesson than the river Deveron. It was love, life, death and forgiveness. It was laughing, dancing eternity – with her arms open to smilingly embrace her children. This was why the salmon returned - every movement of their strong tails was an affirmation of what Rona saw. The land and all its creatures were to her the kneeling celebrant. Sky and river, the divine hand of consecration.

These men were ignorant, unimpressed – they never even looked. Or maybe they looked but just couldn't see it. They moved too fast and they spoke too low. They lacked the tempered assurance of locals, tuned to the reflected beauty all around. Neither man had the glistening puppy-dog enthusiasm of travellers returning to this Caledonian Shangri-la. Garner and Wilson were not part of Rona's serene picture, nor were they were seeking absolution.

Rona remembered that she had noticed these men calling at Billy Stevenson's house, at some time last week. She had seen the Constable inviting them in. No crime had been reported in the village that she knew of however. There had been no rumours circulating. The two men were fishery protection game keepers, she concluded.

They are working for the Duff's, checking on permits for the Laird. The old sod makes sure he gets a slice o' every pie.

Rona returned to her preparations for the funeral party that would arrive very soon. When she looked up again the two men had gone from the table at the window. They had left their drinks untouched. Her suspicions were confirmed. What kind of a man buys a drink but then doesn't consume it? Worst of all - they didn't say goodbye. Rona could see that the man with the piggy laugh was munching one of her carefully prepared egg and cress sandwiches as the two surly fellows went through the outer door. He had pinched it from under her carefully arranged, clean white napkins.

Somers watched through field glasses from the edge of a track leading up through the forest as Garner and Wilson attached themselves to the small crowd of mourners. They tried to avoid attention by standing together, murmuring discreetly to one another.

Good confident start lads! They know each other, so the assumption is someone else here must know them.

They even tried to assume an air of reverence by trying to look glum - but it lasted less than a minute, as Wilson leant over to say something to Garner.

"Impossible!" Somers snarled aloud as he watched his men closely. Sure enough, Ted was whispering in Jack's gigantic ear at the edge of the graveyard. The bastard actually broke into a smile. "You irreverent sods . . . I don't believe it!" No doubt also, Somers knew - though he could only see and not actually hear it - Wilson had begun to wheeze his stifled, piggy laugh. The visual compression of the glasses made it seem that Wilson and Garner were standing right behind the mourners within ear shot, rather than a prudent ten yards or so back as they actually were. Nonetheless Somers felt furious heat rising under his collar. He grunted to himself in rage, lowering the field glasses to look around self-consciously, ensuring that he was not being observed also. The forest was silent but any approaching walker could be on him suddenly, without being noticed. He edged back into cover to look at his watch.

Five minutes into a twenty minute ceremony - plenty of time for me to scan the mourners for possible accomplices or anything else untoward.

Somers brought the binoculars back up to his eyes. PC Stevenson it seemed was looking right back at him, with an obvious look of concern on his face. The man was looking away from the oration at the graveside. He would immediately draw attention away from the dire matter in hand, to the strangers closing in on Harper, "No man! Don't you know anything about surveillance! People will look in the line of sight of someone not paying attention . . . every fucking Sunday schoolteacher knows that!" A pretty young woman wearing a veiled hat almost obscuring her yellow blonde hair, now glanced in the same direction.

The lovely Mrs Stevenson, no doubt.

Somers had almost taken the glasses from his eyes in horror but in the same instant that he caught Stevenson's worried look, the Inspector realised it was Wilson and Garner that the local Bobby was staring back at, not him. He lowered the angle of the field glasses slightly, to play them again over his two subordinates. Somers could see from their movements and smiles that they were deep in some ribald conversation, which was causing Garner to act out of keeping. Wilson was bursting at the seams with barely suppressed laughter, as usual. Somers' kidneys were shouting with adrenalin, his palms sweating as he let out a visceral groan, "You fucking idiots!" he shouted aloud, though he was immediately ashamed of his own lack of control, "It's time to find a replacement for you Wilson," the Inspector murmured angrily to the fir tree he was leaning against. He remembered saying exactly this to himself several times before.

Somers could not bide his time watching the crowd of mourners as he had first anticipated doing but he did check hastily to make note of who was standing close to John Harper. Keith Somers saw the tight anguish on Harper's face and the terrible distress of his close family. The Treasury official gulped back a surge of empathetic feeling for the man. With an awful sense of foreboding he set off quickly down the hill, tucking the field glasses inside his woollen town coat. Sticking close to the tree line he headed directly to a spot immediately behind where Garner and Wilson were standing.

He would let them do the approach work, moving in only to take the sting out of the situation. Now that the Detective Inspector was calmly centred upon the goal, his natural authority resurfaced. He was about to have the last word in a case that had turned the world upside down, leaving all his colleagues chasing shadows. Nothing else really mattered to him now – not the mud on his shoes or the awkward field glasses bouncing on his paunch, the pistol swinging in his pocket - nor the bereavement of the broken little man he was about to interview.

Reverend Blair shook Harper's hand, cupping his elbow with his left hand as though physically raising him up from the grave.

Mourners circled in self-conscious little knots, quietly engaging one another in desultory conversation, some tentatively watching Wilson and Harper family members for their cue to head in the direction of the reception at the Forbes Arms.

Bill Stevenson spoke gently to dismiss himself from his wife's side then turned to move purposively between the lines of gravestones which corralled the living along the gravel pathways. Somers watched the Policeman discreetly approaching Jessie Wilson and saw her hug him. He imagined the man would be burning with embarrassment. Stevenson rubbed a hand over his cropped hair as he struggled for the words to guide Harper's family away from the man at the graveside, in this moment of poignant need.

Jessie turned to look back in Harper's direction, but Stevenson reached out a shepherding arm to draw her away. She looked over suspiciously at Garner and Wilson who waited motionless now, like palace guards. Jessie went to explain something to the girls and to Great Gran then with a gracious hand on Stevenson's upper arm she pushed past him to find Phillip Henderson, the fine looking piper.

The pair looked around and it seemed to Somers that fifty faces were looking at them. Henderson took a deep breath of moist mid-afternoon air and blew it out slowly as he listened to the murmur of the river and exuberant summer birds. Then the piper nodded at Jessie in assent as he drew breath again with a real purpose. A warning keynote from the bagpipe brought pause to every voice in conversation. In a few moments it had risen like the sun over the wilderness into a lovelorn farewell, *Mort Ghlinne Comhann.* Henderson was unsure of his tunes for Buchanan and Drummond. Preferring not to rush his practice or make a mistake, he played what he knew.

Well, none of them will know their clan history and if they did, they would not object.

With Jessie at his shoulder the mourners followed towards the Forbes Arms. As the diverse gathering approached the Hotel *McIan's Lament* scoured the souls of every gentle listener, echoing from the granite of the mill and houses opposite.

Harper stood alone at the graveside for a few minutes with just a scattering of concerned onlookers watching his humped back as he shook, thrown in sorrow. Wilson saw it and paused behind Harper one foot forward, pressing on the rising slope of manicured grass.

Garner moved close on Harper's left, where he could intercept him as soon as he turned to move on from his lamentation. PC Stevenson was observing from a safe distance – concerned only about his neighbour - ready to intervene for his wellbeing. Neither his wife nor Jessie Wilson knew the details but both had questioned Stevenson's need to ask John Harper for clarification about a Police matter, on this of all days. Stevenson would have to live here when it was all over. He had long since traded career prospects in exchange for an easy life with deferential standing in the community. Bill was aware that everyone who knew him either liked him, or was at least prepared to accommodate him.

But if this goes wrong we might as well move to Aberdeen.

At length Harper turned away from Hannah's grave. He stood still for ten seconds with his head bowed, breathing deeply to stretch chest muscles going into spasm from too much time spent shallow-breathing. He was looking at nothing but the mist in his head. Clenching his fists like a punch drunk boxer, he ran the point of his knuckles first into the right eye, then the left.

Garner and Wilson were standing five yards in front of him, on either side of the gravel pathway bisecting the graveyard. Harper sighed as he turned around. He looked right through the two large men as he stepped forward towards them. Somers watched with growing anxiety, hoping that Garner would handle the matter delicately.

He thinks they're from the Co-op funeral service, waiting to finish the business.

Detective Sergeant Garner proffered a clean handkerchief. He waited for Harper to register his commanding physical presence before speaking gruffly, in an East Anglian drawl, tailored to provoke, "A'ye gunna pull y'self together nah boy? We're come t' talk about your plans fer the 'mediate fyootshur." Garner towered over Harper, staring down unblinkingly at him.

Harper looked back at Garner through the irritation of stinging eyes. A feeling of disconnection that had been mounting for days seemed to come over him again as he motioned with his open right hand to decline the offer of the handkerchief.

Who is this enormous, overbearing man? Has he been sent by the King of the Underworld to claim me body and soul, now that the light has gone out of my life? Have all my sufferings been a preamble to this?

For an instant Harper did indeed think Garner might be one of the Co-op undertakers, but his attire was not quite up to their standard and what he was saying made no sense at all. But he definitely knew the man from somewhere on his travels.

"My old gal says never gew aht wi' aht one. I aint bin usin' it to wipe manoor aff me shoes y' know." Garner pointed his chin at Harper, as if to challenge any possibility that he might think he had done.

Harper tried to speak politely in response but merely mumbled broken fragments of the words queuing up in his head, as they stumbled over any notion of sensibility, "Thanks . . .yes . . . I . . . forgot to . . . but no . . ." Wilson's smiling face lowered into view immediately above Harper's left shoulder at head height, all but resting upon the perfect seam of his black town coat. Harper thought the strange gentleman was about to hug him. His mind raced to

337

imagine who the fellow was and why the hell he didn't recognise such an endearing man, although he had definitely seen the other chap before somewhere.

I've been away too long. I can't remember half of the locals who know me.

But Wilson spoke plainly in the casual tones of the tough streets of Bradford, his moist breath playing insistently around Harper's ear, "We've been watching you for a long time old flower. You weave a tangled web, Mr Harper! You cocked the chest like a half-pay Admiral." Harper thought he had been rumbled for playing the expenses game – that they'd put two and two together and got five.

Fuck, Marlene had me taped all along! That tight old bastard Soutar has called in a private detective agency.

"You've summat we wus all lookin' for lad. Nah yer gonna gi' us it back. An' yer gunna tell us all about yer pals."

Stevenson watched with alarm as Wilson placed his right hand on Harper's shoulder. He looked around and could see a small knot of mourners waiting for John on the road in front of the Kirk. They were mostly men who would not want food so much as liquor but who did not wish to show ungentlemanly haste in heading for the reception, without their friend. For now they were staving off the pangs with tobacco. They had the further unspoken motive of wishing to offer condolences to Harper personally. Stevenson noted that the group included close family members and cousins of John's, mostly innocuous but unaware of the two plain-clothes men having approached Harper.

Amid that friendly group of neighbours waiting for Harper was the gigantic figure of the temporarily magnanimous, stone cold sober Donald McIntyre. Standing with him chatting like long lost brothers were two of his acolytes in outrage, Jim Lorimer and Andy Murdoch.

Stevenson knew that if a fight broke out it would be impossible for him to stop it alone.

At least they were not drunk yet, and it might be presumed that Wilson's hand on Harper's shoulder was a gesture of affection. But every once in a while the little coterie of pals glanced over at Harper as they blew out their smoke – he was after all to be their King For a Day. Vicarious interest in all Harper's doings was heightened by the tantalising delay in reaching for that first solid hit of the water of life. The woeful afternoon, now turning to unseasonal overcast, could turn upon that.

Harper took in a long deep breath as he tried to think how to respond to the two roughnecks. He looked over towards the group of men waiting patiently for him to join them. He saw Stevenson tight-faced nearby, looking right at him. Beyond him was a small man whom Harper immediately recognised as a top Treasury Officer, standing aloof but watching with concern. Adrenalin jumped in Harper's guts.

'Fat Man Two', what's his name? - Somers! This is official business. The plates! Nothing else of such value has ever been in my possession. Whatever did happen to those plates?

In that moment the effrontery of their timing struck Harper like a slap on the face. The old rage which had seen him through as a Bobby started to climb up his spine towards the top of his head. He would have understood an approach like this from inept privateers or even a couple of thugs representing a gang of counterfeiters - but he'd risked his life for these fuckers. Bradley had damn near lost his that day back in December '93.

Harper asked himself for the hundredth time why the hell he hadn't secured the evidence properly, requesting it be detailed by Chambers in the squad report? But he hadn't. Now it was all in the past.

His mind raced but his strong instinct was to say nothing – not even ask questions. Surely these two chavs were not going to arrest him at his wife's funeral, in front of so many people.

"I don't like your accusatory tone," Harper stated slowly with a hint of warning ire, glowering at Wilson, "I have no intention of discussing anything related to this matter with you right now. I'll be in Edinburgh in a few days. We can go over it then if you wish. I will help you in whatever way I can."

"Well, there's a remarkable lack of cooriosity for an ex-peeler, wun't ye say Ted? Never even asked us wor it is we're looking for!" Garner mocked with casual understatement, keeping his eyes trained sceptically upon Harper, still baiting him for a reaction.

"Yer, interestin' Jack . . . an' nah 'es givin' us the brush off 'cos 'es got more important issues to attend to." Wilson smirked without taking his eyes off Harper.

"Thinks we're stupid Ted me old tulip! Thinks we've waited for two an' a half year already, so we can just wait another foo days. Only I reckon he'd be half way across the Atlantic Ocean by then. That's your plan ain't it Mr Harper?"

"Look I don't know what information you're basing that assumption on but I assure you its mistaken. Now step aside. Let me get on with the business of burying my wife."

Wilson shook his head slowly, "Nah, I don't think so. We've followed you all over t' entire fucking country pal. This has been the only place we knew you'd be for sure, three or four days in advance."

"We're both sorry for your loss," Garner lied, stepping dangerously close to Harper, "But there's two guys standin' over there behind the church wi' shovels who are going to finish burying your wife for you. You're comin' with us flower. You just tell us everything you know about the missing evidence an' then you can join your friends later. If we don't charge you and lock you away in the meantime that is."

Harper realised that they had not identified themselves. They were trying too hard to be discreet – assuming he would either bolt or comply, at sight of their boss. Harper had only a vague excuse for what he now wanted to do. He'd decided to do it anyway, because their manner had been so crude. Their demeanour was insulting to Hannah and her family. Then he heard her voice in his head and momentarily held back.

"Look I will voluntarily place myself in the custody of Constable Stevenson. He can even hand cuff me if you deem it necessary. I'm sure he won't be missed for a day if he accompanies me down to the West Port to make my statement. I'll even stand the train fare for him. Just let me finish my business here first, will you?"

"Cor, devious little bastard, aint 'e Ted!" Garner declared with a sneering smile. Shaking his head in disbelief, Harper wondered how far they had investigated his personal background. Wilson laughed another squealing, piglet laugh.

Harper shrugged his shoulders involuntarily as he looked down, cranking his fingers into a loose box. Wilson never noticed nor would have realised what the small rotation of muscles presaged. But he was assuming Harper's guilt – and his next statement confirmed it, "Yer's what I heard about him too. Even his own kids said they are about to head off to New York. We know he checked out the ticket prices at White Star," Wilson added, looking across at Garner.

Harper lifted his shoulders again but this time both arms shot forward at a slightly elevated angle. He rocked up on to his toes for a little leverage and power as he snapped his elbows into straightened arms. Harper leant forward into the controlled body blows, which were more a punt directing the hinge joints of fingers of each hand into the upper part of each man's fundus, than levered punches. Right and left flashed well into the stomach area directly beneath the curvature of the ribs of each man.

Garner and Wilson both gaped in speechless agony at the impact. Neither of them made a sound as they simultaneously folded like deck chairs, neatly stacked and stored by a beach boy at the end of a summer day. Harper swept his fists back into an instinctive defence, maintaining Queensbury's discipline not to kick out.

He wanted to hurt them but not finish them. This was no Saturday night donnybrook in Crane's bar where confusion gave vicious latitude to revellers and Police alike. Then there had been brawlers piling in from every direction but these two jokers were down and out. The rage was still in Harper's eyes and he was ready for more. Stevenson moved towards Harper, intending to pacify him. The smokers, now alerted to the spat, were already moving along the path from the side of the Kirk.

Somer's moment had come. He had seen his men drop unexpectedly and had advanced briskly along the path to intervene. He simply pointed the huge revolver at Harper's stomach but said nothing. Harper put his hands up and stood still.

"I take it I am under arrest?"

"Strictly speaking, no Mr Harper . . . but this gun is loaded and I would very much like you to come with us to answer some questions."

"Fuck you, Somers!"

Somers quickly turned to point his weapon at the now rapidly advancing group of onlookers. Stevenson stood in front of them on the path. The local Bobby spread out his arms to stop them getting any closer.

Wilson and Garner were rolling, both blanched white and gagging on the soft green-yellow grass. Neither man could speak, much less stand up or move around. Garner crawled away from the path to empty the contents of his stomach. Wilson was retching tearfully, still gasping for air.

"Well now, Jack," Harper growled, "Just as well you didn't use that hankey to clean the shite aff yer shoes. Next time yer mammy tucks wan into yer pocket you remember me pal . . . eh? And I'll remember you, crawling around in yer ain vomit."

"I'm in charge here – all of you stay back and stand still!" shouted Somers waving his pistol, "We are Her Majesty's Revenue and Customs officials, here on Treasury business. We have powers of arrest. We are taking this man, John Harper in for questioning. I am

Detective Inspector Somers, These two men are Detective Sergeants Garner and Wilson."

Donald edged past the outstretched arm of Bill Stevenson. The huge pistol tracked instantly in his direction, "Dinnae point that fucking thing at me!" growled the butcher.

"Well then, you'd better take a step back before I blow a hole right through you!" Donald looked into the eyes of the little Treasury man, trying to read his quiet tone. He decided for once not to push his luck, for the moment.

"Now!" snapped Somers, with an emphatic tone that had entered his mild voice, "Step back away from Constable Stevenson," he ordered quietly, "Mr Harper may well be free to join you later. Do not make this any more difficult for him. Move away now, all of you!"

The little group conceded with their eyes but never moved an inch back along the path. They were like a wild little herd of summer bullocks showing a strong desire to trample an intruder. He couldn't kill them all.

Somers lowered the revolver to his side, looking back at Harper. Donald and his pals seemed momentarily disappointed.

"DS Garner . . . when you are ready, would you accompany Mr Harper, please?" Somers motioned with his head toward the suspect.

"Shall I cuff him?"

"Yes, I think it best that you do," Somers said grimly, wagging his Enfield Mark Two for both men to see.

"You know the drill," Garner reminded Harper, still gulping air, "Put your hands behind your back."

Wilson lifted his broad bottom to roll into an upright position, sitting down on the grass to get his wind back. Harper stared at him, remembering the admission that this man had taken advantage of his children.

Harper felt the urge to kick him on the side of his head but Somers was now pointing the gun at him. Harper stared down and Wilson glowered back. Harper got the drop on him again though, after

Garner had handcuffed him – this time standing on Wilson's left hand as he walked with Garner towards the road.

"Hey, do what ye want to me lad bu' mek it good – cos I'll get back at ye later on for sure!" Wilson's Yorkshire accent was thickened by pain.

"Did you hear that Donald?" shouted Harper over his shoulder. Wilson looked up at the scowling line of men, with the eager giant in their midst.

"Oh, I hear him, John boy! Jimmy son, go fetch a spade. Let's dig another hole for this cocky little keech."

Standing up, Wilson laughed his irreverent madcap laugh. He looked straight at McIntyre with a fearless, questioning grin of appreciation that went deeper than any game. Wilson saw the black rage of naked enmity but calmly accepted it for what it was. He spoke with measured politeness, uncharacteristic of the man but which did him credit for native intelligence. Wilson had a common touch for people he encountered everywhere, who happened not to be fraudsters.

"Look lads, we have to tek 'im now," he explained, looking along the row of faces and up at the lanky, grim looking Bill Stevenson. He searched for words to give a creditable account to their actions. Then he sized-up straight to McIntyre, like a prize fighter at a weigh-in.

"You know what - it's a long story pal, but your friend was involved in investigating something major. We thor' he was bent, about to flit the country. Either way, right now was the only time for us t' ger 'is side o' t' story. An' that's what were bahn a do pal, funeral or no funeral. We never expected him to lash out, I must say. Could be it points t' man's innocence . . . le's 'ope it does. In which case - fi'st round o' beers'll be on me toneet."

"You hurt that boy an' it'll tak more than beers to get me off your fuckin' tail, sunshine. I'll cut ye up an' mak' a hundred fuckin' butcher's pies oot o' yer fat little carcase," McIntyre vowed – as much a malicious promise, as a naked threat. Wilson smiled his easy smile but this time restrained the urge to laugh like a squealing piglet,

"Gentlemen!" stated Wilson, looking along the row of set faces, "It's been very interesting talking to you. I look forward to getting pleasantly out of focus in your company, at some time in't near future. Assuming we've not cut Mr Harper's hands off in the meantime!"

DS Wilson turned to go but then spun back around to deliver the final thrust of the assassin's stiletto to the overbearing McIntyre, "Or hung him for crimes against the state," he added, with a wink of his flinty eye. He smiled benignly, waiting for McIntyre's riposte.

For DS Wilson this was the sensitive, community-oriented approach to investigating fraud. 'Win over the locals; get them on our side,' Inspector Somers had said, 'Word from Whitehall and the Bank of England is that the Scots currency is very important to us all – believe it or not, this country has been a model of fiscal confidence in difficult times; which we revenue officers have to reinforce and defend. That's why we are here!"

Now Wilson felt he had done his bit. He was even offering to bolster the legitimate currency by spending some of his own hard earned pay locally. Ted's pale blue eyes played with satirical humour around Donald McIntyre's outcrop of a head, waiting for a coherent retort from such an obviously 'interesting' man, but sadly there had been none.

Instead a hail of insults rattled around Ted Wilson's ears as he turned on his heel to swiftly head after Somers, Garner and their captive.

"Bent, is it? You're the one who's fuckin' bent, ye fat bastard!"

"Wilson is it? Fucking Wilson, hear boys? That's a fucking local name – you should be ashamed o' yersel' boy."

"Aye ye fucking Tory rip!"

"I'll no drink wi' you ony way, even if ye are payin' . . . ye fuckin' English cunt!"

"Aye, fuck off back to Yorkshire, ya English shite!" After half a dozen paces, Wilson gave full vent to the raucous, piggy laugh he'd been holding back after Harper's arrest and the ensuing confrontation. Trotting through the church yard to the street, he raised a hand to wave over his shoulder.

Wilson was beginning to really like the place and its people. He delighted in their directness and understated humour. Now he was flattered to discover that they thought he had a local name. Ted looked around at the trees and the river, swinging his arms happily as he loped along through the village. He breathed in deeply, despite still feeling sick from the fierce blow Harper had landed into his solar plexus.

To Edward Wilson, Milltown was 'God's Little Acre.' It certainly beat the hell out of the barren moor lands of the Pennines. He began to speculate hopefully as to whether he really did have living relatives in the area.

The unused entrance lodge of the Forbes estate with its blue granite stonework and round tower, in the style of the castle beyond, was always available to Bill Stevenson as an occasional holding cell for recalcitrant poachers or other abusers of the law. On this melancholy afternoon it served as an interview room for the men from the Treasury. There were half a dozen chairs and an antique card table, a welcoming fire place but unfortunately no fuel to burn. Garner thrust a receipt copy of a search warrant for the house in Edinburgh into Harper's top pocket, as he laid the original Court Order on the table before him to read. It was self-evident and dated for the following day so after a glance neither man commented on it. Garner retreated to the back of the room, to observe with a scowl of naked aggression.

 Somers took full charge of the interview, with Garner and Wilson there to provide details that would back up his line of questioning. He began fiercely, in the knowledge Harper would be reluctant to speak and difficult to crack. At the time of the raid Harper had always assumed the plates would eventually turn up. Chambers would surely have questioned whether the squad had found them in the back of the paddy wagon. Andy Bradley would have told the Sergeant what happened, where to look. But Bradley had been a bloody mess. The poor fellow had been ready to visit the undertaker for a wooden overcoat. Maybe someone else had stolen them? Possibly even Mary Chalmers, or another passer-by? Conceivably one of the ambulance men might have found them. All of these reasoned options had occurred to Harper many times before.

 No-one from The City has ever come to ask me, after that one time when I was in hospital. Chambers and Brodie have had plenty of opportunity at the Lodge and they know where I live.

Somers began his interrogation by speaking elliptically about the heinous nature of forgery and counterfeiting, the just punishment that would accrue to its perpetrators in the courts. His tone moderated suddenly after five minutes or so of the hard line, when he could see that Harper's anger had abated. Harper watched him sceptically, knowing they had no evidence. First he smiled, then began to laugh - which was not in the script. Somer's bluster blew out suddenly, like a hurricane hitting the desert.

"Lemme get this right, Inspector Somers," Harper asked, kicking back in his chair, "You numpties have been following me for the past two and a half years? All over the fucking country. Checking on the hotels I stayed at and questioning who I spoke to? Logging my every movement and as far as possible - listing every contact as another potential suspect?"

Somers hunched his shoulders, shrinking slightly down into his chair. Harper stared at him incredulously, taking his silence as confirmation.

"Look can I have my hands free? They two are ready for me now. I doubt I'd make it to the door and anyway you've got the artillery piece, ih?"

Somers glanced at Garner, inclining his head towards Harper. Garner crossed the room to unlock his well-oiled handcuffs. They were shiny and durable looking – obviously a new standard issue with an internal ratchet that could reduce blood circulation to the wrists - causing measured duress to a prisoner from the moment of arrest.

Harper consciously avoided looking at or massaging his wrists. Garner glanced at Wilson, who registered the same impression.

Tough little bastard.

Garner began to stare hard at Harper, narrowing pale eyes which bored into Harper's. He was still hurting from the fiendish blow to his stomach. Harper resisted the urge to raise his middle finger at him. Wilson sat forward on his chair, which until that moment had

348

been balanced on two legs, Standing up, he took the chair and placed it across the doorway, sitting on it back to front. He smiled a leering smile at Harper across the room, above the head of Somers, then pointed to himself and Garner, clenching his raised fist as his smile faded.

Harper was pleased to read the threatening gesture as one of potential division between the two detectives and their boss. They were incompetent and had fucked up monumentally, so Harper reflected with sad irony. He thought of Hannah and his family. He was angry and just wanted out of there as quickly as possible. Wilson and Garner were lucky to be still walking. Only the Marquis of Queensbury had saved them from a visit to Dr Gray's Hospital at Elgin. Men like these never learn, thought Harper.

All cops lose compassion. They become tainted by the work they do, forgetting that most people are essentially good, if prone to weakness. They are employed because they are hard bastards.

At that moment Harper finally understood that he was better off out of it. He had thought himself naturally talented as a Police officer – now he knew that he had overlooked something vitally important, unclear until this moment. He still had that instinct for the game though and was not about to admit to anything. These jokers had already investigated him thoroughly and could find nothing. Unless – and it came to him in a shocking instant – unless they had planted evidence and framed him purely to justify the expense. Harper knew things like that happened to innocent people as well as to underworld scum. He decided to collaborate as much as possible without showing weakness so these tough men might save face.

"Why the hell didn't you just come and ask me about the raid? I have nothing to hide!"

"Oh no, then why were you planning to emigrate to America, when all the time your wife was dying of cancer, you little rag nail?" demanded Garner.

"Look, you big lardy cunt, leave her out of this or I swear the next time we clash you won't get up and walk away!"

"It's a legitimate question," Somers pointed out calmly.

Had it come from you, it might have been.

Harper decided not to let Garner and Wilson ratchet up the pressure on him. He answered slowly, not wishing to appear keen to dissuade them from their line of questioning, "Let me make it perfectly clear to you from the outset gentlemen," Harper declared, looking around at all three of the squad in turn but avoiding Stevenson whom he assumed was an ally, "I was not planning to emigrate."

"Then why did you go into the White Star booking office in Liverpool last October, to check their sailings and prices to New York?" Garner asked, this time in a more reasonable tone. Harper let the question hang in the air but Wilson, eager as ever to stick his boot in, followed up with an obvious construction of his own.

"Yeah, we know. You went to a lot of trouble to cover yer tracks, didn't you lad? You went all that way to make a booking, when there are White Star offices in Leith, right - within half an hour's walking distance of your new house, in fact."

Harper's temper flared again and he decided to be awkward. If they were not willing to listen to his explanation - and by now he could see exactly where the questions were leading -

Well, stuff 'em!

Harper waited for half a minute before bothering to respond. He knew exactly how to wind them up.

"That is my business and has nothing to do with you, or your enquiry. So, why don't you just get to the fucking point, shit dick?" Harper ignored Wilson, glowering instead at Garner, who had asked the question and to whom he had taken a genuine dislike. Garner read the animosity in Harper's glinting eye, at the same time instinctively feeling the robust disapproval of Somers.

If we press too hard too soon, he will clam up. Get whatever information we can before he demands a lawyer.

Garner rose and turned in one graceful movement – evidently back to normal, despite the heart stopping shock of Harper's blow half an hour earlier, "I'll be right outside the door, Chief," he said, staring back at Harper.

There was a long silence, which Somers used to put pressure on Harper. In fact he was unsure whether to keep Harper or release him - undecided of what else to ask that might clarify his scepticism about the man. Somers knew of his unspoken connection with The Brotherhood. Harper had powerful friends in Edinburgh, who'd already advised the Inspector to back off. That served only to worry the little man more deeply. Then again if Harper disappeared, his boss Chatwin would have him sacked. On the other hand, if Harper stayed where they could all see him, the problem might just fade away.

"When you left school you worked the forge?" Harper felt like groaning. He knew where his inquisitor was going. He stared back at Somers with sceptical eyes.

"You ever fix any guttering, or down pipes? Lay in some lead flashing for leaky roofs?"

"No, we never had the time, too many horses to look after."

"But you used lead?" Harper continued to stare at Somers, waiting for him to make the obvious accusation, "Did you ever consider any profitable side lines? You know like sand-boxing pewter mugs?" Harper couldn't resist, so he asked the question for him.

"Or stamping out half-crowns? Nah, too time consuming old son. We never had the distribution network."

"But you had the opportunity and the skill."

Somers inspired no reaction in Harper, except for an irresistible desire to probe the Inspector's dubious grasp of authority over his men. Wilson seemed the kind of amiable fool he had encountered every night on his foot patrols in Edinburgh, walking at his side in uniform perhaps rather than in the role of a drunk talking up a fight in the Black Bull or the White Hart.

But Garner – Garner clearly had iron in his soul. Harper was angry and sensitive and felt himself slipping ever closer to showing genuine distress. He would channel his animosity, he decided, at Garner, when he came back in from his smoke. Anger would help keep him in touch with reality – distract him from the awful, depressive sense of separation he was now beginning to feel.

In a strange way he was also relieved by their intrusion – bizarre though it was, it took him away from the most painful of social situations. Instead of searching the faces of his friends for inspiration that was not there, he had been temporarily transported back into the world of criminal intrigue. Although he was being unfairly implicated in something he knew nothing about, he knew also that these were men he might have grown used to as colleagues.

He was almost grateful to them. Part of Harper's mind wished he could leave with them, to help unravel the cat's cradle of connections they were reworking. He shunned intrusive thoughts of his family. During any hiatus in their interrogation, mental images of the girls, Jessie and Great Gran came back to mind. They would become more concerned about him the longer this took.

Everyone who lived and worked in the Milltown would know precisely where he was. All would be talking around it, while they waited patiently for him to reappear. This fact alone almost drove Harper to distraction – it was painful to think about. He wasn't worth their love – he'd always had far too much self-doubt but still he was their local hero.

Harper remembered supporters cheering when he used to score at football, or shinty. He thought of shaping broad horse shoes for the Clydesdales, with his step-brother Alex – striking in turn with the long handled hammers until they were perfect and the orange glow began to die away. They were usually right first time and rarely needed reheating. Alex! God, how he had neglected poor dear Alex Harper in his envy!

Somers breathed deeply several times in rotation, like a prize fighter before the next all-or-nothing round. He glowered at Harper unrelentingly, as he composed his thoughts for the next line of attack, "You believe in coincidence Harper?"

"As a Police Officer, no I didn't. But as a grieving husband and father of three - I have to say that I've come to see the entire universe as a fucking accident. Where do you stand, Sir – I mean from a statistical point of view?"

"Look, I know this must be hurtful to you," replied Somers, "But we have to know, so I am not going to spare your feelings, Harper. Just answer my questions."

"Or you'll do what, Sir? What evidence do you have to support keeping me locked up?"

"Do want me to let you out of here?"

"Yes, just as soon as you like!"

"Then answer our questions . . . and keep your temper under control." Harper stared at the wall.

"You have an expensive camera?"

"Moderately so, yes. It belongs to my wife," Harper's voice betrayed hurt, but he quickly added, "What of it?" to prevent himself habitually correcting the tense of his reply.

"You went to a lecture on the pier at Portobello?"

"Oh yes! Blood and sand . . . how many scum bags have you interviewed . . . or did Ali Macdonald tell you that? You men are thorough. I respect that. But why the fuck are you wasting your time?"

"Mr Lees arranged for a package to be sent to you. From an address in south London, to be precise, an order from a photographic laboratory. Yes?" Harper frowned and paused for a few moments before replying, "Oh yes. The shop had a stock of film for the camera, a Blair's *Petite Kamarette,* which the local man, Lees didn't have. One hundred frames on a continuous reel to be precise. What of it?"

"You were in London three times last year?"

"That's another rhetorical question, DI Somers. Where are you leading me that I didn't have a reason to go?" Harper stared at his interrogator with hardening contempt.

"Ever visit a photographic studio in Lambeth, run by a certain Mr Leon Warnerke. Maybe to buy rolls of that film you ordered, with the hundred frames?"

"No actually, never heard of him and I don't take my wife's camera on business trips with me."

"What would you say your political affiliations are? Left; right; centre? Loosely speaking?"

Harper affected a Texan cowboy drawl, "If ya wanna get right o' me boy you've gotta get off the planet!" Somers did not laugh but Wilson and Stevenson did. Somers scowled at them. Harper pondered for a few seconds, "D'you know Sir, I've never really thought about that until now?" he confirmed with alacrity.

"Ever been involved with émigré Russian communards?"

"No, but I suspect one of those bastards tried to spill Constable Bradley's guts, escaping from the engraver's house in Inverleith," Harper began to smile at his own conceit, asking the next question before Somers could, "You boys are getting close to Mr Big, aren't you? Leon Warnerke - is he your printer eh, your master forger?"

Somers glanced over at Wilson. It was a 'tell' confirming Harper's quick perception.

"Ever attend a lecture given by a Polish photographer named Wladyslaw Malachowski?"

"If I had, I can assure you Inspector Somers, I would have forgotten his name."

"Answer the question," both Wilson and Somers shouted together. Harper ignored their intolerance.

"Hmm – so this is a new slant on 'ownership of the means of production' – 'production of the means of ownership.' Oh sorry, what was his alias again, Malakovski? Well never mind, whatever it was – no. No! – I don't know your counterfeiter. I have no association with him at all.

Good old Karl Marx eh? That would keep a man honest in all other aspects of his life: forging bonds and currency to undermine the international capitalist economy, whilst at the same time arming for the overthrow of the political state at home. I think I would lay in a few crates of whisky along with the sand bags – wouldn't you, Sir? I hope no cunt starts counterfeiting that though."

Wilson stared at Harper. He was quietly amazed at his instant perspective on their years of travail. Harper looked back at him, deliberately misinterpreting the Sergeant's apparent moment of confusion, "You know Wilson, for the siege!"

"You know too much for your own fucking good Harper," snarled Wilson, now clearly getting out of his depth. His instinct would have been to resume bullying Harper. But somehow, this time he knew that would not work.

"Well, yer man here did a thorough job of briefing us all back in ninety three," Harper reminded them, inclining his head towards Wilson's boss.

"Are you having an affair with your housekeeper?" cut in Somers.

"What? No!" answered Harper flatly. He was unsure whether to laugh or cry, "What the hell would that have to do with you, even if I was? Did you . . . have you been asking that girl about me?" Harper's face involuntarily coloured with self-consciousness embarrassment.

Now Somers had hit a nerve that Harper had been unaware of himself, until that very moment. This was the nature of the human psyche. There were distinct layers like an onion, ready to be peeled away. It was too late for Garner to rescue him as a hate figure. Harper's feelings were an open book.

Freud is right . . . who really knows what lies beneath the surface? I will say nothing more about Margaret Kemp, or my family.

Somers looked across at Wilson to confirm his impression. Stevenson coughed loudly, shuffling his chair with fellow-feeling and embarrassment for his old friend.

"Why else would a man buy two tickets for New York when his wife was in no fit state to travel?"

"I didn't."

"No, but you planned to. Why did you change your mind and not go through with it? Was it remorse Harper?"

"Why, remorse? I don't understand your question. Remorse for what?"

"You tell me. Indecision perhaps. You realised we were on to you. You spotted Garner on the Peterborough train that time didn't you?" Now Harper was silent.

"Didn't you? Answer me man . . . d'y think we're stupid? You knew we were following you and you lost your nerve – decided to put it off for a while - take the kids with you when you finally made the move. You even told them something of your plan, to prepare them for the shock of leaving."

Harper stared at Somers, speechless with incredulity and concern for the process. He saw how money, even the closely guarded secrets of its manufacture and distribution might totally bend a man's soul from the true path. It struck him like a slap on the face that he felt guilt by association, but without actual cause. He knew that deep inside every common man is the taint of both envy and guilt.

No wonder the Catholics do such good business.

Harper took a deep breath then reluctantly began to explain the story of Hannah's treatment for cancer using the Coley vaccines. Wilson sat back in his chair to listen carefully. This was new information – a fresh perspective. After a few moments the tough, good humoured Sergeant moved cat-like to the door. He motioned once with his head for his taciturn counterpart Garner to come in and listen. Neither man spoke as Somer's Bull Terrier stepped back inside.

Harper continued speaking in his soft Morayshire drawl as he watched Wilson move around the room. Somers listened very carefully, looking at his hands for a rationale he might grasp that was nowhere else to be seen in the evidence.

After a few minutes Stevenson cut the mesmeric spell of Harper's monologue with a carefully thrown hand grenade of his own. The huge policeman glowered at Somers as he spoke, his broad chest muscles flexed with a constrained threat under his stretched uniform jacket, "Anybody in Milltown of Rothiemay, Marnoch, Auchterless - anywhere round these parts . . . half the fucking county, man - could ha' tol' ye this! That no' right John?"

Harper appeared bent and broken, suddenly looking the small man that he really was. His eyes were scooped out from the habit of worry. Normally tight skin on his handsome face was pulpy and wan. He waited for Stevenson to finish his diatribe, thinking it might have greater effect on the Treasury Officers if he didn't speak for himself.

"Why in the name of all the fucking saints who smile upon us did you three wankers see fit to arrest this good man on the day of his wife's funeral – instead o' making proper enquiries? What was the great secret that ye were keeping from me and my Sergeant: Treasury business? Right?"

Stevenson let his chair fall heavily onto four legs as if to emphasise his simple assertion. Everyone except Harper glanced at his enormously long legs. They had not noticed that the chair had been pivoted backwards although his feet were nonetheless flat upon the floor.

There was pensive silence as Somers glared at the local Bobby. When Harper continued his explanation they all looked from Stevenson back to him, like a sombre audience engaged in a Shakespeare tragedy, "I spent months researching a cure for cancer. There are at least three new lines of research which I will not bore you with details of – and you will *not* ask about," Harper spoke with adamantine surety, staring straight at Somers, "Suffice it to say the most effective treatment available is in New York. I did make enquiries of the cost of travelling there, with my wife and family. The least amount of time that treatment would have taken was between six weeks, to six months – *the least amount of time,*" he repeated with emphasis, "I made repeated attempts to persuade my wife to go there, but she refused. A local doctor administered the new treatment successfully and she went into remission," Harper's voice thickened as he reached the dénouement of his story. His hypnotic delivery suddenly slowed and became excruciating for Bill Stevenson to witness. It seemed to him that Harper was forcing the words past his vocal chords, from where they dropped into the shadows of the room.

Harper tersely described how he had tried to persuade Hannah again to go to Sloane Kettering Hospital in New York, once it became clear that the cancer had moved up into her lungs, "She had faith in Payton and in Coley's treatment regime," he explained, looking at his hands with obvious regret, "But the dosages were weaker and for some reason less effective. Finally fluid on her lungs caused pneumonia and a fatal heart attack."

Somers had wanted to interrupt his prisoner, once he began to realise the essential truth of Harper's story but could not find an excuse to do so. He had invited complete honesty. Now he had to suffer along with Harper as the poor chap related the sequence of events that had entailed the need to find out about travel to New York.

Essentially Stevenson is right – we have been over-cautious in our discreet investigation. It has been a 'rolling rock' – triggering an avalanche of paperwork and expenses rather than hard evidence.

Somers realised too late that Harper's eager patron Brodie, would have allowed Edinburgh City Police to take a direct approach that might have saved time and money as well as embarrassment.

There was a pause in the interview as Harper wiped away moisture from his eyes with his thumbs. Then he steeled himself to say something else with a heavy voice, "So, gentlemen, I never could prevail upon my wife, Hannah, to attend Coley's clinic in New York. I will never know whether it could have saved her life," Harper looked around at all four men in turn as if to say, 'But I think it probably would have,' his red rimmed eyes asking a question with broad implications which none of them wished to hear or think about.

"Very interesting!" intoned Wilson with genuine surprise, when Harper finished his brief account and was ready for their further questions.

"Yeah boy, there's an understatement," agreed Harper looking across at the big man, now sprawled across the table leaning on his elbows.

Somers had made mistakes in his career before but none as utterly unpredictable as this. Deep embarrassment resulted from a farcical combination of errors and a remarkable medical discovery which he had never heard of until now.

When he finally spoke again, the Treasury Inspector's priestly demeanour had sobered even further. His tone of voice altered to betray the obvious doubt he was feeling. He spoke like a father, having scolded his child for the first time ever – his voice trembling with compunction. Somers' words carried the logic of the investigation but without conviction, "How do I know this is not a convenient cover story?"

"Can I speak frankly, DI Somers?" asked Harper respectfully, "Right now, I don't care whether you think it is or not."

"I mean who do I speak to – to confirm this?"

"Why don't you just get to the fucking point . . .You clearly think I am part of a network . . . That I still have the plates taken from the printer's house in Leith?" Somers paused before he answered thoughtfully.

"Essentially, yes."

"Well, 'essentially' I do not have them. 'Essentially' you are conducting a high powered internal investigation into some missing evidence. 'Essentially' you are desperately looking for someone to blame because your Polish mechanic is in the wind."

Somers squared his chin at Harper – he was down but not out. He'd handled the approach wrongly but still had questions to ask, "Where did you get the money to buy the house near Queen's Drive in Holyrood Park?" Somers spoke emphatically but seemed to be forcing a connection he didn't believe was strong.

"You mean Lillyhill Terrace?" Wilson looked at a notebook and read out the address, "Right sir. 37, Lillyhill Terrace." Stevenson and Harper stared at him.

"Where did the money come from?"

"It's not a big house, Somers. There are fifty of them in a square of less than a couple of acres. The maze of patchwork backyards never ceases to amuse me. There isn't room to swing a cat, but I like it there. Holyrood Park reminds me of home and it's a pleasant walk up into the town."

"Where did the money come from?"

"I don't need to answer that. What does it matter where it came from . . . I could have saved for the deposit out of my wages as a Bobby."

"But you didn't . . . so answer the question."

Harper stared at Somers. When he answered his voice had thickened with rage, "Not that it's any of your business . . . but it was a wedding gift from . . ."

"Yes?"

" . . . From my father. I'm illegitimate, as you well know, you old twat. My father, my biological father that is - gave me the money through a friend, an intermediary."

"And this friend, might he vouch for you? Could you tell us who he is? Where he lives?"

"I could – but I'm not going to - because this farce is going to end now."

Somers took out his fob watch and sighed.

"If you have more questions, then ask them sharply because my patience is wearing thin," warned Harper.

"What happened to the plates?"

"I honestly don't know. There were plates and I did have them. I thought they were placed in the back of the paddy wagon with everything else. Chambers was in charge – I assume you've asked him?" Somers looked at Wilson who picked this up as a meaningful signal. He began to write in his notebook.

"You went to the Royal Infirmary to guard a man in a coma. You were ill yourself, so when you were relieved later that night you went straight home. You were owed time off and took it prior to your departure from the force?"

"Yes, all of that is correct."

"And you went in to the station when you had recovered, to file your report."

Harper hesitated, "I'm not sure that I'd put it quite like that."

"Well, in your own words?"

"I said goodbye. I went in to see Sergeant Chambers and Inspector Brodie. I chatted with two or three others, who were on duty. It was a working day – they didn't have time and neither did I. I was . . . we were, moving house."

"So no one asked you about the plates?"

"No, Brodie and Macdonald had already quizzed me about the plates when I was still in hospital with pneumonia. They had made a lot of arrests and taken a lot of evidence – my contribution seemed superfluous."

"Superfluous?"

"Well, I had flattened some poor bastard. Thought I'd killed him outright . . . Sat for an hour in a pool of blood with Bradley . . . Spent the entire fucking evening hoping the poor mope I'd punched would come out of surgery alive."

"Did you have any further contact with the man?"

"Which man?"

"The one in the coma, the one you nearly killed?"

"Blum."

"Blum; so you know his name?" Harper looked up at Somers, breathing in deeply through the side of his mouth, "Yes. I read it in the papers and no, no contact. I was pleased that he'd made it through – that's all. I consoled myself that they had tried to gaffe Bradley like a fucking Marlin."

"So, you felt concerned about Blum's continued wellbeing?"

"You might say I was concerned with Blum's continued existence. His well-being, or otherwise, is of no interest to me."

"And had you met him prior to the day of the raid?"

"Fuck off!" Harper folded his arms and scowled at Wilson who was sitting upright at the table scribbling down every word of the interrogation, "You can record that as a negative," Harper remarked.

"Sorrite . . . I can spell 'Fuck off'," Wilson replied with deadpan sarcasm. Somers became silent and deeply pensive. Clearly he was wrestling with some imponderable – some question he knew part of the answer to but was reluctant to ask immediately.

Out of the whirling clockwork of the chromosphere came the Dobie's knock on the door. Garner went to see who it was. In a moment he returned, nodding at Somers who stepped outside into the soft evening air.

There was a whispered conversation with a man Harper vaguely recognised. His name was Chisholm. He worked as a general factotum for Sir William Forsyth. Occasionally Harper had seen Chisholm come with paperwork for Hugh or John senior – contracts to sign off; payments and such, for the lumber mill.

Zachariah Williams has been working behind the scenes.

Harper was becoming impatient. He took his coat off and hung it on the back of his chair, as though resigned to his fate. He drew breath deeply and audibly again – this time sighing sharply as a follow up, his legs stretched out in front of him.

There was a twitchy silence as Wilson waited for Somers to return. By now the eccentric Sergeant was convinced of Harper's innocence. He had done his job thoroughly and his career was safe now for sure, even though the boss wanted rid of him. All he had to do was keep his mouth shut. It was Somer's boat – he could sail it himself.

Chisholm departed and Somers returned busily to sit down as if in a hurry to expedite matters. Garner stood inside the door – an ironic grin spread across his vulgar face.

"Were the premises in Leith secured before you left?"

"Do you mean some twat might have sneaked back in and grabbed the plates?" Somers levelled his gaze at Harper as though trying to read any deceit.

"I was sat outside on the pavement with a man I thought would never make it. I thought he would bleed to death. I honestly do not know who or what was inside during that time. People had escaped through doors and windows. There was a man down on the floor of the cellar – the printing room. Blum. I never even got to check over the whole of the printing room although I locked the door. It was chaos from start to finish, sir. There were peelers everywhere. Until Chambers came back, no – I could not say the premises were secure. The plates were not my primary concern anyway. I honestly couldn't give a fuck where they are now either." Wilson let out one of his suppressed piggy laughs.

"Might you have inadvertently taken them home with you?" Harper thought about this question for half a minute – resisting any temptation to reply. He carefully considered his choice of words before speaking.

"The last time I saw the plates – the only time I saw the plates – was in the basement printing room, when Blum had them in his hand. I put them inside my greatcoat pocket. I have not seen them since."

"Blum says he gave them to you."

"Well, I'm not disputing that. He had them in his hand when I put his lights out. I think he meant to give them to me."

"Why?"

"Why what?"

"Why would he do that – just hand them to you?"

363

"You tell me Somers – you're the one with the Enfield in your pocket. Maybe he thought I had a gun."

"Okay, Harper – whatever happened that day and it does seem terribly disorganised – I am convinced that you are telling the truth. But I place the 'Policeman's Caveat' upon that."

Harper 'hmmd' as though he knew precisely what Somers meant and was about to add.

"Yes Harper?" asked Somers rhetorically, looking through him rather than at him.

"Sure - there is always something more."

"Precisely, Harper, something left out, knowingly or otherwise, which we cannot account for, or even speculate about constructively - because we simply do not know it. But I *know* there is something more, Harper." Somers looked hard at Harper as he stood up and shrugged his coat onto his shoulders.

"No doubt there is sir, but I can't give it to you because I don't have it."

"Tell him Ted!" barked Somers with a surprising hint of vehemence. Wilson stood up also, shuffling behind the table towards the door. He looked down at Harper, swallowing the reflux of his mushroom and bacon flavoured gastric juices before speaking matter of factly, "It was Blum who told us about the plates pal. It didn't feature in any report. Brodie filleted it out. You fucked up, tosser. You fucking lost them!"

"But what you told us today corroborates Blum's part of the story," added Somers, "I have no reason to believe that either of you are lying."

"Why now, if you don't mind me asking?"

"Why any time in particular?" Somers reflected. "We had enough evidence to convict the whole bunch. It pointed to an international organization with 'Mr Big' based in London. I never expected to see the plates. We assumed one of the men who ran from the house on Ferry Road had taken them. When we came to the pre-trial hearings it emerges that Blum thought his behaviour on that day might have helped to reduce his sentence. That's all there was to it really. I described you and we immediately started an internal investigation.

It went beyond Edinburgh City Police authority because you were no longer an employee and the possibility of wider connections made it seem we were on to something significant. We are acting upon the testimony of one man – a known criminal. That is why we have been watching you carefully instead of kicking in your front door with a search warrant."

Harper shook his head and thought for a few moments before he responded, with a distant look in his eyes, "Shit . . . 'Purse Seine' was the worst day of my life . . . on reflection boys, even worse than today. I was really too ill to be out of bed and when I saw what they had done to poor old Bradley, I thought it had all gone to hell. The worst part was feeling isolated though. I felt helpless. I thought the man would bleed to death and all I could think of was how he would feel dying alone. Now I realise, all of us die alone."

There was a long silence in which all four men stared in recognition at Harper and Harper stared at nothing. At last Keith Somers had the last word, "Go to your family now man. I expect to see you back here at nine am when you can make a full statement. I will submit my own record of this interview. At least you will be spared the ignominy of returning to the West Port station. Wilson has the necessary forms and Constable Stevenson can sit in to help you."

Stevenson, who had sat grim-faced through the entire exchange moved over to where Harper sat.

"Somers!" called Harper as the Inspector moved to the door, "What did Chisholm have to say about me?" Somers stared blankly into the middle of the room, then advanced to stand close to Harper.

"I'm sorry to have brought this intrusion upon you at such a time of distress, John. I hope you can forgive it. Let it suffice to say there will be no need for further background checks or action on the search warrant."

Somers offered his hand and Harper shook it firmly. The pulling clasp of his fingers told in essence what Somers knew about Harper and who had spoken up for him.

The Brotherhood.

No doubt there had been a message from the inner-circle saying, 'Stand-off this man. He's connected.' Where would they all be without it? Somers' Masonic handshake made Harper think of the resurrection of the dead - The Archangel helping to lift Christ from the cold slab of the tomb.

Inspector Somers carefully picked up the search-warrant court order as though it was forensic evidence. Without looking at Harper he reached into his pocket to take out a box of Bryant and May smoker's safety matches. He flicked one of the red headed pine sticks along the friction strip on the side and it flared evenly. He held it upside down to allow the paraffin impregnated wood to boil and burn, then flipped it upright, playing the flame onto the bottom corner of the court order. The Treasury Officer glanced at Harper as he held it over the hearth. He nodded to his exonerated suspect once, then threw the flaming paper away disdainfully.

Somers trooped out of the gatehouse solemnly with his bulldogs padding after him. Wilson turned at the door, nibbling his lips and creasing his eyes in a moment of hesitation. Then he turned to Harper who sat watching in silence. Wilson gave him a mischievous smile of approval, winking with his left eye, "See ya later pal. No hard feelings!"

Harper asked Bill Stevenson to leave him alone for a few moments, "to collect my thoughts before joining guests at The Forbes." Stevenson threw him the key to the gate house and left quickly without comment. He would say a few words to the assembled company in the hotel to take the heat off poor John. He had suffered enough of an inquisition for one day.

Harper meshed his hands like a tortured supplicant and banged his thumbs on his forehead, "Were they in my coat, Hannah?" he said aloud. Harper simply wanted to ask her again what exactly she had done with his blood soaked uniform. Had she even looked in the pockets before the rag and bone man called. Had she tried to wash the dried blood out first? The more he thought of her kind motives the more hopeless he felt. He realised she had become a mother figure to him, like she was to the Wilson and Robertson children. He had never really questioned anything she'd decided.

If I had taken a stronger lead, she would still be with me.

The combination of the cold air in the unheated room and the dryness of his throat from talking so long, had worked to draw moisture from his eyes and nose. Harper felt like he was beginning to choke on his own selfish stupidity, curling like a fallen leaf in a springtime thunderstorm, "Oh Hannah, my poor love!" he groaned through pathetic bubbles of saliva and irresistible tears, "Now I can't even ask you a simple question to save my reputation!"

In that moment, sitting alone in the shadows of the folly round tower, Harper's loneliness and anguish were complete.

Chapter Nineteen - *Babes*

When Harper woke early, the distraught faces of his daughters burned directly into his troubled mind. Electrified by the need to help them he groaned with nausea and rolled out of the cold bed. In desolation Harper grasped at the need to love, realising that nothing else would keep him alive. There could be no stronger motive to sweeten his surly temper or lighten his numbed soul. On this the day of their leaving he told himself, nothing was more important.

Love is what everyone needs.

As he sat dressed to his waistcoat, staring into the mirror in Hannah's silent bedroom, he thought of the morning of their picnic at Portobello three years earlier.

So much had shifted to change his perception of the world on that day. Then he had begun to see Hannah as the product of her wider family. Although he understood that the women all had individual motives, he also saw how the act of caring was often a given for them - never conditional.

Hannah's temporary addiction to opiates had revealed an underlying aspect of her beautiful soul as surely as sunlight crystallising silver on developing photographic paper. At her most vulnerable she had become rigorously honest and fatalistic, with humour always shining through. She had been outwardly self-assured, despite the dragging physical tenderness that left her reduced. Around that time Hannah had privately expressed regret to Harper at the inevitable foreshortening of her life. Although she had been stoic, Hannah felt guilty for not fulfilling the hopes of her young family.

He sat on the bed in the grey-pink light of dawn considering this precious legacy of Hannah's as he planned how to get through that final, poignant day at Ramsburn. If he cleared up the statement quickly, double checking to avoid anything incriminating, they might still catch the midday train from Keith. This distraction would take pressure off him indirectly, while giving the children a little more time with Hannah's family. I need not pack their cases as planned. Jessie would organise that, with a little help from Hannah's teenage sisters Jeannie and Betsy.

"God damn it all!" hissed Harper, blunted by remorse, "We're all trapped, as surely as stupid field mice caught by a cat in a larder!" He rose from the bed and headed out to draw water for the kettle.

The leaving was gracious but no less heart breaking. Harper silently swore to what he saw in his heart –

This precious connection must carry forward into another generation. Our babes must remain as familiar with Rothiemay in another twenty five years as Hannah and I have been.

Ultimately that would mean not just maintaining the connection with Great Gran Han and Jessie but with young Uncle Frank, amongst others.

The business with the law was concluded in the collaborative manner of school homework copied before the morning hand bell is swung. Harper went along to the Forbes to settle his bill where he was graciously surprised to meet a full contingent from the evening before, including the reclining doctor Payton and Zachariah.

They looked like wounded men scattered across a hard won battlefield. A mist of white phosphorous from a thousand cheap matches blocked watery sunlight, adding to the impression of carnage - helping to lock their jaws perhaps in hung-over silence. Ardent consumption of alcohol was the only possible rationale for their continued presence in the bar – that and a loose notion that John Harper might return to pay his dues to Will Hendry, the hotelier.

Wilson and Garner, sheepish from over indulgence and lack of sleep, flanked the fulsome, regal looking Donald McIntyre. Today they clearly had different priorities - no one even checked to see if the sun had indeed climbed above the yard arm.

Harper was pressed to make all sorts of affirmations regarding future visits to Rothiemay. Advice came from members of a community as close as family, "You belong here John boy," stated Donald.

"Aye, dinnae forget us!" came the chorus.

Glasses were raised and refilled. Harper thanked his kind friends, raising a measure to them in a toast. And then the bottle went round again. Dr Payton saw the despairing look in Harper's eyes and it was he who finally got the young man off the hook.

"Gentlemen, gentlemen!" he called out to the small assembly of all-nighters, "Ignorant and irreligious bastards that you all are, to a man," he paused for a grumbling roll of protest and laughter to abate, "Nonetheless," he raised his hand and voice together to deflect objections, "May Goodness and Mercy follow us all through the remaining days of our lives. May John Harper and his fine family, each and every one of us and ours, have such and such to thank God for - to laugh and smile about - when tomorrow comes!" he affirmed in hope, raising his glass to all present.

"Tomorrow's here Joe – we've been up aw' night," Jim Lorimer remarked dryly. There was a ripple of amused approval for the young man's observation.

"Slaintje! slaintje!" came the business-like chorus as a dozen or so glasses were tipped and emptied in one.

Propelled with a fond hand on his back and with Dutch courage in his heart, Harper walked the lane through the forest he'd walked so often hand-in-hand with Hannah back to Ramsburn for the last time, alone. He carried every blessing from his friends and could only be committed to hope. Who knew, if he could remain positive, the future might indeed be bright? Like a child repeating his first year at nursery, Harper counted his blessings through a mist of tears.

But to Great Gran and Jessie there was only yesterday. Their misty eyes and cracked voices betrayed profound sorrow at the leaving. Their final embraces spoke only of love forlorn and longing for what had been so precious that would never come again. The more they tried to suppress their sorrow for the sake of his three little girls, the more poignantly their faces told the story. But Harper knew fine, the two women would weep bitterly when all the children's voices on both sides of the family had dispersed and faded. When the door finally closed behind them.

For Elsie, Elizabeth and Hannah that moment of leaving was heart-rending, yet promissory in a manner which only children can conclude for themselves. Adult explanations, like the shadowy legal implications of marriage, inheritance and entitlement, served only to dull their interest, although picking up their lives in Edinburgh would be agony itself. They were leaving their mother behind in the huddled stones of a bleak churchyard two hundred miles from home. Elsie, Elizabeth and Hannah Harper would never take anything in life for granted again.

As the train rumbled through a dispassionately sunny afternoon, the forest green hillsides of that day became frozen in time. Eight charming members of their mother's family: Great Gran Han; Granny Jessie; Frank; Jeannie; Betsy; Kate; Fiona, Elsie not to mention Uncles Alex and Ewan whom they adored, would bravely engage forever in detached pastoral routines on the earth and under the sky. There would be visits, sure but time would pass and their cousins would leave home one by one to become strangers to them. The Harper girl's faces and bodies would change and develop too. The memory of loss and separation would fade as they grew in mind and experience. Time would heal wounded hearts but the scars of love divided would remain forever.

As they rolled along in glum silence it struck Harper that his youngest daughter Hannah was extraordinarily precocious for a three year old. He mused idly upon the comparison between her and her two sisters. Dark haired, genial Elsie at eight years had an appearance of indeterminate age. Sprouting so fast and so personable was she that she might have passed for a teenager. Fair haired Elizabeth, not yet six, was clearly also going to be tall and at times could be sanguine, like her father.

How they change between visits will be remarked upon. It will take on exaggerated significance for everyone who knows them up in Rothiemay. From now on, every meeting and renewed friendship, every homecoming will be tinged with sadness for their mum.

They rode in silence, declining drinks and sandwiches, scowling at the beckoning forests and their own reflections in the glass.

For Little Hannah there was a physical hollowness never experienced before. She had been the centre of attention for two and a half years at Ramsburn. Great Gran had doted upon her, talking with the bairn daily - spanning eighty years of life experience to create a bond of friendship. Aware that time was precious, her mother had engaged intellectually in a way that most parents would have never attempted or have had time for. The child was already a fluent reader and could form words into loosely legible handwriting. She had understood that her mother was dying and there had been no concern greater than that for her. She alone had been told the secret story of the Duffs by her mother – of a little girl left an orphan and taken in by a very kind lady – Great Gran. It had been preparation for the inevitable. She began the habit of saying, "Mammy's Duff and I'm Duff too," and at first everyone laughed at her innocence. But when the inevitable happened, Little Han had been marginalised - ignored amongst the mourners - passed on by proxy to be looked after by thirteen year old Betsy Wilson and eleven year old Kate Robertson, she learned the hardest lesson at the earliest age. Great Gran and Jessie had been too pre-occupied by the practical and social extensions of their own grief to console her.

Harper, aloof and self-controlled, had for the past week seemingly avoided contact with Little Hannah and her sisters, despite his principles. It had been a time for empathy – yet the adults seemed to have none to spare for the children. All of a sudden the discriminations of physical maturation and intellectual development were stripped away to reveal underlying doubt and insecurity.

Hannah could read through their confusion, She was already beginning to make her own deductions.

Grownups don't know what to say when a body dies.

Essential routines stuck through everyone's bare feelings like a rocky shoreline, yet life was definitely not going on as normal. Their mother's passing and funeral had always been a generational battleground without bullets and for their daddy this train journey was the final retreat.

Little Hannah somehow felt guilty. She knew about doing naughty things and being scolded – like when she had opened the gate to the hens and taken Sally in with her. Sally had run at the hens more quickly each time they tried to run from her. It had been a great game full of mad laughter which seemingly the dog and the hens enjoyed as much as she had. The cock had pecked Sally on the snout. But Sally was quick. She barked and chased, knocking him off his feet as he ran away. That was brilliant fun but for once there had been serious consequences.

Great Gran was angry. 'They won't lay if you do that!' The old cock died that night too. So, bad things happen which are not my fault.

Now Little Hannah felt unreasonable sorrow. Grown-ups were clearly even more prone to the same affliction. But the youngest child caught the drift of a profound lesson for life which most forgot, so it seemed, as they got older. Adults were less able to deal with feelings the more they tried to control them. They lied to cover it up. Little Hannah sat on the seat opposite Harper studying his contorted face, searching his eyes for a glimmer of hope that he might stop pretending. Time had passed so painfully slowly for her over recent months that she had become desperate for the relief of genuine contact with her Daddy. Harper was preoccupied though. He was in no mood to be demonstrative, even to the youngest of his three daughters. Not at least under the watchful eyes of her elder sisters.

They had occasionally voiced the notion that somehow Hannah had been treated as a favourite. From Harper's point of view it would do the child no good at all to act in a way that might corroborate that false notion. The fact that Little Hannah had grown close to her mother, whilst her sisters had felt separation, made the dynamics all the more complex. The fact that she carried the living embodiment of her mother's easy humour every time a smile played across her lips, made Harper the more acutely aware of the child's needs as a member of the family. Elizabeth had her mother's looks too but Little Hannah had learned the same voice and tone of expression.

He was already walking the line between generating mutual support or rivalry amongst his children. It was plain to see that Elsie's heart had been broken long ago. She was responsive and lovely but her confidence was shattered. A green light of jealousy and resentment had flashed at times from Elizabeth's quick eyes, which Harper dreaded to see again. He had endured this return train journey too many times. He had always fallen into the trap of trying to cheer them although they were invariably miserable. This day they were inconsolable. He decided to let nature take its course. Harper told himself to give up worrying.

Life is unfair. Opportunity random, unpredictable and discriminatory.

Little Hannah went over to the opposite side of the carriage to look out of the window because Elsie and Elizabeth had placed themselves at either end of the bench on Harper's side. She lifted her slender right hand onto the bottom of the frame to steady herself, every inch a scaled down little-old lady. As she looked back at the distant, retreating scenery her eyes filled with silent grief for all she was leaving behind. In retrospect that image of his youngest daughter sitting aloof in her silence would come to exemplify the period ahead for Harper, of his trek through the wasteland of broken dreams.

During Hannah's long absence many conversational transactions had appeared stilted, meaningless or superficial for him. Harper had come to question people's motives and sincerity. Then in turn, in every fundamental aspect, he was beginning to guiltily question himself. With Hannah's passing, Harper had lost the ability to connect. He knew at the very beginning of his Odyssey that he had no Penelope to return to.

Half way through the three hour journey Harper's meditation was lulled by the trundling carriage into flashing images, then down into the beckoning calm of dispassionate sleep. He was still conscious as dream connections came to him – watching the layer cake of his own distracted existence. Wondering even about the fantastic nature of his eternal soul, he fought the irresistible appeal of exhaustion.

A railway inspector came through the carriage. In tired vigilance Harper heard the man - raising his hand to show the tickets without even opening his eyes. Later, having fully succumbed to the wizard Morpheus, he was still aware of the sweet voices of his darlings as they whispered and stumbled along the aisle to and from the toilet, such was his hyper-vigilance.

By the time the train approached Edinburgh, Harper's head was swimming with fatigue. The effects of his lunchtime affirmations at the Forbes had served to supplement a week of desensitising recourse to the bottle. It had begun on the night of his visit with Zachariah and Anne Williams on the fateful day of Hannah's moving on. Now his stomach burned and his face felt like it had been fried with the morning's breakfast. His tongue stuck to the roof of his mouth. Harper realised with shame that his clothes and breath reeked of stale tobacco smoke.

Now as they arrived at Waverley, waking up was torture. Speaking made no sense at all and his hands trembled like an old man's. Harper struggled with the bags, glowering at a lackadaisical porter who clearly wished to avoid offering assistance. At the station forecourt he hailed a cab, rounding up the girls as briskly as Tex with the flock. Still no-one felt like speaking.

They arrived at the insubstantial little house, devoid of character and memories, in the early evening. Harper dumped the cases in the hallway, locked the front door and exhorted the children to follow his example, "rest for an hour before supper."

In his watchful dreaming he woke slowly but was reluctant to get out of bed. Not knowing what time it was or where he was, he reached for Hannah. The coldness of the sheets told him that she had risen. Hearing her footsteps, he realised she had gone to the lavatory. Harper grumbled in his slumbers, hoping she had not found some other activity down stairs. There was always that pile of laundry and ironing to do. A week of mournful sleep-deprivation had taken over his senses. Harper was deluded, cheated by his own subconscious presumptions. With eyes shut in the dark he felt dizzy, deep in a different reality. His brain was swollen with throbbing pain. Turning to lie face down in the soft caress of linen, he plunged again into the gentle realm of imagination. For hours wandering in the darkness of sweet illusion, he was a bit player in a Bohemian tragedy, embracing only what was unreal. Eventually he lay on his back, soaked in the perspiration of delirium tremens, asking himself where he was.

Harper looked closely at the hands of his fob-watch on the bedside table but time was no longer meaningful. How long had he lain disoriented? What events preceded resting? Where was Hannah? Reality settled in the darkness around him like the concrete of a freshly laid culvert. Harper did not want to move or think. In that warm, neutral place the horrible game had ceased. Something dreadfully unpleasant had temporarily passed him by and he was grateful. He would take as much time as necessary to allow his whisky-soused body to lead him back to wakefulness.

Did my body need the oblivion of sleep, or my mind?

It was twelve thirty am. Harper spent the next two hours resting but marginally wakeful, still in bed. Then the awful reality and what was missing struck him suddenly. In a moment of despair he thought his heart might stop beating. But he did not want to explore reality by thinking. He tried instead to go back to sleep where he could dream of Hannah coming back to bed, or find her down stairs working at the chores. The bleak pain of consciousness was too dire, yet the dream had felt so real.

When he woke fully Harper immediately found himself thinking about suicide again. He knew all about life assurance policies and had taken a great deal of care over writing trust deeds for himself, to ensure the financial security of his girls. He was not morbid, so he told himself but he was certainly thinking about the practicalities of action. He remembered this pattern of his gloomy thoughts from a prior occasion, knowing them to be the same. Recognition told him that depression was merely a sardonic form of honesty - an embittered old friend who'd fallen on hard times, asking to sleep on the sofa.

It was four am when Harper swept the bedclothes to one side, like a soldier blasted by reveille, realising with shame that he was still dressed in his day clothes. Changing into casual slacks and donning a clean shirt and socks, he marched quickly into the bathroom to brush his teeth. Plunging his head into a basin of cold water he rubbed his face and hair dry with a towel smelling of mould.

Heading down stairs to make breakfast, he ground coffee which he drank black, then fried three eggs which had been a little too long in the larder. He toasted stale bread, spreading it with butter on the turn. After chewing the first mouthful of his meal he pitched it angrily into the waste bin.

Harper tried hard to distract himself. The first requirement was to write out a shopping list. Several editions of The Scotsman delivered in his absence offered distraction for an hour. Then he found a hardback copy of Thomas Hardy's *Return of the Native* and forced himself to submit to its timeless magic.

At last sleep lay on his eyelids again, allowing the words to slip past thought and perception, making rivers of white between the islands of black print. Reading and re-reading whole sentences, Harper pushed on until his mind was finally numb. He thought of sleeping there on the couch but knew he would be disturbed by the girls in the morning, so dragged himself upstairs at six am, planning to sleep through until ten. Harper dreamt of the humble Redleman and a Smithsonian cornucopia of human activity which sprang magically from Hardy's gentle touch. A thousand smiling faces drifted past his mind's eye. Only Hannah's was becoming hard to see.

The muted sound of Margaret Kemp's voice electrified Harper's brain. There was a flash of light behind his weary eyelids, as he became instantly alert. When had he established such a deep psychic connection with her? He did not pause to reflect upon this question - but there it was. Harper was more concerned with the negative impression that he might make upon Margaret. He could hear the manner of her conversation with the children - their enthusiastic greetings in the hallway, even though he could not pick out precise words. Harper rolled out of bed and dressed immediately.

There to greet him on the landing as he emerged from the bedroom was Little Hannah. Her doe eyes conveyed a question, holding the natural smiling curl of her mouth in restraint.

"Yes, Daddy is fine angel, how are you?"

"No, you're not fine Harper. I'm not fine. I'm too sad."

He glanced down at her, touching her face gently as he hurried past into the bathroom to brush his teeth.

Margaret was in the kitchen when he found the girls. She had begun to organise breakfast and was happily taking orders. She had prepared the scene well in her mind and was proud of having played her part of staying behind to look after Molly the cat. Basic provisions for every appetite had already been put away in the cupboards. The warm scent of Indian tea greeted Harper at the door.

"Hello John, how are you feeling?" Like a fool she'd blurted out the irresistible question that she had earlier determined to avoid. Their eyes met and Margaret could read the answer in his silence. Colouring with embarrassment she looked away, hurriedly pouring tea and twittering to save his feelings.

"I managed to get to the Castle Terrace Market in town for the last hour. I got you a boneless leg of lamb for half price. I got a fresh cauli and a big piece of cheese for a sauce. I know you love that. I got a stone of Arran reds. So the girls can have roast potatoes with butter . . . I'll make it for you this evening if you like." Elsie and Elizabeth cheered Margaret, begging Harper to let her cook and offering to help her with the food preparations.

Harper self-consciously slid away to grab the suitcases which had been parked overnight in the hallway. He was acting like a machine designed to speed up work processes - an automaton from one of HG Well's novels. Racing up the stairs he bounced the large suitcase containing the girl's clothes lengthways onto Elizabeth's bed, which was nearest the window.

For a moment he sighed deeply, gazing out at what was an unfamiliar view up towards Arthur's Seat. He had always been so pressed for time that there were still aspects of the house he didn't know. Looking around the children's bedroom he planned to work rapidly, sorting out their belongings.

He knew where they kept their clean clothes and quickly checked that they had enough. He had ordered Jeannie to use the Hessian sack for their laundry before they packed and threw it onto the floor at the end of the bed. Other items could be piled onto the dressing table for the girls to put away themselves. Harper felt pressured and uncomfortable in his own house - piqued by an internalised, unspoken pre-occupation with Margaret, which even Somers had tried to raise to cause embarrassment.

He always knew that she had strong affection for him. Now he had a choice to make. Either he kept her at arms-length or she would cause problems. Today he would immerse himself in work of all kinds – *that* would be the best strategy for avoiding engagement with her, which he knew they were both contemplating.

In the instant of turning attention back to organising sufficient clean clothes for the girls, Harper decided to put Hannah in to share a room with Elizabeth. Elsie would protest he knew but it would balance things out nicely if she swapped bedrooms with Hannah. He began to stack items of clothing accordingly, which meant looking closely at the labels. Margaret came upstairs. She tried to take over sorting of the girl's clothes but he managed to deflect her.

"Okay, but your breakfast is waiting. Did you not hear me calling you?" He apologised limply, declining her gently repeated offer of help. Harper knew it was all or nothing with Margaret Kemp – there would be no half-measures. Her sorrowful, tight lips and watchful gaze lifted like an actor's mask – and the resolve of a marchioness returned in an instant. Margaret announced that she was, "taking the girls to the park."

Harper fetched his wallet to give her money to buy them ice cream. She smiled with intimate warmth which he registered with an unwelcome frisson of attraction. Harper stared back without cracking a smile. All four set off noisily down the stairs. Sighing with relief that she was going, Harper sat down disconsolately on the bed.

When the girls had closed the front door and their voices receded into silence he went down to the kitchen. He ravenously consumed two fried eggs on a doorstep sandwich, without sitting down. Swilling the food down with a mug of tea which he replenished quickly, Harper found himself satiating an inner appetite, constantly alert like a hound of hell since Hannah had died. But his appetite wasn't just for food. He needed intimate consolation he could not have. He wanted Hannah – and no-one else. After wiping egg yolk from the plate with his finger and placing crocks in the sink, he went back to the bedroom without washing up.

Whatever desultory tasks were created for Margaret would give him an excuse to avoid her throughout the day. He immediately scooped up the hessian laundry sack which he took to place next to the washtub in the outhouse. Then he headed swiftly back to the bedroom, where he yanked the second case containing his deceased wife's and youngest daughter's clothes up onto the bed next to the first one

Harper braced himself mentally as he undid the leather straps, carefully railing the enormous brass zip fastener to open the case. Overwhelmed by the familiar release of rosewater scent emanating from her clothes, he was reminded of Hannah's smiling spiritual presence.

In a moment that would forever stand beyond time Harper lifted up the top half of the large suitcase with it's laden inside pocket, flipping it backwards onto the land at the end of the divan. He cursed softly as the flap overshot the end of the bed, propelling most of the contents of the pouch onto the floor.

His heart leaped in his chest and he stood in alarm, wondering how he had not anticipated what he saw in that instant.

"Now see my answer to your dilemma," he imagined Hannah saying. Blood rang in his ears as Harper froze, repeating in his mind's eye what he had just seen and heard as the heavy objects landed on the floor. Lying amid familiar items that might comfort and entertain a small child at bed time - teddy bears and bendy clowns; the art satchel with ink-pad; paper and crayons; brass rubbings from Elgin Cathedral, were three heavyweight items that once seen would never be forgotten.

Beside the engraver's plates were artistic copies, faithfully reproduced in various bright colours by the bairns. Harper thought he knew what the heavy objects were with the first glimpse, before they landed on the floor. But the children's paper copies floating slowly back and forth to land on the carpet left him with no doubt at all.

"Well, hunt the fucking dummy! I bet it was Elsie going in my pockets looking for baubles and bells! I should have known it!"

Hannah said they were up all that night with Ella Stewart. If it wasn't for Hugh Harper involving the Brotherhood, Somers would have searched the house and found them. I'd be sitting in a jail cell now, wondering what the hell happened!

381

Harper scrabbled at the end of the bed, pulling madly at the candlewick cover to get at the prize he had glimpsed. The case tipped onto the floor and he cursed as he pushed it away with his feet.

"What was it Elizabeth said? 'Daddy, I have money. Take my money! Take mammy to York.' Elsie offered me her money too! *'New York!'* she meant, not York! Of course."

Harper sat on the edge of the bed, examining the engraver's plates in stunned silence. He was aghast - not so much at the shock of finding the plates or the series of wild coincidences that might so easily have cost him his freedom - but at the remarkable logic of his two daughters. He shook his head as he examined the children's lithographic rubbings of the one pound, five pounds and ten pounds bank notes. He took a real bank note out of his wallet and slid onto the floor, to compare it with the plates.

"Clever fucking bastards!" he intoned softly to himself, pursing his lips and whistling as evil notions flooded his thoughts. Here was consolation. Harper stretched his crooked spine to lie flat on the carpeted floor. He thought he heard Hannah saying ironically,

"Now are you happy, Harper? Your future is secure! Just make sure they get music lessons. Take them to see Paderewski whenever he is in town." Shutting his eyes to imagine the scene he laughed out loud.

Now he could see Hannah's face again. He could hear her voice, even feel her punching him in the ribs. She climbed on top of him. He felt her pin him to the floor. He laughed louder and longer the more he played it all in his mind. The picture was complete. An era had ended but he was safe from his demons. Hannah had been everything to him and he had devoted himself to her cause.

Now she had saved him again. It was a fulfilling end, coterminous to all his recent woes. He laughed in ecstasy – laughed for laughter's sake - for it had been so long since there had been anything to laugh about. Hannah had come back for the final curtain call.

Grabbing one of her blouses from the mess on the floor he held it against his face, breathing in her scent. Imagining the form of her superbly generous breasts pressing behind the reddish purple embroidery, he could hear her incredible, resonant voice filling his head. He imagined that he felt the thrill of her touch running up his spine. With eyes firmly shut, Harper was happy again for one transcendent, amaranthine moment.

However ephemeral this touchstone, evergreen vision from beyond the grave it would tie him into all Hannah and Harper had become in their lives together. It was no less than what they had expected and promised one another. Now he had the distinct impression she had returned at the moment of his greatest need, although she had clearly been too sick to be aware of the girls having the plates in their art satchel.

Even as it was happening Harper knew he would never find the words to relate this incredible experience to another mortal being, yet he was convinced Hannah really was right there with him. He imagined her helping to resolve the issues of his crazy existence in her gently assertive style. His mind reeled with the ecstasy of their timeless unison. Harper laughed until he cried – not with sorrow but relief.

To be continued.

If you have enjoyed reading *Fever Therapy,* here is a sample taken from the next title in the series by Jim Burnside

HANNAH DUFF

It was Thursday the 24th December, beginning of the winter festival –
with Christmas, as well as Hogmanay now seeing-in 1897 by popular
demand. Harper had taken his friend Jeremy to the Spotted Red Bull,
a favourite watering hole where he hoped on the off chance to see the
familiar face of Ali Macdonald.

Outside on the pavement a Salvation Army band were playing
Christmas Carols. A blazing coal fire radiated across the lounge,
warming half a dozen early arrivals while the majority standing at the
bar shivered in raw cold floating in from a door wedged open in
welcome. It was the rush hour prior to an optional holiday and the
SRB, as regulars liked to call it, was filling up rapidly.

'Just nipping down to the *SRB* hen,' as a mid-evening diversion
after washing pots and reading the form or in response to the
demand, 'Where the hell have you been? Your supper's cold!'

'Oh . . . just called in at the *SRB* on the way home, dear.' '*SRB*'
sounded like an altruistic charitable affiliation, possibly a worthwhile
sporting involvement that sat well with hard living patrons.

Pinder had insisted on buying the first round, so Harper went to
grab a table near the fire. The tall, robust man returned with two
pints at speed to the table where Harper was sitting, as though haste
was essential if they were going to drink their fill.

"Tell me the SP, John."

"The starting price, or the State of Play?"

"You know me John, I never bet unless it's a sure thing."

"Yeah, I know . . . and it's never a sure thing," Jez laughed his
brisk, affable laugh and Harper felt obliged to speak easily to his boss
in return.

"I've been looking forward more than ever to spending time with
my family, Jez."

"Oh yes, I agree like bells man. It's been quite a run-up to this
holiday!"

"You mean it's not always this busy?"

"No no . . I don't think it has been in past years, do you? Traditionally conservative Scotland is being influenced, in a positive way mind, by tidal forces of a much larger English economy." Harper nodded pensively and both men sucked deep draughts of their beer.

"Europeans, particularly Germans and of course our wealthy American cousins, started the trend of spending on gifts at Christmas. I think the English and their numerous colonial associates are merely following suit."

"Right, Jez. But it occurs to me that whenever there's money to be made our employers take any trend and promptly turn it into a fashion."

"Oh yes, John that's precisely what we aim to do. But don't knock it. Jenner's and the other large department stores in town have reacted to the consumer trend more than the populace we serve. It's called market creation old son. Edinburgh's citizenry, nestling around their northerly volcanic stump miles from civilization, have begun to feel emblematic of Empire. If not arguably at the very heart of Empire."

"Hmm, but we still feel like a colony."

"I dunno. There has always been a feeling of pride, a general conviviality around our great city which demands recognition."

Both men smiled as they stoked up their pipes. On the cusp of his thirties, Jez was handsome and confident. Opening his overcoat and kicking back in his chair he folded long legs and began to pronounce an economic analysis. Harper imagined Pinder a younger version of Conan Doyle's scholarly investigator, Sherlock Holmes.

"Unlike London, Edinburgh always tries to have a feeling of setting the pace, rather than following it. You've been there haven't you?"

"Oh yes, several times – but never to Lambeth." Jez was completely unaware of the allusion to Polish counterfeiters so Harper laughed aloud at his disarming response.

"Oh, well you missed out on the best whores then. No, John, I think London is too big to care. But when the world wants to celebrate, Edinburgh throws a party."

"Well I know there's a lot of poverty in London, Jez and we are certainly better off for housing, health and education than Glasgow or Manchester . . . but I dinnae see much evidence of investment from central government."

"Who cares if the English neglect us when it comes to investment? forget them, they only ever looked after themselves. Scotland still gets the orders. And not just for textiles John, also for ships and steam engines." Such was the popular invective around Kenningtons, at least among the travelling reps taking orders for manufactured goods. Times were good and employment secure. There was a new corporate identity extending from the top down, which encouraged loyalty and hard work.

When he thought about that conversation with Jez following the Christmas weekend, a couple of typical manifestations of this tenuous economic reality struck Harper. Firstly, he was on holiday with his bairns, following a month of the most manic rush imaginable to take orders and get goods into shops throughout major urban locations of the United Kingdom. This was in fact a holiday Harper was obliged to take because there would immediately follow an almost complete suspension in business in the clothing industry. There were local exceptions – but Edinburgh had long ceased to rely upon a locally generated market economy. The development of rail and ever larger iron ships had seen to that. Despite cold weather, business would not pick up again properly until early March – everyone knew that. And then fashion magazines would see to it that business went crazy again.

Secondly, he was going on a works outing. Although Harper couldn't think of any valid reason why, at that precise moment - seven forty on Tuesday morning, 29th December - he was sitting naked in front of his dresser near the bedroom window, except for the kilt he had avoided trying on since the same time last year.

Staring indifferently at sky above the treetops lining Holyrood Park opposite, he felt a gentle brushing of the cat's tail against his left leg.

"Go on ye daft quadruped. I'm no feedin' ye at this time o' the morning! Ye eat more than I do, fer Chrissake." Instead he reached down to stroke Molly, who jumped up onto the polished elm dresser, where she rolled in front of him, purring in anticipation of affection. Molly took every opportunity to get Harper's attention in this elaborate manner. The tame 'Scottish Tiger' knew him for an easy mark – who often sat alone with her to talk nonsense when he was in his cups.

Now he tickled Molly's belly and the beautiful cat stretched out, pushing her paws against the mirror stand. Harper made a play of counting a double row of black spots on her underside, talking to her like a baby as he prodded them. When he got to ten, near her taut furry abdomen, Molly grabbed his hand with both paws and made a playful feint to bite his thumb. But she was gentler than any cat he'd ever seen and as ever her needle sharp claws were withdrawn.

"Oh well, I'm definitely not feedin' ye now!" Molly continued purring as she rubbed facial scent glands against the frame of the mirror.

In his underwear drawer were the plates. On an impulse Harper took them out to examine closely for the first time since he'd found them in the suitcase six months ago. Knowing perspiration was enough to soften dried ink, he avoided touching the stamp-facings with his fingertips. The built-up layer would be awkward to remove yet metal beneath was not worn.

Their condition speaks of tens, or hundreds of thousands - not millions of imprints. Wouldn't the Treasury love to know. Ha! Sod them.

Harper considered burying the counterfeit Bank of Scotland plates in a Hessian sack in the back garden, or winging them into the tide off the deep water harbour at Newhaven but for some inexplicable reason couldn't bring himself to do either.

I can never hand them in of course – that certainly would spoil things for everyone. I could never explain it all without damaging my reputation, as well as that of the man who investigated and cleared me.

Harper knew Somers would never come back, even though the status of the tentative investigation into alleged missing items was 'open and unsolved.' Harper had seen the search warrant destroyed. On the back of such action came silent agreement that Harper was exonerated. If the plates turned up now it would make Somers seem incompetent. Harper also knew from recent discussions with Ali Macdonald over a pint at the SRB, that there was an active special unit still working the case in a basement room on Bank Street. It gave him pause to think how a good record with the force might have saved him from damaging scrutiny although it had not felt so at the time. In the final analysis the team from the Treasury had taken a leap of faith - seeing him as one of their own.

Harper had not thought much about it until now – perhaps because it had all been too embarrassing. With over six months behind him since the devastating loss of Hannah and the trauma of detention, he could think about it all for the first time without wishing the ground would open up to swallow him.

The Treasury men had appeared at the Forbes late on the evening of the funeral. Between them they paid for several rounds of drinks although a few eyebrows were raised and conversation fell relatively silent for half an hour or so. But Harper read it instantly for what it was.

This is political. Someone high up told them to make amends, to contain any possible blow-back. They need me to keep my mouth firmly shut about this blunder and that's exactly what I will do.

Somers worked quiet charm on local notables, family and friends alike. He spoke freely about shared interests, revealing a little of opinions and personal background but nothing about his work. The Inspector made a firm friend in Dr Payton and his stunning wife, with whom he sat for over an hour talking mainly about symphonic orchestras he'd heard playing in London and his favourite composer, Beethoven. He was gracious but did not outstay his welcome.

When Harper's immediate family began to leave just before midnight, Somers made his excuses shortly after them. With a telling look across the room to John he conveyed the thought, 'You my friend are a special case. We're letting you back in the water but the hook is still in your mouth.'

Harper rose to accompany Somers down the street but the Treasury man made a point of publicly shaking his hand.

"Mr Harper . . . once again let me express my deepest sympathy for your loss. Thanks for clearing up the matter we needed to talk to you about. If there is anything else you can remember please get in touch with me personally."

Harper walked outside with the Inspector to his borrowed motor vehicle, a neat little Farnell truck hired from the Station Hotel in Elgin. Keith Somers gave Harper an enthusiastic demonstration of how it worked, as if all the controversy between them was forgotten. Cranking the starter handle vigorously, he climbed behind the wheel as the engine of the little three wheeler hissed into life. Harper stood with his mouth slightly open as he waited for D I Somer's parting shot, smiling benignly when it came.

"If you find them, dispose of them properly now won't you? Good luck for the future!" Shocked, intimidated and relieved all at the same time, Harper made no attempt to reply. He was still the host and this was shaping up to be a long night.

"For fuck's sake! Enough of bad luck" he murmured as the aptly named Orange Box faded into the velvet night. Wandering down to the river, John needed to smoke and enjoy his own company for a while. He knew if he walked to clear his mind the wake would still be in full swing when he returned. After all the bustle, he'd seen local Bobby Bill Stevenson hemmed into a corner by a table covered in untouched drinks purchased by everyone who loved him. Standing in shadow beneath trees on the far side of the bridge, Harper looked back up the street at noise heard from afar. It was Wilson's raucous, piggy laughter, underlain by Donald's humorous, warm growl - rarely in evidence unless he was thoroughly crocked.

McIntyre had found a true blood-brother and could be heard by the entire village opening his shop to dig out a particular bottle of aged malt he'd hidden there. It would serve to educate the Englishman 'in finer subtleties of the water of life - the best possible way of tying one on, son,' he explained. In Wilson, McIntyre had at last encountered a man as fearlessly balanced on the edge as he was - someone not afraid to open his mouth and speak his mind. Donald was not about to let Ted escape.

Harper smiled to himself at the fleeting recollection of Wilson and McIntyre, enthusiastically playing darts against the outside of the butcher's preparation shed in the small hours of the morning – a fixture he'd chosen to keep well away from. When his pipe was finished and he was strolling back to the lock-in at the Forbes, the compelling aroma of frying fillet steak was drifting along the street from accommodation at the back of the butcher's shop.

Detective Sergeant Garner turned out to be gradually more lucid and friendly as he became drunk that evening. The gigantic fellow stood at the bar all night, buying drinks for anyone who would accept his dubious company. At first there were no takers at all. Then a few. Then by three or four a.m. there was a garrulous forum of old familiars, laughing and shouting across the bar room at one another.

Jack Garner dipped into his pocket two or three times but then found that glasses were filled and paid for before he could take his wallet out to pay. Bill Hendry knew what they all wanted and that they were not about to stop. The hotelier had an understanding with Harper that formed part of an easy tradition. Whenever a man requested a round be bought, all still able to stand up at the bar were included in it, even if their glasses were half full.

When Garner had eventually drunk his fill he'd lost count of what might have been spent, yet was clear headed enough to realise he'd come out well on top. His wallet was still fat, and Rona refused to let him pay. Confounded earlier in the day by his professional status, she now plied him with drinks as if he was a favourite uncle.

Garner wanted to bare his soul to Harper as a former Bobby. "D'ya know, me old tulip, I'm glad for once me quarry has turned out to be innocent. I've never known such a thing in all my years of service."

"I'm glad too Jack . . . and I'm sorry for takin' the wind oot o' yer sails!" Harper held out his hand for Garner.

"Ah, no hard feelings John. Ted an' me, we were taking the piss. At least ye di'nt scuttle me nob." Harper offered a thin smile in response, guiltily thinking of Blum, whose nob he had most definitely scuttled. Garner made several attempts to find the words for something he found extremely difficult to say and in the end he came to it.

"Y' know John . . . what I regret most – I long for my own lost innocence as a white haired boy. D'ye know, out . . . out on the fens, shooting ducks wi' a punt gun."

On the verge of stupor Garner had been poetic in his good humour. Despite the sadness of the occasion this had been a traditional Highland wake and the gigantic stranger had fit in well. His maudlin tone gave cue for recitation and more arcane forms of jocularity. No-one was sober enough to sing but Barber took up the violin and played a couple of sweet laments. Although it was the hour before dawn and blackbirds could be heard rehearsing in the mist-humped forest across the river, Rona came round the bar room proffering an ashet piled high with bacon sandwiches.

Above all else, Harper recalled with satisfaction how Somer's team had taken trouble to redress the question of Stevenson's involvement in Harper's detention earlier that day. If anything, Bill's reputation was enhanced in the end. To cap it all no-one had a fight - not even Jim Lorimer, or Andy Murdoch. Hannah would have laughed and *that* was the entire point of the tradition. All in all it had turned out to be a good way of saying farewell to friends and home for John Harper. At least it had left them all with something to gossip about in Milltown of Rothiemay. And that, he told himself, is what makes the world go round.

As is the case with all the most monumental hangovers, Harper's recollection of the night of Hannah's wake filtered back very slowly. Like all who had ever emerged intact from such a whipping of the cat, Harper hoped there was nothing of potentially greater embarrassment still lurking in the recesses of his mind.

That was it!

The one thing Harper found impossible to envision in reflecting upon the past was the question of what was yet to come. As he held the counterfeit Bank of Scotland plates in his hand, he could hear again Hannah's exalted laughter. Soft, indigo light seemed to appear in the room beside him, as he imagined her thoughtful presence and gentle touch. Harper sighed with bittersweet wisdom, knowing it was time to begin thinking again about the future.

The plates in his hands symbolised Hannah's ribbing sense of irony. Her temporary reversal of fortune with the fever therapy. Even her knowledge that everything in this world is scam, or sham – except the virtue of hope itself. A souvenir of a wild but ultimately happy time, they belonged to no-one now but him.

Harper decided he would clean the plates with methyl alcohol and hide them from the children at the back of his sock drawer. Each time he looked at them from now on he knew all these wonderful, bitter-sweet memories would come flooding back. At last he felt ready to forgive himself.

As he opened the drawer to replace the plates, Molly stamped her front paws into the pile of underpants and socks, tipping one pair onto the floor which she immediately dived after. Harper laughed aloud as he stood up to look with dismay at a hairy paunch, bulging over the adjuster strap of his Buchanan dress tartan.

Muriel had persuaded Harper to order the kilt one night when he was slightly the worse for wear, blatantly trying to impress the girl. The sett was maroon check on buff ground with black stripes running through it, though not as bright as expected from looking in the kilt makers sample book.

What reason have I to be proud of some imagined tradition? It's not Lennox or Hamilton, Campbell or Macdonald, romantically linked to some historic act of valour or treachery. Who cares about the past anyway?

Harper felt no affiliation whatsoever to any mediaeval clan or extended family, much less any minor baronet or laird for whom his ancestors might reluctantly have raised arms in rebellion. But dress tartan was something everyone talked about locally. It figured large at this winter season of celebration, as in the summer when there were games and festivals.

Ali Macdonald had summed up the revived tradition aptly one evening in the SRB – a favourite haunt for off duty policemen, "It's a tradition which differentiates us from the fuckin' English, Harper," This assertion had not required further explanation. All present reached as one in silence as if to say, 'I'll drink tae that.'

There was still shelter in routine and for a time Harper could avoid what was preordained. Margaret Kemp was too valuable to him as a component in family life and routines to dismiss without the disapprobation of her family and a significant number of mutual friends. There was no good reason to do such a thing, apart from the subliminal issue of her trying to insinuate herself into the widower's life and his bed.

At first, indifference to her was protection in itself. She was young and uncommitted. Harper had his family to think about and was de facto her employer. But she had been taken over four years ago in Hannah's absence and was effectively now a surrogate mother to his children. The burning question was to what extent Harper might allow Margaret to become a surrogate wife.

She had one or two male friends and suitors whom she clearly kept, quite literally, at arms-length although whenever Harper met them, the lads patiently pursuing her seemed creditable and keen. By her own confession, Margaret had for a time been genuinely worried about Harper but as the months rolled into years she came to see him as invulnerable.

It was clear to him that the smart young woman was privately committed to grabbing him if she could and had dug in to wait her chance with solemn dignity. Some months ago Margaret had stopped mooning over him – so the boys who called when Muriel stood in added to the tantalizing sexual allure. Apparently determined to express no direct interest until he was good and ready, Margaret Kemp burned with the honest anticipation of an urbanised Jane Eyre.

Evenings when he studied were the hardest for Margaret. She sat in his home waiting for the man she loved to return from night-school, hoping he would ask her to linger and sleep with him. But he always made for the dining room with his brief case, like a monk retreating to his cell after compline. When he turned up the gas lamp and gave her an austere look it meant, 'thank you and goodbye.' Insurance industry examinations were a convenient barrier but the sad and purposeful look in his eyes said, 'this is not a mutual feeling Margaret. I'm not ready to forge another bond, however keen you think you are.'

For Margaret, innate mechanisms of sexuality were understood and accepted, "His memory of Hannah clouds interest in other women," she told her mother, in the kitchen of their home off Willowbrae Road.

"Yes dear, you're far too sage tae doubt it. And it's on'y right that John studies tae elevate his status. Hard work disnae a'ways amount

394

tae happiness. No if ye work every hour o' the day just tae break even, like your faither an' mol'" "

"Hmm, but he disnae need to keep the world at bay as he studies."

"Oh, nonsense. You know where he is, if you have him in your sights," Teresa looked up thoughtfully from the dough she was kneading for onion bread, "Although I think you should find an unmarried man and start a family of your own!"

Margaret did have him in her sights. She teased him proficiently like a kitten playing with a mouse – even though it drove her to distraction wondering about women he might meet and fall in love with on his constant travels. Secretly it charmed her to think Harper was still faithful to the memory of his passed wife. It might take a couple of years before that hurt even began to fade.

Teresa reminded her that, 'In posh society, folk in mourning keep themselves aloof frae mixed company for a year at least.' Margaret laughed but she glanced unintentionally at the calendar on the kitchen wall.

Like a chump, Harper wrongly imagined another effective barrier between himself and Margaret's unsolicited attention was his overtly enthusiastic interest in Muriel. Margaret took it for what it truly was – the foolishness of a lonely, older man, testing his ability to attract the opposite sex. The fact that Muriel was her younger sister and engaged to be married, simply reassured Margaret of Harper's subliminal interest in her.

Muriel Kemp was not only thoroughly delightful in character but also quite exquisite to behold. Her beauty burst out in every sense, like over-ripe fruit - and all the vigorous boys who knew her ached to taste it. She smiled so much, she had developed laughter wrinkles as a child. Creases appearing suddenly around dark eyes that accompanied frequent expressions of delight, would take Muriel from attractive youth to gloriously beautiful woman in a breath-taking instant. Those endearing lines on her face were set in the most fulsome, smooth complexion anywhere to be seen. Jet-black hair tumbled in waves around high cheek-bones and her strongly humorous, fair face. Delightful enthusiasm for everything in life shone through amethysts for eyes no King could purchase for a Queen. Most tellingly, a closer look was always necessary, even when a man had seen Muriel before. Usually the greetings of others were met with an instant, welcoming smile. The amethysts were set against magnificent lashes, a bonny nose and strong, classical brow. Muriel was not so pretty she might snap like porcelain though, nor so matronly she might ever put on bulk, to step heavily on rounded heels. And her voice was laughter itself. It was clear to everyone who knew her that Muriel's sparkling, timeless beauty would always remain.

Unfortunately for the eligible male population of Edinburgh, Muriel had a steady boyfriend, Keith Morrison, who was tall and equally handsome. Morrison was a genial soul who played rugby union for Herriot's whenever he could and was training to be a Secretary in the Diplomatic Service. He wasn't around that much but for any of Muriel's old school chums it would be taking a big risk to chance their arm. She took all their salacious flattery in her stride but when asked about plans for the future would quietly accede that they involved, 'a move to London, then who knows where? Maybe somewhere in the Caribbean if we get to choose.'

She joked about looking beyond Keith's career to their retirement but no-one mocked. Enthusiasm would no doubt carry them forward. It was all a matter of knowing what to volunteer for. Muriel tended to express her worries like her delights – with a sweet smile and shrug of exceptionally contoured shoulders. Then her favourite tight black cardigan would fill reassuringly with the slightest lift of a gloriously proportioned bosom.

Muriel and Margaret played an exceptional and impenetrable double-act. Together they were often raucous in confidence. Muriel, less discreet than Margaret, could be flagrant. Although they usually remained behind the invisible lines of propriety, it was only concern for the feelings of individual people that could stop them in full flow. Where Margaret was dauntless, Muriel was outrageous. Individually they were introvert and extravert but together both became equally charming and hilarious.

Mistakenly trying to use his easy familiarity with Muriel, Harper sought to deflect Margaret from entertaining amorous notions about him. The simple fact was that he could not imagine Margaret's sister as ever having been a child. Muriel had imperturbable balance – she was a gem. Harper realised that she reminded him of Hannah – at least how he might have idealised his deceased wife, unburdened by responsibility in her late teens.

When Margaret teased him about his obvious shine for Muriel, Harper expressed the view that easy friendship with her sister was 'purely platonic, as they say.' Yet he pretended it could be much more. Tuned to one another, the sisters saw through his show immediately agreeing it was no more than, 'typical, red-blooded male behaviour.' Speculating privately whether, 'He might take us both on at the same time,' Muriel and Margaret roared with laughter at Harper's lame strategy. They had no secrets at all – and both women laughed till they cried. Harper had no idea. If he had known how Margaret schemed, or what was in store for him, he might have run a mile – or jumped in sooner perhaps.

The occasion for the wearing of traditional dress was more than just Hogmanay. Working her charms on him one afternoon in late November, Muriel Kemp prevailed on Harper to make a commitment he otherwise never would have entertained. He turned up for a meeting at work with Jez Pinder from Accounts, feeling a little self-conscious. Jez agreed to meet Harper in the staff canteen at one thirty, to give feedback after an end of year briefing with Mr Nichol, the Operations Manager. It was not the end of the fiscal year so Harper was keeping fingers crossed Jez would overlook unevenness in his annualised performance, especially the dry time spent in Northern Scotland last springtime. Harper was also feeling guilty because his commitment to the job had tailed off significantly in recent months.

There can be no team briefing for field reps at this busy time of year. In any case, meetings with Jez are always held on the run. This will either be bad news, or no news.

Straight and direct but with a practical joker's reputation, Pinder was generally thought to be a good sort. Jez was late for the informal meeting and Harper was grabbed by a bevy of machinists on their break. Whatever it was the women were talking about it caused a general buzz of excitement in the atmosphere. Marlene from Accounts was there, sitting opposite Muriel Kemp and two or three other familiar faces.

The Accounts Supervisor asked his advice, "John, you know all the best hotels in Scotland don't you?"

"If I didn't know you better Marlene, I'd say that sounds like a proposition." There was giggling and Marlene conceded her slip with a knowing smile.

"Go on Marlene, please! What's the occasion, someone getting married?"

"No, staff outing!" interjected Muriel over her shoulder. She was turning at one hundred and eighty degrees to talk to a woman on an adjacent table, her voice drowned by two simultaneous conversations.

"Lomond Castle Hotel, and yes as a matter of fact my son was thinking of having his wedding there," answered Marlene.

"Lomond Castle, oh yes, I know it. Very much geared to the tourists but the room rates are no' bad off-season. I visit the local kilt makers. Wool from that area is amongst the softest anywhere, they get so much warm rain."

Muriel turned to join the conversation, "What's the hotel like Harper, tell us?"

"Oh, very grand I'd say, Muriel. Quite traditional. They treat their guests like royalty. The entire place, the hotel and its shoreline setting, has an atmosphere of tranquillity and grandeur that might easily go to your head. They organise ceildiths and boat trips for residents. There are woodland margins with wildlife for miles along the loch side. It's incomparably beautiful there, especially when the sun shines. Of course the whole area is steeped in history - much of it extremely unpleasant," Harper added with a smirk.

"Oh, so there are a few ghosts walking the muir?"

"I'd say there are a few ghosts walking the corridors." The women all laughed, then looking at one another stretched their mouths, pulled doubtful faces or tilted heads in consideration. There followed a cacophony of discussion in which all seemed to finally reach agreement.

"Book it then Marlene!" they all chorused. Glassy eyed with the eagerness of alleviating mundane routines on a subsidised weekend trip, the women turned now to the handsome interlocutor, who'd unwittingly convinced them all to throw in their merk and venture forth together.

"Thanks, John!"

"That'll do nicely then!"

"Well done – we knew we could rely on you!" each of the women called out in turn.

"What do you say John – you're gonny come?" came an enthusiastic suggestion from the irresistible Muriel. There was pause as the request registered with Harper. Then a chorus of, "Aw come on, come with us!"

"You'll love it!"

"We can hae a pic-nic at Rest and be Thankful an' visit Helensborough in the afternoon, if it's no' a wash oot," put in the lovely Marlene, thoughtful as ever.

"Ha'e some fun, while there's fun tae be had!" croaked slightly over the hill Janet Dixon, Muriel's Machine Room Supervisor. A wicked smile played across her eyes that said, "There's no man in my life."

"Oh, go on John, you could get Great Gran to come down frae Rothiemay tae look after your bairns for the weekend! They'd love to see her!" This last suggestion came so fast from Muriel that Harper failed to register fully that it missed an important logical step.

What did register was that Muriel knew his situation intimately. Her idea was a good one, for all sorts of reasons that were nothing to do with a weekend staff outing in the run up to Hogmanay. It flashed through Harper's mind that if Margaret was not invited to come on the weekend trip too, it would cause awkwardness between them. It really would look like he was making a play for her younger sister. Muriel was way ahead of him and she was right. Deciding to prevaricate until he knew more he said, "Oh well, I'll have to see."

"What's that then old son?" Sitting down on a chair that he had reversed, Pinder spread long legs at an angle seemingly impossible for comfort. Sharp creases of his trousers hinted at another juncture in time when serious business might need to be discussed in professional detail. Harper looked down at them in dismay, wondering not for the first time if he had overdone the trips to Rothiemay.

"Oh . . ," Harper began, but Muriel Kemp cut in on him - her face and voice resonant with the prospect of a great holiday adventure, "We're all going to Loch Lomond for the Hogmanay trip. Are you coming too, Mr Pinder? Spouses and friends are allowed but its adults only."

"Wild horses wouldn't stop me darlin' and I plan to sit next to you at dinner!" There were hoots of ribald laughter, followed by affirmations from all.

"This will be fun!" said Muriel, quickly mentioning to Marlene, "I'm gonny need a chaperone!"

"Don't look at me!" protested Janet, her overseer and there were more peals of laughter.

"Only, I need to know now chaps. Jez, could I take a deposit from you? It's all heavily subsidised you know," reasoned Marlene.

"Yes, Mr Nichol says you have to arrange insurance cover," stated Jez in a matter of fact tone, "Give me details Marlene and I'll make the phone call for you. And I will be the first to pay." There was a congratulatory ripple of approval from the machinists as he took out his wallet,

"There now!" Marlene looked across at John in final imprecation.

What could be better - why look a gift horse in the mouth?

He laughed before he spoke to lighten the tone, "I'm tired of hotels and travelling you know, Marlene . . . luxury for me is sitting at home reading a newspaper or going for a walk with my bairns." They all jeered him smilingly.

"Will ye listen to it?"

"Oh, he's spoilt by the expense account!"

Taking Harper's forearm comfortably between her two hands Janet said, "Oh, poor John, you just come home and spend the weekend with me then!" There was outrageous laughter, undermining the last vestige of his reserve.

He held up a hand to stop the barracking, "But I will *reluctantly* agree to this. Since the venue in question is probably the closest I'll ever get to an earthly heaven," again they all chuckled, "On the proviso that I can persuade my children's grandmother to come down frae Rothiemay and that Muriel's lovely sister Margaret travels tae Loch Lomond with us as her chaperone, as much to protect Muriel from Mr Pinder d'ye ken, as from mysel'?"

There was sudden movement of the group back to the looms when Mr Nichol unexpectedly stuck his head round the door. Despite the formality for off-site insurance still to be arranged, Marlene accepted Harper's deposit for two and he stood to leave with Jez, nodding goodbye to all the ladies in the group. Muriel Kemp returned his glance with a smile like the blessing of Athena.

"Oh Jesus!" whispered Harper softly to himself, as he headed after Jez in the direction of the Sales Office, "What *have* I just done?"

Came the day, Saturday 2nd January 1897, Harper dreaded what he couldn't avoid. He had heard all the stories of similar events from previous years with a gentle warning from one of the buyers, Arran Hogg to, 'be careful not to come back with more than you left with.' Whenever he met his 'oppo,' Hoggy, Harper always replied to the last comment from their previous encounter. Aquiline and fair, dependable and outwardly innocuous in many ways, Hogg was nonetheless too fast and witty for Harper. Perhaps he had little else on his mind than making others laugh, since he always seemed to change the subject before Harper had time to think of a suitably droll response. The next time they'd met in the lift Harper asked, "Did ye mean that stag's head in reception Arran, or some of the stamped silverware?"

Hogg just smiled knowingly. As ever he came back with a lame joke to illustrate his word of caution, "Did ye hear about the Haymarket Hector wi' clap, who decided to throw his sel' oot o' a tenth storey window?" Harper smiled and shook his head, "His last words were, "I'm a gonner 'ere!""

Harper wondered if Hogg had first-hand knowledge of such disorders but he didn't ask that. Instead he said, "Hoggy, your jokes would make any fellow jump out of a tenth storey window!"

Harper had to pack briskly to make the pre-booked train journey, meeting Muriel and Margaret at Waverley station. The plan was to catch the early express to Glasgow, where they would have a light morning meal before assembling for the coach out to the hotel. He was slated to share a bedroom with three other gentlemen, whom he identified as Bobby McGregor the eternal bachelor from Retail Sales Men's Wear with a reputation for being a womaniser, Accounts Manager Jez Pinder, and the inimitable Arran Hogg. There would be safety in numbers, even if he might have to endure lascivious anecdotes and Hogg's intermittent farting. Hogg always seemed to leave one in the lift whenever they were going up to Accounts together. The critical issue was whether Muriel would keep Margaret occupied. Harper wanted to treat her - for her to have a wonderful time, without any implication being built upon his best intentions.

From the first moment of the friendly meeting at Waverley there was a light hearted, convivial atmosphere to the entire adventure. Harper felt only a hint of the designs of Auld Clootie as Kennington's clan gathered. Finely dressed, scrubbed up work-colleagues shook hands, engaging in casual chat. Some, with nothing to say to those only vaguely familiar in their daily work routines, nodded politely. Harper decided, with a silent prayer and a thought for Hannah, to remain sober at all costs – to be nothing more than an observer – Odysseus washed ashore on the tide.

Shaking his head, Harper declined a bottle of Dryborough Ale. Hoggy opened his own which he pinioned between his knees before handing one to each of their two room-mates. It was twenty past nine in the morning.

"I'm gonny begin as I mean tae go on," Hoggy informed Harper, clicking bottles with McGregor and Pinder.

"Breakfast!" alleged McGregor with an eager smile.

"Breakfast!" agreed Pinder.

"Breakfast!" Hoggy concurred, taking a swig of the popular brew, "The most important meal o' the day!"

Harper was hoping to make it through to the beginning of the next working week without being implicated in some outrage that might result in him losing his job. But ribaldry, even amongst salaried and management staff present, was such that by mid-morning any illusion of sustaining an element of propriety throughout the weekend had been shattered.

There were two coaches carrying the full contingent of a hundred revellers. Their drivers managed to pace each other steadily, climbing the gentle slope towards Dumbarton. There the road forked left to roll along the Argyll coastline. One coach was a monster from a past era with an internal capacity for thirty with room for another twenty two sitting atop. Originally designed for the run from London to Birmingham, she carried enough coal to run all day and night without stopping but was slow and precariously cumbersome. The other was nimble and fast though extremely noisy in comparison with the old steamer. She had the new internal combustion motor, popularised by the designer Daimler. It had been built so Harper noticed, by an English franchise.

The relative rate of progress of the two coaches and novelty of their design and performance on switchback roads became focus for great levity among the trippers. If there was a notional speed limit of fourteen miles per hour in urban areas, the drivers ignored it out in the sticks - certainly at least heading downhill when new records might be easily attained. Any well-founded concern for country people who might never have seen any kind of motorised vehicle travelling these roads at such speed turned into vaudeville, complete with singing and impromptu comedy. Traditional folk songs and music hall numbers alike were spontaneously adapted to extract the last ounce of foolish banter.

The call and response tune *When the Chariot Comes*, adapted recently by American railroad workers into, *'She'll be coming round the mountain,'* became *'We'll be falling down the mountain.'* Lyrics from Rabbie Burns' *Coming through the Rye*, *'If a lassie meets a laddie,'* were conjured into, *'If a drover meets a coacher, coming round the bend,'* and so forth. When it transpired the driver was a taciturn old cud, apparent to some from the moment of first encounter in Glasgow, they baited the man mercilessly to get a rise out of him. A chorus of: *'We'll be cold mash and mutton by and by,'* began to rattle along the enamelled steel tube within seconds of him meeting an unexpected motorised wagon, coming at speed from the opposite direction on a tight bend.

It was a new phenomenon of the Highlands that in appreciation of Wade, Telford and McAdam who'd built the roads and bridges, those plying for hire or reward lucky enough to be equipped with new internal combustion machines, were going to get the most out of it. Time was money in the most technically innovative country in the world. Yes, distances between major cities and sea ports were great and connecting roads tortuous but it was clear from the outset of fast road transport, regardless of potential hazards, that the Scots were never going to hang around.

Soon enough the coaches stopped at Helensborough. It was a brisk but lovely day, with flat-calm sea and clear blue sky. Whilst some wanted to stretch their legs along the shore others remained on the buses, anticipating an alternative jaunt out to woodlands at Rhu, for those leaning toward temperance.

A dedicated hard-core formed up briskly as 'The Crooked Arm Brigade' to head on-the-double across the road to the Sinclair Arms Hotel, with Harper in tow for ballast, 'After all,' they concurred, 'tomorrow will be a Sunday.'

Several swift swizzles later a slightly raddled Hoggy decided in the clear afternoon air that if Muriel Kemp would not reciprocate his endless, burning desire he would pick her up off the west shore and carry her into the brine.

"If ye'll no marry me I'm gonny droon us both!" he declared. Too late for intervention, Muriel's screams of protest could be heard from afar, "I never said that! I never impugned yer manhood!" Quieter, more quarrelsome imprecations followed as she emerged from the tide sopped through, thumping him gamely on his shoulder. Luckily Muriel was wearing casuals and had a change of clothing for the evening.

"John – do something about this!" ordered Margaret. The She Wolf never roused Caesar's Ironclad Sixth so quickly to skirmish. Hoggy's broad smile turned honest when Harper swept him up in his arms and carried him out to deeper water. The two men wrestled as the coach party applauded, cheering them on. Harper was surprised at Hoggy's strength for a man of average build, how quickly he managed to wriggle free and get purchase on him.

Up in the Cairngorms that evening, so the weather map in the Scotsman had predicted, clear skies were to bring another night of the coldest temperatures on record – minus 41 degrees was expected. Harper remembered seeing this in a flash, as he felt the numbing bite of the Irish Sea on the inside of his thighs. Resolving not to take the ardent fool any deeper, Harper tried to pitch him from where he stood. For his part, the sharply dressed buyer decided to take Harper down with him at all costs.

As the quick minded Hoggy flew in his beige morning suit into the lapping waves, he pulled firmly on the lapel of Harper's jacket. Harper went headlong after Hoggy, taking the salty slap open-mouthed with the jacket yanked over his head. Despite embarrassment he came up sharpish with a triumphant grin on his face. From the shore Harper's attentive quartern of bliss clapped her hands, jumping up and down with her younger sister.

"Good Christ, let's get out o' here afore we freeze tae fuckin' deeth!" Hoggy advised, sitting in the water with waves lapping around his chin. "Fuck me gently!" exclaimed Harper, now gasping for air, "I think Nimrod the Great Hunter has been bitten aff an' carried away by a dogfish!"

"Aye, or mebee it froze solid and broke aff, same as mine!" Hoggy's lower jaw shuddered as he spoke, lurching around in circles to get his bearings as salt water clouded his eyes. Harper let out an irrepressible laugh as a streamer of sandy water ran down from his friend's hair. They trawled side by side towards the beach like shipwrecked sailors, laughing like schoolboys as they stumbled through the shallow waves.

"Who in the blue blazes would want a life at sea?" demanded Harper, still breathless from the Arctic shock of the cold water, "What the hell happened to the Gulf-stream back wash?"

"That's just a summer advertising gimmick to get the English tourists in!" replied Hoggy.

Their coach arrived back from the woodlands at Rhu just in time to save the two men from foundering. Everyone else in the shore party ran to climb aboard in front of them, hooting with derision – to ensure they had a dry seat but mainly to avoid being dripped upon.

"Is this part of the entertainment Jez?" asked Bobby McGregor, tears of laughter floating still in his dark eyes.

"Oh yes . . . and I plan to pay them, Bobby. We'll hae a whip round later tae cover my outlay," Jez replied, creases of amusement puckering his cheeks and lining his high forehead.

Harper and Hoggy were obliged to wait, shivering at the back of the queue as Muriel and Margaret explained their situation, working their charms on the taciturn driver. When everyone else was seated he allowed them to climb up. For the first time that day the frown on the surly fellow's rigid, square face began to melt as he caught sight of the pair standing marinated like Admirals of the Narrow Sea. Clearly he'd seen much worse on a Saturday night in Glasgow.

"Oh well, at least yis are no covered in vomit!" he observed with a guffaw, "Come ahead boys!" It struck Harper that the driver was that rare sort of man who actually delighted only in confrontation.

Hoggy and Harper climbed onto the front platform of the vehicle, where they stood beside the driver smirking back at them. He had to turn away to hide his glee at seeing two toffs in suits drenched to the skin. Glancing across the road at stragglers running back from the hotel he stuck out his thumb, directing Hogg and Harper, "Move down the aisle gentlemen. Yis might want tae hold ontae grab handles on the seats as you drip dry."

"Damn. My socks are wet Hoggy! I hate ha'ing damp socks!" complained Harper. Again there was hilarity and jeering from their audience but Margaret and Muriel shone with delight for their hero.

"Smoke!" demanded Hoggy, "I must ha'e a smoke tae calm ma shaking bones. I thought the bastard was trying tae droon me!"

"What about me, you silly arse-worm?" scolded Muriel, "My new boots are ruined!"

"And her skirt," Margaret added fiercely through baby-blue eye liner, "What about her skirt?"

"Sorry," Hoggy intoned lamely to the floor.

"What was that?" demanded Margaret.

"Sorry!" Hoggy said a little louder, "I on'y did it cause I love you." There was rumbustious laughter along the coach at this beseeching plea for absolution.

"Well, I suppose I forgive you. But you have to polish my boots and pay for my cleaning," Muriel blustered with coquettish dander.

"Now that you've repented, you're absolved of your sins!" Harper invoked above the drone of the motor. Looking around to engage the audience he circled Hoggy with his arms, "So brethren, let us conclude this immersion ceremony. I baptize you, Arran Columbus Hogg - In the name of the Father and of the Son and the Holy Ghost," he incanted, making the sign of the cross over Hoggy. There was more hilarity and now even the taciturn driver began to guffaw, his pot belly rising and falling under the rudimentary steering wheel of his prototype 'frost of ninety-six' motor coach, as it cruised along the loch side road. Harper attempted to conclude Hoggy's confirmation with a Pontifical slap and they wrestled again in the aisle.

The two men made great play of emptying sea water and sand from their pipes, Harper knocking his out gently on top of the younger man's head. With a smile of gratification Jez took briars from each in turn, to fill with dry tobacco. He dutifully provided a dry Lucifer, which he struck and held for them to avoid drips – as if this was the sort of thing Jez was used to seeing every day, up in his carpeted office on the fourth floor.

Surrounded in white tobacco smoke, Hoggy turned to Harper, holding out a hand for him to shake, "Sorry pal – for spoiling yer quiff, ih?"

Harper popped the pipe in his mouth as he reached across to take Hoggy's hand. He respected Hogg and held no animosity at all, "Me too Arran, me too! Unrequited love's a desperate thing, son . . . sorry for gi'in' ye the full sheep wash. At least now we're smoke brothers," said Harper lightly, to take any churlishness out of the matter.

The two men gave up trying to speak in competition with the roaring motor climbing towards Rest and Be Thankful, where the plan was to stop and stretch legs for half an hour while taking in the awesome view. There was a hired photographer on the other coach, intending to use the location as backdrop for recording some of the days' events. Hoggy and Harper moved as little as possible to avoid squelching in their own puddles, or dripping onto people in adjacent seats. When they stopped, the two saturated colleagues stood on the corner of the landing next to the driver, allowing other passengers to get off the coach quickly. Without comment the two men went eagerly to search their overnight bags. Crouching behind the rearmost seats where there was some coachwork to hide behind, they fumbled for dry clothing. Harper found himself smiling unexpectedly as he pulled on a new pair of beige Oxford slacks.

The photographer had his work cut out, shepherding the contingent into rank. He had to persuade one of the drivers to manoeuvre his coach for him to stand on the steps with the tripod adjusted for declination, so he could take in the magnificent backdrop. His frame was a glorious midday with the sun at its zenith above frosted slopes and softly breathing forest. Golden light smiled through virgin blue sky, giving a little comforting warmth to heads and shoulders. Rabbits emerged to investigate unfrozen patches of grass near the woodland fringe. Rising eddies of moisture hinted at all the seasons to be seen in a day, as shadows ran from the sun. But to Harper's dismay, none of the urbanites would wait to ponder the most stunning, natural beauty he'd ever seen in all of magnificent Scotland. Dry cold quickly rose into feet and there were not enough benches for the full contingent to sit down, so the revellers gradually drifted back to consume their picnic inside the buses. This resonant elevation of earthly nature, trumpeting glory of heavenly tides beyond the chasm below, invited contemplation. But Caillech, the blue faced hag had to await another perfect time beyond Beltane for these her youngest children to see themselves as part of her eternal picture.

Margaret noticed Harper still shivering and without a word took off her fisherman's roll neck sweater, tossing it to him as he climbed back onto the coach. The garment was knitted from fine, black Arran wool and would give him the appearance of a field preacher from a past era, but he wore it gladly.

As Jenners' weekend tourists came through Reception at Lomond Castle Hotel, laughter rose and fell amid the chatter. For just a few minutes after they had all passed by, levity seemed to have dispersed along the carpeted corridors of the fine hotel and there followed a little respite.

Slanting sunlight fell through leaded windows, reflecting off Meissen pottery and suits of armour, as the party stowed bags and rested a while in their rooms. But night fell quickly and muted sounds of waiters setting tables, surrounded by the aroma of roasting fowl, told the visitors it would soon be time to dress for dinner.

Bright laughter visited again with a knock on a door and quiet solicitation from a remote corridor, "Hello, is that the Metropolitan Male Quartet?" chimed Muriel.

"Oh no!" answered Bobby, who had opened the door.

"Oh yes, I'm afraid so!" cried Jez the joker from within. There was another chorus of, "Oh no!" from Hoggy and Harper, as the heavy door swung shut and the sisters flounced into their bedroom, ostensibly as Muriel explained, "to advise you boys on your kilt fittings."

The feeling of unwelcome intrusion quickly moderated into one of mild annoyance, instantly accepted by the girls but met with their teasing provocation, "I hope you're all suitably attired, as this will be a grand occasion and we want you all to dance!" demanded Muriel. Harper turned away, smiling to himself.

"Oh yeah!" replied Jez, suppressing a snigger as he checked a close shave in the mirror, running fingers through lank black hair, "I'm suitably attired!"

"I've never been quite sure what's de rigueur for the upper classes?" queried Bobby McGregor disingenuously, ever the tavern fox.

"Me neither," granted Hoggy with a straight face, optimistically looking to Muriel with whom he was clearly smitten.

"Is it tackle in, or tackle out John?" queried Jez, coming to the point with the tone normally reserved for asking directions from old ladies in an unfamiliar town. No one laughed - which was in itself a perilous measure of the controlled hilarity building within the little group. All five looked at Harper, who remained deadpan though a curling line of lips and softening of his voice gave a hint of flippancy to a response that was quintessential Morayshire, "Dinnae ask me guys, I'm no' the traditionalist."

"Oh, but you go to night school, so you're definitely the one closest to being upper class. An' you're a fully apprenticed tailor!" came back the delighted McGregor, roguishly warming to his own line of reasoning.

"What's that got to do with it?" demanded Harper.

"Well, surely it was part of your training to discreetly discover the lie of the land? You know, ask a gentleman which way the pendulum swung and all that?" Harper studied McGregor's expression, trying to think of a level riposte to his baiting humour. Everyone in the room waited.

"Either way Bob, I'm no' showing my dick to anyone, especially not these two poor girls, who may have had too much to drink at lunchtime!"

The dam burst in a tide of warm hilarity, sweeping ornate coving and rattling carefully painted windows. Their vigorous ribaldry might have been overheard outside on lawned gardens and along the adjacent frame of the stone building, though any listener would simply have smiled at their pleasure. There was a pause in the chorus of merriment, then another measured voice, "Oh!" cried Margaret, feigning offence, "I never touched a drop! Muriel . . . how about you?"

"Me neither! I cannae believe he just said that about us . . . that we might want to look up his kilt!"

"It's no you two I'm concerned aboot," testified Harper, again flatly affecting the guileless Northerner, "It's Bobby McGregor."

They all looked at Harper aghast as he paused on the brink of allegation and scandal, "I'm embarrassed tae say it but I think he might be a secret meat-flasher. He telt me he just wants tae get us aw pished, then scandalise the women folk at dinner!" The girls squealed with delight as McGregor's bewildered face puckered with the outrage of undignified ridicule.

"Dye mean in the middle of aw the speeches and toasts?" cried Muriel.

"Precisely! That's when he plans to do it! When the MD, Mr Kennedy is raising a glass tae the vision o' Kennington-Jenner's, or even toasting her Majesty the Queen," said Harper, in a tone of dry innocence and bogus concern.

"Harper is going to great lengths to deflect us from a genuine line of enquiry here – if you'll pardon the expression," declared Jez, looking down at Muriel and Margaret, "I believe he knows the answer and simply will not tell us."

"Yeah Harper, tell us!" chorused Muriel and Margaret, echoed by Hoggy and Bob.

"I think we just grab him and sneak a peek," suggested Hoggy, the manic shine in his eyes seen on the beach at Helensborough returning in an instant.

"Oh no!" stated Harper with his Morayshire drawl.

"Oh yes!" contended Pinder, "We need to conclude this matter now for the benefit of all, or we'll be late for dinner!" Once again the girls squealed with delight. Harper backed into a corner, though it was Margaret and Muriel who led the advance, marshalled by Jez.

Thus it was that the cornered rebel, John Harper, came to entrench himself atop a massive mahogany wardrobe of neo-colonial design while the frustrated but determined Kemp sisters, whose direct assault he managed to beat off, attempted in dénouement to dislodge him by tipping the heavy closet away from the wall.

Certain events in a man's life are unrepeatable and should never be mentioned lightly, even if everyone he knows occasionally speaks of it with a wry smile. Such was the event with the wardrobe. Later Harper was in denial. Eventually he came to sublimate entirely the point in time when, sitting cross-legged on top of the wardrobe, he said to Muriel Kemp in order to stop her tilting it, "Okay! Okay . . . I'll show you what's under my kilt, if you show me what's under your bodice."

This bravura was spoken as much for the lads as for the lasses but if at some deeper level that was in fact what Harper had wanted – well that was precisely what he got. An 'eye-full,' so to speak.

Both Margaret and Muriel folded arms down to their waist and in one movement lifted outer garments and trusses up to chin level. Harper's eyes nearly jumped out of his face, as once again the laughter hit the rafters.

As senior man Pinder read his cue, slipping out of the bedroom with an endearing smile and casual salute to Harper, squatting just below the high ceiling. Jez was followed by the hooting McGregor and mildly scandalised Hoggy, who affirmed later he would gladly have swopped places with Harper. In retrospect Hoggy told his friend, "I am deeply grateful to you Harper, wishing only that my gaze dwelt longer on the astounding wealth of fleshy delight revealed to entice you down from that wardrobe. In fact I'll probably go to my grave thinking about it!"

As they scooted along the corridor there was a yell of finality from within the bedroom, followed by an almighty crash, as Harper leaped towards the nearest bed and the wardrobe went flying to the floor. The three men accelerated their pace guiltily towards the staircase, laughing uncontrollably all the way down into the bar. But there it was – a choice moment in life that no-one could have imagined or scripted.

They were decent girls for sure. The event simply showed how men tend to underestimate women, also the lengths they will go to if directly challenged. There was also an important caveat in Margaret and Muriel's view, that Harper really did need a 'boost' so to speak, "Or a 'boob' maybe?" Jez quietly insisted, when Muriel tried to justify her actions to him later that evening in the bar.

END OF EXTRACT

Lightning Source UK Ltd.
Milton Keynes UK
UKOW07f1826050215

245776UK00001B/1/P